W9-CHM-044

FIC   Kuniczak, W. S.,
        1930-

        Valedictory

DATE			

VALEDICTORY

Valedictory

W. S. KUNICZAK

DOUBLEDAY & COMPANY, INC.
Garden City, New York 1983

Library of Congress Cataloging in Publication Data

Kuniczak, W. S., 1930–
Valedictory.

1. Great Britain. Royal Air Force. Squadron
(Polish), 303rd—History—Fiction. 2. World War,
1939–1945—Fiction.   I. Title.
PS3561.U5V34 1983   813'.54
ISBN 0-385-15267-1
Library of Congress Catalog Card Number: 79–8022

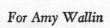

For Amy Wallin

CONTENTS

AUTHOR'S NOTE

I have made every effort to assure accuracy in the historical content of this novel. Its facts and figures are correct, its conclusions reflect the time in which it is set. Persons who have become a part of recorded history are depicted here under their own names. All other men and women appearing in these pages, and in particular the commander and pilots of the 303 Squadron (Polish) RAF, are literary inventions and are not intended to portray their living counterparts. The surviving Polish airmen who flew with the Royal Air Force in the Second World War still live in Great Britain, in the United States, in countries of the British Commonwealth, and in Western Europe. Even though this is a work of fiction, I hope that they will accept it as a memoir of their times.

W.S.K.

Everything that grows
has the right to perish.

GOETHE

PROLOGUE

An Enemy
Long Ago

THIS IS A STORY that no one wanted told and, perhaps, it might have served a better purpose, both public and private, to have kept it buried in the archives. Can words raise the dead? Can they right a wrong? Nothing can change what happened, confessions least of all, and since all the memoirs written by men who helped to make this story carefully avoid a mention of Ludwik Toporski (or Ludo, as everyone called him then), or of the men he led, or of the specter of an armed rebellion among three hundred thousand angry Poles we feared in those last, tense months before the Victory Parade, it's fair to ask why this tale of betrayal, blighted hopes, and spendthrift waste of lives should be resurrected after forty years.

That war is over, its moments are history, and even the world that we had tried to serve no longer exists. Yet in that spring and summer when war itself seemed to have become the enemy for both sides, and men, like their machines, continued to kill and destroy for no greater purpose than that war should end, all hopes of lasting peace left the world forever.

Why, then, recall past bitterness, resurrect dead follies? Perhaps, like an uneasy spirit finally laid to rest, the story of Ludo will cease to trouble both memory and conscience once it has been told. In that one shocking act he staged on May 3, 1945, ten thousand feet above the cliffs of Dover, the truth about the war, about himself, and about the sort of lives that all of us would live thereafter, stood revealed so sharply, that thinking about it even now shatters peace of mind.

Chance ruled that the last great air battle of the war in Europe would be fought by Ludo and his squadrons, and that this unexpected clash between patrolling Poles and embittered Germans (neither of whom, in victory or defeat, had anything but a battle to win at this stage) would be witnessed on the ground by several hundred journalists, most of them neutral or American, who had been brought to Dover for quite a different purpose.

Chance placed them, along with several members of the Cabinet, most of the Allied service chiefs, a covey of visiting American politicians, my mortified Minister and myself, under a cloudless sky that made a perfect backdrop for the hurtling aircraft, the white streaks of crystallizing coolant and spirals of black smoke, the flower-bursts of flame and scattering debris, the black-and-white crosses of the Germans and the white-and-red checkerboard insignia of the Poles. We had come to Dover on a peaceful mission, to watch the King present the George Cross to that Channel fortress. None of us, I am sure, understood at first that this was a battle in which an uninvolved observer might be killed.

The Germans had come across the North Sea (from Denmark, as a survivor's memoir would reveal much later) on a mission that was partly vengeance against fate and partly an assertion of their worth as warriors in the last moments before the humiliation of defeat. They flew in an impeccable formation that made them seem like a back-turned page of history. The slow and vulnerable Heinkel He 111s, the poorly armed Dornier Do 17s (the famous "Flying Pencils" that had littered the English countryside in the autumn of 1940 and spring of 1941), and the straddle-winged Stukas that had been knocked out of English skies in dozens, hadn't been seen over Kentish fields since the Battle of Britain, when Ludo and his men had shot down more of them than any other squadron in Fighter Command.

Now they were here again, like a bad dream, flying with a theatrical stateliness as though expecting everyone to applaud. A solitary Junkers Ju 88D bristled among them like an eagle in a flock of crows. The luck that comes from indifference to one's own survival had brought them safely past the fleets of Mustangs, Tempests, Airacobras, and Typhoons that combed the skies of Germany in search of a target. The dread that they had represented only five years earlier glinted from their wings.

The Poles fell on them in a loose formation of squadrons and flights, coming out of the midmorning sun where they had been invisible. I heard a senior air officer catch his breath. It was a classic ambush, its single-minded savagery was antique, and I thought of falcons I had seen in India during a maharaja's hunt: dark, compact killers with elliptical wings striking a flight of herons.

In moments, the sky had cracked into speckled fragments; fire, sharp as talons, flashed yellow-and-white. The thick, oily coils of smoke that spiraled to the sea seemed as obscene as torn birds.

In moments (actually, it was seven minutes), three of the Poles and twenty German machines were either blown apart with cannon fire or sinking in the cold, choppy waters of the Channel, and the scattered remnants of the enemy armada had turned grudgingly for home. We watched them as they receded in the east along with their pursuers, falling one by one in the spreading distance, trailing smoke like blurry exclamation marks until all but one were gone. Then, in the suddenly emptied air overhead, a solitary German bomber droned on into England, a Spitfire beside it.

—Magnificent! someone said, loud in our general relief, and *God! What a sight!* someone else cried out, and an American correspondent wanted to know how we had managed to stage such a show. An Air Vice Marshal murmured injudiciously: *The Poles, I believe, to judge by their markings,* and Willard Loomis, an American journalist who had his own Polish cross of guilt and grief to bear, shouted:

—Ludo's people?

I heard my Minister sigh and say under his breath: That's all we need at this moment, thank you very much. Winston will be *so* pleased. Oh, bloody . . . *bloody* hell!

Thinking of Ann and Ludo, and Ann as I had seen her last in her hospital bed (her face quite bloodless, and her eyes askew with a bitterness I couldn't understand), I was sick with an anger of my own.

Had this been all, the story would have ended there and then. I, certainly, would have felt no need to say any more about it, and the correspondents would have forgotten it in another moment. The sky had almost emptied and I waited for the excitement to abate, for the babble to cease, and for indifference to return. As I remembered such things from my own early days in India, one is not really touched by a witnessed battle until long after it has taken place. It takes time and distance to rearrange the memory of immobilizing fear, the shock that comes with the realization of danger, and the euphoria of relief. Death had appeared above us at ten thousand feet, and each of us had felt the breath of its passing. Now each of us was looking in another's face for a reflection of our own guilty joy at having stood so close to danger without injury so that, at first, the final act of the drama overhead didn't have an audience.

Then our loud, nervous laughter ceased, we could ignore each other, and we began to watch the lone Spitfire flying beside the Junkers as if escorting it, flying so close that the pilots must have been able to see each other's eyes. They flew together in perfect amity, the Pole and the German, as if suspended on twin strands from a single puppeteer's hand, and I felt unaccountably impoverished on the ground.

Something terrible—and beautiful, perhaps—was happening up there. A final and irrevocable decision had been made, and the depth of our silence showed that each of us had sensed it.

Then the Spitfire turned sharply toward the German bomber. Impossible as it may sound in the telling, since what we watched took place at least two miles above us, we heard the rending crash a moment after the Spitfire's airscrew sheared off the bomber's tail. Perhaps we felt it. Our cry was general, brief, sharp as pain, full of outrage. It was like watching the murder of a cripple or an execution. The bomber fell through silence like a stone and vanished in the sea. The Spitfire climbed steeply. It hung motionless for a moment, as if riveted to the streaked sky by its scarlet spinner, defying gravity and our own comprehension, then dived into England.

Loomis cried out redundantly: He rammed him! You could see he did! It was . . . *must* have been . . . deliberate!

His red-rimmed eyes were full of tears and he seized my arm with both his hands, as if in championing Ludo and his Poles he were paying off a debt that could wait no longer.

—What kind of medal will you give him this time, you cynical English sods? The Royal Shaft with clusters? Can you still see it in your conscience to keep these poor sons-of-bitches out of your damned Victory Parade?

—Please, Loomis, I began, conscious of others within hearing, and caught the stricken look in my Minister's eyes.

—You'd like it if it wasn't Ludo, wouldn't you, Loomis said and hiccoughed. That'd make it easy. Just one more angry Pole ramming his head against a wall, eh? But it *was* Ludo, and you know it, and you won't be able to sweep *him* under a rug. Not Ludo, old buddy! So what are you going to do about *that*, Colonel Hudson, sir?

I did my best to laugh and said in a voice designed to soothe him and disarm him: Take it easy, Loomis. We don't really know who it was up there, do we? And the ramming could've been an accident, you know.

—It's Ludo, I tell you. Everybody knows that scarlet spinner. And if it's Ludo then it wasn't any accident, the American said as he swayed and clutched at me for support. Poor old bloody Ludo, he's really given you something to think about this time! As . . . if I may hark back to the unmentionable . . . he did in your damned Battle of Britain, right?

—A bit early to get soused, old man, don't you think? I said, and tried to move away, but he'd have none of it.

—Ah, so that's your story?

—Seriously, Colonel, another correspondent said. Was that your famous Ludo? It might make a story if it was.

—I really don't know anything about it, gentlemen, I said.

Soon afterward, a harsh yellow fog began to roll off the water, swallowing everything. The bright morning sky gave way to low cloud as we left the coast and drove toward London in the Minister's black Bentley, and for several miles of unremitting silence our mood matched the scene.

We knew by then that we were dealing with Ludo (that scarlet spinner angled against the sky had been unmistakable), and we discussed various ways of limiting the effects of what he had done.

Normally, if anything said about a war could be described as normal, such disregard for his own life and contempt for death would have been deemed heroic. But at this juncture of political expedients that were about to doom such men as Ludo to the bitterness of exile, his gesture—whether quixotic, desperate, or merely contemptuous of victories and defeats alike—would cause acute embarrassment in Washington and Whitehall. The sad truth was that our Polish allies had become very inconvenient. They had served us well, as Loomis had reminded everyone by invoking the Battle of Britain, but now we had to do our best to make them invisible among us so as not to irritate the Russians to whom President Roosevelt had given the Poles' country, or to remind our own people of Winston Churchill's role in that betrayal. As the Minister was quick to observe, this was no time for headlines about heroic Poles.

Moreover, there was more than just the correspondents' reaction to consider. The mood among the Polish troops in Italy, France, Germany, and Britain was highly explosive. We thought it possible that in their frustration they might take desperate steps. General Prus, whom they had loved and trusted, had blown out his brains in a dingy London boardinghouse only nine days earlier. Ludo, their other hero, may have just signaled his own contempt for us. Attempted suicide, with the mind's balance disturbed, was the desired explanation, the Minister believed. But Ludo's name had been a household word for too many years, he had friends in surprisingly high places, he couldn't be explained away without a special effort.

Derek Bellancourt, who was my cousin and Ann's brother, was the first to break the silence in the car.

—I suppose he must have preferred to die well than to live badly, don't you think? What's left for him? I mean, he can't go back to his own country now that the bloody Reds are moving into it. His life as an officer in his country's service is over. His career is finished. His private sense of purpose . . . his identity . . . are gone in one stroke. He must've asked himself: What is this all about? What could come next that could mean as much as everything that had gone before? There's the bloody Hun, he'd say, and I'm out of ammo, and why not end it all and be done with it? So he dives headlong on the Jerry, rams him deliberately nose-to-tail, and out he goes!

—But he didn't, did he? Go out, as you put it, I said, conscious of my dislike for Derek. The word from the rescue people is that he got his Spitfire down in one piece, what was left of it. He cracked it up after landing.

—Instinct, Derek said and shrugged and smiled disarmingly at the Minister. He's too good a pilot to crack up a plane if there's a way to save it. Nothing wrong with getting it banged up, that goes with the job, but his every instinct would be against losing it in the air. It's like that Conrad story about the sea captain who turns the steering wheel with a hand that isn't there, saves his ship, and doesn't know how. Our chap makes up his mind to go out with a bang, prangs the old Hun, and as far as his mind's concerned it's all over and done. But the body does what it's been trained to do. It brings the Spit safely down, just the way it's been doing it for years. The hedge, the telephone pole, well, that can't be helped. The Spit cracks up, Ludo's legs are gone, and he can't help that either. It could have happened like that, Minister, couldn't it?

The Minister appeared distracted, his attention masked. His pouched, protruding eyes were fixed on Derek in a speculative manner, and I wondered how much each of them knew about the other's connections with Ann. As Ann's and Derek's very distant cousin, who had loved the one and detested the other from their infancies, I trod with caution near both these men and envied them their easy access to my brother's wife.

Derek went on:

—Odd chaps, these Poles. Oh, quite splendid, really, in an archaic sort of way. I remember when Ludo showed up in Lisbon after the fall of France, a wreck of a man. Barged into my office, eyes of a fanatic, and nothing would do but we must ship him off to England at once! Wouldn't wait his turn. Stole a Lufthansa transport, flew it to Casablanca where the Frenchies tossed him in the clink. Broke out of there with a bunch of other mad Poles, stole a coastal steamer, and sailed that pitiful old scow all the way to Oban. No charts, not a sailor among the lot of them, and damn the minefields and U-Boat torpedoes! The Poles filled up the papers for a week, with that one.

But the Minister was no longer listening.

—Supposing, he said. Just supposing, mind you, that the Huns were coming in to surrender? Wouldn't that solve the problem?

—That's quite brilliant, Minister, Derek said. The Huns come in to surrender and the Poles attack them.

—The journalists will never buy that, Minister, I said.

Hugh Wadsworth-Jones, my department head and former classmate at the Royal Military College, said immediately: Why the hell not? It'll shift the onus. Turn the whole thing around. Is that what you've in mind, Minister?

—I don't quite know what I have in mind, the Minister said sharply. I'm asking for ideas.

I said that it had looked to me as though the Germans had

come to fight rather than surrender. —They did knock down three of the Poles, after all.

—Perhaps the Jerries changed their minds, the Minister suggested. The Poles *did* attack them! What were they doing over there anyway, Hudson?

I said that it had been the Poles' last war patrol, as far as I knew, a valedictory flight they had arranged for themselves. They were supposed to stand down the next day and prepare for demobilization.

—No one expected anything to happen so far from the actual battle zones. And since today is one of their national holidays, one that they tend to get emotional about, it was thought better to send them up than to keep them brooding on the ground.

—What sort of a holiday is it, then? Hugh asked.

—It's their Constitution Day. Ironically, it preceded a Russian invasion and partition in 1793 and led to more than a century of foreign occupation. The parallels are quite uncomfortable today, as I'm sure you're aware.

—And now they've lost the war that everyone else is going to win, Hugh said and shook his head as if the ironies of history were just too much for a simple soldier. I don't wonder they're all a bit around the bend these days.

Bitterly, and with sarcasm that Hugh decided to ignore, the Minister said: We didn't win this war entirely unassisted. That help has its price.

—Pity it wasn't our own chaps up there, Hugh said. The Canadians, perhaps. It would've been quite a good point to make with the Americans, don't you think? They do talk so much about winning the war single-handed.

—I'd rather not think about the point that was made, the Minister said sourly. But I suppose we must. And why didn't we know that the Germans were coming, Hudson?

I said I supposed the Germans had come under the radar screen, which wasn't all that reliable north of East Anglia and did, occasionally, fail over the Channel. And with the war being so close to an end, perhaps things were getting rather slack along the radar chain.

—Damn people sleeping at the switch, Hugh said. Shoot them a rocket, Hudson, and a strong one. We might have been killed.

—Winston might have preferred that to what actually happened, the Minister said. He does *not* like surprises of this kind and he doesn't want to hear any more about Poles. How will you handle the foreign press on this?

—We may be able to delay things in Censorship but not for very long, I said. A "D" Notice will silence our own people.

—Then make sure that Censorship kills any references to Poles, the Minister said. *An RAF fighter squadron* should be quite enough. Who was that drunken Yank who did all the shouting?

I described Loomis as an American correspondent, not accredited to any one newspaper, whose wealthy wife owned a newspaper of her own.

—Can he be managed? the Minister asked, smiling. Is he responsible?

We laughed then, as the Minister expected. We had heard those phrases spoken by President Roosevelt about Joseph Stalin at both the Teheran and the Yalta conferences. In our department—the Allied Forces Liaison and Coordination Committee (AFLACC) of the Foreign Office—this had become a mocking way to describe a hopelessly mismanaged situation. I said that Loomis had deep personal feelings about the Poles. He had been in Poland when the war began. He had had a brief and tragic love affair there. The woman was, in fact, one of Ludo's cousins. She had lived for a time with General Prus. She had been killed during the siege of Warsaw. Loomis had enjoyed few sober moments since then.

—Is that his only interest in Ludwik Toporski?

—No, Minister, I said. He thinks he created Ludo.

—Are you trying to be amusing, Hudson? the Minister said coldly.

—Not really, sir. He's been writing obsessively about Ludo since the Battle of Britain. The Ludo legend . . .

—I know the Ludo legend, the Minister said and made an irritated gesture.

—Yes, Minister. Loomis seems to see him as a possible savior of his lost love's people.

—And what about Ludo himself? Hugh wanted to know. Is he also mourning a lost love?

I thought of Ann, blue-lipped in the glare of the overbright hospital bulbs, gray-and-yellow as one of those dusty waxwork mannequins one used to go to see at Madame Tussaud's. Bloodless and weightless, she had seemed suspended from an iron gibbet by plastic yellow tubes, her white-painted cot like an illusionist's unnecessary prop. She had chosen to injure herself with a straightedged razor (Ludo's, I supposed), a horrible ear-to-ear slash across her throat that seemed intended to disfigure as well as kill her. It had taken all of my authority to induce the hospital registrar to enter her in records as a victim of a flying bomb.

Shaken with such sudden hatred that it terrified me, I said: I don't know.

Derek, whom I would never detest more than at this moment, laughed.

The day, as I recall it now, was dry but without sunshine, the kind of day that is known in England as *mild*, and the late spring colors, usually so vivid in the Kentish countryside in May, seemed to have run into each other, blurring definitions.

The land appeared more gray than green, more weary than hopeful. Some spindly-legged cows grazed among the wreckage of vandalized Horsa gliders scattered in the hedgerows where the invasion landings had been practiced the summer before. The mounds of air-bomb casings that lined the country roads, and the crumbling roadblocks that went back to the near-forgotten days when it was England where invasion had been expected hourly, created artificial mountains mile after mile. Already, all of these remains had started to slip into the past. They had become part of an alien intrusion into an orderly insular existence. The war had moved to Germany. Its unwanted debris was but an uncomfortable reminder of everything that had had to be done, both glorious and ignoble, to bring it to an end. An act such as Ludo's inconvenient heroism could be resented, along with the rest of the monstrous human aberration that was finally ending. I could believe that he and his kind had earned their extinction. Heroism had become archaic in war-weary eyes, almost a matter of bad taste, and yet we who were closer to the political machinery that controlled the war continued to need heroism and heroes. Their innocence gave a veneer of respectability to the quite disreputable acts of the politicians.

I was aware of my own confused feelings in regard to Ludo. Almost everyone for whom he cared was dead by this time, dead or heading toward one of various disappointing endings, and, as we drove toward the Minister's country house, I thought that I might be able to approach the truth about myself as well if I could understand what the Pole had done.

I asked myself, as I had asked for more than two years: What kind of a man was it to whom Ann could give herself so wholly without reservations? Ludo and I had met three times: first, on the eve of war in Warsaw, at a party given by his sister, where I had gone to represent the chief of the British Military Mission; then on Bloody Sunday, September 15, 1940, at an English airfield, when he and his men mourned lost friends and celebrated an astounding victory; and finally, thirty-four months later, in Ann's borrowed rooms at the edge of Mayfair.

The last of those meetings had outraged all my hopes; it erased all doubts that he was Ann's lover, and it struck a mortal blow at my own love for her. I found that I could hate him then, not only in my own behalf but, curiously, for my brother Patrick whose marriage to Ann I had always envied even though that marriage had been a disaster for them both. Yet hatred is never a straightforward business. It works best in England if, like love, it is never mentioned. I had begun by liking and admiring him, and some of that remained. Ludo fascinated me, being quite different from anyone I knew. I had studied him as though he were a rare ornithological specimen, both beautiful and deadly.

We didn't drive all the way to London with the Minister. That year, he lived in an ugly Edwardian villa near Edenbridge, in Kent, and took the ten o'clock morning train to London from Tunbridge Wells each day. When we arrived, he asked me to walk with him privately in his garden. He showed me his collection of medieval sun-clocks and gave me my briefing out of the others' hearing.

—Sorry to hear about Lady Ann, he said, as though a formal

apology from him would erase all my bitterness. These are such brutal times. Your second cousin, isn't she? And Patrick's widow, of course? Anything I can do?

—I don't believe so, Minister, I said. She's doing reasonably well.

—Friend of that Polish squadron leader, wasn't she?

—We both know she was.

—Yes. Quite. Hugh Wadsworth-Jones can be an insensitive ass sometimes, and I must say I fear for Derek's soul. Nasty business, in any event. Do you suppose the Pole had something to do with it?

—Are you suggesting, Minister, that he cut her throat?

Startled, the Minister gave me a long, calculating stare.

—Good God, no, he said. But there are other ways to inflict an injury. I don't suppose you knew that Ann did a little work for us?

—I had begun to think so, I said. But she never told me.

—She was particularly anxious that you shouldn't know.

—Did Derek know? I asked, and found it suddenly difficult to breathe, but the Minister chose to evade an answer.

—One never really knows about Derek, does one, he said and smiled coldly, and went on in a distant, musing tone: I've never understood the suicidal impulse. Nothing can be so unbearable that one can't live through it. And this . . . this seems so trivial, a wartime love affair. It's no more logical than what we watched this morning.

—Logic? I said. Yes, I suppose everything must follow some sort of logic. But what kind of logic? Motives and attitudes aren't interchangeable between nationalities and cultures.

—That's just what I was thinking, the Minister said and smiled.

—In what reference, Minister?

—Several references. You have a private interest in this matter of Ludwik Toporski. And, of course, you've no reason to be fond of him, isn't that correct? We also have a public interest in him as part of our duty. The Poles look up to him . . . quite literally, I suppose. He's become a symbol that they'd follow far more readily than their politicians, especially in their present state of mind. We should control whatever influence his reputation gives

him, or, if that proves to be impossible, we should be in position
to re-evaluate his record and present him in a different light. We
may find a perfectly good solution to everyone's problems, both
public and private, in some unexpected facet of his character that
a careful investigation might reveal.

—Minister, I asked incautiously. Are you telling me to ruin the
man's good name?

—Would that worry you?

—I believe it would.

—Then simply be fair.

—Fair, Minister? You want me to be fair?

—What else could I ask for? Objective, devoid of sentiment,
even skeptical. Those are the elements of fairness. Think of your
researches as a purely intellectual exercise in which your special
knowledge of the man gives you an advantage. You shouldn't
make a moral question out of a purely political assignment.

Carefully, knowing that I had begun to sail in murky waters, I
asked: Weren't there some other political plans for him?

The Minister had stooped to sniff at a rare bloom and kept his
back to me as he said, with what I thought to be a studied carelessness: There may have been. But . . . man disposes, don't you
know, and fools decline to listen. Perhaps there's a lesson for you
here, Hudson. True opportunity is never offered twice.

—Yes, Minister, I said.

We had come to the end of the garden and the Minister
stopped there, among the greening rosebushes he tended himself
and the Italian sundials that were his special passion. He was a
tall, stooped man whose eyes seldom seemed to move or rest
directly upon any object. He stared by habit into that middle distance which is the preserve of Englishmen of his kind.

I knew that Ann and he shared a distant moment which had
been both scandalous and tragic, that he had been responsible (at
least in part) for her many years abroad, and that his interest in
Ludo was quite possibly as personal as my own. I thought then of
how dependent on his good opinion I had become in the last four
years. At forty-two, my hold on my career was tenuous at best. I
had done little regimental service. With the war's end, my acting

colonelcy would revert to my substantive rank of captain, Indian Army, followed by retirement at half-pay. It was a prospect almost as unenviable as that of the Poles. Ironically, it had been my knowledge of the Polish language that had given my career an unexpected burst of life just before the war, deferring the unappetizing vista of a furnished room in a boardinghouse and lone walks by the sea. I had mastered those reptilian sibilants as my obligatory second language at the RMC, thinking that a posting as a military attaché in a second-rate capital like Warsaw was the more likely prospect for a young subaltern with meager connections than one in an important embassy like Paris or Berlin. But now my expertise with Polish and the Poles had no further value. I had every reason to view my future with distress unless I could secure a full colonelcy, that most difficult step in British promotions, before the war ended. Then, as the Minister's briefing was clearly suggesting, I could look forward to retirement in five or six years as a brigadier, perhaps to a knighthood and a charitable directorship or two in the City.

As though the thought had traveled from my mind to his, the Minister turned and said:

—Soldiering is such an improvident occupation, don't you think? You people have so few opportunities to render some singular service to yourselves. You serve your country. Year by year, you advance in rank, authority, privileges, and social position, and suddenly it's all gone. One day a thousand men move at your command, the next day you launder your own shirt in a shared bathroom and darn your own socks. It all ends with such terrible abruptness, doesn't it?

—Yes, Minister, I said.

—Not very fair, is it?

—It . . . isn't something one should think about, I said.

—I wonder. Shouldn't faithful service be faithfully rewarded? That Pole, now. Think of his circumstances. He's . . . what? Forty-four years old?

—Forty-two, Minister, I said.

—Forty-two. Like you. Too old to think about starting a new career. He doesn't even have a pension to look forward to since he's not a British officer and his own government has neither

legal standing nor any money of its own any longer. He must
have had all that in mind when he rammed that German.

—I rather doubt that, Minister, I said. The Poles don't think
in quite such practical terms.

—But wouldn't it be fair to assume some sort of a mental
derangement under his circumstances? An awareness of the end
of things with no illusions left must be the most painful state of
all.

—Yes, it is, Minister, I said.

—I wonder what I'd do in his place. Or in yours.

The sun-clocks were arranged in a circle, like a faery ring, as
though time had neither a beginning nor an end. Nothing that
men could do would affect its flow in any measurable way. I wondered what could have happened between the Minister and Ann
all those years ago, why he had never married, and then I thought
I knew. He stood in the middle of his circle of time, poised in the
center of turbulent hours, and he'd be quite impervious to the
fleeting touch of human emotions. It was a quality that ensured
survival.

Softly and kindly now, as if regretting the need to explain, he
said:

—One tries to do the right thing, one tries to be fair. But the
Poles must slip into oblivion, vanish, disappear. They mustn't be
allowed to draw any favorable attention to themselves just now.
It's most important that no voice should be raised in Britain to
ask why these rather gallant people, who may have rendered quite
exemplary service in the war's darker days, should not be honored
with the other victors and have their cause upheld. We have a national election due sometime this year and the Prime Minister
may not hold the country.

—Wouldn't it be simpler, Minister, just to let them march in
the Victory Parade and then do their vanishing? Don't the
damned Russians have what they wanted, in any event?

—It's not the damned Russians, Hudson, that we're concerned
about. It's the damned Americans. They've let themselves be
gulled into giving half of Europe to the Communists and we're

obliged to take our cues from them. Britain's economic future will depend on their largesse for years to come.

He stood with his back to me and passed his long, well-bred hand in slow, measured movements across the face of a medieval sundial. He stroked the tall Roman numerals gently, with affection, and I was struck once more by the inevitability of defeat, no matter what men did to save themselves.

—One tries to do the decent thing, the Minister was saying. We're not in the business of manufacturing libels. One can be properly sorry for the Poles, but our feelings are irrelevant. The Prime Minister has determined a certain policy which depends upon a certain truth, and we can't have that truth questioned by anyone, no matter how deserving. There is nothing we can do for or about the Poles, in any event. To attempt it would be like trying to turn back the shadow on one of these dials. And when we serve a greater truth we serve a greater master. Such service is invariably rewarding.

Then we were walking back toward the others and the Minister did something I'd never have expected. He took my arm, the first gesture of friendship and affection that I had ever known him to make to anyone, and I was strangely moved. Here, I thought, was yet another man crying out in anguish and doing all he could never to be heard. I could not speak and when he went on to say, *Things beyond value have no value, the priceless is worthless*, he was speaking for me as much as for himself.

—People believe only what they touch, he said finally. Or what has touched them. The rest they believe conditionally on the testimony of those who claim to have touched it. If they remain untouched, truths need not be painful, as I imagine you've found out by your own experience.

Remembering everything I knew about Ludo and Ann, I said that I had.

I went to see Ann at the hospital the next afternoon. She was too weak to talk but she would live, the nervous young doctor assured me. She had been found in time. Indeed, Mrs. Smallwood, a friend of her mother's, had been at the point of entering Derek's flat as Ann, the razor in her hand, had fallen on the rug.

Help had been summoned quickly. The scar on Ann's long and graceful neck would probably remain.

To die by choice is an act of primitive absurdity that is not without its comic element. To do so horribly is nothing short of madness. Ann had been self-indulgent, promiscuous, careless about her name, and destructive to anyone who loved her long before she had met Ludo, but she had never been mad. Whatever passed through her mind as she grasped that razor must have been too terrible to bear. Yet what could it have been other than a return to normalcy, to ordinary living, to a future free of unconsidered emotional commitments? She could have had no illusions about the fleeting quality of such lives as Ludo's. Their natural purpose was to circle ever closer to the flame until they entered it. Yet, if he had been the determinant in her last, dreadful choice, I wanted to maim him.

What could I say to her? Her arms were lifeless, connected to tubes. Her eyes reflected the harsh white glare of the electric light bulbs as shattered prisms might do. They contained no light of their own.

It was no time for questions or recriminations. Even sympathy would have been out of place. The scene was vulgar, a commonplace of sculleries and war. I couldn't understand what had happened to Ann's sense of her own worth and value. How could she have been brought down to the level of a jilted cinema usherette? But I felt neither anger, nor pity, nor sorrow, nor even regret at the waste of my own misunderstood emotion. Watching her, I found myself thinking of England herself: noble, depleted, fallen from her standards, reduced to the melodrama of a Victorian novel written for kitchen maids. It was a view with which the Minister happened to agree.

Finally, I could begin to think of Ludo as I had seen him last in Derek's tidy and delineated flat: Ludo's long white legs swinging to the floor off the disordered ottoman, Ludo standing naked with a courtly smile as Ann, giggling like a schoolgirl, pulled up a sheet to cover her own glowing nudity. I had stood immobilized in the doorway they had been too preoccupied to secure, as he reached for a robe while indicating an armchair in which I might

sit and as I wondered when I might wake safely from that nightmare.

I could have killed him easily then, as naturally as I had wished
for my brother Patrick's miraculous disappearance from the wedding chapel while our bewildered country-parson father droned
the ceremonial verses and I, desolate beyond all sense of loss,
fumbled in my pockets for the wedding ring.

He was at ease and cordial and I hated him. He was amused
and smiling. But his mouth remained closed and the smile
suggested that, while it might be feasible, there was no reason for
it. The smile made a crooked diagonal on his lower face, meeting
beneath his right eye the upper diagonal of the scar on his forehead. Through some kind of transference of my tension, or
through his own effort to keep his smile in place, the scar on his
forehead began to move. His body had acquired that ridged
solidity on which disfigurements seem painted.

The robe had parted with one of his gestures, and I saw that
the skin of his upper torso and right thigh was seamed with tissue
that had survived a burn. The fire had taken whatever gloss of
softness he might have possessed. The clean white nipples made
by bullet wounds lay like crude embroidery across his chest and
shoulders. A thought came from nowhere: the image of a Roman
legionnaire's cuirass that I had seen unearthed from some Tuscan
field made me think of him as an artifact, pierced and scarred by
weapons and years, rather than as a man.

Taller than I, he was looking down, speaking from a height.
His English was flawless, perhaps excessively so, and it occurred to
me that his urbane amiability was a ploy on his foreignness, as if
to suggest that he couldn't be expected to act like an Englishman. His eyes were hidden under thick green spectacles that
made him seem mechanical, antihuman. His false, lopsided smile
seemed like yet another disguise.

Ann rose, wrapping the sheet about herself, and smiled at him
over her shoulder as she left the room. He made an effort to be
agreeable. His gestures showed a quality of breeding I had not expected in a professional practitioner of violence.

Later, I would remember only his last three sentences, and
those I overheard on my way down the stairs. I managed to turn
around without a word to Ann as she returned with a tray, a bot-

tle, and glasses, her long, brown, Anglo-Irish legs as symmetrical as scissors under her insufficient sheet. Halfway down the stairs I heard his deep, overloud voice asking Ann a question. Cruel Ann laughed and said through her crowing laughter: *It doesn't matter what he thinks, what anyone thinks,* and then Ludo was correcting her with a saddened urgency as though he had been disappointed once again: *No, no, Ann. Not think but* believe. *If people thought, if they were able to think, they'd never be able to believe what they were thinking.*

Ann mocked him gently:

—I thought that soldiers weren't paid to think?

I didn't hear his answer. Now, knowing why he finally turned against Ann and the rest of us, why he left her, I wondered what he had said.

In my desk, I had collected extracts from his service file, a bureaucratic rendering of a life at war which had chipped at him a little at a time: half a hand here, another injury there, a family and friends killed and buried in every corner of the world. It is the sort of bloodless arithmetic that dissolves a man in a mass of numbers which, in his case, included twenty-seven thousand hours in the air, one thousand and twenty combat sorties, forty German aircraft shot down (with an additional ten "probables," unconfirmed, and fifteen others damaged), and thirty-two major and minor wounds in fourteen engagements. He had been shot down four times in six years, bringing his crippled plane to land three times out of four, and had been cited for gallantry thirty-two times in Poland, France, Great Britain, and North Africa. He had been decorated twice with our Distinguished Service Order, twice with the Distinguished Flying Cross, three times with the Polish Virtuti Militari, with the American DFC, the Czech Order of the White Lion, and the French Croix de Guerre with palms. There was no reason to suppose that these medals were unearned.

In 1945, he was forty-two years old. He had been thirty-six when the war began in Poland in 1939. Born in 1903, in what had been a province of the Russian Empire, he had been orphaned in 1919 when the invading Bolsheviks and rebel Ukrainian peasants had murdered his parents. He served in the Polish-Bolshevik War (1919–1920) in the cavalry of General Janusz Prus and then as a fighter pilot in a squadron organized for the Poles by American adventurers.

His family, tabulated on a single page like a matched set of tombstones, listed a father (Jan August Rymwid-Toporski, 1873–1919, landowner); a mother (Lucyna de Jauneville Toporska, 1882–1919, concert pianist); three brothers (Piotr Secundus, 1908–1944, Major, Polish Army; Jan "Norwid" Tertius, 1912–1940, Commander, Polish Navy; Jan Zygmunt Quintus, 1918–1940, Ensign, Polish Army Reserve, university student); and a sister (Wlada, 1916–1943, actress and chanteuse, m. Romuald Modelski, diplomat, 1937).

I thought of him as I had seen him for the first time in his sister's home on the evening before the war began. I had gone there with Loomis, who was then in pursuit of Lala Karolewska, and with Prus's nephew, who had fought (together with Loomis) in the Spanish Civil War, and who had invited both of us to Wlada's unforgettable party.

Ludo had puzzled me that night. I thought him arrogant and aloof despite his evident fatigue. The eyes, not yet hidden under tinted glass, had been gray, hooded, widely spaced, unprepared for pain. The mouth was wide, thin-lipped. The effect was triangular, unpleasant in conjunction with high cheekbones and a flattened chin. I thought him sharklike, capable of cruelty and evasion. All his movements were economical and swift.

Here was the quintessential soldier, I had thought. If I knew anything about his kind of European, who stood astride all his centuries simultaneously, I could expect no complaints from him. His rigid personal codes would allow him the most appalling excesses in the name of honor, country, duty, and the reputation of his family. To such men, suicide was preferable to life with dishonor. But, I had thought then, as I wondered now: Could one have the ancient Roman virtues without the Roman vices? It hadn't seemed likely.

Yet there had been something else about him at that gathering in Warsaw, a contradictory aura of affection that made him the center of whatever group he happened to join. His brothers and his sister obviously loved and honored him, his peers deferred to him, and this respect and love glowed on him as though he were a mirror, so that I thought him dazzling.

Had Ann been equally dazzled by his reflection of her love for him? She was too intelligent and far too experienced to make such mistakes, and yet she must have made them where he was concerned. She must have seen in him a light of his own.

In my thoughts, determined to retain that cold, intellectual objectivity that the Minister demanded, I moved to the beginnings, to the day before my path first crossed Ludo's, and to the long, careful talks I had had with men like Prus and Auerbach and Bettner, and to what I knew of a world in which none of them would ever live again. History is made by heroes but written by people incapable of heroism, and the propaganda of the victors often becomes the story of the vanquished. But sometimes conscience festers long enough in the most unlikely of unheroic men and then the truth is told.

PART ONE

As It Was in the Beginning

Thus saith the Lord, Set thine house in order;
for thou shalt die, and not live.

II KINGS 20:1

CHAPTER I

EARLIER THAT DAY, the last in the month of August, 1939, there had been no reason to suppose that Ludo would see his brothers in Wlada's vast apartment on Koszykowa Street.

Wlada had given orders to close the apartment, and Krolik, the janitor, got drunk. He was an old man, jealous of his dignity. He had been a corporal in the rural gendarmerie of a Russian Tsar. Each time he was asked to do a little work, he drowned his humiliation and fueled his anger with a bottle of grain alcohol flavored with cold tea. Now he was staggering up and down the stairs under packing cases, littering the chestnut parquet floors with straw, coal chips, and the mud that had dried through the summer on his boots, and Zosia, once the savior of the family and now the cook-housekeeper, was shouting at Krolik and the maids who were taking down the tapestries and paintings. Janek, the youngest of the brothers, was putting on a performance of his own.

Like several thousand other youths in Warsaw, he had read his mobilization orders half a dozen times. He had dusted his long, spurred, handmade riding boots and he had shaken the mothballs out of the pockets of his military greatcoat. Now he was practicing the mindless curses of a cavalry cadet-officer and barking orders that everyone was too busy to obey, striding through the rooms in lancer breeches and in the red silk socks that junior officers of his regiment affected, and then the doorbell rang . . . and there was Piotr—dusty and unshaven and grinning from ear to ear—and Zosia cried out: *All Spirits praise the Lord!*

—So they damn well should, Piotr said, coming in.

His battalion had arrived from its eastern garrison only an hour earlier and Piotr had come to Koszykowa Street in search of a bath after a week in trains, as he and Norwid and Ludo did whenever one of them happened to be in Warsaw.

—Piotruś! Wlada said, unsurprised. What are you doing here?

—What does he ever do when he comes to see us? Janek cried

and ran to embrace him. He eats! He uses up all the hot water in the tank. He falls asleep in Romuald's armchair! Welcome home!

—Home? Piotr said and looked around the empty spaces of Wlada's apartment, and the others laughed.

It was a place the brothers often ridiculed, calling it *The Circus*. Wlada herself thought of it as little more than a ten-room stage for her entertainments and a convenience where Janek might live within walking distance of the university. Their real home, where all of them had been born and then so cruelly orphaned, was an abandoned, fire-blackened ruin which none of them had thought to visit since the night of their parents' murder twenty years earlier. They used to tell each other that they never went there because it was so isolated, so provincial. It took days to get there, first by train and then in a rented two-wheeler or on horseback. But what made it really inaccessible for them was another kind of distance; the horror of their parents' fate had displaced the manor in a remote and sealed-off era.

Gagging on his cigar, his first as it happened, Janek said: Well . . . not home, then. Welcome to the Circus!

—Ooof, Piotr said and stretched and yawned and rubbed his dust-streaked face. Let me tell you, a week in those cursed trains is enough to break a man's spirit. And must you smoke that stinking rope, little brother? You'll gas us all even before the war begins.

Janek had become quite pale, regretting the cigar. He took a deep breath, said uncertainly: I hope the fighting lasts long enough for me to see some action.

—How long can you stay this time, Piotruś? Wlada interrupted.

—Long enough to take off my boots, I expect. That's a soldier's definition of home, little brother. Anyplace where he can take off his boots and not have them stolen.

—And then what? Janek said eagerly. Then where?

—Wherever the geniuses of the High Command decide my boots ought to take me.

—I bet I'm in Berlin before you, footslogger! Janek cried and grinned and dodged the cushion that Piotr flung at him. Everybody knows the Germans' tanks are made of plywood and cardboard. It's all a huge bluff! We'll ride through them like a chicken through a bag of corn.

Wlada looked at the strutting, posturing young man and felt her own long nails in the palms of her hands.

—Twenty-one, the age of faith, she said with sadness, pity, and contempt. The perfect age for a soldier to die for his country.

—The last year when a woman can marry for love alone, Piotr said and grinned gently. The final age before compromise begins.

She smiled, it was a practiced smile: the actress wielding the tools of her trade, the woman her weapons. Yet she thought herself better equipped for the days to come than anyone else she knew.

—Imagine the impudence of those Germans! Janek was orating. Trying to scare us with tinfoil and cardboard.

—I wouldn't be too sure about the cardboard, Piotr said.

—Oh, Janek said airily. That's defeatist thinking. The Germans will get stuck in our autumn mud, whatever their tanks are made of, and we'll ride rings around them. Everybody says it'll all be over just like that.

He blew a wavering smoke ring to show how effortless their victory would be. He choked, and his eyes began to water, and he looked about for an ashtray where he might dispose of the cigar without appearing to give in. The blue-gray strands of smoke drifted in the sun-streaked morning air among the crates and bales and Wlada's modernistic Art Deco furniture and the framed paintings stacked against the walls. In the sun's slanted rays, the room seemed on fire.

War would come soon enough, Wlada knew, and it would take them all away from her—Janek and Piotr and Norwid and Ludo —and they'd return as Ludo had done in the year of their parents' murder, aged beyond his years.

If only we could stay exactly as we are, she thought. If the eroding process of time and experience could be halted so that life would continue in easy affection, and if we could stay forever as each other's trusted allies against the future and the past, then neither bluster nor reticence would be necessary in our lives.

—Did you come here to bicker with each other? she chided them gently. You men are such children, all of you.

—What else would you have us do, little sister? Piotr said and shrugged and looked at Janek, who shrugged and looked at him. Ought we to sit about telling military lies? He's not going to frighten the Wehrmacht with his scarlet socks, though I don't mind telling you that the rest of our war equipment scares the hell out of me!

—We should enjoy ourselves, Wlada said. We should make the most of our time together.

—It's hardly a time for celebration.

—Of course it is, she said. Warsaw is full of people who scurry about and try not to look at anybody else. All that dreadful tension! We ought to create some wonderful memories for ourselves! We might not see each other for months, even years.

—Oh, we'll be home in six months, Janek said. Everybody says so.

—And if you're not? Wlada said. We should do something about all that gloom.

—Easy enough to say, little sister, Piotr said and rubbed his eyes where dust and his own sweat had caked in the corners. But how? We don't even know how much time we've left.

—We should have lights, laughter, music, and all our friends around us! Wlada said. We should celebrate the fact that war still hasn't come . . . Oh, Piotruś, you know what I mean! Who knows when we'll see all our friends again?

—Or each other, Piotr said somberly.

On cue, as though they had rehearsed it, Norwid telephoned. Norwid, from whom they had last heard earlier in the summer from Rio de Janeiro, was in Warsaw on some mysterious Navy business and wanted to spend the night. He'd be on his way back to his ship, docked at Oksywie in the Baltic, by the first morning train.

—*And the Word became Flesh!* Zosia cried, bringing them the news. It's a miracle!

—We can certainly use one or two of those, Piotr said.

—But this is unbelievable, Wlada said and laughed. When was the last time that so many of you were in Warsaw at the same time? Three years? It's at least three years. Now, if only Ludo would make a miraculous appearance!

—Oh, by all means, Piotr said. The more miracles, the better.

—Do either of you know where they might have sent him? Well, it doesn't matter where they sent him, Wlada said. We'll just have to find him.

—Just like that, Piotr said. An army of a million men is being deployed on a battle line that stretches around half the country, and she's going to find one officer among them. Not even our father was such an optimist, may he rest in peace.

—Oh, she can do it, Janek said. Honestly, you've forgotten the power of this woman. Death alone can stop her, once she's set her mind to a certain course.

—Would you mind not talking about death? Wlada said sharply. And will you take your filthy old spurs off that hassock, Piotruś? You know how frantic Romuald gets about his possessions.

Piotr sighed, grinned, said: When men take orders from a woman, that's a point at which civilization crumbles.

She cried, as they'd expect her to: Perhaps that's where civilization will finally begin!

Piotr said: I hope I'll never live to see the day.

—But I'll bet ten *zlote* we'll see Ludo here if she wants him here, Janek said and ran toward Wlada and lifted her toward the chandeliers. There's never been such a woman anywhere before!

—Put me down, you bear!

—TUM-ta-ta-TUM ta-ta ta-ta, Janek chanted and waltzed her through the room while Piotr grinned and nodded, and Zosia clasped her hands over her eyes, and the maids peered giggling through the doorways.

—Do you think anyone can say no to *her*? Janek cried and laughed. She's fluent in five languages and she doesn't understand a refusal in any of them! Well, Piotruś? Do I have a bet?

—Enough! Wlada cried. Put me down! Don't you ever run out of breath?

—Time enough for that when I'm dead, Janek said.

—Put me down, you fool!

The qualities that Wlada prized the most, she knew, were reasonableness and reason. Premonitions had no place in such mental processes as hers. But Janek's pale face, hanged in its aureole of smoke, had become a strangely tilted mask from which light had fled, and Piotr's stocky body had subsided into a graven stillness under the dust of his journeys.

Back on her feet and wrapped against a sudden chill, the actress glanced swiftly into mirrors and retrieved her smile. The woman would make good use of it, she knew. She made a marginal note to mask all her fears.

—A party, then! she said brightly and made swift, fluttering motions with her hands. We'll have a family gathering. We'll ask all our friends. It'll be something for all of us to remember later. Is there anything unreasonable about that?

—Unreasonable? Piotr murmured. Did I hear the word *unreasonable* mentioned in this country? Who'd ever dare to accuse us of anything like that?

But Wlada had already run to the telephone.

In turn cajoling, helpless, scornful, and imperious, she dipped into her repertoire for the voice and manner of a woman who'd be oblivious of the trouble she was causing; indeed, one who'd be unaware that anyone would view her requests as unreasonable, no matter how harassed they might be in preparing their country for a terrible war, how frightened to see the paucity of the country's military resources, how close to exhaustion or sure of disaster.

—Hello? she said. Pawel? Is that you? But how tired you sound, poor dear. . . . How terribly . . . What? What? But of course I care! Friends must help each other, friends must be concerned. . . . Of course I'm concerned! What else is friendship for?

She offered a diversion, relaxation, a moment of merciful oblivion in a time of tension that had become almost tangible. —And do bring that odd, amusing Englishman who speaks Polish. And that American journalist! Yes, we *will* have a wonderful, carefree time. . . . We must, you know. We will!

She had never taken no for an answer since she became the woman of the family after her mother's death. She would have puzzled and upset her mother, whose ethic had been to submit with grace.

—We mustn't be negative about anything, these days, she said. We mustn't think that *anything* is impossible. . . .

And then: Hello? Hello? Stasio? Is that you? Oh, my poor dear friend . . .

As she spoke, she listened. The theater had taught her to improvise on cue. She heard the weariness, the fear that bordered on despair, the agony of hatred and suspicion, and she watched her brothers who had been so carefully brought up to fearlessness and duty and family affection.

Fearlessness, they were taught, was to courage as sainthood was to the mere doing of good, or as pure evil might be to the shabby intricacies of suburban vice. Fearlessness was better than courage because it was simpler, and simplicity was the key to dignity and grace. They had been taught contempt for money and commercial matters, and to avoid the poses of grandeur, and she thought them all doomed to extinction before they were born because their country's spirit had never been related to its time.

And: Hello? she said. Hello? Yes, my dear friend, there *is* something that you can do for me. . . . It's Ludo, of course. How can we have a family gathering if he isn't here? Surely, *you* know where to look for him, how to find him! And, once you've found him, you could tell me where I might speak to him . . . and then you could arrange for me to speak with him. Surely that's not too much to ask of such a dear friend? What? Well, of course friends must be able to rely on each other, it's part of our caring. . . . Oh, of course I care. You know that!

Listening somewhat wearily to herself, she remembered her murdered father who had taught his children a quality he called *invincible elegance,* a refusal to accept defeat long after the point of impoverishment and failure.

Up to the moment when the bivouacking Cossacks had begun to nail horseshoes to his hands and feet, and when he saw his own tenants bringing the wood drill and the ripsaw with which, eventually, they blinded and dismembered him, up to the irrevocable moment when his wife was butchered and he saw all his verities disproved, the old gentleman had been an almost professional optimist who read *War and Peace* at breakfast for more than twenty years because (as he'd put it) reading about so many dead Russians gave hope for the future. He was a foolish and ineffectual man, perhaps, yet there had been generosity in his life. It had been possible to live unselfishly in such a world as his.

The nervous voices that shrilled over the wires of the telephone tried to tell Wlada something altogether different.

—But why? she said. Why is it impossible? And what does that word mean?

Janek cried proudly: *Brava!* That's the spirit!

—No, I don't think I'm being at all difficult, she said. Hello? Are you still there?

Yes, she quite understood that war might break out at any moment, that the borders had been closed since noon, that foreigners were leaving the country in droves, that the political situation was worsening each hour. She could imagine . . . (Of course I can imagine!) . . . how exhausting it must be to move all those regiments, and to mobilize an army in secret so as not to irritate the Allies and provoke the Germans. (Of course I understand!) But it was precisely because of these things that she had to find Ludo. (Surely that is clear?) Otherwise, would she have been forced to bother her dear friend at the General Staff . . . at the Foreign Ministry . . . on the Air Staff of the Minister of War . . . in the Presidential Palace?

Watching and listening with the same sense of wonder that bemused Wlada's every audience, Janek said: I suppose that since these are military rather than spiritual requests, she won't have to call her dear friend in the Archbishop's Palace.

And Piotr said: Lights, music, laughter . . . it might be worth the trouble and the price. One miracle's as good as another, when all is said and done. And if you're part of a nineteenth-century army going off to fight a twentieth-century war, it's just as well to do your laughing early.

Wlada's logic, or her pretense of logic, was unassailable as always. Within an hour she was saying: Thank you! Thank you, my dear, dear friend. I knew I could depend on you. You'll come to the party? Ludo will be so pleased, and I'll be so grateful. . . . Yes, about eight or so. . . . Oh, you know I do.

And shortly afterward, a small red light, the signal for a high-priority message, appeared on a mobile switchboard in a forest clearing forty kilometers northwest of the capital, and the duty telephonist sent a messenger on the run to get the squadron leader. The squadron leader had been either in the air or on his feet for two days and a night and he was trying to get a little sleep.

CHAPTER II

HE HAD SLEPT LONGER than he had intended, but nothing around him appeared to have changed. Indeed, the land itself seemed to deny the possibility of change. Yet, he thought, in the aftermath of his recurrent nightmare, our past is handing down its verdict even now.

At dawn, as the sun began to gleam through the tree crowns like one of those ten-ruble gold *chervontsy* his father had kept buried in a trunk at the bottom of the apple orchard, as the day began, he had taken stock of his fatigue, judged himself too tired to make intelligent decisions, removed his soiled military blouse and boots, and told his orderly to wake him in an hour. Then he stretched out on the narrow canvas cot in the tent he shared with Papa Bettner, the squadron adjutant, with his two flight leaders, Reszke and Wardzinski, and with the squadron cat. But Papa Bettner had seen to it that Ludo's order wouldn't be obeyed. The squadron had been walking on tiptoes all morning so that he could sleep, and, in that conspiracy of silence, he had fallen into a deep and puzzling dream in which he flew forever between the horizons. He awoke gritty-eyed to take Wlada's call.

Looking at the forest, at the deep and dark expanse of woodland and meadows and reed-grown streams and marshland and sandy tracks and stillness that was full of soft brown scurryings, the forest to which he and his men and their machines had come two days and a night ago, he was aware of leaves, of individual trees, of the soil in which they were rooted, of the textures and colors of their bark, of the smell of the pine, of the enameled weight of red-and-yellow canopies spread over oaks and chestnuts, of the age of the trees. He saw them all separately and together and knew what each of them was and what they represented. The trees had been there centuries before his arrival; they were familiar with such gatherings as his.

The hiss and crackle of the radio-telephone was a violent intrusion.

He sighed, said: How did you manage to get this connection?

Wlada trilled crystally; there was no other way to describe her laughter. —Oh, that's a military secret! When can you be here?

—My dear mad sister, Ludo said. Do you have any idea of what I'm doing *here?*

—I know perfectly well what you're doing *there,* Wlada said. But Norwid is here! And Piotruś! And Janek is packing! You know what that means. You know, I'm sure you know (and now her voice had darkened, dropped in pitch; she was no longer playing the role of an irresponsible scatterbrain) it might be quite some time before we're able to see each other again. I shall be closing the Circus in a day or two. I'm to stay with Romuald's cousins in Lwów, young Catherine and her family, which should be rather pleasant. But I'm sure that nothing else is going to be pleasant! I think that you should make a real effort to come home tonight.

—Impossible, Ludo said and knew that this was another word his sister didn't understand.

—You owe it to us, Ludo, Wlada said, and then there was only a distant humming in his ears and the stale taste of interrupted sleep in his mouth.

His orderly, Jacek Gemba, who claimed to have been a waiter at the Europejski, brought him a cup of coffee and a moistened towel and began to fuss with Ludo's boots and jacket. He kept up a breathless stream of comment on the weather, on cows that had apparently invaded the airstrip at night, on the hayloft generosity of local village girls—on anything that might divert attention from his failure to awaken Ludo—and Ludo realized that the boy expected ruthless punishment.

Instinctively, he looked up at the sky, judging the known parameters of his world. He sniffed the air, testing it for danger as a stray dog might do outside a strange village. The sky was cloudless, as it had been all month, providing neither refuge nor cover for ambush, and for a moment he let his attention settle on a flight of crows that hung crookedly above the meadow, riding the thermal currents. The air was morning-fresh, but warming. The day would be hot. The wind had shifted once again; it came from the east, rolling like a tide from the shattered islands of his past, and with it came the smell of woodsmoke and the memory of fire. He had become a flier not out of love of flight but from lack of mercy. In his recurring nightmare, he destroyed, again and again, the murderers of his parents and the village in which he was born.

Jan Karol Bettner, not yet called Papa in those days, had seen this act of vengeance as a tragedy in which he, as Ludo's closest friend, had his own role to play. The view from the observer's seat of the wobbling Farman "Goliath" bomber must have been shattering for a man who needed a clear conscience to rationalize his own unappetizing life; the price of his silence would be great, Ludo knew even then.

Now this prematurely aged reservist, whom horror and conscience had sent on a twenty-year alcoholic search for something fine he might believe about himself, was coming toward him across the sun-drenched meadow, and Ludo ground his teeth. He could see the young soldiers grimacing and mocking the middle-aged adjutant behind his bowed back. Like making love, self-doubt and self-contempt should be private things, he thought. Bettner's public display of his own nightmare was unforgivable.

—Well, what's on the menu, then? he said and reached for the papers that Papa Bettner began handing to him one by one.

Years of work among the paper shufflers of the General Staff had given the middle-aged lieutenant an ability to speak like a ventriloquist's dummy, with teeth on show in a wooden smile and lips scarcely moving.

—First, Papa Bettner said, they've five aircraft and reservist pilots ready for you in Warsaw. We'll have to send a flight leader after them. Who do you want to go?

—I'll decide that later. Who are the pilots?

—Nobody we know, Bettner said and hiccoughed. Intellectuals. One's a concert pianist. One writes books. One is a sculptor. One's a university lecturer in mathematics. One lives by his wits.

They're all checked out for P-11 fighters, if that'll make you feel better about them.

—Nothing about the extra guns I've asked for? And what about our fuel allotment?

—No guns, no fuel, not yet. That's still somewhere on the road, rattling about in a peasant cart. But we might find something lying around the replacement depot if we keep our eyes open.

—What about the new birds?

—Ah, well, Papa Bettner said bitterly. That's the nicest surprise of the lot. Two P-7A monoplanes, 1930 vintage. One RXIII general-purpose reconnaissance machine. One Czapla observation crate. And one Farman Goliath. Do you suppose it's the same Goliath we flew to kill those poor, half-human bastards twenty years ago?

Ludo snatched at the specification sheets, scanned them, and stared at Bettner.

—Is this a joke? These things are useless to me. I run a fighter squadron, not the air museum.

—It's no joke, no mistake. I've checked. It's our allocation, Papa Bettner said and made a helpless gesture. I'll put in the usual protest, that goes without saying, but since we're to achieve full combat readiness by oh-five-hundred hours tomorrow, there's not a lot of time.

—Have they gone mad in Warsaw? Ludo said. Are they asleep? Drunk? Stupid? Haven't they heard about Messerschmitts?

His vision blurred and, for an irritating moment of dizziness and blindness, he watched liquid circles skip and dance in the corners of his eyes. Out on the airstrip, a cow was bellowing mournfully, in need of a milkmaid.

—You're entitled to an official protest, Papa Bettner said and went on to caution: Please, Ludo, don't leap without thinking. Go through channels first. Bureaucrats never forgive if you go around them, they've so little to work with to justify what they do. And . . . this isn't the Ukraine in 1919.

—I know what year this is, Ludo said savagely. Who's in charge at the matériel replacement office, these days?

—I don't know, Papa Bettner said. But it wouldn't be anyone

we know. All our friends are out in the field with the flying squadrons.

—There's somebody we do know at Okęcie Field, Ludo said and smiled. Auerbach's still there.

—Don't do anything drastic, Papa Bettner pleaded. You can get twenty years' hard labor for what you are thinking.

He had been drinking, that was clear at once. Nowadays, the querulous self-disappointed man was nearly always drinking, as if the advent of yet another war would resurrect all his gibbering ghosts. Ludo knew him to be a kind, decent man, even generous; but it had been so long since there had been a clear purpose in his life that he had forgotten what it was. Stiff as a lead soldier, he was both fragile and hollow; the air within him would be stale and flat.

—How do you know what I'm thinking? Ludo grinned.

—I know you. I know Auerbach. I remember what we and he and Wyga did in 1919. But they don't give you medals anymore for doing things like that. They lock you up and throw away the key. Forget about Auerbach, file your protest, and put in a new official requisition. It's just some poor reservist up there in the allocation office who doesn't understand the difference between one kind of airplane and another.

—There's no more time for that, Ludo said. What kind of liquor do you drink nowadays?

—Well . . . I don't know, Papa Bettner said and licked his dry lips. This and that.

—Have you a bottle of good cognac?

—I believe I might have . . .

—Lend it to me, will you?

—Don't do it, Ludo, Papa Bettner said. Take what they've given you and move it through channels. The days when you and I and Auerbach and Wyga fought a private war are long over and gone.

—Nothing is over till you decide it is, Ludo said. And if young men's lives depend on something that'll keep them flying five minutes longer than some other thing, you get it any way you can.

—I'll call Auerbach for you, if you want me to, Papa Bettner said.

—No, Ludo said. I don't want you involved in my problem. Not this time. Besides, remember? One doesn't call Chief Auerbach. One goes to see him and brings him a present, and one sits down and talks about old times.

—And one gets court-martialed, Papa Bettner said. And the young men still fall out of the sky like apples in autumn. And in the end it doesn't make a difference, one way or the other.

—Go get the cognac, Papa, Ludo said.

The wind had freshened, quickened.

Earlier, before the sun had risen, there had been a fog that closed and opened above the field and forest like the mouth of a giant fish feeding at its leisure. Now the fog was gone. He listened to the sounds of the village church bell tolling for matins in a steeple that rose above the trees. He heard the creaking of the weighted well beams, the calls of young women driving geese and goats, the shrill and frantic barking of a hungry dog.

Jacek Gemba waited to hear his sentence and his doom, and his young pilots waited, and Ludo looked at the sweating, cursing squads of Air Service soldiers who dug slit-trenches and latrines, and rolled oil and fuel drums from one clump of chestnuts to another, and struggled with tents and got themselves entangled in camouflage netting. They were all doomed men, caught up in the awful business of preparing for a war that couldn't be won; it would be a boon to get away from them even for a moment.

He watched his three duty pilots sprawled among the trees, three others coming to relieve them: Reszke, Borowicz, Gerlach getting to their feet under oaks red as flame; Wardzinski, Straka, and Wilchurzak walking toward them with mess tins full of coffee steaming in their hands. They were in full flying gear; silk scarves, leather helmets, and goggles hung around their necks or dangled from their fingers. He could hear the creaking of their leather suits, the sharp snap of harsh young voices laughing in fresh air. He saw them as six fresh new lives emerging from six histories, each separate and distinct and aimed toward whatever optimistic futures might enthrall young men. Yet the attitudes they expressed belonged to past centuries. They knew themselves to be the historical coin with which their country paid for its continuity.

Starting from sight-alert, it would take them six minutes to reach sixteen thousand feet in their P-11 "Pezetelki." Flying without oxygen, they'd have no chance to get above the echelons of Heinkel and Dornier bombers that would be overhead before they left the ground. The high-cover, twin-engined Messerschmitt Bf 110 "Zerstorers" would be coming down at them from twice their service ceiling, the sleek Bf 109 "Emils" would be all over them at twice their climbing speed. With eyes closed against the sun, he could imagine them climbing into a sky full of swift enemies and cannons, climbing laboriously minute after minute, ineffably romantic in their open cockpits; climbing, then burning and exploding before they could bring their own puny armament to bear; then falling from the sky with black-and-scarlet streamers unfolding behind them.

He wished for better planes, heavier armament, greater speed, a rate of climb, and a service ceiling that might give the Messerschmitt Zerstorers and Emils a dangerous run. If that were too much to expect, he wished for himself a ministerial shallowness of perception and that moral numbness with which generals move multicolored pins around paper landscapes. But the imagery of extinction couldn't be erased.

He swore, and Jacek Gemba stared at him in terror, and he rubbed his eyes—not to see better, but to allow his anger to subside. A certain (how was he to put it?) *necessary blindness* . . . a willful inability to see things as they were was needed . . . because there had to be that absolute, unquestioning commitment . . . because one did have to love something blindly, after all, to be able to die for it on demand.

He supposed then that he must have started smiling. The thin-lipped grin felt as tight against his teeth as a laced purse; he thought it an appropriate image for a paymaster of historical coin.

Jacek Gemba waited for punishment or reprieve, encouraged by the smile which he misunderstood. The tips of his fingers were white in the regulation manner against the seams of his coarse blue wool regulation trousers, and his eyes were apprehensive yet not without hope. His round peasant face, normally vacant or impertinent, assumed the expression of a frightened child that had cried itself to sleep.

—More coffee, sir? he offered.

—Thank you, Ludo said.

—You'll be going back to Warsaw, then, I expect, sir? To see Chief Auerbach?

—Yes. I expect I will.

—That's . . . a terrible man, sir, Jacek Gemba said. Not that I'd ever say one word against him, as God is my witness.

—What's so terrible about him? He's just an old soldier.

—They say he's got more ways to get things done than the Devil himself, Jacek Gemba said and shuddered and stared at Ludo with wonder and fear.

—That's useful, sometimes.

The young man's eyes contained something that might have been love but was probably only trust. Perhaps that was better than love, perhaps it kept going after love withered and died, in which case it would last longer than any love that Ludo had known or expected to find. Suddenly, Ludo wanted to tell the young man that he should trust no one.

Instead, he said: Find Lieutenant Bettner. Tell him to give you a bottle of cognac. Put that, and a clean shirt, and my service uniform in my flight bag. Then find Lieutenant Reszke and tell him to get ready for a trip to Warsaw. He and I and Bettner will fly there in the afternoon.

—Yes, sir. By your order, sir, Jacek Gemba said.

—Then go to Chief Wyga and tell him that you're to be confined to barracks for twenty-four hours. That might teach you to obey my orders.

—Yes, sir, Jacek Gemba said and Ludo turned away from his shocked, angry tears.

—You must obey orders, he heard himself saying and knew that he was speaking to himself as well. You're not to question motives. You're not permitted the luxury of evaluation. Civilians can afford to think and to argue. Soldiers obey orders.

Jacek Gemba had become quite pale and Ludo said quietly: Of course . . . there are no barracks here in which to confine you, and *Pan Szef* Wyga is a very literal man. You're being punished metaphorically, if you know what that means. D'you know what it means?

—N-no, s-sir, Jacek Gemba said.

—A literal man sees things only as they are, not as they could be or should be if we're to remain sane. He won't confine you to a barrack if there isn't one. He'll ignore a metaphor because he doesn't understand it. Metaphors frighten people like *Pan Szef*. You, on the other hand, have every reason to be scared out of your wits by things as they are. Learn to think metaphorically and you can be a hero like the rest of us. Do you understand me?

Terrified, the boy regarded him as though he had gone mad.

—N-no, s-sir . . .

—Metaphors confuse you? They're something you invent to give yourself an acceptable reason for doing your duty.

—If you say so, sir, Jacek Gemba whispered. By your order.

—Oh, yes. By my order.

The morning, which had begun quite badly, had many hours to go and none of them, he was sure, would offer him a reason for confidence, contentment, and a sense of pleasure with himself.

And now the earlier breeze had fallen away. The treetops were still. Unnoticed, the sun had moved higher into the sky and the morning had begun to ebb. The heat had acquired an almost tangible solidity in the breathless shadows under the oaks and chestnuts where the ready pilots sat among their machines. The waiting Pezetelki gleamed with lubricants and oil, their broad upraised wings seemed to tremble in the heat, so that he felt a near-overwhelming urge to stroke their dark noses and pat their hot flanks and to speak to them soothingly as he would to nervous thoroughbreds. In 1933, they had been the most advanced all-metal monoplanes in Europe; they had made Poland something of an air power. But now their day was gone. To send young men against the Messerschmitts in that kind of warcraft was like putting them before a firing squad.

Every Polish pilot knew about the superb PZL-24F pursuit planes that were sold abroad to balance the budget while they— the pilots—awaited the Luftwaffe in machines no other air force would take as a gift. Their weapons were the 1930 prototype P-7s armed with two machine guns and able to wring out a hundred and ninety miles an hour at sixteen thousand feet, or the P-11s which (sometimes) carried two additional machine guns and flew fifty miles faster, two thousand feet higher, or the wooden, hundred-and-thirty-mile-an-hour RXIII two-seaters armed with a single gun.

Anger had robbed him of breath. He had to stop then and lean against a tree while his duty pilots rose to their feet around him and Reszke offered him a canteen full of cold spring water. He swallowed his curses while his vision cleared.

Slowly, as if he were obliged to weigh and measure every word, the young lieutenant said: You're not going to accept that flying garbage they have for us in Warsaw, are you, sir?

—What would you like instead? Ludo asked and smiled while his glance darted away from the expectant faces and moved back and forth across the horizon.

—Something that'll stay up in the air long enough to do a bit of good, Reszke said.

Gerlach, Wardzinski, Straka . . . all of them . . . laughed politely. Reszke didn't laugh. His eyes were full of questions that Ludo couldn't answer; he had clear answers only to questions of his own.

. . . Courage, contempt for death, self-sacrifice for the sake of principle, these were the guideposts for such lives as his. One thousand Polish years stood as guarantee of the supremacy of the spirit over mechanical devices! And if his young men's lives were to be the price of national prestige in foreign marketplaces, if they were to be shot out of the sky because they didn't have the weapons that might keep them there, everyone would grieve for them and honor them in speeches and bestow on them the immortality of legends. Someday, he thought, someone would have to hang for this.

—Pity we can't have some of those beautiful birds they're selling abroad, Gerlach said.

Dryly, Ludo said: Yes. It is a shame.

—One would suppose, Reszke began again, and Ludo interrupted: Suppose, Lieutenant? How long have you been with the squadron?

—Going on ten years now, sir, the lieutenant said.

—Then you should know better than to hope for the impossible.

Pale blue-gray eyes regarded him calmly. He approved of Reszke, wished him well, seeing in him something of his old expectations for himself. What he wanted to say then was: *Tell me what gives you joy, what fills your life with pleasure,* but, of course, he could say nothing of the kind. Sentiment wasn't foreign to either of them—they'd hardly be able to call themselves Polish without an inclination to the sentimental—but war was marching toward them with great strides and everyone was learning to conceal what they treasured most.

Gerlach swore. Fear was very real then, the fear that comes from rage so deep that it threatens reason. If he could find them all together, Ludo thought, all of them . . . the ministers who spent a millionaire's ransom on forty regiments of horse cavalry while limiting the fighters' service ceiling to save the cost of oxygen equipment . . . the statesmen who flirted with Hitler until it was too late for anything but death or surrender . . . the generals for whom an air force was something that flew above parades . . . he would kill with pleasure.

In his blind fury, he could see everything as clearly as though he were still dreaming: those charming men of lofty principle and imperturbable dignity who had led their country to the brink of an abyss and then stepped aside, ever courteous, mouthing their historical metaphors . . . the sky from which fire would fall . . . the terrible innocence of the victims digging their own graves for a thousand years.

There was a certain logic to all this, to be sure: a very Polish logic which called for death before resurrection; he could understand it in much the same way he understood the function of the air he breathed. But understanding didn't bring forgiveness.

CHAPTER III

THEY FLEW TO WARSAW shortly after noon. The flat land reeled away mile after mile. Here (as he looked down, fondly) a small market town, there a row of poplars strung along the edge of a reed-grown stream. Then fields of wheat, cabbage, and wheat again, grassland, potatoes, cabbages, and turnips.

A dusty village street wound among yellow-brown roofs woven out of straw, and he banked the little red-and-silver avionette and cut its airspeed so that he could drop down just above the huts. Children had run out of a barn that might have been a schoolhouse; they deserved a show. He wobbled his wings between a metaled church tower on the right, and a redbrick railway station on the left, and began to climb in a lazy spiral while the children waved.

A manor house, set in a grove of chestnuts, reminded him of home.

Warsaw gleamed gray-and-white in the near distance: not his world, not entirely, and never by choice, but he returned to it again and again. He didn't love this city of his middle past. He used it warily although appreciatively, as he used his women: with competence and courtesy, with the detachment due to any distraction, with the minimum affection necessary to maintain an illusion, and (always) with caution. Like his women, his most persistent ghosts, it was a city best viewed from a distance and preferably from above. It glittered with metal roofs and iron monuments and with the hot glare of windows taped against concussion.

Someone had told him once that if a line were drawn from Lisbon in the west to the Ural Mountains in the east, and if another were inscribed from the northernmost peninsula of Norway to the southernmost promontory of Greece, they would intersect here, in the Vistula, between Warsaw on the river's western bank and the suburb of Praga on the eastern one, and that this tilted cross, an unwitting symbol of a nation's endless journey toward Golgotha, would mark the geographic center of the continent of Europe.

The city slipped under his wing and he viewed it coldly, as a German armada commander might in a day or two: a target, no more. Nine hundred years' worth of stone and brick and mortar and monument and spire. Sharp, silvery roofs sheeted in tin and lead. Lead and copper piping. Gilded cornices. Cobbled thoroughfares in the Old Town, asphalt in the New. Narrow stone houses pressed against each other, each with its inward-looking rows of windows peering into courtyards from the four corners of its own small world.

Then they were in the northwest corridor, slanting across the town, and Ludo eased the throttle, thinned out the fuel mixture, and cut the airspeed to begin the long descent toward Okęcie Field. It looked no larger than a green-gray postage stamp pasted in the top-right corner of the city, awaiting cancellation. He flew toward it, banked, and dropped into the rectangular landing pattern that would identify a friendly aircraft, dropped lower over the newly dug machine-gun pits and sandbagged revetments, and observed long lines of machines parked between the hangars: old Potez 25s, Breguet 19s, and Fokker F7s; it was as if the memories of his youth were lined up for inspection. Then, unbelieving, he watched the most reluctant memory of all: an ancient Farman Goliath bomber bumping across the grass.

He took up the Aldis lamp and began to wink and flash the squadron's coded recognition signal to the control tower, but there was no reply. He cut the throttle, the engine sighed into silence, and the ground tilted suddenly toward them. They could hear the humming of the wind in the struts and wires, the hiss of the air.

And then the wheels had touched the concrete runway and they rolled toward the gray cold buildings of the air base.

The corridors of the base administration building were full of officers in tunics of an unfamiliar cut. They carried cardboard files and brown-paper folders. They clutched briefcases and gestured with portfolios. They consulted each other gravely in the open doorways of their offices. They were punctilious about the deference due to each other's rank. They barked harsh orders at the orderlies.

Distrustful, cautious, assessing but allied nonetheless, the regulars and the reservists regarded each other with mild apprehension. Bettner had paused to fill and light his pipe while he stared about, but whether this was a pose of thought, perplexity, resignation, or resolve, Ludo didn't know.

—It won't be easy to deal with that lot, Papa Bettner murmured.

Knowing that he was no longer fully trusted, the adjutant was anxious to point out a difference between himself and the other hastily uniformed civilians, but Ludo would have none of it.

—Just don't fail me, Papa.

—Fail? How often do I fail? I don't remember failing you at Shepetovka in 1919.

—Neither of us is the man he was at Shepetovka, Ludo said as gently as he could.

—And a good thing too! Papa Bettner said. Nevertheless, I think the balance is still in my favor. I think that both Auerbach and Wyga would bear me out in that.

—We can consult later with Auerbach and Wyga, Ludo said. In the meantime, you're to get our fuel. If your reservist friends won't tell you what they've done with our allocation, then make damn sure you find out where they're keeping theirs. And if you so much as think about a bottle, I'll break it over your head.

The adjutant feigned lightness: A midnight requisition? They shoot you for that.

—Only in wartime, Ludo said. You're quite safe till then.

—If someone *doesn't* shoot us, Reszke said, grinning, we might be reservists the next time around.

—Can't we be rational in our lunacy? Papa Bettner pleaded. You know you can depend on me, but . . .

—Can I? Ludo said.

—You *know* that you can! In Shepetovka . . .

—For Christ's sake, move out of Shepetovka, Ludo said. I burned that place down twenty years ago.

He heard the slight hiss of Reszke's exhalation, and then the adjutant was walking away, walking stiffly among the other middle-aged reservists. His limp, an advertisement of a wound he suffered as a flier, had become pronounced.

—I thought you liked him, Major, Reszke said quietly. Isn't he your friend?

—I don't adopt my officers, Lieutenant, Ludo said.

Unchastened, Reszke nodded thoughtfully and said: He's lost his nerve, hasn't he.

—No, dammit! He has not, Ludo said and suddenly found himself explaining both the adjutant and his feelings for him: He talks too much. He has some memories he finds difficult to live with. He doesn't lie to himself enough. He's . . . an honest man.

—That sounds like you, Major.

The insolence took Ludo's breath away.

—You also talk too much!

—A privilege of innocence, sir, Reszke said with a rare smile.

—There's no such thing, Lieutenant, Ludo said.

—Yes, sir. But unlike you, sir, I'm not obliged to demonstrate cruelty that I don't possess. It's a . . . ah . . . wingman's privilege, if you know what I mean.

—And what is a wingman's privilege, may I ask?

—To let the flight leader do the killing while you watch the sky above and behind him, Reszke said.

They could laugh then. Even Reszke laughed. He didn't laugh often. He had been orphaned in a manner similar to Ludo's, and he had been raised by Jesuits to discipline without charity, and he had come to the Army on his eighteenth birthday in lieu of any family or home to which he might return. Now he said, with an air of assumed indifference: You protect Papa Bettner every day, Major, yet you don't respect him. Why is that?

—I respect what he was, Ludo said. I admire the courage he once had. I pity him for his struggle with himself.

—I don't even know what *courage* means, Reszke said. Is it like honor, money, things like that? The things that people talk about when they haven't any?

—Good God, what did the Jesuits teach you in that orphanage?

—They taught me *will*, the young man said quietly. The will to attack and to go on attacking even when you know that you've lost, giving up only when you're dead. They taught me to believe without understanding, and to love blindly but clear-sightedly.

—That makes love tragic, Ludo said.

—But isn't that what being Polish is about?

To break their sudden closeness, Ludo sniffed and grimaced.

—It stinks in here. What is that damn smell?

—Eau de Cologne and mothballs?

—Of course, Ludo said. Mobilizations always smell of mothballs.

—I must say, sir, that this isn't quite how I had imagined the coming of a war.

—What had you expected?

—I didn't know what to expect. But I had hoped . . . yes, *hoped* . . . for something less provincial, if you know what I mean. All this is so much like a garrison theater performance. Ill-fitting costumes taken out of storage, fumbling spear carriers worried about their entrances and exits, and lots of desperately serious people who are scared that someone'll laugh at them. It's a bit unnerving the first time you see it.

—It doesn't get any better the second time around, Ludo said.

—I mean, sir, Reszke said, how do we win a war with that kind of army?

—You place your trust in God and in the enemy's reservists.

Too close to the truth, Ludo veered away. A recruiting poster hung at eye level: three bronzed young men in partly superimposed profile, a cornflower-blue sky, three shining arrows shot into the sun. In the fly-speckled glass of a window, he stared at his own gaunt face. The eyes were cold as metal. He searched in them in vain for something of an earlier man and a simpler faith.

Then it was midafternoon and the sun had dipped over the western suburbs. A dry, hot wind blew across the parched brown grass of the airfield, and he was soaked with sweat. Inside the corrugated metal hangar, where rows of aircraft waited for assignment to the forward squadrons, the heat was like a hand pushing against his chest.

—Chief Auerbach? he said, coming in, and a young mechanic pointed respectfully into deeper shadows.

Once a sailor, once before a savior, the balding, bandy-legged line chief walked with a rolling gait as if the concrete hangar floor were a ship's deck at sea.

Their hands clasped and held.

In the hot, dark corner of the hangar that housed the line chief's office—a littered kitchen table, a workbench and a lathe, a metal filing cabinet from which papers spilled—Ludo rummaged in his flight bag and retrieved the bottle of cognac he had brought.

An old affection, born of trust, hung around them like a curtain drawn against intrusion. It was a moment for recollections of shared triumphs and disasters, but Ludo found it difficult to begin. He forced himself to look past the bowed, balding head with its untidy strands of rusty gray hair, past the glittering little eyes in their plain wire frames, and through the hangar window at the parched field and the obsolete machines. What he saw there were days that neither of them would need to recall for the other. Nevertheless, he did so.

—The last time I put one of these on your workbench was after you had saved my hide. This time, he said, it's before the fact.

—Other times, other customs, Chief Auerbach said. But it'll take more than glue and bailing wire to fix the junk you're to fly this time.

—I remember how you fixed me up the last time. You and Wyga came forty kilometers behind Budyenny's lines to get me and Bettner out of Shepetovka. I didn't think a bottle of Napoleon's best was wasted on you then.

—And now, I suppose, you want me to fix things for you again? Times have changed, Ludo. We live by the book. You stick one finger outside the regulations and they chop it off for you at the neck.

—I'd be the last man in the service to ask someone to break a regulation, Ludo said and grinned.

—Sure, said Chief Auerbach. And Bismarck wasn't a German. And goats don't eat paper. Listen, if I'm old enough to be pensioned off, which is what some people around here are starting to say, then I'm old enough to know when a pilot's buttering me for a roasting. But I'll tell you straight out, like I've always done, the only way I can give you something other than what's been assigned is if some damn fool of a young mechanic paints your squadron numbers on the wrong set of birds.

—Could that happen? Ludo asked and smiled.

—Not if I know about it. And if I don't know about it, then it hasn't happened, if you get my drift.

—I read you, Ludo said.

—Of course, Chief Auerbach said and scratched his close-cropped head on which a few long, lifeless strands of hair defied combs and water. Of course, there's always miracles to pray for.

—And old times to drink to, Ludo said.

—Old times. How come old times are always said to be the

best? How come nobody remembers the blood and the shit? They weren't better times. We were just younger, that's all. That's what we remember, ourselves when young. A man does stupid things when he's young. Age is supposed to bring a little wisdom. How come we never smarten up enough to remember how stupid we were?

—Because then we'd be too smart to pray for miracles, Ludo said.

—Hmm. Yes. When's this war coming, then? A week? Two?

—Perhaps even sooner. I'm supposed to effect full combat readiness by dawn tomorrow, September the first. Allied intelligence tells us that the Germans won't move till the fifteenth. It could happen any time between tomorrow and midmonth.

—Hmm, Auerbach said. Tomorrow? Two weeks, you say? If there was some kind of a mixup here, I mean if somebody fucked up on the allocations, nobody would know about it for at least a month.

From the pocket of his grease-stained coveralls, the old line chief took a pair of old-fashioned reading glasses and positioned them carefully on his nose. He picked up the bottle and peered at the label.

—Asbach Uralt, he spelled out the syllables. German, is it? As good as the last time?

—Bettner never drinks anything but the best, Ludo said.

—Hmm. Good for him. That's the way to make your way in the world. If you don't demand the best, nobody'll give it to you. Yes. Two weeks . . . and then a war begins. And I'll bet my pension that the first bomb is going to hit right here.

He pointed to the dark shadows of broad wings and graceful fusilage and Plexiglas canopies and oiled propellers.

—Right in the middle of the most beautiful birds you've ever seen, he said.

—Mind if I take a look?

—You're my guest.

They walked among the shining, factory-fresh machines and Ludo found himself suddenly dry-lipped and short of breath. This was what was needed but how many of his friends had come close to that kind of aircraft? They were to stop the Luftwaffe with a hundred and forty P-7s and P-11s and eighty-seven wooden RXIIIs.

—Nice, eh? Chief Auerbach said softly. Twin twenty-millimeter Oerlikons. Four seven-point-sevens. That Gnome-Rhône power plant cranks up to nine-seven-oh HP on takeoff. It'd take you to thirty-four thousand feet in under five minutes, and you can wind them up to three hundred miles an hour. And tight? A nun doesn't have anything on these beauties. There isn't a bird in the air that turns a tighter circle.

—A dream bird, Ludo murmured.

—So dream a little, Auerbach said and grinned. That much is allowed by the regulations.

—How many have you got here?

—Ten, as you see. There's another five at Dęblin, at the training center. But there's a hundred and eighty-eight of them in crates waiting to go to Greece. Fifty went to Yugoslavia just last month and forty to the Turks.

—Someday, my friend, Ludo said. Someday, I'd like to see all those great leaders of ours propped against a wall, you know?

—I know, Chief Auerbach said. And they know what kind of good wishes you have for them, which is why you're still only a squadron leader and why they send you garbage. A man of your experience ought to know how to play the game.

—That's why I come to you, old friend, Ludo said.

—And what d'you suppose I can do for you? The days when we used to steal a chicken from some poor, lousy Ukrainian peasant anytime we felt like it are long over and gone. This is 1939 and these aren't chickens, lad. A man would have to be out of his mind to try and steal a whole fighter squadron. He could get himself a front row seat before a firing squad for a trick like that.

—A man would have to have nothing to lose, Ludo said.

—I hear you, but I'm not listening to you, Chief Auerbach said.

Then he scratched his head, hawked, spat, wiped his mouth fastidiously with a handful of clean waste, and said: Still, it's a shame. Where's the sense in sending old junk to a squadron, where it'll be safely hidden in a forest, and letting beautiful birds like this get bombed all to hell? You see any sense in that?

—None at all, Ludo said.

—Damn shame to see them turned into junkyard scrap just because somebody forgot to hide them in a forest. You'd think they'd want them dispersed on a forward field along with all our other first-line aircraft, wouldn't you?

—Indeed I would, Ludo said.

—Yes. Well. But it can't be done. They're the personal reserve of the commander-in-chief, whatever that means. D'you know what it means?

—It means that every squadron leader in the service is pulling strings to get them and nobody has enough pull to decide the issue.

—It also means that nobody can touch them.

Back at the littered kitchen table, the line chief hunted for clean glasses he might fill. His eyes, narrowed into slits, were fixed on the deep shadows of the hangar and, perhaps, on more distant shadows as well. Whatever he was thinking he'd keep to himself until he was ready, and Ludo knew that there was nothing he could do to move the game along. Even so, he felt immense excitement and relief.

—Beautiful, beautiful birds, Auerbach was muttering. A man who'd take 'em and hide 'em in a forest would be doing the country a service, I would think.

Then he said: Nothing begins big. Everything grows, and that goes for stupidity as well. This may be our last week on this fucking planet and they want to put me out to graze? I ought to give them something to remember. They want to give me a one-way ticket back to the pissy-ass little town I swore I'd never see again. A job as postmaster. Twenty years' service and you end up teaching fucking peasants to lick stamps. Ah, it's a dog's life, any way you see it. Maybe this new war will put an end to it. Maybe we'll get a chance to start out all over again.

—I'd like to keep my pilots alive as long as I can, Ludo said.

—And I'd like to keep these beautiful birds from getting bombed to hell. But the only way any of that'll happen is if some damn fool of a young mechanic fucks up on your squadron numbers.

—And that just couldn't happen, Ludo said. Could it?

—Oh, it could happen! Chief Auerbach said. It's hot. Everybody's tired. It's going to be a long night, what with a dozen squadrons filling allocations. I've got a feeling that some damn young fool is sure to foul up on your numbers.

Then the old line chief squinted upward, grinned. His small blue eyes peered brightly from their nest of wrinkles.

—As God's my witness, Major, he said in a voice loud enough to carry through the hangar. I wish I could do something about that junk they gave you to fly. But what can I do? It's not like the old times.

—The more's the pity, Ludo said in pretended sadness.

—Yes. When a man's got to leave his past, it's like his life's being closed out, you know? Maybe I'd better put in for that retirement they're talking about.

—You're not old enough for the iron handshake.

—Oh, I'm old enough. I feel old enough. And it seems like I haven't gotten any smarter than I was as a damn young fool. It's time to go back to the fucking peasants, I expect. Ah, by the way, do you still get your spinner painted red?

—It's become a sort of tradition in the squadron.

—It isn't a bad one. Lets people know who's sending them to hell. Which is a lot more than most people can tell nowadays. Well, I'll have your birds ready for you at first light tomorrow.

—Will you be here when I come for them?

The line chief's small eyes had retreated deep into their nest of wrinkles, and a crooked grin split the weathered seams and creases in his face. Teeth, stained and gapped and leaning on each other like unattended tombstones, glittered with new metal.

—This is the last place on God's planet I'm going to be at first light tomorrow. Like I said, somebody's sure to fuck up on your numbers. I don't want to know anything about any mistakes.

Then he peered myopically at the cognac bottle. His military moustache moved up and down, betraying rare emotion.

—Asbach Uralt, eh? Not bad. Does it seem to you as good as the French stuff we had that other time?

—Better, old friend. Much better.

—Pity I couldn't do anything to earn it, Chief Auerbach said, grinning. But . . . that's the way things get done these days.

When he came out of the hangar, night had come. The sun had slipped from the sky several hours before and now a nervous, electric tremor hung in the low night clouds. The cognac bottle had been a barometer of a kind and his mood had lifted glass by glass as the level in the bottle dropped, and he was full of stormy optimism by the time the bottom of the bottle appeared.

It might work, he thought. It might not be so bad if his new pilots were up to their jobs, if there was time to show them how to handle their high-performance fighters, if . . .

And there, of course, he stopped. *If* was the start of every confident assessment of the situation in Poland these days. If the rains came and the roads became impassable quagmires. If the Allies moved swiftly and decisively against the Germans when the first shots were fired. If the regular army could hold off the onslaught until reserves could be mobilized and massed . . . if there was any luck. There were too many *ifs* in Polish military plans and calculations, and too much self-delusion. There was a great shortage of everything else.

But courage and determination were in plentiful supply. There was a plethora of set, determined faces. There was hope that the war, when it came, might be fought memorably and with minimum damage. There was faith in the invincibility of a valiant army, trust in God's mercy and in the ringing phrases of foreign politicians. There were assumptions—oh, so many of them!—about the strength and goodwill of the Western Allies.

He grinned in the dark. He had watched the fueling and arming of magnificent machines, watched the metallic yellow paint dry into familiar recognition numbers on the thin steel fabric. The business of his day was done.

The storm clouds hovered close above, dark as death ships, and he said loudly: *It'll be all right.* A harsh rumble of dissent, booming and clattering like toppled masonry, came from overhead. Lightning and the hot red umbrella of reflected neon that hung above Warsaw tinted the clouds with electric colors.

In the rattling taxi that carried him toward the center of the town and Koszykowa Street, in the tremulous, thunder-laden air of a city that never displayed its anxieties in crisis, he composed the lines of his face into a mask of confidence and serenity.

CHAPTER IV

THE TIME WAS midnight when he reached the party, and he wondered what was delaying Reszke and the new pilots whom Reszke was to bring. He was alone, the sole airman among groundlings who bewildered him.

He had ascended four long flights of stairs toward sharp voices, laughter, polite argument, speculation, malicious gossip, Piotr's music at the piano, Wlada's bittersweet French ballads, and the click and clatter of cutlery and glasses. He hugged and kissed his brothers and embraced his sister. He listened distractedly to rhetoric from a poet, Zygfryd Bunt, who regarded himself as the conscience of the nation, and to the crisp civilities of a British major who spoke to him in Polish. He drank champagne and shared a salver of caviar with General Prus's nephew, Pawel, and with the American correspondent whom Pawel had brought, but everything seemed to be happening just beyond his grasp.

—Who's the Englishman? he asked.

—The name is Hudson, a decent enough fellow, Piotr said. One of Carton de Wiart's aides from the British Military Mission. He came with the American who is the last foreign journalist left in Warsaw. Pawel brought the Yankee. The rest . . . well, I think you've seen them here before.

—There's no way to get away from them in Warsaw.

—Or anywhere else, it seems, Piotr said, drank, and laughed. They're the cream of our society, I'm afraid.

—The cream's turned a bit, then, Ludo said.

—Isn't that the truth?

They listened to the others talking about war as though it were an intellectual exercise, like a discussion of Molière or Kafka by

academic critics who had never written an original word, heard
well-rounded phrases formed like battalions on review. Someone
said: *Everyone knows that one of us is worth ten of them.* . . .
And someone else said: *It'll take six months, no more, everyone
agrees.* . . . And yet another person said: *Still, Paris is so enchanting at this time of the year. Perhaps a short visit* . . .

A sound intruded from outside, the wail of a siren, faint at the
edge of the swelling conversation, and then the metallic crash of
something falling and rolling right under the windows.

—I wonder if the outside world sees us all like that? Piotr said,
shrugged, and looked about with mild distaste. The bombs will
fall and they will still be arguing and striking moral poses. I think
their main concern is to make sure that they die intellectually correct. You're like a breath of fresh air here, Ludo. My God, it *is*
good to see you!

—It's good to see you.

—I wonder . . . when will we see each other again? Where? In
what circumstances? I have a feeling that this is going to be the
bloodiest of our wars.

—Perhaps it should be, Ludo said. There's something wrong
with the way we've been living.

—Wrong? What do you mean *wrong?* And why pick on us?
We live like others do, no better and no worse. We're neither
more noble nor corrupt than anybody else. D'you think you'd
hear something more intelligent at this kind of party in Paris or
London?

—I don't care about Paris or London, Ludo said and smiled to
take the bitterness from his words. I care about us.

—We are what we are, Piotr said. There's nothing you can do
about that, Ludo.

—Perhaps it's time for someone to try? Perhaps after the war,
we can break with our past and begin all over again. . . .

—Cleaner? Finer? Wiser? With a new vision of ourselves and
of our place in Europe? Each time I see you, you sound more like
our father, Piotr said and added, grinning: No, not *that* Father,
but our earthly one. There's not much point to objecting to stink
in a stable unless you're willing to crack a few windows.

—It might have to come to that in the end, Ludo said. Don't
you think?

—No, Piotr said. We're the wrong generation for coups and revolutions, and you're too much like Father. Now *there* was a faith for another century, remember? And the advice he gave us! That too was designed for the last century before the Deluge.

—I can't help thinking that he lived a better life than we have done, Ludo said.

—I hope we die easier, Piotr said and laughed softly. Listen, I know what you're thinking. We ought to be better than we are, but what if we're not? And why not make your peace with that? The reason I've never married is because I know that every man gets the kind of wife and government he deserves, and I suspect that's the real reason you're still single too.

Piotr smiled, winked, and turned away, and Ludo watched him as he made his way among the party guests to the piano where Wlada was preparing to sing another song, and then Norwid had appeared beside him with two chilled champagne glasses in his hands. They had always been closer than the other brothers. Fair, blue-eyed Norwid resembled their dead mother more than any of them. Tall, big-boned Ludo was a replica of their murdered father. At times, he thought that their parents' passionate devotion for each other had become resurrected in Norwid and himself. But now it seemed to Ludo that he and Norwid were looking at each other through bulletproof glass.

They were embarrassed by their own constraint and helpless to do anything about it.

—What brings you to Warsaw at this time? Ludo asked.

—I came for the Fleet War Codes. We are putting out to sea tomorrow afternoon. We'd be as good as sunk, tied up at the piers. The Baltic is a German lake these days, and so's the air above it.

—You needn't tell me about the air, Ludo said.

—No, I imagine not. How long *do* you think we'll be able to hold out?

—On the ground? I've no idea. Two or three months, if the rains come and the Allies move. In the air? We've pilots and machines for perhaps two weeks. We're outnumbered by more than twenty-five to one. If the British attack the Luftwaffe at once, as they're obliged to do by their treaty with us, we've a decent chance. If they don't, we'll be finished in three days.

—You say it so coldly. You're so matter-of-fact.

—Can you think of a better way to say it? Ludo asked.

—No, I can't, Norwid said.

—And what about you, then? What are the fleet's chances?

—We're going to leave you, Norwid said. The destroyers are already in England. The submarines will stay in the Baltic as long as we've a base. After that, we're to fight our way through the Skagerrak into the North Sea and get to English ports. Nobody in the fleet feels very good about that . . . but what's the alternative? Perhaps the real answer would have been to make a Czech choice.

—Thank God you'll be in England.

—Still, that does contradict everything we've been taught, doesn't it? Oh, Jesus, Ludo! Norwid cried suddenly. We *will* get through it all, won't we? I mean courage and loyalty and devotion and love of country still count for something, don't they? Things couldn't have changed all that much everywhere in the world.

In the sudden silence, one of those weary interludes that descends on every gathering that had gone on too long, his voice carried through the room, and then they heard Janek crying out: Man for man and saber for saber, we've always been a match for anyone!

Ludo and Norwid touched the rims of their glasses. Their smiles were seamless, opaque, unrevealing.

They had come out onto the balcony, into the cooling air; and an air-raid warden shouted up at them from the street to blot out the light that poured from behind them into the still night. The storm clouds had passed. The sky was brilliant with strange stars. A great white moon had risen in the west and touched the darkened windows with a cold, pale fire.

Below them, a troop of cavalry was clattering on the cobblestones—the men hunched in their saddles, drab in khaki, the horses burdened with field gear and weapons—and then came wagons, fieldpieces, more ranks of bobbing horsemen, machine-gun carts, ambulances, a field kitchen and an ammunition tender, then more animals and men. Dark in the moonlight, the column seemed to stretch into forgotten centuries: a cavalry brigade riding for the border.

—You ask about our chances? Well, there they are, Ludo said. It's what we have instead of the finest war machines in Europe. Do you know what we could have had?

—Well I did hear about your PZL P-41 "Wolf," Norwid said. But that never made it past the flight tests, did it?

—Poor old Wolf, Ludo said. Killed, stuffed, and mounted on a budget table. It would have been a real flying miracle for us. But at twenty thousand *zlote* apiece, the only engines we could get for it would've cost as much as twenty horses for the cavalry. And, of course, we had to have the horses for the cavalry. Tradition has to ride on something.

—I heard the rumors, Norwid said. They're hard to believe.

—Why? What's the mystery? We couldn't find an engine for the Wolf anywhere in Europe. The British wouldn't sell us their Rolls-Royce Merlin III and we don't build our own. The American Pratt & Whitney R1830-13 was perfect in the flight tests but at a thousand dollars each, at twenty *zlote* to the dollar . . . well, you can see how the Budget Office would react to that.

He laughed emptily, went on: Of course, it could be argued, since the cavalry is supposed to fight on foot, and its horses are just a means of transportation, that if you put twenty lancers in a truck that costs fifteen thousand, you'd have a motorized rifle platoon and five thousand *zlote* saved toward an engine for the world's best fighter plane. And if you put eighty lancers in four trucks, you'd have a mechanized rifle company and a complete engine. And if you didn't feel compelled by visions of past glories, by ignorance, and by suspicion of all mechanical objects, to spend twenty-eight million *zlote* on the nags of the Army's eleven horse-cavalry brigades . . . if, in fact, you'd risk professional suicide by suggesting that our military leaders are technological illiterates . . . you'd have two motorized divisions and a thousand engines! All for the price of twenty-eight thousand nags that eat thirty thousand *zlotes'* worth of oats a year. But would anyone listen to that kind of arithmetic in Warsaw?

—If nothing else, we'd have had sanitary parades, Norwid said. Then each of them was alone in a private silence.

Hungry, he went toward the kitchen. In the kitchen doorway, he collided with a terribly drunken Krolik who was staggering out with a basket of empty bottles on his shoulder and who dropped the basket. The basket fell, snapped open, the bottles rolled and smashed, and Krolik flattened himself against a wall.

Zosia glanced at him, flushed from the stove, still pretty. Her lean, dark face had acquitted itself well through the years, the few white strands were hardly visible in her pale hair, and he wondered how she had created the illusion that time could be stopped.

—That old fool, she said. Thinks he's still clanking about the village in his spurs and saber and waving his whip. Is there anything like an old fool for remembering things that never happened?

Ludo spooned hot *bigos* into his mouth, sipped the scalding tea she had set out before him on the kitchen table, said: Some things are worth a memory or two.

Always serene, often pensive, sometimes impudent, she had a way of smiling which (quite literally, he thought) used to stop his heart, and an abundant, articulated body that he knew (remembered) as intimately as his own. The woman he had been raised to need was to be dignified and graceful, but she—this once-upon-a-time source of discovery in an apple orchard—had taken care of that.

They were of one age, of one country, born within a kilometer of each other, but this distance might have been measured in continents and oceans. He was one kind of creature in a world of passionate hatreds and profound devotions, and she was another, and there was nothing he had been able to do about that at fifteen years of age. Sent away, he had been obedient. Later, he knew that to return to love in a time of need, having left it voluntarily in a time of abundance, was an abasement his pride would not permit. By that time, he had discovered for himself what fighting men almost never talk about: that you can make love to

war, nursing it and magnifying it, even making out of it a shield
against memory and conscience.

Now, when she spoke to him, it was in the dialect of her village, and he replied in kind.

—Do you ever miss the old days?

—No. What's to miss?

—Innocence, I suppose, he said.

—I don't remember much of that, she said. Nobody ever put
me to sleep with fairy tales.

—There wasn't much of that in my crib either, he agreed.

—But I do miss some things. When I remember them.

He forced himself to ask: Your family?

—No. Never. I never think about them. I miss . . . ah . . .
looking forward to things. You understand? The feeling you'd
have that something special might happen before nightfall. Ah,
but who's got the time for such foolishness now. It's best to live
without remembering anything.

—I remember you and me in the apple orchard, Ludo said.

She bared her strong white teeth, said: Ah, then there is something worse than an old fool. There's a young one.

—They're the worst kind, he said.

—Don't talk so much. Eat. That's what a mouth is for when
you're in a kitchen.

—And in an apple orchard?

—That's where you eat apples if you've any sense.

—Listen, he said so harshly that his voice startled him. There's
one thing I've never thought about. Wouldn't let myself think
about it, I suppose. Were your brothers in the village when I
bombed it?

—It took you a long time to get around to asking.

—It'll be twenty years this October, he said.

—I don't know, she said. I wasn't there, was I?

—No, you weren't, he said.

—So how would I know? Maybe they were, maybe not. I don't
think about it.

—But they were your brothers.

Her voice had remained soft throughout, she had never raised
it, but now she faced him squarely, her back to the stove and her

arms clasped tightly under her breasts, and the harshness of her voice was a match for his own.

—If you killed them, you killed them. I watched them kill your father and mother. Your mother was good to me and I loved her and I loved you too. I didn't love my brothers. But even if I did, it wouldn't have made any difference. It took an hour for your mother to die. But what do you want from me now? You want me to tell you it was all right for you to kill all those other people? That's not for me to say. You're the one that did it.

She turned her back to him and busied herself among her pots and pans. She was a woman of her time and people, a creature of rare honesty, and he thought that he could see her shoulders beginning to quiver as he went out of the kitchen and back among the guests.

Wlada's guests were his own and he was obliged to be polite to them. He moved from group to group. He spoke and he listened. He watched two imitations of Hitler, one of Chamberlain, three of Mussolini. He heard and watched a cruel parody of a recent speech by Marshal Smigly-Rydz, who had inherited the mantle of Pilsudski. (*We won't give a button, not a single button!* cried the parodist and seized himself by the navel and the fly.) He blew a kiss to Wlada, who blew one back to him as she sang "J'attendrais." He raised his glass to Piotr, who raised one to him.

He spoke to a little ballerina who stared at him with enormous eyes, to a Wagnerian mezzo, to a tall dark actress and a small blond one, to a sly gossip columnist who was stuffing himself with caviar even as he denounced the artificial values of the haute bourgeoisie, to a fat bearded academic person who called himself a critic of the arts. The men were charming, often brilliant, sensitive to insult, and totally ineffective. The women flirted with him in calculated terms. He couldn't fathom a society which produced such an abundance of conceit with such little minds.

Nothing seemed real then, the party and its guests least of all. He watched them with pity and contempt, and he didn't quite know whom he was pitying or what he despised. The sounds they made seemed like one harsh, metallic whisper, so that he thought of upright serpents swaying on their tails and hissing at each other. The focus of their curiosity and malice shifted back and forth. The air itself snapped and crackled with their witticisms, their jealously defended self-importance, and their inadequately shielded fear. In search of victims who might deflect their own uncertainties about themselves, they fixed upon Lala.

She had come in while he and Norwid had been out on the balcony, and she had come alone, and this—more than all the gossip that could be hissed about her—exposed her to the flickering malice of the party guests. At once, he looked for General Prus, who should have been with her, but this old friend and mentor wasn't there.

—This is one of the surprises I had for you, Wlada murmured. I ran across Prus and Lala at a Foreign Ministry reception a few days ago. He's been called back into the Army, you know, and she looked as though she needed a friend.

—She won't find many here, Ludo said.

—She has us. And the American correspondent seems smitten.

—Why didn't Prus come?

—I think it's all over between her and Prus, Wlada said. I don't know why. But it was obvious at that Ministry reception that something had happened. I know that it's a tragedy for her.

—It's hardly the sort of tragedy that kills you, he said and went on quickly so as to take the sting of cruelty out of his voice: She seems to be bearing up under it.

—Men! Wlada said. Why can't you ever credit a woman with some self-respect? Not to mention intelligence! A little compassion wouldn't do you any harm either, at this of all times. She didn't choose the society in which she was born, nor a marriage to a musty old academic faker, nor did she go out looking for a man as exciting as Prus to whom *you* introduced her, anyway. She fell in love. Women do things like that, you know. It isn't something she should be punished for. And she *is* our cousin! We *do* owe her our loyalty and affection.

—I'm sorry, Ludo said, immediately contrite. You're quite right, of course.

—Of course she's *bearing up under it*, as you put it. What else would you expect? But the pain is there, for all that.

—I'm truly sorry for her, Ludo said.

—Twelve years! Wlada said. How could she and Prus take all

the personal and political opprobrium heaped on them and still keep their dignity? It's something to admire.

—He'd do it by ignoring it, Ludo said. She would accept it as inevitable.

—You'll speak to her before the party's over, won't you, Ludo? She always liked you more than any of the rest of us.

—Of course I will, he said.

She left him then, joined Lala Karolewska in the middle of the room, among the stabbing glances. The two women linked arms, their glances locked and their heads raised proudly, and Ludo thought that he had never seen two women who looked so very much alike and yet who were so entirely different. Wlada could command armies, if she put her mind to it; Lala had been born to be misunderstood, embattled, and commanded.

She had been the prettiest of his many cousins. In the unspoken understandings between their two mothers, they were supposed to have been raised for each other to marry. But she had married a steadier, older man, and he (Ludo) had chosen a life of different service. It was, of course, just as well that this should be so, but his responsibility to her remained.

And, suddenly, something strange began to happen to him. The party began to fade, the guests to vanish. In their place, he saw his sister and his brothers dead, his young pilots dying, and he couldn't remember anybody's name. He had allowed himself a moment of affection and he was paying for it. Neither Lala nor Zosia might have phrased it quite like that but they knew, as they had always known, that as soon as intimacy is allowed to start then a shared history begins, and with a shared history comes the certainty of loss. Cursing his fate and the cognac and champagne he had drunk, Ludo struggled against a grief to come. But, at that moment, Pawel and the American correspondent came up on one side of him, and Reszke and his flock of pilots appeared on the other side, and he concealed his sudden terror in politeness.

—Having a good time? he asked the pilots, who chorused in reply: Yes, sir, thank you very much.

Always afterward, he knew, he would remember every word said to him that night, but he'd never remember the names of his new pilots. He thought of them as the Author, the Concert Pianist, the Mathematician, the Eminent Sculptor, and the Philosopher, which is how Reszke introduced these reserve lieutenants. They were nervously polite in the presence of their squadron leader. They were awed by Wlada. They looked at everyone else with diffidence and respect.

—Sorry we're late, sir, Reszke said. But it took quite a while to process everybody's orders. That's where Papa Bettner is right now, sir, processing the orders. He's very angry to have missed the party.

—Is he still sober?

—Moderately, sir. Not unreasonably so. But all his work is done.

Men who fly have never been articulate, Ludo knew. They know themselves to be alive only in the air or in the company of their own strangely isolated kind. Grandiloquence confuses them. The clustered lives of the earthbound have no meaning for them. Their struggle is with the elements, not against other men. But as he looked at Reszke, it occurred to him that this was one life that had to be preserved at all costs. The future, he thought, will need him; his was a generation fated for great things. It was as if a transference of some kind were taking place, as if something which had passed from the harsh, uncompromising soil to himself twenty years before were now moving from him to the younger man. He had to make sure that Reszke understood it.

—We must have replacements, he murmured to himself and Reszke nodded without comprehension.

—We're in fine shape where that's concerned, he said. What with these new fellows, and the flight left with Captain Wardzinski at the forward field, we've more than a full aircrew complement. What kind of aircraft are we getting, by the way?

—PZL-24s, Ludo said.

—That's wonderful, sir! How did you manage that?

—God was kind.

—I doubt if he'd be that kind to anybody else! Congratulations, Major! It's . . . like a miracle, you know?

—If you'll bring the new pilots to Okęcie just before first light, you'll see how modern miracles are made, Ludo said.

—Yes, sir, Reszke said and looked at the little ballerina, the Wagnerian mezzo, the tall dark actress, and the smaller blond one. Permission to enjoy ourselves?

—Permission granted, Ludo said.

Time had passed, it was then perhaps two hours before dawn, and some of the guests had begun to leave. Lala had left before he could speak to her. Reszke and the pilots were the next to go. Wlada was singing "Chansons d'Amour," and Piotr, who must have been at least as tired as Ludo himself, began to play a modest composition of his own.

Ludo and Pawel and the American correspondent sought the cool night air on the balcony. They stood there, looking down in silence as the young pilots vanished down the street.

—No matter how often I watch this kind of thing, it's always like the first time, the American said.

—What kind of thing? Pawel asked.

—This, the American said and pointed to the dark end of the street, where the last of the pilots had hailed a dilapidated horse-drawn cab. It's like the ball in Brussels before Waterloo. The handsome young men disappearing one by one, and only the old men and politicians left to dance with the ladies. This is about the sixth time that I've seen it, but I can't get used to it.

—You fought in Spain? Ludo asked.

—I'd rather not say what I was doing there. Or in Ethiopia. Or in Manchuria before that. I swore I'd never get involved with my own stories again. But I've a drunken sort of sense of destiny at the moment, if you know what I mean. It isn't a comfortable way to feel.

—Lala has had quite an effect on our American friend, Pawel explained to Ludo.

—She has a way of doing that, Ludo said. And, God knows, she needs someone to treat her decently.

—A cousin of yours, isn't she, Major? the American asked.

—If there's one thing you ought to know about us, Loomis, it's that we're all related to each other, Pawel said. Or we know each other. Each of us is a skeleton in someone else's closet, which is why there are no family secrets in Warsaw. Which also makes for uncomfortably tight family obligations.

—I like that, Loomis said. Maybe that's why I go back to the United States as seldom as I can.

—You dislike your country? Ludo asked.

—I love it, Loomis said shortly. I don't have to like it. But God help anyone who doesn't feel about it the same way that I do.

—You must forgive Loomis, Pawel said to Ludo. European disasters are his bread and butter. And he did overhear you and Piotr talking about revolutions.

Aware of the sudden silence and the questioning eyes, Ludo shrugged and said: All I meant was that we shouldn't leave our country in the hands of people who make nineteenth-century decisions.

—But isn't that what life in this country is about? the correspondent asked.

—Is that how people see us in America? Ludo countered.

—Well, they don't see you with *your* eyes, that's for sure, the American said. And, anyway, we're all too busy back home, making money now that the armament factories are starting at full capacity, to see much of anything in Europe.

—And what do you see here? Ludo asked.

—I see a country that belongs in a museum case. I see a fine, gallant, intelligent, energetic people who are going to be wiped off the map in a week or two because they don't belong in the twentieth century. I don't see anybody anywhere else shedding tears about it. What do you see, Major?

—A need for change, and no time to bring it about, Ludo said.

—Oh, it's not as bad as all that, Pawel said and grinned. Is it? We've come a long way in the last twenty years. Of course, I'm still going to ride to war on a horse, but I'm not complaining. I like horses. They're almost as intelligent as our politicians and a lot more useful. As for a need for changes . . . the future and all that . . . I'm not concerned about it because I don't expect to be around to see it. Me and my horse both.

—Welcome to history, then, Ludo smiled and said.

—Don't be in such a hurry, Pawel, the correspondent said. What has history ever done for you? But I'd like to hear more of your opinions, Major. I don't mind telling you that you're a bit of a surprise. I'm used to hearing a different line in Warsaw.

Pawel was humming a song under his breath and Ludo wondered whether he was doing it on purpose. The song was a sentimental military ditty about Lady War, a most unsentimental mistress. The beat of explosions was the pounding of her heart, her favors came high, and a wise man avoided her embrace as long as he could. But she would have them all soon enough: the fools together with the wise, the brave with the cowardly.

—A soldier isn't supposed to have political opinions, Ludo said.

—I know, Loomis said and smiled. They're forbidden by the regulations. But so were apples in the Garden of Eden, Major, and we all know what happened there.

—Well, then we'll just have to wait and see what happens here, won't we? Ludo said. There'll be time for opinions after the war is over. Right now, it doesn't seem to matter much what anyone thinks.

It was cold then, the last and coldest hour before dawn, and the moon had gone. Out on the balcony, there was an odd silence. The cold hush in the graying air was all the more remarkable because this city was never wholly silent. Life pulsed and throbbed in Warsaw no matter what the hour, but not on this night.

The streets (as he saw them and would remember them) were gray, lifeless, stained with pools of shadow. There were no streetcars, taxis, hooting trucks, creaking peasant carts, coal and water wagons, pushcarts, sidewalk vendors, peddlers, shrill beggars, washerwomen, haggling merchants' wives, barking dogs, and clattering horse-drawn cabs, and then the sound, heard before, came again in that unnatural stillness: a far-off booming, a moan and a clatter, and then a great, deep roar.

He heard and recognized the dull thud of bombs, the tinny crash and rattle of responding antiaircraft artillery, the thin drone of motors pulsing overhead. The blue-gray dawn had turned to scarlet and gold.

—Dear God, dear God, someone began to pray in the room behind them, as the hot wind of a nearby explosion blew them back into the light, off the balcony, among the party guests. They were all on their knees, their faces wet with tears: the little ballerina with enormous eyes, the Wagnerian mezzo, the tall dark actress and the small one, the sly gossip columnist and the fat, bearded academic person.

—*Jeszcze Polska nie zginęła*, Wlada began to sing in a clear soft voice while tears ran down her face. Ludo and Piotr and Norwid and Janek collided in the doorway.

Their eyes were wide. They searched each other's faces. Each asked a mute question that none of the others was willing to answer. All their answers, Ludo thought, were echoing outside.

And suddenly they were all in each other's arms and, as suddenly, apart. Their embrace had shocked them, the upsurge of their love for each other had caught them unaware, and they recoiled in mutual protection as if their acknowledgment of affection would mark each of them for loss.

Then he was running down the stairs. He led the way, as always, and the others followed: Piotr, Norwid, Janek—the brothers he had brought up to duty and to service as their father would have done had he lived. But hadn't he missed a whole universe of feeling? Wlada alone remained. Home, or whatever passed for their home in Warsaw, had fallen behind. Outside, the war waited.

Running, he shouted over his shoulder: Take care of yourselves, hear? And remember . . .

But whatever it was that he wanted his brothers to remember was lost in the sound of a very near explosion. Smoke filled the stairwell. Dust blinded and choked him. It choked their replies. And then they too were invisible, and he was in the street, running past a wailing beggarwoman who huddled in a gateway, past a dead horse and a terrified policeman who was firing his rifle blindly into the sky, past an overturned streetcar and a broken body.

Gray, venerable, stony-faced, obscured by smoke and brick dust, Warsaw shook and quivered to the beat of explosions.

CHAPTER V

STATUES PASSED BLINDLY as he ran into what had been a quiet tree-lined square where, under a striped awning, he used to drink Viennese coffee and read the Sunday papers. One monument, that of a poet whom years of inattention had turned a bilious green, pointed a finger upward; another, that of a military hero who had lost his head, pointed a broken saber toward a stormy future. Somewhere under the sound of bells, sirens, fire engines, erupting masonry, and explosions, he thought he could hear music.

His first clear thought was: I must get to a telephone.

His favorite café was gone, the draperies were ballooning out of shattered windows, and the small marble-topped tables lay about like vandalized tombstones. But a radio was playing military marches on the serving counter and, next to the radio, a telephone was ringing.

—Hello! he shouted, but the line went dead, and he began to punch the holding-forks for a dial tone while the radio addressed him and the rubble in which he was standing.

. . . Today at dawn . . . in contravention of existing treaties . . . without a declaration of war . . . an unprovoked attack . . .

—Get me a clear line! he shouted to the operator then. This is a military emergency!

But the woman had become hysterical and sobbed in his ear.

. . . Fierce fighting continues around Częstochowa . . . around Katowice . . . German irregulars are attacking the Silesian coalfields . . . German-born residents of Bydgoszcz are said to have fired on our troops . . . a battle is raging in and around the Tuchola Forest in the north and near the naval base of Gdynia and Oksywie . . . the Polish post office in Gdańsk is under attack . . . Air attacks continue against all major towns and cities and civilian casualties are said to be heavy . . . In Paris . . .

—Paris is so enchanting this time of year, he muttered savagely. Perhaps a short visit?

As seen through smoke, through the fallen ceiling, the sun was scarlet in a sky of cornflower blue. The Dorniers and the Junkers gleamed there like polished silver ornaments, seemingly immune to the little flower-bursts of shells that blossomed under them. They flew as if on parade, with wing tips in precise alignment, with their protecting fighters stacked in layers around them. The Stukas dived and wheeled, rose, wheeled and dived again. They seemed to hang motionless in the air as their bombs leaped free, so many crooked crosses pinned to smoke.

He thought at once of Gerlach and Wardzinski and the others he had left in the forest clearing, and he thought of Reszke and the respectful pilots whom Reszke had brought to the party, and then he did his best not to think at all.

Looking up, trying to see through layers of smoke, powdered brick, and concrete, he went on thinking nonetheless. *Perhaps they are up there? If not . . . well, then, perhaps they've a chance.* It was as if only his presence among them could defer their deaths.

At once, as though his thoughts had been read, he saw a scarlet fireball falling from the sky: a P-series fighter tumbling down in flames. In a miraculously unsoiled corner of the sky, a parachute had opened; it hung there for a moment, delicately tinted by the sun, then flared redly and was gone.

Hatred exploded in him. Thinking himself a realist, which is what every romantic believes himself to be, he had been sure that he was moving forward into life, no matter what his destiny, and (always before) he had been able to find an antidote to despair in duty. But now he saw life as dark, unpromising, and without hope. It had become merely a matter of winning or losing, not of right or wrong, and the chances of some overriding personal victory had become exceedingly small for him. He knew that nothing would ever be the same for him again, that he'd be unable to find simplistic assurances in his family's resurrection. He wanted to be able to kill simply and unemotionally until he was shot down and killed, and—as far as he was concerned at that moment —the sooner the better.

He heard the thin, wailing scream of a diving bomber, and watched the black machine hurtling down, saw it grow and swell and become defined as a deadly weapon aimed straight at himself, and he felt a dizzying touch of exultation. He noted the bent wings, the heavy undercarriage, and saw the dive flaps lift, and watched the gleaming five-hundred-pound bomb detach itself and leap free as the Stuka's nose jerked into the air, and then he heard the howl of the siren attached to the bomb.

The moments between this sound and the next, the roar of the explosion, seemed frozen so that nothing moved, and he noted people huddled in a doorway, looking up and praying. The air was red with brick dust and a blood-red haze hung between him and everything he saw, so that, for a crazed moment of his own, Ludo thought that he had returned to his nightmare.

. . . Fierce fighting in Pomorze . . . in the Silesian basin . . . heavy attacks in the Bay of Gdańsk . . . a battle rages in the Carpathian passes . . . an all-out attack by the Allied armies is expected momentarily on the western front . . .

He was thrown to the ground by a rush of air so hot that he thought it burning.

The telephone receiver was trembling in his hand, and he began to mutter obscenities into it, and then, miraculously, he could hear the humming of the wires and he began to dial the only number at Okęcie Field that he could remember.

Time, a commodity in very short supply, was passing too swiftly, and he was conscious of every minute of it, and he looked savagely at the sky through what had been a ceiling painted with sylvan frolics; gone from his field of vision, the Germans must be over the airfield, he thought. He listened to the sharp ringing of the telephone that nobody answered and to the crackling radio but all he heard were the names of cities under air attack and border towns that had fallen. He heard a loudspeaker.

. . . ATTENTION! ATTENTION! I HAVE A WARNING OF AIR ATTACK FOR WARSAW . . . FOR KRAKÓW . . . FOR LUBLIN . . . FOR LWÓW . . . ATTACK ON TORUŃ . . . ON POZNAŃ . . . ON BYDGOSZCZ . . . ON GDYNIA . . . I HAVE A WARNING OF ATTACK FOR THE NORTH-CENTRAL REGION . . . FOR THE SOUTHERN REGION . . . FOR RADOM . . . FOR KIELCE . . . FOR ŁÓDŹ . . . ATTENTION! ATTENTION! ALL CITIZENS MUST REMAIN CALM . . . MUST REMAIN IN THEIR HOMES . . . IN THEIR PLACES OF WORK . . . ALL MILITARY AND POLICE PERSONNEL MUST REPORT IMMEDIATELY TO THEIR UNITS . . . ALL MILITARY LEAVES ARE CANCELED . . . ALL RESERVISTS ARE

TO PROCEED AT ONCE TO THEIR MOBILIZATION CENTERS . . . ATTEN-
TION! ATTENTION! I HAVE A WARNING OF ATTACK . . .

The entire country must be under one immense air attack, he
thought. The massive onslaught was simultaneous so that no city
could send help to another, so that road and rail systems would
be destroyed everywhere at once and communications down
throughout the country, and so that everyone would be helpless
from the first moment on. The Germans must have left their
bases long before dawn to be poised above all their targets at first
light.

Well, he thought, they can do it. With four thousand first-line
aircraft, they can hit everything worth destroying at one blow.

—*Psia krew*, he muttered into the telephone receiver. Will
somebody answer?

A *special session of the National Assembly has been convened
in Paris*, the radio informed him. *In London, a debate has been
announced in the House of Commons . . . Sir Neville Henderson
is to fly to Berlin with British peace proposals . . . a Swedish emissary is flying to London with German peace proposals . . . President Roosevelt has appealed to Hitler for restraint . . .*

Damn them, he thought. They'll go on talking until we're all
dead. He knew then, although he'd never know how he knew it,
that no help would come from the Western Allies, that they
would break their solemn treaty obligations, and that the war in
Poland would be swiftly lost.

But, at least, the telephone was no longer ringing.

—Hello? Yes! Who?

—Where the hell are you? Papa Bettner shouted. Everyone is
here! I'm having a hell of a time keeping them on the ground!

Weak with relief, Ludo was unable to speak for a moment,
then said: I might have known I'd find you in the bar of the
officers' mess. Speak up, I can't hear you.

—I said: Are you on your way or not! We need you here,
Ludo!

—Taxis, he said bitterly, are a little difficult to find this morning.

—What? Well, we've been hit hard, the place is a shambles,
but all the pilots are all right and your new birds are safe. What?

Dammit, Ludo, will you make some sense? I can't hear a thing. I think my eardrums are gone.

—Don't let anyone go up until I get there, Ludo ordered. They wouldn't stand a chance in a climbing fight.

—Ah, you've discovered that, have you? Well, of course I wouldn't! What do you think I am? But you tell me right now how to keep young pilots on the ground when everything around them's getting bombed to hell! What? Of course I'm sober! The officers' mess took a five-hundred-pounder and that, believe me, is the real tragedy this morning.

—Get through to the forward field, Ludo said. Get Wardzinski to bring his flight here. Then . . .

—Wardzinski is dead! Papa Bettner shouted. So's Borowicz! Gerlach, Straka, and Wilchurzak are here. I have them and Reszke sorting out the new men into flight echelons.

—What happened to Wardzinski?

—The Emils got him. You should've been here, Ludo.

Coldly, Ludo said: I'm aware of that. Give me a breakdown of the morning's action. Quick!

—Can't that wait till you get here? Well, all right, as Gerlach reports it, it was still dark when the German first wave came over the field, which is maybe why so few of our people got hurt. They got four Stukas before the Emils went to work on them. Wardzinski flamed one Emil, and Gerlach and Straka both peppered another, but he got away. Gerlach saw Wardzinski go down right after that. Borowicz blew up, they must have got him with cannons through the gas tank. Then Gerlach's own plane got hit, caught fire, and he bailed out. He cracked an ankle on landing. Straka took a piece of twenty-millimeter through the shoulder. Wilchurzak has burns on his face to scare a dog up a tree. But they're all out of shock now and ready to fly. Of course, there isn't a P-11 left that doesn't look like a sieve, but there are the new birds.

—They're safe, you said?

—I told you! Not a scratch on them. Auerbach had them hidden in revetments. But you ought to see what the Stukas did to the rest of the place. And the Goliath . . . remember the Goliath? That's finally gone! What? What? Ludo, I can't hear you! What? No, I don't know what happened to Wyga and the others. Why don't you ask Gerlach when you get here? And will you please get here? It's like the end of the world from where I am standing.

—It isn't the end of anything, Papa, Ludo said. And, listen, let me say it before it's too late: you were right, I *can* depend on you. You're in command until I get there.

—What? I can't hear you! Papa Bettner shouted. Will you please speak up?

Then the line was dead. He dropped the receiver. The radio went on talking in the shattered room.

. . . *In Moscow, Foreign Minister Molotov has expressed his government's confidence in German intentions and has pledged full support for the terms of the German-Soviet alliance . . . Once again, as for so many centuries, the vultures that surround our country are looking forward to sharing the spoils . . .*

He went outside, where the blackened sky was clear of Germans.

An hour later, he was in open country, among small shuttered villas and vegetable gardens, tall fences of unpainted weathered pine, and sunflowers tethered to their posts. The air there was thick with the cloying stench of rubber and burning paint and lubricants and fuel. Okęcie Field, visible in the flat distance under its own pall of greasy black smoke, glittered with blue-and-yellow fires.

The first of the day's air attacks was over by the time he reached the airfield. Bettner had not exaggerated the destruction there; the field had been raked with bombs from one end to the other, no building stood untouched. Huge craters had appeared in the concrete apron where direct hits had been made on the arming and fueling bays. Crowds of soldiers and civilian volunteers were filling the holes in the runways with gravel and sand. The antiquated aircraft that had been lined up as decoys were a pile of rubble.

Then he and Auerbach and Bettner were entering the first of the sandbagged revetments, where the mechanics had a PZL-24 running on low revolutions with the canopy slid open. The spinner had been painted scarlet, his squadron identification numbers gleamed in white-and-yellow on the fuselage, and Auerbach handed him a leather helmet with wires for his radio. He buckled on his parachute harness, climbed into the cockpit, and settled in the familiar narrow seat.

Bettner was asking him: You won't wait for the next raid, then? You're going out to meet them?

And, finally, he could speak.

—Try to get through to the forward field. Tell Wyga to be ready for us with ammo and fuel. I want a turnaround time of no more than fifteen minutes for the lot of us. He can expect us to start coming in about an hour from now.

—You're uncovering Warsaw? Where are you going, then?

—They come from Allenstein. I want to start killing them over their own soil, in their own damned sky. And don't worry about Warsaw, Papa. Both we and the Germans will be back here soon enough.

—A good move, Auerbach muttered his approval. You'll have a hundred and fifty miles to fight them in before they're back here. And you'll be the last thing they'll expect to see in their own airspace.

—I hope we'll be the last thing they ever see, Ludo said.

—Well, Bettner said, be careful. Nobody's ever seen a dead fighter pilot, ask anybody in the infantry, but there's always the first time.

—And I can't go and get you this time, Auerbach said.

—This time, you can buy the cognac, Ludo said.

Then the old line chief jumped down off the wheel, and he and the middle-aged lieutenant backed away and signaled to the crewmen who crouched by the chock lines. Ludo checked the panel and plugged in his earphones. He set the R/T frequency. He pulled the stick hard into his stomach and opened the throttle, watching the engine revolutions, oil-pressure and temperature gauges. The engine roared, and he waved to Auerbach, who shouted: Bring her back in one piece! I wouldn't want anything to happen to the C-i-C's personal ree-serve!

Then he was ordering the linemen to pull away the restraining chock blocks, and Ludo throttled down to taxi out of the revetment, and watched the flat, blunt noses and widespread wings of other machines edging out of their bays, and smelled the hot wind and the acrid stench of lubricants and oil, and then the machine was bumping on scorched grass toward the concrete runway.

Left and right—beautiful, gleaming, dangerous—nine machines followed him at increasing speed. He pushed the throttle wide open and eased the stick forward, and the machine leaped under him as though he had struck it with a roweled spur. It bumped once, then once more, and then the tail went up, and he watched the scarred and pitted surface of an imprisoning earth rush toward him and disappear under him, and he closed his mind to all guilt and fear that belonged to the earth, and then the wheels were free of the ground and he was climbing.

The thick black smoke rose high into the sky as he circled upward. The city lay under a blood-red cloud. East and west, as far as he could see between the horizons, smoky gray columns slanted into the air as if the entire country had become one vast burned offering. As yesterday he had noted crops in fields of rye, wheat, cabbages, potatoes, and beets, and found in them a texture of a people's life, so now he noted the reverse of the image: an antlike stream of soldiers winding through parched stubble, a smoldering farmhouse, dead cows in a meadow, dead horses piled beside a road, a bridge tossed into the dry bed of its river. Then more marching soldiers, horses, ruins, craters, dead animals, burned farms.

Grief blurred his vision then, and he looked away.

He glanced back over his right shoulder to where, normally, a wingman would be weaving back and forth, a hundred feet above and behind his flight leader's tail. But on this day, short as he was of men and machines, there was no one in the blinding ambush zone between him and the sun.

He glanced down, lured by a gleam of sunlight reflecting off armored Plexiglas, focused on Reszke and Gerlach, who led their three-man echelons two hundred feet below him and spread to the right. Straka, the Author, and the Concert Pianist were stepped a hundred feet below them and another hundred to the right. He was the high man, the Man on the Roof, and they would all pivot on him if the attack would be to the southwest, as

Ludo expected. The sun would be behind them and blinding the Germans. Reszke and Gerlach and their wingmen (the burned Wilchurzak, the Philosopher, the Mathematician, the Eminent Sculptor) would strike at the Emils. Straka would take his men wide around the main German formation of bombers and Zerstorers and fall upon the flock of Stukas that brought up the rear. Ludo would start it all by punching through the screen of Bf 110 Zerstorers, hitting the heavy bombers in a single pass, and drawing the high-cover Emils after him. It was a maneuver he and his squadron had practiced at least a hundred times in their P-11s.

He leveled out at eighteen thousand feet, set his fuel mix on COARSE, drew a breath. The PZL-24 droned on medium revolutions, the horizon gauge tipped gently, then recovered. He checked the panel. All instruments were reassuringly in order. He looked down, saw a boiling black cloud pierced by innumerable red-and-yellow flashes: a battle was in progress around the town of Mława. Left to right, and then from right to left, he swept the empty sky above and to the front.

He switched the R/T set to SEND, said: Radio check, flight leaders.

At once, alert young voices crackled in his ears.

—We're crossing into Prussia now, he said. Fix your landmarks and your reverse bearings. You'll be flying back alone or in pairs and you won't have time to look at your charts. Watch the sky. Stay alert. They're on their way, you can be sure of that.

—Won't they be surprised to see us here? Straka laughed and said.

—It looks so peaceful here, Reszke said.

—Ten minutes ought to change all that, Gerlach said.

—Now, listen carefully, Ludo said. I don't want to see any circus aerobatics, they're useless in combat. You'll have altitude and the sun behind you, so hit them and break and go back to the ceiling as fast as you can. Break under the bombers but above the fighters. Never fly a straight line until you're ready to shoot. Stay in pairs and never follow a German to the ground without somebody to watch out for your tail. If you find yourself alone, hug the ground and run home. There'll be ten of them to every one of us, so watch out for each other. We won't be re-forming as a squadron after the first pass, so stick with your wingmen. Understood?

One by one, they said it.

—About the Stukas, he said then, they break to the left. They dive from a long right-echelon formation, a sideslip or a half roll, and then drop at full throttle straight as a candle flame. They re-form in line astern and fly home in sets of staggered Vs. Hit them as they start to climb back into their formation and you'll be able to knock them down like clay ducks at a country fair. You'll find the fighters massed in layers all around the bombers. It's a tight, controlled, maneuverable shield, and a head-on, line-abreast attack would splinter against it. Hit them from the rear.

Then: Watch the Emils, the Bf 109Es and -Fs. They fly on the best-designed wing in Europe, but that's been weakened to make room for ammunition magazines and the landing-gear wells. Hit at the joint of fuselage and wing, an Emil goes out of control. They're heavily armed in front, just as you are, but they're vulnerable from the rear. Their pilots sit on their fuel tanks, and that might make them nervous. Once you have one in your sights, give him everything. They don't hold still for long, and they're fast and deadly. The bomber isn't your enemy, that's only your target. Hit them, scatter them, break up their formations, and a lot of them will turn and run for home. Your enemy is the fighter. His job is to kill you.

—Now, he said. Listen carefully. I want total silence in the ether from now on. I don't want to hear one word of Polish in my earphones until after the first pass, and the man who breaks that silence had better not come home. You understand me, pilots?

—Yes, sir, Reszke said.

—Understood, said Gerlach.

—I heard it, Straka said.

—And I, Wilchurzak said.

One by one, the others added to this quiet chorus.

—Then switch your sets to RECEIVE, Ludo said. Now.

Then there was silence in his ears, the soft hiss of air, the quiet hum of motors, and then the green woods of Prussia appeared below them.

There was no smoke in this East Prussian sky. The deep woods and lakes and sharply delineated roads and the neat clumps of red-roofed farmsteads and gleaming village spires were still and undisturbed. Such peace was an affront to him as he remembered Warsaw, the cratered Polish roads, the litter of dead bodies in the checkered fields. Left to right, and then right to left, he swept the empty sky.

Left to right . . . still nothing. Right to left . . .

A deep dark cloud glittering with ice? A layer of smoke? A black migration of huge birds hung crookedly against the western sky? The air above them seemed to crackle with reflected light: the sun stood trapped in a hundred prisms there. Almost immediately, he began to hear their chatter in his earphones.

They were at ease, unsuspecting, safe in their own sky, exuberant as schoolboys who had done their homework and were not at all apprehensive about the possibility of a test. The air was theirs, as was the present and the future of the world below them; they were free of any doubt about themselves as if whatever they believed about their destiny and mission made them immune to failure. But no one, *no one*, Ludo thought as he peered beyond and above the bombers, should take anyone else for granted.

At first sight, the Germans appeared to fill the sky; there seemed to be no end to their gathering column. The long, thin bodies of the Dorniers gave them the look of gigantic dragonflies. Their bulbous crew compartments looked like huge, watchful heads that flashed with the glitter of a hundred eyes. They flew in three deep columns, ten echelons to the column, on a course opposite to his own at thirteen thousand feet, and he saw these ninety Dornier Do 17s as two hundred and seventy thousand pounds of high explosives falling upon Warsaw.

He found the escort fighters where he expected them. The twin-engined Bf 110 Zerstorers were stacked in slanting layers at fourteen, fifteen, and sixteen thousand feet; the Emils flew in staggered groups of twenty at various altitudes beside, below, and behind the bombers, with five hundred feet between their interlocking layers. The lead fighter squadron would be stepped back under the head of the column unless it played the role of the Man on the Roof as well.

A time check, then. A rapid calculation of distances and angles. The Germans were assembling ten miles away and closing at about three hundred feet per second. Ten miles behind the heavy bombers, forty Stukas had begun to gather at nine thousand feet. Ten Emils were climbing on either side of them. Another ten or a dozen (it was difficult to count them at that distance) had just begun the slow, leisurely turns that would take them to high-cover altitude about a mile and a half behind the dive bombers.

One more quick, careful look around. Nothing in the sun. The Dorniers and their Zerstorer screens would begin to pass him on the left in less than half a minute. Below, Reszke's white face was pointed toward him, and he thrust his arm into the airstream and pumped it down sharply. One by one, his pilots rocked their wings, acknowledging his order. He banked his machine gently to the left and began the pivot.

He picked his target, a bright blue Dornier with red-and-yellow markings on the fuselage and tail, an echelon commander who flew about halfway down the center column under the triple screen of twin-engined Zerstorers. He closed his canopy, pulled down his goggles, and began to count the intervening seconds. On five, he set his guns on FIRE and swung into the sun. On seven, four thousand feet above the topmost Zerstorers, he crossed the head of the enemy column at right angles, rolled to the right, and dived.

Falling, he counted seconds. Each represented four hundred feet between him and the arrogant procession that slid under him. Nine, ten, eleven . . . He sharpened his angle of descent and increased his speed. Twelve, thirteen . . . A Zerstorer floated into his sights. The Zerstorer grew. The layers of aircraft under it had blurred. Fifteen. Sixteen. He pushed down on his stick, forced the nose of his machine into a steeper angle. His circular gunsights stroked the length of the enemy machine, centered on the crew compartment just behind the nose. He calculated his lead and deflection, blessed the blinding sun at his back, kept counting steadily.

Twenty-four seconds, twenty-five. On twenty-six, he was four seconds away from a head-on collision. Two hundred feet away and angled toward the German at seventy degrees, he pressed the red button on top of his control stick, felt the convulsive shudder in his wings.

Huge now, and staggering like a stunned ox, the Zerstorer hung in his sights. He knew that he had killed the pilot. At fifty feet, he watched the Plexiglas shattering, saw a white goggled face, saw a lick of flame, and then the black machine was rolling away, spinning down, and he was through the hole. Twenty-nine and . . . thirty!

In moments, the sky was full of fire and smoke and blue-and-yellow flashes of exploding high-octane gasoline, and coolant vapor trails, and red streams of tracers.

In his earphones: a cacophony of voices crying, *Achtung! Achtung!* Break! Break! Look out, Author! Oh, my God, help me, somebody! Hans, watch out! Watch him, Gerlach! Look out at four o'clock! I've got him! Turn, Sculptor, turn!

Nine hundred feet below him, two seconds away, the Zerstorers sideslipped to left and to right, uncovering the bombers. They watched his dive, he heard their cries of warning. The Germans' high squadrons were too tightly massed to follow him down through the scattering formation but that, he knew, wouldn't last long. This time, he opened fire at long range and watched his new explosive ammunition brush an engine cowling with small dancing flames, saw (for a chilling fraction of a moment) a great black cross that obliterated every other sight in his field of vision, saw a vast white belly sliding along the twin concentric circles of his gunsights, and squeezed the cannon trigger.

His concentration was so total that he heard the click of the solenoids before the cannon fired. Ten dull thumps meant two seconds. A blue flash blinded him. He fell into an envelope of smoke, felt more than heard the rattle of debris against his wings and fuselage, rocked to an explosion, then he was out and beyond the last of the Zerstorers. Six hundred feet below him, just beyond the outer ring of the gunsight, gleamed the crystal facets of the crew compartment of the bright blue Dornier, and now a broad-based cone of green-and-scarlet lights ascended toward him and crossed behind him, and he slid along the invisible wire that ran through the center of that web of lights.

Down and down and counting: Thirty-five, thirty-six . . .

His gauges were steady. Airspeed three-sixty and rising rapidly;

altitude twelve thousand, ten-five, distance narrowing; attitude and angle at eighty degrees. Temperature, oil pressure, and engine revolutions as expected. He had not been hit.

And suddenly, his canopy shattered over his head. The pressure-molded Plexiglas, supposedly bulletproof, slashed into his face. The machine staggered as though it had been kicked heavily in the side, and he knew that the high-cover Emils were coming down behind him. Too late, he saw them in his rearview mirrors: eight Bf 109s in two groups of four, hurtling through the hole he had punched in the Zerstorer screen. Their spinners and their engine cowlings were painted bright orange and each of them had individual markings on the wings, and sharks' teeth had been lacquered on the underside of their air intakes in short, uptilted grins.

Too late, he could curse the fascination of his fall, too long a time spent in a straight line pressing the attack. Break, break, he muttered to himself, but his altimeter and airspeed gauges had wound off their springs, and he knew that at his speed the force of a sudden turn would tear off his wings. There was a choice to be made in the fraction of a second that remained as his safety margin: to roll out and slip away or to continue the attack . . .

His dive was nearly vertical. One hundred and fifty feet away, the Dornier filled his sights. He pressed his thumb on one trigger, clenched his fist on the other, opened fire with all his armament (four 7.7-millimeter Browning FN machine guns, two twenty-millimeter Oerlikon cannons), felt the blow of the recoil cutting into his speed, saw the glassy head of the blue dragonfly disintegrating in slow motion fifty feet away.

Then: right stick, right rudder. The machine was shuddering along its whole length. His instruments were telling frightful lies. Somewhere close to the roof of his consciousness, a maddened animal was bellowing in pain . . . and then he was rolling in smoke, spinning out into a flat, revolving carousel of brown-and-yellow fields.

A flaming PZL-24 curved past his line of vision and he thought: Which one's that? Not Gerlach? Please, dear God, not Reszke? His earphones had filled with the high scream of a man trapped in a burning cockpit. And then it seemed to him that all the shrill young voices shouting in his earphones were just one voice, one language, one terrible obscenity.

He switched his R/T set to SEND, said: This is Toporski. Come in, Reszke. Reszke? Gerlach? Anyone?

But there was only silence in the ether then.

It had been twenty minutes since he had first sighted the assembling enemy armada one hundred and twenty miles to the north, and now the battle had taken itself eastward toward Warsaw. He was alone in an empty sky. An unexploded cannon shell had smashed his instruments. His oxygen line was severed. His wings—and he thought of them as his, rather than his machine's —were pitted with holes. He had been cut about the face and hands when his canopy was punctured. Time, rather than frozen gauges, told him that he was almost out of fuel. His cockpit reeked of spilled and seeping oil.

One adds up the pluses and the minuses at such moments. One plays the dreadful game of historical accounting. He had shot down two Zerstorers and a Dornier. Gerlach had set fire to another. He had seen two Emils going down after Reszke's attack and one more had exploded in the dogfight. The Stukas, caught in their slow climb, had fallen like apples in a hailstorm, and the battle wasn't over yet. But he also knew that once the Germans had recovered from surprise, their revenge had been terrible and swift. He had seen two PZL-24s on fire, another locked in a hammerhead spin, at least two blowing up as cannon shells hit them. He had seen no parachutes opening above any of them. One adds up numbers at such moments, one never thinks of names. One does not remember the shrill young voices, whatever their language. One makes a formidable effort to forget the screaming of the burning man.

Figures and numbers, then. Very well. The honest workman may take pride in his labor. The score would stand at seventeen to five. He could claim a victory. As the day went on, the weight of numbers would tip the scales in favor of the Germans. But, even so, the scoreboard would remain anonymous. He was glad that he had not had time to learn the names of the new pilots he had led that morning.

Close to the yellow tree crowns, he turned the nose of his machine toward the southeast, then climbed as high as lack of oxygen permitted. Modlin, a fortress built for a war two wars before this one, passed under his wing. Modlin was burning. Its brick-walled maze of magazines blew up in brilliant colors. The woods were on fire. Within the radius of a hundred miles, forty towns were burning. Time and again, this country had been reduced to ashes and had been reborn or reconstituted, or whatever politicians called it as they sat down at a conference table to redesign a map. But what of the lost lives?

He flew above ruins, wreckage, and the litter of terrified humanity on the move. The roads had become riverbeds in which a gray tide of animals and people flowed hopelessly toward no imaginable refuge. He could feel their inability to understand what had happened to them. Nothing stood untouched. No life was immune to loss and to grief, his own least of all.

Another time check, then, so that he might estimate his remaining fuel. (It was only ten o'clock in the morning, the war was five hours old.) Judging by the sun and the shadows of the trees over which he flew and, here and there, landmarks he recognized, he was about thirty miles northwest of Okęcie.

And then the Emils found him.

His gold pocket watch had been made in Vienna for an adviser of a Russian Tsar. It played a minuet when its lid was opened. It fell out of Ludo's hand when the first bullet struck him in the back. For quite some time, he remained unaware of pain but his left arm was useless. The watch continued to play the minuet as he dived and twisted among trees, high-tension towers, and under a bridge, while multicolored streams of incendiary ammunition glittered around him like so many fireflies, and instinct joined skill.

Fear, if it came at all, would come later, he knew. At the moment, there was only cold skill, faith in his luck, and a grudging admiration for the German who led the eight Emils. It was the squadron with the orange spinners once again, the humorous sharks, and he was sobered by the skill, depth, and devotion of the enemy. It was perhaps characteristic of himself that he didn't wonder whether they found him difficult to kill.

He blessed the anonymous airframe designer who had given

him a machine that could turn a circle standing on its wing tip. Gaining height in a series of tight spirals to the left and right, he kept himself inside the turning radius of the Messerschmitts, avoiding their cannons. He didn't have the speed to get away from them in level flight. Tight turns and steep dives into a flat turn at the bottom kept him in the air.

There was no more schoolboy chatter in his earphones then; only one voice was speaking, a quiet Viennese drawl thick as coffee cream.

—Put yourselves in his mind. Watch him. He's a tricky one. Stay alert, stay alert. . . .

The minuet went on to its end and Ludo had begun to laugh, having understood the role he had been assigned: a mother cat was teaching her kittens how to kill a mouse. Quick, sharp commands in that creamy voice gave him an advantage. Sooner or later, his tormentors would make a mistake and he would break out. In the meantime, being able to hear them and to understand them was an unexpected bonus.

They worked in pairs, each two pairs grouped into a finger-four; it was a wonderfully controlled formation, so called because it looked like the tips of a hand's four fingers swooping this way and that. In each quartet, only two men were shooting. The others watched the sky.

—Lead him, lead him, the calm measured voice of the German squadron leader instructed his pilots.

Ludo had done the same thing so often in air combat training that he could almost anticipate what the German would say.

—Box him on top, Hans, that's the lad. Put a lid on him. Watch for the break, Jurgen, he breaks to the right. Stay with him! Now! Now! Tighter! Tighter! *Ach* . . . by the perforated balls of Saint Sebastian, you'll have to do better than that!

Ludo swung out to the left, rolled to the right, and saw the pert squared tail of a Messerschmitt in his center ring. He squeezed the cannon trigger but nothing happened after the solenoids' click. Too late, he thumbed the Brownings' button and felt the convulsive shudders in his wings, but the Messerschmitt had turned belly-up and rolled out of sight.

—Watch him, he's first-rate, the calm German voice ad-

monished his pilots. You're not in flight school now. Are you still
with us, Kurt?

—*Jawohl, Herr Oberstleutnant,* a shaky young voice replied.
But, *Heiliges Sakrament,* I thought . . .

—Tell us about it later, the commander drawled. After you've
changed your pants, eh? This fellow can kill you. Now, by the
flayed balls of Saint Albert, will you please wake up? Concentrate,
concentrate . . . Now! Now! *Ach* . . . *Meine Herren,* you fly like
pregnant ducks!

In truth, they flew superbly. They clung to him like shadows.
He couldn't get away from them, no matter what he did. Whoever led them on that day, he thought, certainly knew his work.

Then he spun out again, free of them for a moment, and only
the German leader followed him in a tight climbing turn. Red-
and-yellow tracers streamed past him overhead. He throttled
down and hauled the control stick hard into his stomach. The
PZL-24 stood motionless on its tail for a count of one, then
snapped nose-down and dived and he pushed the throttle wide
open, watched a whirling yellow field, an onrushing haystack, a
terrified cow . . . sensed rather than saw the long shadow of the
German lifting over him . . . and twisted up with all his weapons
firing . . . and then it was the German squadron leader's turn to
break, roll, and dive.

—Now . . . by the breathless balls of the smothered innocents
. . . that was *not* flying, *Kinder.* Jurgen, you've just missed
becoming the youngest Jagdstaffel commander in the service.

A master at his trade, the German could afford to laugh at
himself. A predator with a sense of humor was the most dangerous enemy of all.

—Gather round, children, he said then. Let's do it right this
time. Get on his tail, Jurgen. . . . That's the way, Hans. Stay with
him. Watch him. *Ach* . . . by the wet balls of Saint Christopher,
here is a man who deserves to die with a certain dignity.

Ludo had gained some height and looked in vain for clouds in
which he might hide. The running fight had taken them above
the center of the city, a mass of thick smoke lit by rapid flashes.
This offered him a desperate kind of refuge.

His vision blurred, and he fought an overwhelming desire to

lean back, close his eyes, and allow himself to slip into his recurrent dream, and then the pain—hot and sharp—sent the adrenaline flowing. He knew that he was breathing far too quickly, but his mind was marvelously clear, and he wondered in an abstract, impersonal way what the German squadron leader was like. Was he young? Youngish? Would he die with the name of Adolf Hitler on his lips, conscious in that final moment of his own mortality? Would he experience the sweet soaring joy that Ludo was feeling? But the German leader had become impatient.

—All right, now. We've played long enough. Let's get this mouse boxed. Get under him, Erich, force him up. Jurgen, you cover his break to the right. Hans, watch him on the left. Second echelon, stay high and keep awake. Watch him . . . watch him. . . .

Then there were only two of them in his rearview mirror. One had dipped out of sight. In a moment, he'd raise his nose and empty his guns into the belly of Ludo's machine. Aerobatics never worked outside war fiction and the cinema; the trailing fighter would blow him out of the sky simply by raising his own nose if he went into the classic inside loop, the Immelmann turn. Nevertheless, he had a second to live, and knew it, and his rearview mirror was empty just long enough to risk everything on the unexpected.

Shaking with silent laughter, he went up and over at full throttle and began to fire at the top of his turn. The Messerschmitt (Hans? Jurgen? Kurt? It was suddenly important to remember a name) was coming head on; he was seconds away from collision and must have known, as Ludo knew, that there were no more choices to be made. The first man to break away would either bare his underbelly or expose his cockpit to the full armament of the other, and at this range it was impossible to miss. He (Ludo) had no further need for any kind of metaphor. Cold as ice, he watched his tracers disappearing in the silver blur about the orange spinner, and felt the hammer blows on his own wings and cowling, and knew, as surely as a priest knows his God, that he would not break.

—*Heiliges Sak* . . . !
—Break, Hans! Break! *Ach*, by the crucified balls . . . !
The pale-blue belly of the Messerschmitt lifted before him and

began to pass with agonizing slowness across his stream of fire, and he could see the great holes appearing among the neat stitching of rivets and overlapping metal sheets, and felt the heat of the fireball that bloomed over his head, and then the enemy was gone and he himself was diving into the heart of the burning city through a reddish twilight. He fell in a glitter of tracers that sparkled on his wings, felt flames, smelled the burning oil, and then smoke engulfed him.

It was dark then. He had been hit again but he couldn't tell where. Oil had splashed his goggles and he tore them off his face and threw them away. Pain seized him by the scruff of the neck and shook him as a terrier might worry a rat.

He flew through canyons whose walls were made of fire. Ten . . . twenty feet above rooftops, he searched for landmarks in a landscape that had become wholly desolate, looking for the river. The Vistula, where all the European currents of civilization intersected, would be a bright path to follow.

It was too soon to think, except in terms of moments, images such as a sixteen-story tower blazing in every window, a green roof to be avoided, the hot updraft of an obliterated square. Evaluation would come later, along with trembling hands. He did this and I did that. . . . And if he had done that and I had done the other . . . well, then, I wouldn't be here to tell you about it . . . there'd be no need ever to say anything again.

And then he was busy among sudden spires, the pylons of a bridge, the sunken shipping in the river, and climbed out of the smoke into a soiled sky, climbed at full throttle so that he might dive again and put out the flames that swept back from his engine cowling into his shattered cockpit. He didn't see the Emils with the orange noses. Indeed, he saw nothing.

—Gentlemen, the coffee-cream voice was drawling in his earphones with immense respect. Remember this man if you don't manage to kill him today. Remember that red spinner and thank Field Marshal Goering for free laundry service. But, by the burning balls of Saint Joan, I'd advise killing him at once.

Three quick explosions threw him into a barrel-roll and suddenly his machine was out of control. The stick was dead in his hands, the rudder pedals offered no resistance. The sun was brilliant, blinding in his eyes, and a Messerschmitt was on his tail with white lights twinkling around its orange nose. A massive blow knocked the stick out of his hands and threw him headfirst into his shattered instruments.

In moments, the cockpit was a mass of flames. He struggled to turn the machine over on its back, but the heat was so intense that he felt himself beginning to faint. So . . . was this to be the end of it, then? Piotr . . . Norwid . . . Janek . . . Wlada . . . Zosia . . . Lala . . . shouldn't they make their last farewell appearance? He knew then that he would never see any of them again . . . and then he was aware of an immense relief.

—*Auf Wiedersehen,* my friend, the coffee-cream voice crackled in his ears. I'll see you in hell. . . .

Gradually, with agonizing lethargy, as if unwilling to bring this exhilarating moment to an end, the machine rolled over and began to flutter slowly toward the ground, back and forth like a leaf, and he had fallen from the cockpit. He was free of flames and falling through whistling air.

PART TWO

Roads and Journeys

Your country is desolate, your
cities are burned with fire: your
land, strangers devour it in your
presence, and it is desolate, as
overthrown by strangers.

ISAIAII 1:7

CHAPTER VI

HE LAY IN A HOSPITAL for a month while his country fell. In what seemed like a single thousand-hour day, eighty-two thousand Polish soldiers were killed or wounded, thirty-six thousand civilians died in the ruins of their cities or in flight along the open roads, and seventy-eight thousand others had been rendered homeless. Three hundred thousand disarmed and bitter Poles were driven to captivity in Germany and another million vanished in the Siberian wastes of the Soviet Union. The Germans listed twenty-seven thousand of their soldiers as killed or badly wounded, along with three hundred and forty armored vehicles destroyed and two hundred and seventy-four aircraft lost in air combat. The Russians, who seized more than half of Poland's territory, claimed the greatest victory in their history at the cost of seven hundred lives. Neither the French armies nor the British Air Force fired a single shot at a German target in the west.

Some people approach their tragedies as they do life itself: tenaciously, egotistically, and with a knowledge of doom, expecting a reward for their real or imagined sufferings. Ludo expected nothing of the kind. He had been burned about the face and body and he believed that he was blind for life. He had been machine-gunned as he hung in the shrouds of his parachute, and no one, least of all the doctors, saw much hope for him. Each time the orderlies passed the mattress on which he lay in a corridor, they were surprised to find him still alive.

He lay in a black stupor while the morphine lasted, a stupor from which he awoke into agony to lie, hour after hour, staring into darkness. Never a moralizer, he resented the humiliation of his country quite as much as the wrecking of his body, perhaps even more. The suddenness and swiftness of Poland's defeat had made him, like every Pole, seem worthless in his eyes. Uneasily poised between wakefulness and nightmares, he saw again flaming machines that fell from the sky and listened to the screaming voices of young men. It was then, when he cried out his own incoherent warnings and commands, that Jacek Gemba or Auerbach or Bettner or his brother Janek, or whoever happened to be sitting with him at that moment, would run to get help. But there was rarely any help to be found in that littered corridor that led from the operating tables to the grave.

Something extraordinary happened to him then. As the shamed image of his country dwindled, so his own increased. He saw each as a separate living organism that had been crushed by a single blow. It would take months for any such organism to struggle up again and regain vitality. Its wounds went deep, the inner scars would never heal entirely. But life would continue with the persistence of unfinished business and he—and his country—would make the best of it. He made only one vow to himself: never again to endure defeat.

His days and nights were one, indistinguishable in their lack of light. Sound, and the voices of his visitors, helped him to position himself within that strange, agonized calendar of anger and regret. One day, he heard the deep, troubled voice of General Prus, a man whom he had loved more than his own father, asking if he'd survive a long journey on a stretcher. The general, it seemed, was planning to break out of Warsaw before its inevitable surrender with whatever remained of his command. The weary surgeon said that Ludo was as good as dead.

—There's nothing we can do for him. We've nothing with which to do it here. We've no supplies left, our surgeons are falling asleep at the operating tables, and there's been neither water nor electricity since the third day of the siege. It's a miracle he's lasted as long as he has.

—I know him, the general murmured. He's too stubborn to die.

The surgeon laughed bitterly, said: Say rather that he's too stubborn to admit he's dead.

On another day, he heard the voices of Loomis and Lala Karolewska, who spoke about him as though he wasn't there. Their concern was for each other, rather than for him. It was as if they were speaking of someone who had been dear to them but who had emigrated to another country, someone whom they had come to see off at the dock, only to find that the ship had sailed before they got there.

—Do you see now why it's impossible for me to be anywhere but here? Lala asked the American correspondent. If they can't all go to America with you, how can I?

—God, the American said with something like despair. I can't wait for all this useless horror to be done with here. The waste is just too much for any good that might come of it.

—It's never done with here, Lala said. No matter what anyone does to save himself, it's never quite over.

—If anything should happen to you, the American began, but she cut him short: Nothing will happen that isn't supposed to happen.

—Why did all *this* have to happen, then?

—God knows, she whispered, as if in reply to Ludo's own dark questions.

And then one day, or perhaps it was night since Auerbach, Janek, Jacek Gemba, Bettner, and one or another of his former pilots seemed to be always near, no matter what the hour, he heard this conversation:

—The end's almost here. They'll be surrendering the city in a day or two.

—And then what?

—We go on, like always. France, England . . . maybe the Mountains of the Holy Cross . . . maybe the forests in the Lubelszczyzna. . . . There isn't going to be any official surrender of *this* country, you know that. Nobody's going to ask the Germans for an armistice and peace terms. The war goes on.

—So where do we go?

—Winter's not all that far away, Gerlach said. The snow gets higher than a man in the Carpathian passes. So if we're going that way, we ought to start soon.

—And what about the major, sir? Jacek Gemba said. We can't go anywhere as long as he's like this. . . .

—War doesn't stop because a man's been hurt, Reszke said.

—No, and the more's the pity, Papa Bettner said.

Janek, who had come back from the war so ashamed and bitter, carrying such a burden of self-contempt and guilt that he seemed to have become twice his age, said furiously:

—Stop all this talking. You sound like everybody that I've ever met. Talk, plan, consider this and that, and in the meantime the

world ends! You'll still be talking, planning, and considering
when they prop you up before a firing squad. If we're to go at all,
then let's do it now!

—Where shall we go, Lieutenant? Auerbach asked politely.
Hungary or Roumania?

—Does it make a difference?

—Just about every difference in the world, I'd say, Gerlach
said. One way means Germans. The other way means Russians
and the Ukrainian peasants, and the traitors of the Red Militia.

—The idea is to get to France, not to be killed in Poland,
Bettner murmured softly, and Ludo wondered whether this old
friend, whose courage had become a daily struggle to conceal his
fear, could ever become an open enemy.

—The idea is to start killing our enemies again as soon as we
can! Janek said.

As always in the past, Auerbach's lilting accent provided a measure of logic and reason, and Ludo thought of all the moments in
which this extraordinary man had lifted him and others out of
doubt, uncertainty, and unavoidable disaster. So now again the
rollicking southern drawl of the old mechanic soothed and chan-
neled the distraught patriotism of the younger officers who had so
little to qualify them for war beyond a vast, pathetic bravery.

—We'll go because we have to, Chief Auerbach said. Nobody's
ever given a soldier the luxury of choice. But where to go and
how to get there is another matter. The siege will be over in a day
or two, the German lines will open, and there'll be ways to make
it to the border. Now, there's a lot of men that'll prefer to stay in
the country and go to the forests. That's all right for them. But
there's not going to be any machines to fly in the forests so, the
way I see it, there's no other choice for us but to get to France.

—I agree, Gerlach said. And the shortest way is southwest to
the mountains and then to Hungary.

—Not all of us are fit to play a mountain goat, Lieutenant,
Chief Auerbach said. Maybe the longer way might be the better
one. Maybe we ought to try for the Roumanian border.

—How about north to the Baltic and then a boat to Sweden?
Janek said.

—I was born in the mountains, Gerlach said. My family's still
there, as far as I know. I can get us across the high passes with a

sack on my head. If we leave Warsaw before the snows come, we
can be in Budapest in a month.

—And the major? Auerbach said quietly. Can he also get across
the high passes? There are no mountains between us and Roumania. There's just a river to cross.

—There's also all of the Russian Zone to cross, Reszke said.
From what I hear in town, that's become sheer hell. Mass deportations, shootings, drumhead tribunals . . . and the Russians
aren't doing it alone. We can trust almost anyone to help us in
getting around the Germans, but we can't trust anybody in the
Russian Zone.

Time returned to its proper subdivisions shortly after that. The
days acquired their displaced minutes and hours. Until light
began to reappear in his eyes, time had been marked only by a
change in sounds.

First, the radio lost its human voices. Day after day, each less
believable than the one before, the radio had cried out its warnings and announcements through the moans and sobbings of the
wounded. Then it ceased to speak. Its voice became reduced to
the opening bars of Chopin's "Polonaise Militaire," which it sent
out into the world as a signal that Warsaw was still fighting. Day
after day in terrible monotony, hour after hour, these ten notes
had drummed through his personal darkness so that always afterward he would associate them with hatred and despair. Then all
sounds gave way to a deep exterior silence. Soon afterward, he
knew even before it happened, he'd hear the clipped clatter of
German commands in counterpoint to the moaning of the Polish
wounded. After that, his visitors would be fewer.

Yet, even then, with Warsaw fallen and the Germans in control of their half of the country, he was not to be left entirely
alone. Auerbach, dressed incongruously in the leather apron of a
garbageman, came with plans for Ludo's escape from the hospital
which, by that time, had become a cage for prisoners of war. He
saw the old line chief through inflamed, suppurating eyes as his
first clear and welcome image in a haze of shadows, and knew
that he'd be neither blind nor a cripple nor a prisoner of war, and
that his war would continue.

—You can see me?

He nodded, and saw the old man's military moustache move up and down to mask a rare emotion.

—Well, then God's not on vacation as I thought He was, Auerbach said. Now, if we can only get you out of here, we can be on our way.

—France?

—France it is. But now's the time to get you out. Not after they've got you caged behind barbed wire in Germany. Reszke and Gerlach jumped out of a prison train, but they didn't have a dozen holes in them. We've got to find a way to carry you out.

—Maybe I'll grow wings, Ludo said. Since the age of Polish miracles doesn't seem to be over yet.

—And maybe I'll paint you yellow and call you a canary. No. I'll have to think of something else. We carry dead men out of here every day, but the German doctors have to certify a corpse before he's bundled out.

Slipping once more into unconsciousness, Ludo whispered: Damned if I oblige them. . . . How are all the others?

—Reszke and Gerlach left for the mountains just as soon as the Germans folded up their siege lines. They'll be in Hungary before the snow starts falling. They said to tell you they'll have a bird warmed up for you when you get to France. The rest of us are hiding in the city.

He had another visitor, a Luftwaffe oberstleutnant who came to offer his compliments to Ludo and to ask whether there was anything that he could do for him. It was a piece of Old World courtesy that went with the well-remembered Viennese accent of the oberstleutnant.

Other than a swift reversal of their roles, Ludo could think of nothing that he wanted from him. He lay in his own stench on his soiled mattress while the impersonal rubber hands of German military surgeons dressed his burns, caked his eyes with ointments, and tagged him for shipment to a prison camp. He was delighted that he could neither see nor touch himself and so could sustain the illusion that he too was bathed, shaved, neatly uniformed, and erect. The German was the victor and he was one of the malodorous vanquished; yet a mutually understandable current passed between them even as the soft, drawling coffee-cream voice of the oberstleutnant identified him as the commander of the Messerschmitts with the orange noses.

—We never expected you to give us such a fight, the oberstleutnant said. But one does learn from the unexpected, does one not? And one does go to the trouble of identifying an enemy like you.

Ludo said nothing to the German. They were linked by a current as strong as destiny; they'd have to meet again, he knew. In the meantime, the gulf between them was measurable in decibels of pain, and the oberstleutnant was staring about the littered ward with obvious distaste. His face was weathered, narrow, and surprisingly lenient. The body was slight, slim, compact as a dancer's. On his right-breast pocket he wore the golden Spanienkreuz, the badge of the veterans of the Condor Legion who had fought in Spain, and the First Class of the Iron Cross with 1939 engraved on its bar. His name, he said, was Walther Reinecke, commander of Lehrjagdstaffel VI, on temporary duty with the SS, the Gestapo, and the Golden Eagles of the Nazi Party who were moving into Warsaw on the heels of the combat soldiers. He did nothing to hide his contempt for the policemen and the politicians.

—We'll move you to a good Luftwaffe hospital in a day or two, the oberstleutnant said. That's the least we can do.

—And then? Ludo's dull, muffled voice astonished them both.

—And then? Well, that's for *them* to decide. In any event, the war is over for you.

—I wouldn't count on that, Ludo said.

—By the upside-down balls of Saint Peter, I'd shake your hand if you had a spare one, said the oberstleutnant and, for the first time, looked thoughtful and bemused. A small civilian in a leather trenchcoat and a Tyrolean hat and wire-rimmed spectacles had accompanied him, pointing to this wounded man or another, consulting his files, and a noncom in a coarse black uniform tied cardboard shipping labels around the necks of wounded officers.

He knotted each loop like a small hangman's noose and laughed as he did it.

—Just an innocent little bit of fun, he said and grinned as he caught the oberstleutnant's eye. Anyway, this other burned mummy over here smells like a Jew to me.

The glance which passed between Ludo and the oberstleutnant contained elements of pity, shame, and bitter promise.

What the troubled oberstleutnant seemed to be saying then was: Look, you've got to understand this, we're not all like that. You and I are fighting men. We kill each other, but we don't humiliate each other. We can appreciate each other's qualities more than any other kind of soldier because we are airmen! What happens on the ground has nothing to do with us. We don't even live here. This is groundling business and you and I both know what that's worth. So let it pass, forget it as quickly as you can. Neither you nor I can expect anything worthwhile out of our own element.

What Ludo's glance was meant to convey to the German in reply was: Never mind all that. One day, I'll have to kill you to erase this moment.

That night, the autumn rains began. The rain that turned the Polish country roads into impassable quagmires every year, and for which the whole nation had prayed throughout that parched September, seemed like the last ironic stroke now that the war was over. It flowed down the cracked walls, through the shattered ceilings. It flooded the corridor. Ludo couldn't sleep.

Half awake, half drifting in a nightmare, he listened to the sounds of a captive city: whistles, distant commands to halt, and shots. The night was dull with pain, fear, sudden death; he thought he might go mad. He listened to the gurgling hiss of the man on the mattress next to him. The man, who was known simply as The Burn, had neither moved nor made any kind of sound before. He was swathed in grimy bandages that robbed him of features. The yellow-gray rags that formed what must have been a face, in much the same way that Ludo's own face had been wrapped by surgeons, were punctured by one small, dark hole, and it was out of this that the sound was coming. It was less a

whisper than a creaking sigh, and Ludo had to harness his entire
attention to make out the words.

—Have you . . . hands? creaked the awful whisper.

—What? Hands? Yes, he said.

—Ah . . . and mercy? Have you some of that?

—Nobody has that, Ludo said.

—But you're an educated man? An officer?

—For what that's been worth.

—You'd not be . . . ah . . . inhibited by superstition, then?

—No more than anyone, Ludo said.

—Then . . . can you kill me?

Appalled, Ludo found himself unable to speak for a moment.

—What are you saying, man?

—I hear you talking to yourself, the whisper hissed and gurgled. You talk about escaping, fighting . . . killing people. . . .
Why don't you kill someone who wants to be killed?

—Nobody wants to be killed, Ludo said and felt his own cold
sweat inflaming his wounds.

—I do, the Burn whispered. It would be . . . Christian charity.

—Then ask someone else.

—Whom should I ask? the strangled whisper hissed. Where
should I look for it?

—I don't know. But you won't find it here.

—Not anywhere, it seems. Listen. I hear you talking with your
friends. About getting away. I can help you there.

—How can you help anyone?

—Who leaves this place and goes free? Corpses leave it. You
need a corpse to switch your label with. The corpse stays as you,
you leave as the corpse. Kill me and you've got what you need to
escape.

—You must be mad, Ludo said.

—You've got to do it. You've killed men before! Look, every
sound I make is agony. Spare me the need to argue. End my pain
and you're as good as free.

—For God's sake, be quiet!

—I too am an officer, the Burn hissed and gurgled. Oh, not
much of one, I admit. An imitation officer, as it's said. But, even
so, that ought to count for something. If you won't kill me out of

hatred . . . and not out of mercy . . . will you help a brother officer? It would be . . . your duty.

—For God's sake, no! Ludo said.

In the last graying hours before dawn, when the shadows were still mercifully dark, the burned man said that he was a forty-six-year-old reservist, an actor by profession, and, as a Jew, destined for the garbage dump in any event. He pointed out with the icy logic of a man for whom pain had no thresholds that he was a corpse whether he breathed or not, that even if, by some miracle, he survived the hospital, he'd be killed somewhere else, and that no SS guard would give more than a passing glance to a dead Jew carted out for unrecorded burial.

—An . . . unrecorded burial, Major, he hissed. A point worth the making. No fuss. No questions. Out of the door . . . and gone. So be a Jew for half an hour, Major. Why don't you? It's not all that bad. And . . . anyway . . . you'll recover from it.

As for himself, the Burn would masquerade as Ludo in Ludo's bed and with Ludo's shipping tag around his bandaged throat. One set of dirty bandages wrapped around a head looks much like another. So who'll know, eh? asked the dreadful whisper. The worst thing that might happen to him now was a Christian burial, he said, and God was sure to understand it and forgive it.

—No, Ludo whispered. I can't do that.

—*Antysemita*, hissed the Burn. You'd do it for a German.

—Leave me alone, said Ludo. Why don't you kill yourself, if that's what you want?

—I've no hands, the Burn said.

Then, gurgling: Can you imagine an actor . . . at the Yiddish Theater . . . with no hands?

—No, Ludo said.

Then it was morning.

The one thing that had kept him relatively sane in his weeks of pain, sleeplessness, and blindness was his fevered determination to escape. But how? Even the damp, cold weather conspired against him. His wounds had opened; some had become infected. Deep sleep (the senses all but shut off and only an occasional drift of thought) had become impossible, so there was little difference between wakefulness and sleeping. Morphine had changed his hormone levels and his biological clock had slipped out of gear.

In the dark, wet ruin of the corridor, among the not-quite-dead who couldn't be saved, he drifted in and out of a ninety-minute cycle of nonsleep and a never-quite-alert state of waiting for a dream in which he might be safe from either misadventure, memory, or imagination. He listened to the softer whispers of Auerbach and Bettner.

—He can't walk, Bettner said. So how do we move him?

—If you're supposed to be a German, as your name implies, why don't you think like one? Auerbach said. He dies and we take him out to the garbage truck.

—And what do we do for a real corpse to show to the Germans?

—Listen, Auerbach said. If there's one thing in this town that we're not short of these days, it's corpses. We're digging up a couple of hundred every day.

—We're supposed to be taking them out of the hospital, Papa Bettner said. We're not supposed to be bringing them in.

Classified as ethnic Germans by the conquerors, they had been assigned jobs in the city's civil administration: Bettner as a records clerk in the municipal Office of Births and Deaths, and Auerbach as a garbageman whose horse-drawn, rubber-tired lorry doubled as a hearse in the early weeks of the occupation. It would be several weeks before the Gestapo weeded out such poisonous plants as they from the ordinary Volksdeutsche, the genuine German minority in Poland, who formed an eager network of Gestapo collaborators and informers. Their rewards were special ration cards, exemptions from police curfew and arbitrary seizure in the streets, and the confiscated property of Poles who had been their neighbors. In the meantime, Auerbach and Bettner had freedom of movement and official functions which took them in and out of the hospital every day.

Awake, Ludo smiled up at them and they smiled worriedly at him.

—There really isn't a great deal of time, Papa Bettner said. The Wehrmacht is handing over control of the city to the Gestapo and the Party people, and there aren't any *Kaffee mit Schlag* gentlemen among *them*. They're shooting people a hundred at a time in the Pawiak prison. They have mass street hunts every day and anybody caught without an *Ausweis* or an *Arbeitskarte* gets to be a *Häftling*.

—Just because they've labeled you a Volkser, you don't have to talk like one, do you? Auerbach said.

—It's catching, Bettner shrugged and said.

—So's the plague, Auerbach said. But who'd want to catch it? If you'd learn to think like one of them, instead of just talking, we wouldn't have any trouble in finding a good corpse.

He nodded at the Burn, whose sudden gurgling sound could be identified as laughter.

—I'd say that a man who killed that poor son-of-a-bitch would be doing him a service.

Then they were all quite still, not looking at each other, each aware of one cold thought they shared. Then Ludo fell back on his sodden mattress and whispered: No. Think of something else.

—Didn't you hear what Papa said? Auerbach asked quietly. There's no time for that.

The man who had been known simply as the Burn died during the night. His name was Izydor Kaminski. Because he was a lieutenant in the Army, albeit a reservist and a Jew, his death was recorded by Bettner on official forms for the International Red Cross, and Auerbach carried out his body (Ludo) in a sack to his unofficial hearse. Ludo's own death was recorded the following morning when Kaminski's shrouded corpse was found on Ludo's mattress. For propaganda purposes of their own, the Luftwaffe gave him a military funeral with all appropriate honors.

CHAPTER VII

IN NOVEMBER, equipped with documents that Papa Bettner forged or stole from the Germans, they left Warsaw as Volksdeutsche volunteers for fortification work on the German-Soviet demarcation line that bisected Poland.

In the beginning, all of them believed that they had put their pasts behind them and that only a future lay ahead of them. Even Janek, who seemed to have lost his faith in everything, made optimistic plans for a return in spring. The French were expected to move their vast armies as soon as winter ended. They and the British and their great empires were sure to crush the Germans and their Russian allies, and the Poles would have their country once again. But the Roumanian border and what it represented to them when they began their march became something altogether different by the time they reached it.

The journey through the looted and dispirited wasteland of their country hardened and embittered them and finally convinced them that there was no escape from a past such as theirs.

They walked in rain, in darkness, through a sea of thick, loamy mud that sucked their boots off their legs and clung to their clothes and tainted everything they ate. They lived on what they could beg or steal on moonless nights. The villages they passed were lifeless, shuttered against intrusion, and even the dogs had a mad, tormented air.

As long as they were moving through lands held by Polish peasants, it was possible for them to knock on any door, whisper a greeting, and walk away with bread, milk, apples, or a cheese, and (sometimes) even an excited little boy to lead them to a forest path that went around a roadblock. But these hospitable moments became rare once they crossed the demarcation line. There, in the Russian Zone, patrolled by Cossack cavalry and the Red Militia, the eyes that looked at them were filled with hostility and suspicion and (all too often) a lad would be sent to get the NKVD while villagers distracted them with evasive answers. The Ukrainian peasants hated Poles as deeply as they hated Russians, and they took pleasure in using one set of enemies to destroy another. Nor were they content to leave it at that.

Sometimes it was impossible to avoid passage through small market towns, and they split up and edged, singly or in pairs, through dark, glowering crowds to whom a stranger was anathema. Jacek Gemba, whom the hardships of their journey had thinned down into the semblance of a fourteen-year-old, pretended then to be a lad who was leading his blinded father (Ludo) to the local dealer in miracles and herbs. This was Jacek

Gemba's country, anyway; he had run away from it when he was a child, and there was nothing about it or its people that he didn't know.

—This is where I'd get a fist in the ear for breakfast and a kick for supper, and only my own knuckles to chew in between. It's a hard land, sir. Death counts for nothing here.

—I know, Ludo said. I remember.

—Walls full of saints and a hungry belly, Jacek Gemba said. And if one man's got to take his cap off to another, he'll live on hate until one of them's dead.

In one such small town, they stood in a crowd against the wall of a shuttered wooden church, chewing sunflower seeds and wheat stalks while a pale young man in a leather coat harangued the crowd from the back of a Red Army truck, and they watched two bloodied officers led on halters by the Red Militia and locked in a pigsty, and they saw the peasants beat and drown another in a water barrel.

—A man'd be a fool to look for mercy here, Jacek Gemba said.

They walked at night and hid during the day in woods, marshland, misty copses of poplars and pine, and on the reed-grown banks of streams. Then, as the meager stands of birch came to an end, as the land flattened further, they moved with greater caution, sometimes walking no more than five miles in a night. Thousands had gone that way before them, they could tell; at each step through these southeastern woods, in roadside ditches and by wayside shrines, they came across the flotsam of a great migration: discarded pieces of uniforms, broken weapons, and—occasionally—the stripped and mutilated bodies of stragglers caught by Ukrainian peasants. If any portion of this drab and gloomy land had ever known love, it was not evident. The peasants hunted for them in the woods, the Red Militia occupied the villages, and Russian cavalry patrolled the muddy tracks on shaggy-haired ponies. None of the fugitives looked anything like soldiers by that time—indeed, to Ludo's eyes, they hardly looked human. But to those who hunted them they would be as obviously Polish as if they were still in uniform. Time and again, they'd come across bleached corpses, loosely covered with brushwood and leaves, each with a crushed skull or a slit throat: young

soldiers who had accepted peasant hospitality on their way to the
Roumanian border.

—It didn't have to be like that at all, Papa Bettner said in one
such moment of a horrible discovery. We're the same race; we
were all one people at one time. What difference does it make if
their priests marry and ours don't? In God's name, how do such
things begin?

—In God's name, Janek said. And doesn't *that* tell you something about it all?

—No, Bettner mumbled. That's not what this country was
meant to be about.

—Tell that to the Ukrainians and to the Red Militia, Janek
said.

—People have to begin to forgive each other, Papa Bettner
said.

—Why? Janek asked bitterly. Hating is easier. And . . . you
can get a lot more pleasure out of it.

Almost at once, a light machine gun chattered at them out of a
stack of felled timber at the far end of the clearing, and a hand
grenade curved toward them darkly in the moonlight, and they
scattered and ran. Janek carried Ludo slung across his shoulders.
The woods around them echoed with shots, calls, cruel laughter,
and, in the ever-growing distance of their headlong flight, with
the dwindling sound of church bells rung in the nearby village.

Finally, the night began to end. It was to be their last night in
Poland. The river that marked the Roumanian boundary lay only
half a day's march away. They reassembled at the edge of the
woods where, normally, they'd spend their daylight hours. But on
that morning, after that night, they had to risk open ground in
daylight.

Then, as the sun climbed higher and the concealment of the
night was taken from them, they met a peasant leading a small,
shaggy-haired pony loaded with panniers of firewood. In open
fields, there was nowhere to hide.

He studied them quietly, then said: May God be praised.

—Forever and forever, they replied in chorus.

And had they come far?

Three hundred miles lay behind them, the hardships of their march were stamped on their faces, but to tell the truth would be dangerous.

—Not far, Little Father, Ludo said in dialect.

The peasant smiled and nodded. He was a gentle, fatherly old man with twinkling blue eyes in a weather-beaten face, and, for an instant that recalled every moment of innocence and childhood, such words as kindliness and honesty had some sort of meaning.

—Such times, such times, the old man said sadly. That God should permit it.

Could one still hope, then, for a human impulse? The clatter of pursuit had fallen away but the images of the night were monstrously clear. Yet what could be more reassuring than this elderly villager in a frayed straw hat and a white homespun shirt belted with a strap?

—We bow to God's will, Ludo murmured then.

—In his hands lies our peace, the peasant replied.

He wore a pair of Polish military breeches tucked into muddy bast boots. He had watched them calmly, unafraid, as they emerged from the last of the woods, and there was something so disarming in his lack of fear and suspicion that each of them felt an immense relief. Surely, not everyone was an enemy!

The old man smiled and nodded as they told their lies about being travelers from another village, and offered them cheese and black bread and a quart tin of sour milk to share. Shyly, as if fearing a rebuff, he offered them shelter. He had a barn, he said, not too far away. They could sleep there on dry straw. They could rest up for the last stretch of open country between them and the river. The river itself, he said, was high at this point, and swift with all the rain, and they would need all their strength to swim it. His own son had been a Polish soldier and had *gone over* several weeks before. He would be honored to feed and shelter the comrades of his son.

Bettner was grinning from ear to ear, and Auerbach had sat down on a tree stump and allowed his huge shoulders to sag in weariness, and Ludo himself felt all his tensions ebbing at the prospect of rest, perhaps some hot food, a chance to dry his clothes, to take off his boots, perhaps even sleep. Sleep . . . great God in heaven! When had that been possible for more than an hour at a time? The temptation was almost impossible to resist.

—As you've guessed, Little Father, he said cautiously, we're not really travelers from another village.

—If not from one village, then from another, the old peasant said. Every man comes from somewhere, and a guest in the house is like God in the house.

Ludo began to smile and to nod as the old man droned his kindly invitations, and all the others smiled, and death stood grinning at them in the form of the fatherly, inoffensive peasant. Who could fear such openness, such kindness? It was Janek, whose finest instincts had been burned away, who whispered in Ludo's ear that there was dried blood on the military breeches the peasant was wearing, or what looked like blood.

—And what are all those brown stains on the shaft of your ax, Little Father?

The peasant said that he had killed a chicken earlier in the morning, a fine plump hen they could share with him and his wife after they'd slept a bit. As for the breeches, proper soldier breeches, they had belonged to his son, the soldier, a corporal in the cavalry, no less. He had brought them home when he came back from war. That's where the blood came from, he supposed, if that's what it was. The Pany Soldaty would know about such things better than an old man who had never walked further than ten miles from his village. War's a bloody business, didn't they agree? Perhaps his son, the corporal, had slipped in some blood . . . Perhaps that's where it came from . . . But, as Saints George and Michael would attest, he had nothing in his heart but pity for the tired comrades of his son, and sorrow at their suffering. His home was theirs, his barn was theirs too. They could rest, eat, sleep. The border would be there to cross tomorrow as it was today.

—Well, Ludo said and looked at the others. What do you think?

—What's there to think about? Papa Bettner said. He's a kind, decent man. We have to trust someone! All this hatred and suspicion . . . it's got to end sometime!

The old man had taken off his straw hat and bowed from the waist, and Jacek Gemba brought his clenched fist down on the old man's neck, and the old man crumpled into the mud.

—What in God's name . . . ! Papa Bettner cried, and Jacek Gemba said softly: No peasant ever killed a chicken. That's where the eggs come from. That's cash crop in a village. You eat a chicken if it dies but you never kill one. And them there . . . them's officer's breeches, sir. No corporal in the cavalry ever wore a fine pair of twill pants like that.

In the panniers, they found an officer's Vis pistol and a hand grenade and seventeen silver eagles cut away from military caps. They took the hand grenade and the pistol. They took the peasant's bast boots. They tethered the small horse on loose reins so that he might graze. They hanged the old man on the strap he used for a belt.

—Why are we doing this? Papa Bettner asked and pleaded for the old man's life. How does this make us better than the other murderers? Wouldn't it be enough just to tie him up and gag him to be found by someone after we are safe? The border is six hours away at most!

But Ludo said no. His eyes were full of tears.

—Just tell me why? Papa Bettner pleaded.

—Because it's . . . necessary, Ludo said.

—Necessary? For the war or for you? Or to keep hatred alive?

Then Bettner said nothing more and none of the others said anything to him.

They spent the day, their last day in Poland, hidden in the wet, dank undergrowth of an abandoned graveyard, and waited for the sun to set in the gray sheets of rain that continued to fall in the west. The steep banks of the river, which they would cross at twilight, had become the final limit of their possibilities.

They knew by the muffled sounds of footfall and the click of shod hooves on the occasional stone, that the patrols were moving all around them, and they wondered how soon they would be found. The Cossack cavalry would herd them to captivity, the

Ukrainian peasants would torture them to death, the Red Militia would drag them off to the nearest city to parade a triumph before their Russian masters. . . . But, Ludo thought, it wasn't likely that the Red Militia, as hated by the Ukrainian peasants as the Poles themselves, would wander far from their village billets.

As they waited, they talked in low voices.

He listened to them and to the hiss of the rain, and he slipped in and out of unconsciousness as if crossing back and forth between a dark room and an illuminated one in which all the moments of his life were stored.

What was this war about? A soldier doesn't ask that kind of a question. But the peace that followed would have to be so rewarding, so full of assurances of a better future, that all of the horrors of the past could be dismissed from memory and conscience.

Why, suddenly, should he be troubled by conscience?

(*You owe it to us, Ludo,* Wlada said invisibly through the hiss and crackling of the radio-telephone in a forest clearing, and the phrase, which had been merely irritating, had become a verdict.)

He muttered: Nothing! I owe nothing!

And Jacek Gemba said at once: What's wrong, sir? Can I get you something?

—Nothing, he said. A stray thought. Not worth mentioning.

—Yes, sir, Jacek Gemba said with no conviction in his worried voice. If you say so, sir.

Perhaps the fault lay less in himself, Ludo knew, than in the Polish language in which the word for *owe* is the same as *guilty*. I owe nothing, he had said aloud, but what he really wanted to hear himself saying was that he was innocent of anyone's death.

Jacek Gemba was staring at him with concern and he closed his eyes so as to be alone. Alone, he counted ghosts. He sought explanations. In Poland, the past was always ready with unsolicited advice which had nothing to do with the realities of the present. He felt again the vague but poignant urge to grasp his life, embrace it, know it all at once, and insist on a reasonable course for it; but he knew that the more one strove to bridge the gap between things as they were and as they ought to be, the harder it was to evade futility.

To his surprise, he slept. In the dream, the recurrent nightmare which appeared when he was very tired, the past and the future were coming together. He was a child running away from home while cavalry trumpets played, and then he was flying, and then he was destroying the murderers of his parents and the village in which he had been born. He was alone. Everyone else was dead. A city or a village was burning below him, a huge red heart was beating. Wrenched with nausea, he twisted away from the booming in his ears, dived into inner silences, sought cover in the clouds. He was in flight from something invisible that pursued him and drove him toward something threatening that awaited him. Maddened peasants were hunting for him in the ruins of their fire-bombed homes. He would be safe in the ruins of the manor, in his brothers' nursery; the peasants wouldn't enter that scorched maze of stones because of the ghosts. But he had lost his way; he couldn't find the ruins in which he belonged.

Then he was falling, burning. He saw a red embrace unfolding below him; saw it through a blood-red haze booming with explosions. A wind had seized him and was shaking him, but he was dead and he could not awake.

—Wake up! Wake up! a distant voice was calling, and he said: To what? What's the point?

—The sun is going down, Janek said.

Awake, yet feeling as though he were still dreaming, he looked around and saw an edge of scarlet appear beyond the screen of rain. The silhouettes of the gravestones had darkened. Crouched in the mist, they seemed like milestones.

—Looks like it's time to get moving again, sir, Jacek Gemba said. Are you hurting much?

—Enough to share it if anybody wants it.

The young man hooted softly and showed uneven teeth in a crooked grin. —Is that one of them *metafory* again, sir? And what's going to happen now? I mean, we *are* going to come back home, aren't we? Sometime?

—We'll be back, Ludo said. You can depend on that.

—Because if we don't, sir, Jacek Gemba said. If . . . well, if something happens and we can't get back from that place we're going to, then everything that's happened here will've been for nothing, don't you think? I mean, sir, that France, that's all very well, but this is where we come from. And if that's where we come from, that's where we belong.

—Out of the mouths of babes, Ludo said and smiled. You don't make things difficult for yourself, do you?

—I'm not smart enough for that, sir, Jacek Gemba said. I leave that to people that's been educated. But I never did see why things have to be hard when they can be simple.

—It's not too late to turn back if you don't want to go, Ludo said. Nobody will think badly of you if you do.

—I'm your orderly, sir, Jacek Gemba said. I go where you go. And all them foreign places—well, sir, that'll be something to talk about when I'm an old man.

The river was only five kilometers away at this point, the mist was thinning everywhere, and the western horizon had become a blurred crimson haze. If they could leave at once, they would be at the border in an hour.

And then what?

Roumania, Hungary, Yugoslavia, Italy, and France . . . the names fell like stones. Bettner sat on a burial mound, his head in his hands. Janek stared westward without a word, his eyes were remote. Ludo himself felt as if he'd do anything to delay the moment of departure; to leave now, to turn his back on Poland, would be like deserting, no matter what the reasons for the journey.

He watched the others, and saw them watching him, and he listened to the trilling of the waterfowl around them, and he sniffed the damp air and peered into the mist.

—Time to go now? he asked.

—Not yet, I think, Auerbach said. Listen.

—To what?

—The birdcalls, Auerbach said.

—What about the birdcalls?

Sometime during their flight through the woods, Auerbach had lost his glasses; almost blind without them, he turned his head this way and that, listening, and then he passed the edge of his hand across his throat.

—*Ryzuny*, he said simply. I never thought you'd forget that sound.

—*Ryzuny?* Janek said. What's that all about?

—That's how they talk to each other, the bastards, the old line chief said. They've found us, that's what it's about. It will be death to move.

Again, as if to mock them, the harsh nasal call of geese came from the tall grasses that surrounded them. The sounds, sharp as a butcher's knife, had more than just personal menace in them; peasants goaded to slaughter were part of the history of these eastern lands. Their birdcalls fluttered in the mist and rain, and Ludo had an overpowering feeling of futility. To have come so close to the end of the journey, and to fail, was almost more than he could bear. The past—his past—waited like a creditor and the payment could no longer be deferred.

His wounds, he noted, had opened again. His chest and shoulders were covered with blood. The birdcalls, so familiar from the night when he had crouched in the ruins of his home, had become insistent.

—Who has the Vis and the hand grenade? he asked.

—I do, Janek said.

—Give them to me.

—No one is going to disarm me again, Janek said.

—Do what you're told, boy, Ludo hissed, and Janek shook his head.

—I'm done with doing what I'm told. From now on, I make my own decisions. All my life I've been the coddled little brother, looking up to others and playing the fool. You and Wlada and Piotr and Norwid gave me everything. It's time to pay for it.

—Don't be a fool, Janek, Ludo said. Give me the weapons, and then all of you go down to the river. I'll join you there as soon as I can.

—How can you join us anywhere? Janek said and grinned.

—Maybe I'd better stay instead, Auerbach said. I'm an old man, I've had my good times. And I can still move fast when I've got to.

—Enough of all this, Janek said. I'm staying and that's that. It's my turn, don't you see? You've had your wars. This one was mine and I lost it. And . . . anyway . . .

—Please, Janek, Ludo begged. If you've ever loved me, give me the pistol and the hand grenade and get down to the river.

I'll hold them off until you're well away. Dammit, it's my duty!

Pale in the slanting rain and grinning like a skull, Janek said: Sorry to disappoint you, Ludo. Indeed, I'm sorry about a lot of things. I've been a fool, living in a fool's world, believing the slogans. War was going to be such a wonderful adventure! Well, even a fool has to grow up sometime. The adventure is over.

—But they'll kill you here! Ludo cried.

—Not necessarily, Janek said and grinned.

Then he said: Don't worry about me, I'm not suicidal. I intend to get across that river too. So you just wait for me at the first kilometer stone on the other side of the Kuty bridge.

—For the last time, Ludo said. Janek, I beg you . . . if you've ever loved me.

—What does love have to do with anything? Janek said and raised the pistol and the hand grenade. This is what counts. I'm making my own decisions now. Isn't that what you brought me up to do?

Ludo wanted to say something more, to protest and argue and to issue orders, but Auerbach picked up one end of the improvised stretcher on which he was lying, and Bettner picked up the other, and he lost consciousness almost as soon as they set off, trotting at a crouch. The pain of his wounds, the fever of infection, the hunger and exhaustion carried him into a miasmic world. There were sharp, hostile sounds in that vague world through which he was carried: cries dimmed by memory and distance, the *crump* of a bomb. In the cool, moist air of the riverbank, he regained consciousness and stared at a gently moving sea of rushes and reeds.

Bettner, who sat beside him, held his hand.

—Where's Janek? he said.

—He said he'd meet us on the other side, Bettner murmured and turned his head away.

—We're still in Poland, then?

—Still in Poland. The river is fast here, a lot of debris. But the bank is gentle on the other side. Auerbach and Jacek are making a raft.

—Hasn't Janek come yet?

—It's only been an hour, Papa Bettner said evasively. An hour's not so long. You and I hid out in the ruins of your manor a lot longer than that.

—Were there shots? Cries? Anything? Did you hear anything?

—We heard some shots. We heard the hand grenade.

—And you did nothing? You just went on running for the river, you damned drunken coward?

—For God's sake, Ludo! Bettner cried, pale with grief and pain. Will you please have some mercy for someone before it's too late? Mercy . . . understanding . . . affection . . . has that become quite impossible for you? If your brother chooses to give his life for yours, does that mean that everyone must die in return? (Then, clumsily, because in tears and close to collapse:) He made his choice, Ludo, for good or for evil. Don't try to take the meaning out of it.

—But to leave him like that . . . with those butchers . . .

—It needn't be the butchers, Papa Bettner said. There was some rifle fire. There was a burst or two from those Pepesha machine pistols that Russian noncoms carry. That means the Cossacks got there. They have a high regard for personal courage, they wouldn't let the peasants get to him. Christ, they despise those peasants as much as we used to.

—You offer me sick comfort, Papa, Ludo said.

—What other kind do we have to offer each other? Anyway, the boy has a damned good chance. He's brave, he's resourceful. He's full of rage and cunning. He sees very little value to any kind of life, and that's the sort that lives to a ripe old age. Don't buy any masses for his soul until you know where he's buried. He might just surprise us all.

—You don't really believe that, Ludo said.

Bettner shrugged, looked away. —Ah, now you're asking the impossible of me. I haven't believed in anything for more than twenty years. Anyway, we'll wait for him on the other side, as he asked us to.

The brown muddy water was swift and cold and full of debris carried downstream from the old wooden bridge on the Kuty road: some planks, half-burned logs, the wreckage of a wagon, a dead horse or two. All of this, including one bloated, air-filled carcass, went into the making of Auerbach's raft, on which they floated out into midstream, where the current seized them. Lashed to the logs and timbers, while the others clung to the raft with one hand and paddled with the other, Ludo listened for sounds in which he might read some hope for Janek's survival, but all he heard was the grumbling of the water and the panting of the paddling men.

Never a broad, important waterway, as this small untended corner of civilization had never been more than a dimly seen backwater of Continental history, the river twisted among brown ravines. It spilled into broad, stagnant pools full of hidden currents and unexpected eddies; its muddied depths held a variety of sunken objects designed to impale or to ram. Its Polish bank was high and forbidding and overgrown with rushes from which waterfowl rose in great screaming clouds.

The birds wheeled, settled, and rose again. The sun climbed whitely in its own gray clouds and, as the raft spun in chaotic circles toward the flat and sandy bank on the Roumanian side, Ludo was sure that he would never come back. No exile ever did, not entirely. The intervening days would change everything. Whatever lay ahead would have to have its own existence, unrelated to his disappearing past. Yet, without some deeply personal link to this vanishing moment, there'd be no point in going on at all. Janek, he knew, had provided such a link for him.

They spent the rest of the afternoon, all of the night, and a good part of the following morning sitting beside the first kilometer marker on the Roumanian road which led from Kuty, on the Polish side of the river, to the small Roumanian market town of Calimanesti. The day was sunny, mild. The flies were somnolent and easy to kill. The passing peasants gave them curious glances. Poland lay hidden under mist and rain as if the river were a boundary between seasons.

As long as they could see that mist, the smoke of village chimneys, and the small black figures of the Russian sentries pacing the north end of the Kuty bridge, they could maintain the illusion that the air they breathed was still theirs and not a foreign one. None of them spoke, each had retreated deep into his thoughts, and when Ludo finally broke the silence with an oddly harsh formality and said: *Ensign Toporski isn't going to join us,* they stared at each other as if awakened from a dream.

—God rest his soul, said Chief Auerbach.

—God rest all of them, Papa Bettner said.

The sound of village church bells came from the south on the warm, dry breeze so that, for a moment, the illusion was complete. The fat, lazy flies. The shyly grinning peasants. The barefoot children with enormous eyes. It really seemed as though the nightmare had ended.

—Well, dammit, what are you waiting for? Ludo said.

Chief Auerbach came to attention, clicked his muddy heels, saluted. —Orders, sir.

—Route step, forward . . . march!

Auerbach and Bettner picked up Ludo's stretcher. Jacek Gemba fell in step behind them, carrying the knapsacks. The white dust of the limestone highway rose swiftly behind them and obscured the miles one by one.

CHAPTER VIII

WHO, HAVING MADE that journey that autumn and winter, could ever forget it? They crossed Roumania, Hungary, Yugoslavia, and Italy on foot, in wagons, on the undersides of trains. They begged for their food. They were in rags, gaunt, and unrecognizable by the time they reached the French-Italian border at Modane one hundred and twenty days after leaving Warsaw. All of them were ill.

It was March then, but the Alpine winds were still the winter ones, and the nights were freezing. The winter of 1939 in Europe was the fiercest since the beginning of the century and the snows were deep.

For many of the hundred and twenty thousand Poles who made their way to France after the fall of Poland, spring was a time they'd recall as one of mending, renewed hope and determination, and a refurbished faith in victory and return. Nothing was lost forever. Everything was yet to come. Their reconstituted government was entirely new. It was led by General Władysław Sikorski, who had had no access to power before the war. The ineffectual heirs of Piłsudski, who had contributed so much to their national disaster, had been swept aside. In that alone lay much of their hope for the future.

For Ludo, Bettner, Auerbach, and Jacek, France had been a beacon, less a place of temporary exile than a great armed camp from which they and their allies would march to free Poland. It had sustained them through months of privations. Yet when they finally stood at the top of the last of the Alpine passes, and looked into France, they were unable to move. The air was thin and icy in their lungs. The light was bright, hard-edged, as a great white moon rose above the mountains. The distances they had crossed had become a burden that pinned them to the ground.

Looking down through wisps of torn cloud at the neat tourist town, with its hotels and esplanades and resorts for the tubercular rich, Ludo felt as if he had come to the edge of the world. Snow blinded him, he couldn't speak. Beside him, Auerbach had sat down on an iced outcropping of limestone and clutched at his chest. Papa Bettner dropped into the snow. Ill with frostbite, the middle-aged lieutenant was convinced that he would lose both his feet as soon as he fell into the hands of the surgeons, and there were no lies that Ludo could invent to comfort and encourage him, or to give him a reason for living.

—Easy, easy, Papa, Auerbach tried to soothe the distraught man as they helped each other along the mountain path. You'll be all right in a day or two. You'll see.

—They are going to cut off my legs, Papa Bettner said.

Ludo could think of nothing he might say. He heard the words but he didn't properly understand their meaning. There was a strange, twisted feeling in his throat and belly, something—he realized at once—that was as close to madness as he had ever gotten. Blind will drove him on, but to what? Not life, to be sure. He had spent his life in pursuit of a moment that might illuminate all the roads he had taken, and grace them with meaning, but there had never been any clear answers. Service and duty had been simple road signs. Too simple for what was needed now, he thought.

—Think, he said then. Tomorrow morning, we'll have breakfast at the Grand Hotel. There, that long white building with the balconies. Brioche and croissants. And cream in your coffee. Polished silverware.

—And people playing on a violin? Jacek Gemba asked.

—Oh, there's sure to be a few of those, Ludo said.

—Like in the Europejski?

—Just like in the Europejski. White tablecloths and napkins, and a waiter in a swallow-tailed coat. Flowers on the table.

—Ah, Jacek Gemba sighed.

—Leave me here, I beg you, Papa Bettner said.

—And then tomorrow . . . Paris, Ludo said. Paris . . . our own people around us again. Our own squadrons forming. In a month or two, we'll have forgotten that we were ever tired. Just a few more steps down this mountain and all these months of effort will be over.

Long past his limits of endurance, Papa Bettner had begun to weep, and the tears froze whitely in his beard and moustache.

—I've never asked for anything, he said. I've always done my duty. But there is nothing more that I want to do. Leave me here, I beg you.

—I can't do that, Ludo said.

—Why not? What difference can that make to you? You may have some sort of a future down there, but what do I have? I know what gangrene smells like, even in this cold. I know what'll happen to me in a hospital. Do you want to watch me selling pencils on some damn street corner, is that it?

—Don't be a fool, Papa, Ludo said.

—It's a bit late for that kind of advice, don't you think? the older man cried fiercely. You owe me something, Ludo. No matter what you've asked me, no matter how terrible it was, I've always done it, haven't I? So will you let me do something for myself for once? Haven't I earned at least that much gratitude?

—Be quiet, Papa! Ludo said.

—Oh, certainly. Be quiet. Be tractable. Do what you are told. Bomb a damned village. Hang an old, mad peasant. Never question orders. But when do I get something I can live with?

—Not on this earth, my friend, Auerbach said and sighed.

—You owe it to me, Ludo, Papa Bettner said. Leave me here and all our debts will be paid in full, I promise. There'll be no hard feelings about anything. You'll have done your duty as a friend. But if you take me down there, I'll find some way to kill you, I promise you that too.

—I thought that . . . you were done with killing? Ludo murmured and knelt beside the frightened, injured man, and took his hand in his own.

—In vengeance, Papa Bettner whispered then. I'd do it in vengeance.

They brought him to his feet. The four of them clung to each other, supporting each other in the icy wind, and Ludo could feel his own tears freezing to his face.

—I don't want to be a cripple, Papa Bettner said. I never could stand to look at them. I've had this phobia about crippled beggars since I was a child. What are we doing here, anyway? What's the point of this?

He staggered in the icy snow. He slipped and would have fallen but for the grip of Auerbach's arms around him. He dragged his frostbitten feet in small, clumsy circles. The towering white mountains echoed his despair, and, suddenly, Ludo didn't know who he was, or where he had come from, or what he was supposed to do. His own injuries, he knew, were less a matter of the body than of the mind and spirit.

—We've lived in the past, a nation of cripples, Bettner went on in a plaintive whisper. And what's it all going to mean in the end? Just one more illusion.

Then he cried out: No! We aren't supposed to have more than one war to a generation! And this is our third! I'm . . . ah, God, forty-six years old. If this war lasts six years, I'll have spent a third of my life in this murderous trade. It's different for you, I know. You have your absolutes, your damned sense of service. May they serve you well! May the pigeon shit lay lightly on your head when you've become a national monument! But what does any of that have to do with me?

—Easy, take it easy, Papa, Auerbach said and stroked the unnaturally pale, luminous cheeks of the frostbitten man.

—God, how I hate winter, Bettner whispered then.

—Winter's over. It's spring.
—God, how I hate spring, Bettner said.

They made their way down the mountain, in the harsh white light of a galloping moon. Had it been entirely up to him, Ludo thought, had he and Papa Bettner been alone in the hissing wind on the mountaintop, unseen by the shocked eyes of Auerbach and Jacek, he might have complied with his old friend's request. A man had a right to die as he wished and, in that chosen moment, to justify his life. It might have been the last gift of friendship, a way to say: Go with dignity, all of your life's indignities notwithstanding. But they had not been alone to make such decisions.

A quick, bright death was always better than a lingering one, he thought as they entered the town at the foot of the mountain. But not at the expense of duty.

A cold, pale sun had risen by the time they had come to the town. It gilded the mountains. It brushed against the icicles that hung in rows from the eaves and balconies of the great hotels. It seemed to light a thousand welcomes in the windows.

Indeed, lights were on everywhere. There were few signs of war in Modane. Gloomy reservists sat at coffee tables at the railway hotel. The mobilization *avis* outside the town hall had been spattered with mud. As the morning passed, as the shopkeepers rolled up their metal shutters, and as listless shoppers appeared in the streets, it seemed to Ludo as if he had come to a country where everyone had agreed to ignore the war. The crowds along the esplanades were self-absorbed, depressed. Their aura was one of hostility and rudeness.

—It doesn't seem like we've come to the right place, sir, Jacek Gemba attempted to joke. Maybe we made a wrong turn at the last mountain? Maybe these are Germans?

Auerbach, too ill to respond in kind, jerked a thumb toward the *Tricouleur* that snapped in the wind outside the *mairie*.

—It's the right place, he said. But the time is wrong. They don't want to see our kind of tourists here.

Looking around, sniffing the brisk air as if to test it for signs of rot, Jacek Gemba said: They'll see another kind if they aren't careful.

—*Parlez français!* a woman hissed at them in passing, and added angrily: *Sals polonais!* Who wants your war here?

Hungry, they went toward the Customs House, where a bored *douanier* muttered and snapped his fingers while they hunted in their clothes for their frayed paybooks and identification cards, and then, as if the dress uniforms on their photographs were a final, unforgivable insult, he ran out of the room and slammed the door behind him.

An hour passed, then another. One of Papa Bettner's boots had burst, and the sweet stench of gangrene filled the overheated room. The sun was scarlet in the fly-specked windows which had been nailed shut and couldn't be opened. The heat, the stench, and their terrible fatigue drained the last of their strength.

He had to ask himself then, as Bettner had asked: What are we doing here? The war was in Poland. There, in that scorched charnel house where people were dying by the hundreds every day, the war made a dreadful sort of sense. Here, in this comfortable civilization where patriotism was an object of derision, he and his kind would be as welcome as plague-bearing vermin.

Their many miles mocked him. A blue-green fly had awakened between the double windows. Its insistent buzzing brought to mind other sounds, heard in other places: the drone of aerial engines fading in and out, the whine of a Stuka, the hiss of air in a shattered cockpit. When he closed his eyes, he could hear Kaminski's dreadful whisper in the hospital in Warsaw, and then the trilling of the waterfowl at the river's edge.

Bettner fainted then. They made him as comfortable as they could on the floor, putting their bundled coats under his head, and Auerbach slit open the remaining boot, exposing the greenish-white, swollen flesh streaked in blue-and-scarlet. Between the windows, the fly seemed to go mad. The *douanier* returned, grasped his nose, and ran out again.

—Sir? Jacek Gemba whispered. Sir?

But Ludo couldn't answer. He could neither see nor hear anything as it was. All sights and sounds had become one and none of it made sense. The gray room revolved so that, for an icy moment, he thought that he had been shot down again and falling in a spin. Warsaw burned below him, fire filled his cockpit, and he couldn't find the controls that might flip the machine over on its back. A voice kept calling to him in the receding distance: *Loo-do! Loo-do!* He was aware of sadness, nothing more.

In the hospital, Ludo's collapse was total. He neither moved nor spoke. He couldn't give his name. He was bathed and his wounds were probed, and his inflamed eyes were prepared for a new English process that allowed burns to heal without bandages, but the surgeons could do nothing to save his right hand. They took three of his fingers. They amputated both of Bettner's feet. After the operations, Papa Bettner raved in a drug-induced nightmare about the corpses of children he kept tripping over in a fire-bombed village, and Ludo vomited on the starched percale sheets, and the nursing sisters—young nuns with faces smooth and cool as wafers—turned their serene eyes to the crucifix on the white-tiled wall.

Later that night, he awoke to deep, booming groans that he thought were his own. Bettner, as ghostly white as his sheets, was still unconscious and talking to himself in thick, strangled gasps.

Later still, after the blue-gray light of dawn had brushed against the windows, he tried to murder Ludo.

It was a nightmare, he thought and watched the large, round, trembling head, the huge swollen nose, the veined cheeks of the drinker straining with the effort. The mouth was open in a silent scream.

Bettner had swung his legs out of bed and took three steps toward him, a pillow in his hands, and Ludo thought: My God, he's no bigger than a child, so fragile and wasted. . . . And then he thought: My God, he's standing on his ankles!

In that insufficient light, the mouth was a black hole in a shining, colorless surface, and the eyes were glazed. The man had taken his stand upon agony for so many years, his rage had such logic, that this ultimate expression of his pain made considerable sense. Papa Bettner took one dreadful step after another, his amputated bones clicking against the floor, his fingers buried in the pillow he clutched to his chest, and Ludo thought: At last. Finally. God be praised. As Kaminski had convinced him in the hospital in Warsaw, death by suffocation wasn't particularly painful.

He felt a savage joy, a thankfulness, and added his own silent scream of encouragement to Bettner's. He waited in an ecstasy of submission: the lover at the threshold of attainment . . . but Bettner failed and fell.

The women who came in the morning with buckets and mops found them like that, both apparently unconscious: Bettner face down on the floor, Ludo staring blindly at the ceiling from his sweat-soaked bed. Since Ludo was still unable to speak, he couldn't be questioned. But Bettner told that story many years later.

Moved to the Polish military hospital near Coetquidan, the great base in which two Polish infantry divisions, an armored brigade, and a special brigade of mountain troops were in training, Ludo mended quickly. Discipline was the basic element of such lives as his and he accepted injury without question or complaint. One by one, he buried all his ghosts.

His hard, lean body responded to the gentleness of the nursing sisters as if its collapse had been a sort of death needed before true resurrection could begin. The wounds closed and grew new coverings for themselves. His eyesight proved to be faultless, although he did take to wearing dark glasses from then on. The surgeons had left the thumb and little finger on his right hand with which, he was sure, he'd be able to control an aircraft in flight and press a trigger button. Some slight modifications would be needed in the cockpit of an advanced machine, where the left hand did most of the work in any event, but that was something that any skilled line chief could arrange. His inner wounds were another story.

There, a lone, dark battle took place in those weeks of silence and recovery, a struggle between the image of his country as it was and as it ought to be. Vague notions of justice, dignity, and pride fought against obedience. It wasn't enough simply to do one's duty. One had to fight one's country's enemies inside as well as outside its borders. Yet how was one to do that when so few people seemed to be able to see that anything was wrong?

Bettner who, Ludo realized, had served as his conscience, was gone. There was, perhaps, a lesson to be drawn from his final madness. Yet, had he been mad? Wasn't there a deep sense of remorseless logic in what he had tried? If you hate something to such an extent that it might drive you over the borders of reason, isn't it your simple duty to oppose it? It would be either that or a bullet in the head, and to the Devil with the consequences.

Visitors came to see him. Piotr, now a major commanding a battalion in the Mountain Brigade, brought him news of Wlada. She had vanished from the home of her husband's uncle in Lwów and all attempts to find her had failed. She was most likely to have been among the hundred thousand people transported to Russia, a tragic fragment of the forced exodus that had depopulated all of eastern Poland. Janek, however, was alive. He had not been killed by the Russians on the border. The Polish underground organization had released lists of officers imprisoned by the Russians in three camps named Kozyelsk, Starobyelsk, and Ostashkov, and Janek was among them.

—To be alive is always better than to be dead, no matter where you are, Piotr said. Don't you think?

—As long as there's still something one can do.

—He'll be all right. Don't worry. He might surprise us all. And . . . who knows . . . I might be seeing him quicker than we think.

Piotr's brigade was to be part of the Allied Expeditionary Force that was to fight the Russians who had invaded Finland in the winter, once the Norwegians and the Swedes had granted to the Allies transit rights across their territories.

—Obviously, this extends the war, Piotr said. The Russians are now going to be everyone's enemies, not just ours. But at least there won't be any questions now about our eastern borders.

—I didn't know there had been any, Ludo said.

—Not among us, of course. But our allies might have had a different idea. They guaranteed our borders, but they've done their best to ignore the Russian invasion. I wonder why they've

decided to defend the Finns, when they wouldn't lift a finger to
help us? But it's all coming out the way it should be.

—The war is going to last longer, Ludo said.

—But when it ends, there won't be anyone left to fight, Piotr
said. We'll go home to peace.

—And then what? Ludo asked.

—Well, Piotr said and laughed. That'll be up to men like you,
won't it? General Sikorski is a man of vision and conscience. We
can believe in him. The old gang is finished. There's room now
for ideas such as yours, and you won't even need to make a revolution.

—It won't come in time to save men like Bettner, Ludo said.

—Nothing can save men like Bettner, Piotr said. They're
doomed the day they're born. They are what keeps the past alive,
and so the past kills them.

—And since when have you become a philosopher?

—Since I discovered that fixed bayonets don't stop a Panzer division, Piotr said. Get well soon, Ludo. We need you on your feet
even more than we need you in the air.

His brother-in-law, Romuald Modelski, also came to see him.
They had detested each other for years, but now that Ludo had
become an official hero, and that political plans were being made
for him, there was obvious value in such a family connection.

—I must say, I don't think it fair, said Romuald Modelski. A
man might spend years in politics, maneuvering from one position to another, and nothing extraordinary ever happens to him.
And then another fellow comes out of nowhere, shoots down a
few planes, escapes from a hospital, and everyone talks about him
as a future leader of his country. Let me warn you about one
thing, though, brother-in-law. You can get killed with words as
easily as with bullets.

—I don't intend to get killed with anything, Ludo said.

—Well, that's obvious, isn't it? Romuald said and laughed.
How did you manage to arrange that funeral in Warsaw, anyway?
The Germans showed it all over Europe in their newsreels. Your
return from the dead has made complete fools of them. Everyone
in Paris is laughing about it.

—A man died, Ludo said. I took his place. He took mine. That's all there was to it.

—Is that so? Romuald observed. How very convenient. I wish that some of my arrangements could come out as neatly as that.

—Don't envy what you don't understand, brother-in-law, Ludo said.

—Ah, you mean there was a price to pay? I thought that there might be. Still, I imagine it was worth it, what? You've been awarded another Virtuti Militari. There's some talk about promoting you and a staff appointment. All of a sudden, your career looks brilliant and all it took was a Luftwaffe funeral!

Softly, then, savoring his contempt for Romuald Modelski and for everything that he represented, Ludo said: Yes. That's all it took.

—Who'd think I'd ever have anything to learn from you, brother-in-law? said Romuald Modelski. But I suppose one must adjust, hmm? One must try new ways. For the first time since I married Wlada, I don't regret our family connection. I have a feeling that you and I are going to be close friends.

—I wouldn't build a career on that hope, Ludo said.

—Who can tell? Romuald wondered as he prepared to leave. Politics are said to be the art of the possible. What is possible is often dictated by the unexpected. You and I can be useful to each other in a variety of ways.

—I doubt that, Ludo said.

—Well, we'll see, won't we? said his brother-in-law. War is such a chaotic, disorganized business. All sorts of things can happen. The thing to do is to be able to seize an opportunity when it presents itself, and you seem to have learned that very well. You will keep in touch?

Ludo shrugged, turned his face away, said nothing. Shortly afterward, Romuald went away.

In April, there was other news. The Franco-Polish-British Expeditionary Force had sailed for Norway. The Finnish expedition was forgotten. Norwid's submarine, which had escaped from the landlocked Baltic in a feat of seamanship that had captured headlines all over the world, was reported missing, overdue from patrol in Norwegian waters. Piotr, whose battalion covered the retreat of the Allies from the Fjord of Narvik, was severely wounded. At the beginning of May, Ludo was discharged from the hospital.

He traveled to Paris, where, in the peaceful neighborhood of the Bois de Boulogne, he went to see Papa Bettner in the psychiatric hospital to which he was confined. He sat at Bettner's bedside for an hour, but neither of them spoke. What was there to say? There was no doubt in Ludo's mind that both of them had gone through a moment of madness. He had anticipated death with such joy that only some sort of a derangement could explain it. Bettner's failure to kill him didn't erase that moment.

There was no history of madness in his family, although who could tell? Had his father's lifelong optimism about human decency and goodness been entirely sane? Didn't his death prove that aberration? Had Janek made a rational decision on the Roumanian border? Did Piotr's mild cynicism mask a darker, self-destructive purpose? And how normal had Ludo been himself in all the harsh decisions he had made? Everything seemed right in the moment of an action, including the senseless, but no plans could live longer than the moment in which they were made, and no course of action made sense in retrospect.

Madness, under such circumstances, he thought, was something to envy.

Having drawn four months' arrears in pay, he happened to be solvent, and he left two thousand francs with the hospital's administration clerks to cover whatever small luxuries Papa Bettner might want from time to time. He was aware that this was blood-money of a kind, a way to ease his conscience, because he knew that he wouldn't come to see his friend again. Sharing a silence, and the guilt that lay within that silence, would eventually destroy all possibility of friendship.

Outside, in the sun-speckled shadows of the park, where madmen wandered about on their own private journeys, he asked for directions back to the center of the city. It amused him to think that a lunatic would point out his way.

Next morning, he reported to the officers' selection board of the Polish Air Service in the Hotel Lafayette and traveled north to be a flight commander in a fighter squadron on the Belgian border. According to those who knew him at this time, he was a man who had begun to live entirely alone. He seemed to trust no one and to care for no one. He discouraged friendships. When he wasn't flying, he took long walks in the untroubled green French springtime countryside and wrote long letters that he never mailed. It was a sort of temporary retirement from mankind, a suspension of all his human faculties but one. The French pilots of the pursuit squadron to which he was attached would describe him later as a killing machine and attributed his silent, cold ferocity to their own sentimental notions of what it meant to lose a country. He neither intellectualized nor mourned, and he rebuffed their offers of sympathy politely but firmly. By preference, because the high-strung argumentative snobbery of the French bored and irritated him, he spent his off-duty moments among the Hurricane pilots of the RAF who shared his French station. They were a mixed group of English professionals, Canadian volunteers, mild-mannered innocent young university reservists, and one genuine Indian prince. They were quiet men, restrained to a fault, and embarrassed in the presence of imagined tragedies, and they didn't bother him with questions.

He fought his war, which resumed when the Germans flooded into France, with a savage, single-minded fury, as if each of his aerial encounters were to be his last. In one day, he attacked an entire squadron of Bf 109s, shot down three of them, and was himself shot down and wounded again, but he landed his bullet-ridden Dewoitine D.520 fighter safely in a pasture. He was decorated with the Croix de Guerre. The French surrendered before he could receive it.

CHAPTER IX

FRANCE FELL in eighteen days. Holland was overrun in twenty-four hours. Belgium surrendered after three days of fighting. Ten days sufficed to break the French armies in the north and the British Expeditionary Force took itself off the Continent. In June, he was on the road again, walking in the familiar yellow dust among hordes of demoralized French *poilus* who were heading home. His mood was cynical and cruel as he passed the vast columns of abandoned French and British vehicles, the artillery parks full of heavy guns that had never fired a shell, and the landing fields on which French soldiers guarded rows of spotless aircraft against the possibility that some pilot might take one up against the Germans or fly it to England.

He felt neither bewilderment nor shame among the trailing mobs of this ruined army armed with wine flasks and carved walking sticks, for whom the fall of Poland had been supposed to buy the time to prepare a summer offensive. The French had spent three seasons huddled in their fortifications, and no order could make them fire their guns at sunbathing Germans in fear that this might cause the Germans to fire upon them. The shrug of the staff officer who had taken Ludo on a tour of the front had been évocative. *They've spent ten years waving the Red Flag*, the officer grimaced and said. *Would you expect them to fight for the Tricouleur?* Their answer to the German onslaught on May 10 had been flight and surrender. Their officers, who in moments of crisis behaved like civil servants, had been the first to abandon their troops. Now the defeated armies drifted in huge, dung-colored masses back and forth across the central plains, and jammed the roads and bridges, and waited for someone to capture them and take them away. They had cried, *Nous sommes foutus*, when the first German shell whistled over their heads. *La guerre est finie*, they said with satisfaction now.

For the first two weeks, Ludo walked south, looking for fighting men he might join or a machine he might fly. Only a quarter of French territory had been overrun when he began his march, huge armies were intact to the south of Paris, the world's second-largest war fleet was yet to fire a shot, and on the African shores of the Mediterranean were all the resources of a great empire. He thought it reasonable to suppose that a second Battle of France would shortly begin.

Then he was told that the French government of Premier Reynaud had dismissed itself, that the new French chief of state, Marshal Pétain, had asked the Germans for an armistice and that all French troops everywhere were to lay down their arms at noon the next day. The date was June 22, 1940, and there was nowhere in France or the French possessions where Ludo might find a war.

One had to find something to remember about a day like that, he thought wryly. Dust and demoralized armies just weren't enough to mark the end of a civilization. He would remember it partly as a day on which he came to a small town where he saw old men and women attacking a platoon of Senegalese soldiers who, faithful to their warrior image of themselves, had had the temerity to construct defenses.

—*Pas de combat! L'armistice! La guerre est finie!* the pale, brittle voices creaked and cracked.

The stench of defeat was palpable in the crowd; its aura was hysterical, close to joy.

He would remember the black, bewildered, good-natured faces of the colonial soldiers, who did nothing to defend themselves. They stood in neatly ordered ranks while the old men and women beat them with brooms and hoe handles, and only in the depths of their maroon-rimmed eyes was there a measure of dark understanding.

Then, as he moved off the road into the shade of the poplars, to eat and to bathe his feet in an irrigation ditch, a large black Renault roared past him in a cloud of dust. Two German noncoms sat in the front seat, three French officers sat in the back and stared fixedly ahead. He had a glimpse of pale, aristocratic faces, aloof and proud as conquerors. They were exquisitely uniformed and smoking small cigars.

At once, as though its glorious civilization had never existed, France disappeared from Ludo's consciousness. So much for *La Gloire*. It simply wasn't there anymore for him, and he transported himself mentally to England, where Reszke and Gerlach were flying RAF Hurricanes, and where everyone else he knew would be heading now. Instinctively, he turned toward a rough country track that curved away from the highway at this point and wound among the sand dunes to the sea.

The road ran along high coastal cliffs among gorse and bracken and, for most of the morning, he walked in its soft, furry dust, thinking that he had never seen a gentler and more placid sky, a more peaceful landscape, a more promising day. On his left, sheep grazed and distant villages trailed smoke. The sea at his right was a gently rolling blue-green turbulence that sparkled with reflected sunlight. The waves boomed among the rocks. There was no wind, no clouds. There were only noisy seabirds wheeling overhead.

His feet were swollen and blistered and the water in the road-side ditch was warm and thick with green slime. A diet of stale bread and apples and raw peasant wine had given him the runs. He pulled down his trousers and bared his buttocks to the road just as a long dappled column of green-and-brown British Bedfords began to file past. The trucks were filled with sun-browned, singing German infantry, and he thought that he had never heard young men who were happier and more confident. Well, why shouldn't they feel good about themselves, he thought. In forty-two days, at the cost of twelve thousand casualties, they had either scattered or demolished the armies of four nations. They had taken a million prisoners and captured four countries. And last year, in September, there had been another. . . .

A noncom roared, *Eyes left!* and the Germans cheered as he hissed and groaned. Dignity and diarrhea don't mix very well: it was a situation to make a dead man smile. One of the laughing, shirt-sleeved Germans threw something toward him, a metal object that flashed in the sun, and Ludo hurled himself face down into the ditch; then he remembered that in *this* country, on *these* roads, such objects were unlikely to explode.

It was a tin of English cigarettes, fifty Gold Flakes stamped H. M. FORCES ONLY. He wished the laughing young German soldier a quick and easy death.

On the beach, he stripped, swam, ate some dry bread, and drank a little wine. He was dazed by the sun, depleted by his journey. He viewed himself with the same cold, calculating objectivity with which he looked at everything and everybody else. He neither blamed anyone for anything nor found excuses for them. Nothing that he had done in the ten fierce days of fighting before the Germans overran his airfield, and before his own French ground crews had immobilized the squadrons, seemed extraordinary to him. The fall of France exasperated rather than distressed him; he didn't think of this disaster as his own. Another chapter of his life had closed; it would be followed by another, and then another and another until there were no more, and each of these distinctive subdivisions would tell its own story. If there was one connecting theme to these various stories, it was never again to care for any people other than his own, and never to surrender.

Someone else shared his beach at a distance, a tall, thin woman in a white dress who walked at the edge of the tide, looking down. He noted hair so black that it seemed edged with blue, and bare arms and legs as deeply stained by the sun as his own face and hands. A hot, swift wind came off the water and ballooned her skirt, and stirred some sort of memory in him, like an echo in a long and dark corridor that had closed behind him, but he let the image and the memory slip out of his grasp. She could have been a child or a crone, it made no difference to him. His body, flat as a stone slab laid across the mouth of a cave, was disinterested, a damaged but workable instrument at rest. He made no effort to cover himself; there was no reason why he should.

She sat for some time at the far edge of the beach, looking at the water, and he watched her only long enough to determine that she was alone, that her interest in him was minimal (indeed, his first thought had been that she was irritated to have found him there), and that she represented no danger to him. Then he lost sight of her. He ate some bread. He drank the rest of his wine. The raw, red wine, the hot sun, the hiss and slap and mutter of the waves put him under quickly. He slept and dreamed of violence that he could not remember afterward. Strange fiery shapes twisted, arced, and fell. A great red heart was beating. The air through which he flew was cold and very dark.

When he awoke, everything had changed. The wind had died down. The sea rolled heavily, thick as a pool of oil streaked with flames. Wide, placid, sated at this time of the year, the Bay of Biscay spread toward the disappearing sun. The scarlet disk had set both the sea and the sky on fire, and the flame leaped to the white wisps of cloud and high into the aquamarine space beyond, and shot across the water, and then sped on through dark folds of land to the somber foothills of the Pyrenees. The blaze was sharp and, for some reason, he thought of it as anguished. Then it sank into a deep crimson glow, as though a city were on fire beyond the horizon.

The woman was gone and, for a moment, he thought that she had been part of the blue-edged darkness through which he had flown. She had the aura of an accusing ghost that would inhabit nightmares. Perhaps he had imagined her as well as the vague memory she evoked: some long lost moment of a human closeness. . . . But she was still there, at the top of the rise, a white patch sewn to the dark fabric of the night, and he looked past her in search of something dangerous.

An owl hooted, quartering the fields in search of prey. He heard the thin, distant whining of a truck. She made no sound in the shadows of the trees where she waited. Her hair seemed heavier, bulkier, and he realized that she had wrapped a black knitted shawl over her head, holding the fringed ends crossed at her breasts and throat.

He walked toward her, said: Who are you? What do you want?

Her laughter was harsh, coarse, cruel as she mocked him: And what do *you* want?

—Nothing, he said and gestured down the road toward the small white town, the semicircle of silvered beach and the rows of bathing cabins there. I'm just a soldier coming home, the gesture was supposed to say.

—The resort is closed for this season, she said and went on laughing. I imagine the Germans will reopen the casino in a month or so. But, at the moment, it's a crushing bore.

—What's the name of it?

—St. Jean-de-Luz, for all the good that does you.

—What sort of a town is it?

—Franco-Spanish, Basque, virtuous, and dull. Little men with big strings of onions, and everything smells of sardines fried in olive oil. But it's the last town this side of the Spanish border, very convenient for shopping in San Sebastian and the bullfights in Pamplona. Much cheaper than Biarritz, and thus full of slightly shopworn Englishmen who'd rather not go home. An excellent place in which to drop from sight without vanishing altogether, if you know what I mean.

—I don't, he said and moved to pass her, but she barred his way.

—And who are you? she said. What were you doing on my beach?

—I am a Basque, he said, remembering the beret he had found in a ditch, and then he grinned and shrugged because he knew that she couldn't possibly believe him.

—Certainly, she said. And I'm the Empress Eugenie. If you're hoping to find someone in St. Jean-de-Luz to take you to England, you're wasting your time.

—Why would I want to go to England? he asked cautiously, and she laughed at him.

—I couldn't imagine. You just look and sound like the sort of Basque who's very anxious to be in England now that war is there.

—There've been others, then?

—At least a dozen every day. But don't worry. The French are amused by them. The Germans ignore them. The Spaniards catch them on the border and send them somewhere else.

—Do you live in St. Jean-de-Luz?

—I live there, she said and gestured to a villa that stood behind a white wall at the turn in the road. It's called *Mon Repos*. It's really not as awful as it sounds. We could have called it *Happy-Enda*, or some such damned thing. The expatriate English are the most vulgar people on God's earth.

—Are you English, then?

—Not to hear my relatives on the subject, she said and moved closer to him. A touch of the Gael in the old bloodstream, you know. It makes for a certain instability, for wild Irish flights of the imagination, for brooding walks by the sea. No, I don't suppose you could call me English.

—The Germans, he said and looked into the darkness, but she made a quick gesture of impatience.

—I told you not to worry about Germans. The *Boche* is most correct in this part of the world. I don't know where you've come from, but you won't find *that* kind of occupation here. It's business as usual for the valiant French, the utmost in Teutonic understanding for resident foreigners. You'd hardly notice that there was a war.

—I should have thought they'd intern the English, Ludo said.

—Why should they? You don't find the Churchill type of
Englishman living on a remittance in St. Jean-de-Luz.

—Is that what you're doing here, then? Ludo asked so that he
might dismiss her as a neutral, neither someone who might offer
shelter nor sell him to the Germans. Living on a . . . ah . . . remittance, was it?

—I live here because I want to live here, she said with a sudden
hopelessness that astonished him. Let's just say that I'm a permanent English visitor abroad.

—Oh, so you are English, then.

—Only to the extent that I don't play the bagpipes or eat
leeks. But I don't suppose that means anything to you. If I were
to call myself *British*, which I most certainly am, someone might
think I was Welsh or a Scots lassie with chapped knees, and I
couldn't bear that.

Quietly, and meaning every word of it, he asked: Are you mad?
Have you been ill? Is that what it is?

Her laughter gurgled upward and broke on a high note and he
waited, icily polite, while she wiped the tears that ran down her
dark and hollow cheeks.

—Oh, that's wonderful, she said. That's precious. That is priceless. That is exactly what it is—if you were to ask my loving relatives and my loyal friends. Are you always so wonderfully direct?

—It saves time, he said.

—Oh, does it ever, she said. What sort of a Basque are you,
then? You don't speak French fluently enough even for a Belgian.
Austrians speak German the way you speak French. Let's see, not
a Greek, I know one when I see one. . . . Are you a Czech with a
Jewish mother? Or a Dutch general with a guilty conscience?

He took a deep breath, said: I'm a Polish fighter pilot.

—Well, it was close, she said.

Then it was his turn to laugh until tears came.

Her name was Ann, that was all she'd tell him, and he was
quite content to let it go at that. The villa was spacious, cool,
furnished with a variety of delicate objects that he could never recall in detail afterward. The rooms were high-ceilinged, airy,

paved with coarse slabs of fieldstone over which Persian carpets
had been thrown. There were untidy heaps of books and sketch
pads everywhere. The ashes in the great stone fireplace had been
allowed to accumulate almost to its top. All this suggested an attitude of such careless contempt for leisure and wealth, and such
a natural assumption of superiority to censure, as to remind Ludo
sharply of Wlada and the Circus. Yet there was something clsc, a
quality he thought plaintive, as if an attempt had been made to
bury memory alive.

She took him on a tour, pointing to this and that (the view of
the mountains from the balcony upstairs, a cracked clay pot with
an Etruscan symbol of death and resurrection, and next to it, and
treated with equal reverence, the cheapest of carved peasant objects). It was an eclectic collection of personal mementos that
seemed pointedly to exclude such costly trappings as a camel sad-
dle of hammered gold-and-silver she used for a footstool. Watchful, he looked for more personal acquisitions. But the only evidence of a man's presence in the villa was of a transitory nature:
a briar pipe in which the ashes had turned into stone, a disreputable hat, and a wide Paisley tie she used to secure her bathrobe.

She insisted on talking about herself in clipped, derisive terms
that he would identify later as a practiced fraud. The more she
loved a person, an object, a place, or an idea, the less good she
found to say about it. Her words were barricades behind which
she crouched like a poorly armed insurrectionist, the images she
painted were artful camouflage. Yet some truth was sure to be
there and, testing the strange, dark, honeyed corridors that she
began to open up before him, he listened curiously to an accounting of disasters presented as a joke. There had been a marriage to
a second cousin much older than herself (*a hopelessly botched
flight from the ancestral home, don't you know, a sort of death
march straight from a cold schoolroom into the even colder hell
of an old man's bed*), followed by frantic leaps into the unknown,
indiscreet attachments, scandalous behavior, recriminations,
threats and (finally) banishment. (*It didn't go as far as the Archbishop of Canterbury, you know, but it might as well have done,
for the noise that was made.*) The way she said it, it might have
all happened only the day before or, with equal disregard of prob-
ability, in another era. Somewhere along the line, there was a dis-

graceful episode in Oxford, the Paisley tie was a memento of it.
There was an Italian archeologist and a brother-in-law who lusted
after her. (That, he thought, would have been the cracked pot
and the pipe.) No, she had no plans to return to England at this
moment. Everyone she knew would be in uniform. It would be a
bore. St. Jean-de-Luz was a rotten sort of place, full of disastrous
people—lecherous stockbrokers and absconding bishops, penny-
pinching Frenchmen and fanny-pinching Spaniards—but war was
hell, was it not? Somehow one would endure. . . .

Some kind of plea for mercy (he'd have none of it!) hung like
a thin, dark veil over everything she said.

Ann's bed was wide, hard as a monk's pallet. An ugly, tortured
Christ hung above her headboard. Her sheets were fresh and cold
and smelled of the sea. *Making love* wouldn't describe what they
did there, although, toward the end, they acquired a sort of grateful gentleness that approached affection. They tore at each other
with a savagery in which pain seemed to be the greater part of
pleasure; each deprived for too long, they were careless of the
other's needs. She, after memory had provided the cold distances
needed for introspection, was loud, athletic, a profane contor-
tionist, a crazed mount, and (in her turn) a rider to the hounds,
a darting bird of prey, a museum of outrageous fantasies. He,
lifted above the moment, focused upon the night sounds outside
the open windows with a mechanical ferocity. A madwoman's bitter cries (surely she was mad, surely a shocked, resentful world's
complaint was to be heard in all that bellowing!) spurred him toward cruelty, brutality, contempt; his own uncompromising image
held him back. He was fascinated by the long, twisted mouth
that moved over him and that he hadn't even kissed, by the dark,
lean body that became a vise which threatened to crack his bones.

—You are disgusting, she hissed into his flesh at one point. Oh,
Christ in heaven, you'll burn in hell for this.

—And what about you?

—Me? she cried. Of course *me!* Who the hell do you think I'm
talking about? Oh, Christ, lover, there!

Christ? Lover? The Byzantine horror on the cross had tilted toward them.

—Oh, damn you! she cried. Damn you for a bitch!

Then it was over, just like that. No alarms, trumpets, imitation

earthquakes. No great white blinding light, transcendence, trans-
formation. She was spread out darkly as if for a crucifixion of her
own, white palms turned upward and awaiting nails. He thought
she was dead.

They had fought their battle in the dark; she had refused him
light. Perhaps her body, which was not as young as she might
have wished it, had something to do with her need for shadows
and concealment. Tracing it with the fork of his maimed hand as
she leaned forward in the glow of her cigarette, the dark face con-
templative and unshuttered, he thought that the years had been
kind to her, at least in one respect. Her body might be safe from
fatuous eulogies, but she had no need to be ashamed of it.

He thought that they were of an age, perhaps she was older by
a year or two. Either way, it wouldn't make a difference. Her
body was dry and cool where his was wet and hot, and she
aligned herself to fit him exactly as if he were a mattress tailored
to her measure: hip upon hip, knees upon his knees, the long flattened instep laid along his own, her sharp elbows digging into his
chest, her chin in her hands. Her eyes were huge and black, deep
as wells; the whites were faintly blue. Her mass of jet-black hair
made her deeply tanned olive skin seem pale by comparison and
gave her an illusion of fragility.

—What now, bloody man? she said.

—Now? Nothing, he said and took her cigarette and filled his
lungs with smoke.

—The journey continues?

He watched her quietly, finding pleasure in the unpredictable,
watched the gradual widening of her eyes, then nodded and
looked toward the windows, where the quality of the light had
begun to change. Had she not pinned him down, he would have
raised his head to look at the mountains.

—It may not be as easy to get away from here as all that, she
said.

—You see yourself as some kind of Circe, then? he said.

—Ah, she laughed softly. The pleasures of a classical education.
No, not at all, my lovely rooting hog. I had the Germans in
mind, don't you know. Not to mention the mountains.

—If one can't go through the Germans, one can go around them.

—You don't seem to have done it all that well, she said and began to trace his scars with a long fingernail. And, as my countrymen have begun to say in an attempt to limit unofficial travel, is your journey really necessary? You may not find exactly what you're looking for in England, you know.

—Some surprises can be very pleasant, he said and grinned, and she slapped him lightly on the forehead.

—Disappointment is the general rule, she said. One really ought to know more about the English before venturing among them.

—So far, I've had no reason to complain.

—Disgusting man. Pig. Greedy hog, she said and showed her white teeth. Don't do that unless you mean to finish the job. Anyway, the lady wants to talk.

—Why? What about?

—All sorts of things. Life, death and the frailty of dreams. What the Archbishop said to the Mother Superior. I'd hate to think that this is no more than a sort of wham-bam-thank-you-ma'am kind of interlude on your journey to bigger and better moments. A pit stop, so to speak.

—What else can it be?

—Oh, come now, she said. Brutality does have limits, even for someone as primitive as a Polish pilot.

—I didn't wait for you on the road, he said. You waited for me.

—Bad hog, she said in a sad-little-girl voice. Cruel hog. And a conceited hog too, it would appear. What makes you think I waited for you?

—You spent too many hours looking at the sea. You collect flotsam, don't you?

—Ah, she said. You've had all *sorts* of educations, haven't you. But then, so have I. The best that England has to offer a lady of family and station. Don't be surprised, however, if you're asked in your next English bed whether you had indoor plumbing in Warsaw and if you eat with forks.

—I'll tell the lady not to talk with her mouth full, Ludo said.

—No, wait, damn you, she said with an odd note of panic under the impatience. I do want to talk! Call it another sort of necessary hunger. . . . But why should that worry you? What can you lose in one night? There's not a lot of danger of complications, I expect.

There was something about her that was very private, no matter how impiously she offered herself. If she were lost, then she was longing to be found while hiding. Of what, or rather of whom, did she remind him? The murky image that rose in reply was, somehow, a threat. He damned the night, the violent airs she stirred in his interior darkness. . . . Oh, shit, he thought, why the *hell* do they always want to talk?

As if she were able to read his mind, she said: Don't be so bloody selfish. Your war won't run away. In a friendly and uncomplicated way, the lady is trying to do you a kindness. Forewarned is forearmed, and all that. Some friendly interest in return wouldn't come amiss.

He didn't want to carry anything out of this moment into the next mile of his journey.

—My interest is self-evident, I should think, he said.

—If I had wanted pompous prigs, I would have stayed in England, she said, sat up and straddled him and crossed her thin arms in front of her chest. Damn, but life is becoming such a bloody bore!

Had she said, during her derisive litany of disasters, something about a nervous breakdown, slashed wrists, a bottle of hydrogen peroxide? He caught her scarred wrist between the thumb and solitary finger of his own disfigurement, pulled her down.

—What's the matter, he said, suddenly furious with her. Wasn't the razor sharp enough? Next time, try a cutthroat!

She pulled her wrist away, hid it against her breasts, and spat into his face. Two hectic spots of color appeared in her cheeks.

—Scars worry you? How droll. One suicidal maniac censuring another! Well, well, will the lady never learn about hasty judgments?

She was unbelievably strong, her muscles bunched and bulged in his grasp, and it took all his strength to hold her down, to pinion her upon him with both arms, and then she was suddenly quiet, relaxed, unresisting.

—Yes. Well, she said and leaned across him to drown her cigarette in his glass of wine. Perhaps one really oughtn't to expect more than the occasional competent fuck, everything considered. Ah, well, once more into the breach and all that, then. Perhaps we can talk later.

His face was wet where hers had pressed against it in the struggle, and he thought: Oh, God, not tears, not that damned blackmail water, and he held her still and peered upward, choked by a sudden disgust with himself, but she had jerked her head aside and hid in the dark mass of her hair. The windows were full of light, day had come, and they were both exposed.

—Listen, he said, if it's all that important, if you'd rather talk . . .

The harsh, grating laughter mocked him as before and, unaccountably, he felt both saddened and impoverished.

—Not to worry, laddie. I'm told it's rather nice to find that you actually like the person you're fucking but it's not biologically necessary. One can, as the saying goes, do without the frosting on the cake.

He held himself very still. The image then was one of a dangerous animal in ambush, scenting the air and peering into darkness where other and equally dangerous animals had begun to move.

CHAPTER X

THE NECESSARY GENTLENESS and consideration of each other's needs began the next morning, and grew in the course of the ten days Ludo spent with Ann, so that he knew that if they met again they'd see each other as lovers rather than as mutual exploiters.

In those days, Ludo searched the border for an unguarded path where French and Spanish patrols didn't wait for him and found his entry blocked at every point. Once he disguised himself as a border Basque by hanging a string of huge onions around his neck and marching through the Customs posts with a market-day mob. The French gendarmes laughed; the grinning Spanish *guar-*

dias slapped their thighs with their leather hats and pointed him back the way he had come; Ann laughed herself into a mild fit. On another morning, he climbed with smugglers along a goat trail, supposing that the guards would seek safer footing, only to find a toll collector on top of the mountain. The smugglers paid their fee and went their way; he trudged back down into France.

The Germans seemed oblivious of all this. They took care not to interfere with anyone in the early days of their occupation. They were under orders to be polite and to pay for everything they took, and to molest no one, and they provided a brass band that played Offenbach and Strauss (both Johann and Richard) in the pink bandstand on the beach on Saturday afternoons. The *Sturm und Drang* found expression much farther to the east.

Hatred, always a private matter, took time to develop. The patriotism of the bourgeoisie—the keepers of the bars and brothels and restaurants and gift shops—was counted in the till. It wasn't until the Germans' Russian allies had become their enemies that the Communists of France began to organize resistance. Until then, life in St. Jean-de-Luz went on as if the Germans (*les touristes*, as they were called with the exquisite French touch for the proper word) had never arrived.

Yet not even such contempt as his could be universally applied. Everyone in the port, in the *estaminets* and bistros and the boardwalk cafés, knew who he was but no one turned him in. It was as if his journey had become their own, both a symbol and replacement of their need to climb the Pyrenees, cross hostile Spain, or grow wings and fly across the Atlantic. They listened to the London broadcasts of de Gaulle, looked at each other fiercely, shrugged and bought Ludo a drink. *La Patrie* had never had such sons before, they could assure themselves. And then they told him about yet another path, known only to God and the mountain goats, that he'd try the next day.

The mountains . . . well, the mountains. The damned Pyrenees. Great round hills piled on top of each other, a barrier that he could neither bypass nor climb across, snow-covered passes winding among the clouds. Each morning, as he stood on Ann's balcony and watched the sun sliding past this mocking barricade of granite, watched while the woman yawned and stretched and called him back to bed, he began to wonder if he too would spend the war playing dominoes in a seaside café, making love, and complaining about the quality of the wine.

—Would that be so terribly awful? she asked on another day of his disappointment.

—No, it wouldn't, he said.

—Well, you could stay here if you like. It's up to you, you know. It's not as though you'd be violating a cardinal principle, is it? The war doesn't need *everyone's* involvement.

—I've people waiting for me in England, he explained.

—What people?

—Pilots.

—Can't they survive without you?

—It isn't a chance that I'd like to take. They're my pilots, you know. It's . . . almost like a family to me.

—And we must never disappoint our families, must we, she observed unkindly. Tell me about your real family.

—That's the last thing I want to talk about, he said.

—Try. Indulge me. Did you have brothers? A sister?

—Three brothers. You might have heard of my sister. She was . . . is . . . an actress. Her name is Wlada Modelska. She's quite well known in Europe.

—That was your sister? Ann said and sat up to look at him carefully. Is there no end to the surprises you've in store for me?

—You've seen her?

—Of course. In Paris at the Comédie Française. In Rome. I thought she was quite wonderful in *El Ansuelo de Fenisa*.

—Yes, she was good in that.

—Good? She was wonderful. What was she like offstage?

—Is, not was, he insisted suddenly and went on swiftly to cover the onrush of grief: She's ruthless, loving, manipulative. The word is *insistent*. I think that's the word. Loyal to those she loved, careless with people she didn't care about.

—That could be said about any of us, Ann remarked. Still, it really isn't all that difficult to see that she is your criterion for what you think your women ought to be.

—She may be one of the criterions, he murmured.

—Criteria, Ann said.

—Criteria, then. I've not thought about her recently.

Ann laughed and touched the side of his face, an admonitory gesture. —You make an awfully unsuccessful liar. But it is nice to know that you can love a woman as deeply as that.

The sun was setting then. They were on the beach, and the night looked and felt exactly like the one which would define June 22 for him ever afterward. As a milestone, the fall of France meant less. The long sunset shadows had striped their naked bodies in anarchic colors. Black-and-red, she had become a banner of disorder. By an odd trick of angles, the splintered light had illuminated the scars on her inner wrists.

He watched her quietly and somewhat warily then. Sooner or later, with that odd, atavistic female need to know the roles of other women in his manufacture, the women in his life interrogated him about Wlada, as though they sensed instinctively that there could be no place for them in a life and culture such as his. They would know, of course, that there was safety in reaching out for something that must stay out of reach, that withered when you touched it . . . something that might consume their own lives if they came close to it.

—Well? Ann said and turned into what must have seemed an easier path to the same objective. If not about your sister, tell me about your mother.

—Why must I tell you anything at all?

The wariness was very real then, and she could sense it, but there was a limit to how far she would retreat before any man, so she said: Because I want to know.

—She was . . . affectionate, he said finally and moved to distract her. And overprotective with her children, as we Poles always are.

—Is that all? she asked.

—What more should there be?

—Something human, she persisted. Something that another woman might appreciate.

—She knew the meaning of self-denial, Ludo murmured then. She knew how to submit with grace.

—Is that what you expect from your women? Graceful submission? Invisibility? You'll have a sad and disappointing life if you do.

—I don't expect anything, he said defensively.

—Hope, then? Is that what you hope for?

She had sat up, dark and edged with the red glow that crept toward them from the sea, and her long black hair fell about them both. He laughed, and the false laughter rattled in his throat like a dry pebble in a metal box. He reached across her for a cigarette, so that speech might become impossible for a moment.

—Because if you do, you must believe in miracles, she said, and he could smile then.

—I believe in what happens. When it happens.

—My God, Ann said and laughed. What happened to that wonderful directness? The way you twist and turn, I sometimes wonder how any German manages to shoot you down at all.

—They don't very often.

Ann sighed then, and pressed her lips together, and judged him quietly, and he found himself quite illogically content to be assessed. Some kind of a decision was being made about him, the skeins of his life were being taken from his hands, and he was aware of a peacefulness that he had never been able to imagine before. After a time, her hand moved to his body and began to trace invisible hieroglyphics among the scars and ridges she encountered there, and he was very careful not to move at all.

—They seem to have done well enough, she said. But you are not fighting for your life just now; you're not under attack. You are with a woman who cares for you quite a lot . . . possibly more than good sense should allow. My bed is not a battlefield, though that's not something that too many men have been able to understand. Can't you take off your armor even for a moment?

—I am as naked as I can be, he said quietly.

—I don't want to be a replacement for anyone, she said. I am not your sister. I . . . don't think much of . . . permanent arrangements. But I think it's possible for me to change my mind.

—Wouldn't you rather keep to the safety of a life without illusions?

—I think not, she said. I think that's really being dead without knowing it.

—How wise of you, he mocked gently. How perceptive. Is that the word? Perceptive?

—Every time you want to dodge the issue, you ask for an En-

glish lesson, she said and laughed quietly. You really don't have
to hide from people who are fond of you. The word is *not* perceptive, and wisdom has nothing to do with it. It's love, not wisdom,
at least I think that it might be if given a chance. You might consider it in your lighter moments.

The careful silence stretched as far as he could take it, then he
asked:

—Do you really think that there still are any choices we can
make?

—I can't think of anyone who can make them for us, Ann said.

—Someone else gave me a choice a few months ago, Ludo said.
To abdicate my responsibilities. To give them what they thought
they'd earned. It may have been a kindness on my part, but I
couldn't do it.

Harshly, as though a disfigured beggar had clutched at her
wrist, Ann said: Spare us the awfulness of kindness. Spare us
charity. (And then, making her own retreat, she said mockingly
to Ludo:) Was it one of your grateful but possessive women?

—No. Just someone I once led to disaster in the name of vengeance.

—How unkind of you, she said, suddenly introspective. And
how foolish of him to have followed you.

—Well, people do things like that when they love someone,
don't they? Or trust someone. Or when they feel that they can't
trust themselves any longer.

—Yes, don't they just, she said bitterly. I do have some such
memories myself.

She rose and gathered up her clothes and walked toward the
villa, and he watched her powerful, long stride receding up the
beach. Then she vanished in the darkness and he felt relieved.
His sense of purpose had a way of tilting in her presence. Their
roles as each other's interrogators, he reflected, had begun to du-
plicate each other; he was as full of questions about her as she
was about him, finding every scrap of information a matter of
great moment. But she had begun to defend her privacy from
him as though it were the city of her birth and he, shooting his
arrows out of ambush, was the barbarian at the gate.

He knew this much about her: she was forty-one (he had searched her papers and found her passport and was suitably astonished), married (she had told him that much) to an officer in the Indian Army who had fled from her as though she were the bearer of a plague, the daughter of a rich (and apparently titled) family that had brought her up to leisure, to civilization (*And to be useless in six languages,* she had said). He knew from the people with whom he drank his *fines* in the port cafés that she had lived in St. Jean-de-Luz for ten years, that she disappeared for months at a time to places like Tangier, Casablanca, Fez, and the Aegean Islands, that—unlike all the other English in the town—she was not a heretic but went to Mass on Sundays, and that men in expensive cars sometimes visited her with flowers.

Her sketchbooks were full of arrogant young faces: a Greek fisherman, an insolent Moroccan tout, an Italian shepherd, a French steeplechaser; and he experienced moments of sick, jealous rage at the sight of every one of them. *Mon Repos* wasn't a place he'd remember as being particularly restful. But just as his collapse in Modane and Coetquidan had brought him to a pit in which his body had been forced to mend, so here, on the gray volcanic beach, in her dark bed, in the connections with his own recessed humanity that she offered him, another and invisible process of repair was taking place. She had restored some peace to his interior air; he had to be grateful.

. . . And would it really be so bad to stay here with her? She wanted him there, she had made that clear. Whatever it was that she found in him was, apparently, sufficient to her needs. What, then, of his own? The war had abandoned him, not the other way around. It had taken itself across the English Channel to torment a people who had sat and watched while his own country burned on a funeral pyre they had helped to light. They would fall as the French had fallen; no one who had seen the Wehrmacht in Poland and France could have any doubts about that.

When he got back to the villa, Ann was in bed, asleep. She slept untidily, carelessly, spread out in black-and-white and murmuring to herself. He was unable to sleep. He stood by the window in which her broken and disjointed image became superimposed upon his own. He was mocked by mountains. The sleeve of a Persian robe that he had found and borrowed had snagged on a long splinter along the window frame and held him fast as duty. He jerked at his captive sleeve and felt a seam give way at his shoulder, but the window and its curious images held him, and he looked through her long white reflection at his own dark foreshortened one, and icy sweat began to run into his eyes.

—Come back to bed, lover, Ann murmured then, but he was suddenly quite certain that she was speaking to another man.

They had reached that stage between sexual excess and easy intimacy that either terminates an affair or takes it into other realms, and both of them knew it. He could leave now, and that would be that. He owed her for nothing more than a moment of forgetfulness, of unusual pleasure, of consideration and acceptance in a land of strangers. He knew that there could be no limits to his obligations as a lover, if that was what he was destined to become with this Englishwoman. If, as she implied, she had begun to fall in love with him, his privacy would become intolerable to her, and there was much that he feared to confide, even to himself.

As she emerged from sleep and turned and muttered in the residue of an uneasy dream, and as the night advanced toward a troubled sunrise, he paced up and down. War, he thought, had been a much less demanding mistress.

When the solution presented itself, it was so simple that he couldn't understand why it had taken him so many days to find it. He suspected that, having found something for which he thought that he might want to live, he had accepted those high, cold mountain peaks as impassable because he didn't want to cross them.

He had spent yet another night on a footpath above the timberline, thinking that not even goats would risk such a crossing in the dark, and he had been caught shortly after sunrise by the same bored Spanish *guardias* who had caught him several times before. (The climb was easy on the Spanish side.) This time, they took him down the mountains to Pamplona and locked him up in the municipal jail, and the gray-haired, tired Spanish captain who interviewed him there gave him a choice of moving to another frontier zone or spending the war years in the Miranda concentration camp, where three thousand other Poles, caught on the border as he had been caught, were learning the art of patience in considerable discomfort.

—Be reasonable, *amigo*, the Spanish captain said. Repay my understanding with some of your own. You have become a byword in my zone, you are bad for discipline, my men are making bets about you instead of catching smugglers. As a man and a Spaniard, I admire your determination. It is, of course, the manly thing to do. But as an officer responsible for eighty kilometers of this border, I can't have my zone turned into a joke. Go and create a problem for somebody else. Next time we catch you here, you'll go to Miranda. I assure you that you'll sleep less comfortably there than you do in the bed of the beautiful Lady Hudson in St. Jean-de-Luz.

—You're well informed, Captain, Ludo murmured.

—What do you expect from an officer whose job is to catch smugglers? French tongues wag and Spanish ears listen. Take my advice and go to Perpignan.

—The peaks above Perpignan are even taller than here, Ludo said.

—Possibly. There is, however, a railway station at Perpignan, and trains run through tunnels. And do pay my respects to the beautiful Lady Hudson. I've admired her, from a respectful distance, whenever she has visited Pamplona.

Returned to France through the Customs post at San Sebastian, Ludo caught a ride aboard a swaybacked produce truck, then hitchhiked, then bumped along in a lorry loaded with baskets of sardines. He was in Perpignan in the afternoon. After sunset, he reconnoitered the mouth of the tunnel, the first of several tunnels that followed each other into Spain, each with its own entrance and exit through a succession of mountains. Only the entrance to the first tunnel was guarded on the French side. It would be reasonable to suppose that the same was true on the Spanish side. The mountains here were particularly forbidding.

He sold his watch to a merchant from whom he bought a thick sweater, a pair of heavy boots, a pocket compass, and a flannel shirt. He traded his carved walking stick for a lightweight ruck-sack.

He took a room for the night in the hovel-home of an exiled Spanish loyalist, a grief-stricken man for whom the Pyrenees were a border between life and death, and who looked at Ludo with such naked envy that hatred would have been easier to bear. Nevertheless, next morning Ludo found himself hitchhiking back to St. Jean-de-Luz.

The mountains, then, were no longer a barrier; even so, they mocked him, and he stared at them with a dull, dispassionate loathing, having come to the end of all the lies he could tell himself. He could no longer blame the Pyrenees for keeping him in France. The war seemed very near then; its summons had come with exquisite timing at the exact moment when he had been ready to believe that he had no more debts to pay. Perhaps after the war there would come a time when commitment to another human being made some sense, he thought, but it would have to be a totally different world.

He found Ann on the beach. He told her about the Spanish captain, the tunnels, and the plan he had begun to make. Hungary, Yugoslavia, Italy, and France itself up to the interlude in St. Jean-de-Luz had been an education in illegal journeys, so that he expected to encounter nothing new in Spain. In Portugal, where the British Embassy ran a reception center for men like himself, there'd be false passports and visas to Shanghai (to protect Portuguese neutrality), and ships that formed convoys in Gibraltar and sailed to ports in Scotland.

—So that's that, then, she said.

Her profile was sharp against the lighter backdrop of the starlit sky; the nose was straight and long, the full, long mouth turned down at the corner. Her eyes were turned toward the sea, dark and reflective and unreadable.

—Don't count your borders until they are crossed, she murmured to herself, but he was not thinking of her; he thought of Spain and Portugal and of the distances to be covered on foot, in the backs of trucks carrying vegetables to market, on the undersides of trains, across fields and orchards.

—Once before, in Modane, I thought that this journey was as good as over, he said. But this time I really believe that it's just a matter of walking. Once I'm on the other side of the Pyrenees . . .

—Then England, home, and beauty, she said bitterly.

—How can you hate your own country so much?

—Oh, don't be such a fool! she said. Of course I don't hate it. I love it. I hate its disapproval. And . . . I can't be faithful to people and places I can't see.

—Then why not go home?

—This is home! she said fiercely. I may not like it very much, but this is where I live. Occasionally, something rather pleasant happens to me here. From time to time, I even think it might last.

—Come to England, Ann.

—*Follow* you there, you mean? I don't *follow* people. And I don't compete with other women, wars, or occupations. If you've found out anything about me, you ought to have discovered that much for yourself.

—At least I've discovered your name, he said quietly.

Her laughter was short, cold, artificial, and he hated it. She had begun a retreat of her own, he knew, and perhaps that was just as well.

—How fascinating for you, she said. And which name might it be? There have been a number.

—You're Lady Hudson.

—There's no such thing, she said. It even *sounds* ridiculous. This kind of title is used only with the Christian name, if it is used at all. My poor, bewildered Patrick, who did his insufficient best to live up to it, had nothing to do with getting it for me. Daddy did that by selling lots of beer. You ought to learn about that sort of thing if you're going to be a success in London.

—There is no *Lord* Hudson, then?

—Not to the best of my knowledge. There is a Brigadier Hudson, now busy propping up the Empire somewhere near the sunrise, and there's a hopeless, panting, balding puppy dog named W. W. Hudson, better known as Wally, who lusts for his brother's wife. But Lord? *Lord?* Oh, dear loving Lord. Not even such ambitious second cousins as the Hudsons could aspire to that. Who told you about the Hudsons?

—About you, not the Hudsons, Ludo said. You have an unknown admirer in Pamplona.

—Impossible, she said. My admirers always make themselves known. Not that I ever know them very long.

He sighed, said: You don't have to say things like that to me. I've thought about you much more carefully than you know.

She laughed, said: How nice to know one has had some effect. But don't worry, lad, you'll get over it.

—I don't want to get over it, Ludo said.

—That, she said, would be making a terrible mistake. I say it as your friend, this is one lady who doesn't wait for the boys to come home from the wars. Johnny comes marching home and there's Tom and Dick and occasionally Harry, and that's when things really become confusing for everyone. However, I don't think you really mean what you're saying, dear boy. You've found a way through your bloody mountains and now you feel obliged to make a sentimental gesture.

—Is that what it is?

—It could hardly be anything else.

Afterward, he would wonder now and then what would have happened if he had gone back with her to the villa. When and where would they have gone together, how would they have lived, for how long would they have been able to bear each other's disappointed silences. . . . It was the kind of crossroad one occasionally reaches at the far edge of youth, the sort of point in almost everybody's journey that should be clearly marked: one chance, possibly the last one, for ordinary human happiness . . . and then nothing but desert for a hundred miles.

He stayed behind after she left the beach. He saw the lights go on in every window of the villa, and, sometime later, he heard the growling of her little car.

Time passed, and then a great white moon sailed into the sky, and then he watched stars. He thought of Reszke and Gerlach and Straka and Wilchurzak and of Messerschmitts and Spitfires, and watched the meteors and shooting stars fall into the sea. Responsibility for the lives of others would call for a special and continuing ruthlessness on his part. Gentleness could become a habit, and what would happen to fearlessness then? Fearlessness, and that necessary carelessness about his own welfare, would guarantee the others' survival; yet he longed for the solace of a deep emotional commitment as a replacement for the gentleness that he had discarded.

Piotr . . . Norwid . . . Wlada . . . Janek . . . the names reappeared and skimmed the ripples of his memory, and he struggled against the tide of remembrance, and strove to keep his face rigid and his thoughts noncommittal so that this night—and all of this uneasy interlude stolen from the war—could continue as a barrier against future loss.

When he went up to the villa, Ann had gone. The house was wide open and all the lights were on and she had packed with obvious haste; her clothes were scattered through all the upstairs rooms.

Tangier? Fez? The Greek fisherman? The Moroccan tout? He damned them all to hell and he was sick with bitterness and longing.

But she had the last word; she always would, he thought. She had left him a note. Her handwriting was angular, sloped, sliding off the page, slashed with erasures and spilled ink. *Don't find the lady too ill-mannered,* she had written. *She is simply too bored with living backward. Affection, for lack of courage to use the stronger word, is too dangerous to attempt again. It's just too depleting in the long run, don't you see, if it's allowed to have any run at all. Caution IS the better part of valor, lover, so take note and heed. Ave atque vale is the cleverest thing the Romans ever said.*

Should he reach Lisbon, she wrote, her brother might be useful to him. His name was Derek Bellancourt and he made his living as a military attaché at the British Embassy. *He's a nasty, selfish, cunning little beast, not to be trusted ever—but employable. He takes malicious pleasure in being helpful to my discarded lovers.*

To his amazement, he found the note wrapped around a rosary.

In the first week of July, he went into the mountains below
Perpignan, bypassed the first tunnel, dropped into the mouth of
the second, and walked along the rails until he reached the last
tunnel but one. Later, if forced to talk about it to the journalists,
he'd joke about flattening himself against cold, wet granite walls
while express trains roared past, a hand's breadth from his sucked-
in belly, or about lying facedown in the gravel between the rails
and the wheels. At the time, when he could swear that he could
hear the tens of thousands of tons of earth and stone creaking
overhead and settling down upon him, there wasn't much to be
amused about. Dead, shredded animals, trapped in the tunnels
while the trains went through, reminded him at each step of his
folly. The cold, fresh mountain air between the tunnels made
him drunk with pleasure.

This journey through the underworld left him spent and
stunned when he climbed into the mountains to bypass the last
tunnel and the Spanish sentries at the other end. He climbed
with something approaching desperation; he couldn't climb high
enough, he thought, to get away from the memory of his own
debilitating weakness, the sense of entrapment in the dark,
enclosed environment, where it would have been so easy to lie
down, surrender, admit the uselessness of the attempt, and betray
his purpose.

But the cold, clear roof of the mountains displayed familiar
landmarks, the stars were out in their glittering millions, the wind
was a well-remembered mass pressing against his face . . . and he
slept in gratitude among the granite boulders, Ann's rosary—that
incongruous gift—wrapped around his fist.

PART THREE

Never So Few

You may well ask why I write. And yet
my reasons are quite many. For it is not
unusual in human beings who have witnessed
the sack of a city or the falling to pieces
of a people to desire to set down what
they have witnessed for the benefit of unknown
heirs or of generations infinitely
remote; or, if you please, just to get the
sight out of their heads.

FORD MADOX FORD

CHAPTER XI

ANN RETURNED to London in the first week of August. Quite un-
consciously—at least she'd never admit afterward that the choice
was conscious—she had followed Ludo's route to England.

She had driven from St. Jean-de-Luz to Lourdes in Unoccupied
France, the rump state left to the French after they had made a
separate peace with Hitler's Germany, obtained the necessary
Spanish transit visas on her British passport, and traveled to Portugal by train in a first-class compartment reserved to herself. She
entered Spain through the same tunnels that Ludo had crossed,
rode under the same mountains, supposed that she was skirting
the same narrow valleys and ravines through which he had crept
past the small white villages with bullet-pitted walls, and she was
conscious of all of this every mile of the way. The Spanish Civil
War, a fierce and recent memory in the shocked consciousness of
Europe, had littered the countryside with rusting debris, and the
landscape through which she traveled was only a degree more lenient than the savage desolation through which he had come. He
had inched his way at night along the dangling rails of a great
wrecked bridge a hundred feet above a mountain torrent; she saw
that bridge as a gaunt skeleton hanged in the sun-drenched air on
a quivering horizon.

How else could he have come? She thought of him as riding on
a donkey, sharing a truck with a load of sheep, walking along the
dusty tracks and clay roads, hiding in olive groves and in the
winding alleys of small towns before he slipped across the far
edge of the Spanish plain into Portugal. He would have waited
there for the heat of the noon sun, when everyone had gone into
the shade of their shuttered houses, when even the dogs had
vanished. She, when asked on the Portuguese border if she had
anything to declare, said: *Yes. The service on this train is con-
temptible. The food is tasteless and the wine is corked.*

In Lisbon, when Derek had asked her why she had chosen this
of all possible times to go Home (England being spoken of and
toasted as Home in capital letters), just as the air campaign over

the Channel was coming to an end and the assault on England was sure to begin, she had laughed and shrugged and said that she had been moved to patriotism by onions; and then she told him about Ludo's unsuccessful masquerade on the Spanish border, and she was furious as she did so because she found her own laughter too revealing.

(*Onions or garlic or whatever it was,* she said in that harsh, careless, artificial voice that she used to hide depth of feeling and to mock her listeners as cruelly as herself. *I mean, the wretched man was malodorous! So if he, with his delicate Continental nose, could make such a sacrifice just to get to England, well, I mean to say, what could a genuine Briton do? Duty called and all that, don't you know.*)

She flew from Lisbon to Southampton on a regularly scheduled Pan American "Clipper" flying boat, having the embassy courier and his diplomatic bag for company, and she was letting herself into her brother's Mayfair flat at just about the time that Ludo—gaunt, footsore, weary, and looking more than a little mad—sat down to wait outside the door of Derek's Lisbon office.

A shared journey? An experience that might bind them closer? Not quite, not by a long shot, she thought, grinning derisively at the rain-streaked windows of Derek's apartment. He, as a story in the newspapers revealed shortly after her arrival, had stolen a German airliner at the Lisbon airport and flown it to Casablanca, where the Vichy French authorities had thrown him into prison. He had escaped the next day and, with the help of twenty other Polish airmen and soldiers, had *liberated* a six-hundred-ton coastal steamer which he had navigated to a port in Scotland. So, not quite a shared experience. Not this time, she thought and laughed without amusement and went to stare through a window at the darkening, misted grayness of Green Park.

In the park, graceless young women in bulky battle dress and ammunition boots were polishing big guns. The street was lined with rubble in which flowers grew. The sky was overcast with low clouds, and the barrage balloons lurked there like a school of whales stranded in a foggy sea, and—beyond them, at the edge of vision—a small brown humpbacked fighter plane climbed like a homesick angel. Derek's flat was the kind that needed a coal fire in July, and she, having lived for so many years in the sun, was chilled to the bone. She had become a stranger to mahogany drum tables and antimacassars, to the damp wind that whispered platitudes in the grate, to hunting prints and riding trophies and to the process of presiding over tea. The dull, dark weight of Victorian disapproval, shot through and through with hidden passions and perversity, hung in the mist outside Derek's windows. Ludo, she thought, would find these institutional landscapes just as foreign as she.

The face that stared back at her out of the streaked, fogged glass was tranquil enough. The great black eyes were full of exterior motion, images, and reflections, and she saw the crabbed, foreshortened military women—so ugly in their terrible usefulness—moving about in each of them like maggots. The dark, unlined, youthful face framed in blue-black hair had the quality of a ceremonial mask for bitter rituals. It was a face to be shown with caution to selected viewers because its narrowed, sharp intensity was such an open challenge. The mouth was straight, long, generous, and much misunderstood, she thought; men fell upon it as though their own lips were clenched, punishing fists . . . which struck such unmemorable blows. Ludo had promised to be something different.

She was determined not to think about him, or to credit him with any part of her decision to return. Impatiently, she told herself over and over in those first few days that she was a woman who made all her own decisions, for good or for evil, and she accepted the responsibility for the consequences. No matter what she did, she was sure, the end result would add to her collection of regrets. She was quite sure that she wouldn't see her accidental Polish lover again; yet for some irritating reason that she refused to think about, she found herself looking for his blunt, triangular face above the collar of every foreign uniform she saw in the street.

London—even this different, nervous, wartime London—assaulted her with a rush of memories she had thought safely put behind. It had been both her playground and her pillory. England, or what she had schooled herself to think of as England, in turn enraged and bewildered her. Her return appalled her, and yet she couldn't understand how she had managed to stay away as long as she had.

My God, she thought, eighteen bloody years! And nothing (except for the crushing vulgarity of a war) had changed! The mannered, icy beat of self-centered little lives went on as before, she was sure. The same lies were being told. Men (and women, too) who had been raised to Empire, to a natural assumption of superiority over less fortunate categories of mankind, still spoke and postured on the same old stage. . . .

Ten years in St. Jean-de-Luz, two in Taormina, an optimistic eighteen months in Tuscany. (*And how, she asked herself, could one be optimistic in a Tuscan village with or without an Italian lover who brought her flowers and threw fits, who was the raging antithesis of everything that was measured, mannered, tepid, and restrained . . . home, husband, hearth, and the sense of never having been alive . . . ?*) A desperate year in the Aegean Islands had come before that, a year best not thought about in any circumstances, preceded by the isolation of her first home of exile: the white mountain villa among the lemon groves and Crusader castles perched on the green slopes of the Kyrenia Mountains, on the north coast of Cyprus, as far away from England as she could get in the Mediterranean without the need to be anything but English. She had been twenty-four before she tasted bitter lemons and knew that almonds flowered in April! Each step thereafter took her nearer to the country she had been so determined never to see again, as if an invisible wire had been looped around her neck.

Eighteen years!

And now she felt as though she had never left at all.

On Sunday, she walked to early Mass at the Brompton Oratory, but when she got to the church she found that she couldn't pray. She had taken a long way around the park, making her own personal stations of the cross in the Mall, around the clubs of Mayfair, near the gilded iron gates at Hyde Park Corner (where it had been such fun to hang policemen's helmets), in Knightsbridge, and in the white cold silence of Belgravia, where she was careful to avoid her parents' shuttered mansion. (It had been known as *Yeast Castle* in her contemptuous girlhood.)

The streets were swept clean of people so early in the morning.

The pavements were immaculate, the grasses manicured and rolled, the trees were wrapped in little wire cages to discourage dogs. She passed sandbagged monuments and fortified museums and porticoes inscribed with names like *Malplaquet* and *Balaclava* and *Khartoum* and *Ypres*, and rows of tall, white-pillared houses grouped in crescents, and cobbled little mews, and each step took her deeper into a picture-postcard world. At almost every step, she recalled faces and events—routs, balls, shimmying on marble tabletops, climbing lampposts—and couldn't understand why she felt no part of any of it. Perhaps, she thought, that was because none of it had become a part of her.

Perhaps there's this to say about England and the English, she thought in the damp gloom of the Lady Chapel, in the smell of old stone and stale sandalwood and confessionals: that no matter how much the exteriors change, and the spaces narrow, and the possibilities dwindle, they (we?) remain committed to their own survival. The rest of the world can go to hell on a haycart, but England will survive, detached and floating in space like a moon if that's necessary, and all the English know it with absolute conviction, and all the lesser peoples (the Germans, and the Americans, and the French, and the Hindus, and the Hottentots) accept that English evaluation of the English role because they've no other way to explain their own endless failures.

The church was full of people, mostly men in uniform. She had been away too long to realize how unusual that was for her countrymen, for whom religion was a comfortable ritual at best. But this dark, dank atmosphere was charged with emotion; these people prayed as though they believed that their prayers were heard. She noted the harsh, lean faces on which lines were etched deep as saber scars, heard the precision of their Continental Latin; their strange, foreign hymns thundered among the Gothic arches like demands.

Conscious of undermining her own vanity (*But, then, these were only foreigners, after all!*), she put on her glasses, looked about, read the name of their obscure little nation on the sausage-shaped tabs they wore on their shoulders, and thought: *How clever of us to label our allies. Once something is labeled, you don't have to wonder what it is.* The red-and-white tabs that

said POLAND made her think of stored, addressed packages to be
sent at Christmas.

The habit of childhood had seated her in what had been her
family pew (the name was quite clear on the brightly polished
small brass plate) and she thought, angrily: What are they doing
here? Can't they read? Up to a month ago, she had never heard
of them as more than just another unknown race, living in probably quite unsanitary ways in a distant corner of the world, and
now, it appeared, she couldn't get away from them. She resented
the sense of being an intruder within her own past in which,
unaccountably, foreign rituals were taking place. The priest cried
out to God and they responded in a harsh, deep chorus, and none
of them had to open a missal to do so. She began to watch them
and to listen to them and to sense the pulse of their civilization,
their unyielding purpose.

Damn them, she whispered, and damn him too! She felt as if a
net had fallen all around her, drawing her into commitments she
had long abandoned and to faiths that had betrayed her time and
time again. Such single-minded love for an intangible ideal was
sheer suicide, she knew.

After the service, the last soaring hymn that seemed to her
more like a promise and a battle cry than a plea to heaven, the
church emptied quickly and by the time she had reached the
street all but a few of them were gone.

She had paused on the steps because a thin, cold rain had
begun to fall, and she had come without an umbrella or a coat
(having forgotten about the constant need for such things in England), and one of them—a tall, stooped man with one sleeve
pinned up under his elbow—who had walked down toward the
staff car that waited at the curb, looked back toward her in her
carefully simple black silk Paris suit, and returned to ask where he
might take her. Later, all sorts of foolish and unimaginative people would mutter darkly about coincidences; she made no such
mistake. Her life was full of detours, unexpected turnings, and accidental meetings in which she could sense the presence of a plan,
a logical progression in seemingly random moments, and she
knew that nothing was ever wholly a matter of chance. Once

something happens, as Ludo had happened to her in St. Jean-de-
Luz, other things must happen. Chaos, she knew, is the art of
order running with equal logic in reverse.

He introduced himself in the formal Continental manner as
General Janusz Prus. She was familiar with the stiff little nod and
simultaneous salute, the slight click of the heels, the name stated
firmly as he bowed over her gloved hand, and neither of them was
surprised a few moments later when she said that she had met another Polish officer in France and found him congenial. Once
named, Ludo created a common ground for them.

—I've known him since he was a sixteen-year-old boy, the general said. Sometimes I've felt guilty because I cared more for him
than I did for my own son.

—He seemed . . . durable, she said.

Suddenly pleased, the general nodded and said: I'm very glad
to meet you. Forgive my abruptness, but I've not had much practice, lately, of talking to a woman. I'd like to give you dinner, if
that's possible.

She hesitated only for a moment, then nodded in her turn.

—It's possible, she said. But tea would be better.

—Ah, tea, he said and smiled. Of course. I've not had time to
get used to the English tea.

—And I've had all the time I want to have forgotten all about
it, Ann said and laughed openly. So let's compromise and have a
lunch instead. Tuesday?

—Tuesday.

She had lunch with Prus the next day, as well as on Tuesday.
On Wednesday night, they went to hear Vera Lynn singing
about a time when the lights would go on again all over the
world, and had dinner in a Soho restaurant whose Italian owner
assured them tearfully that he was a Frenchman, and got lost in
the blackout, and sat in the depths of an Underground station
while antiaircraft guns cracked and boomed overhead, and talked
until three o'clock in the morning. Each of them had sustained a
loss, each was hungry for untrammeled human contact, each felt
displaced among people who knew either not enough about them
or too much. Sooner or later, Ludo would become the subject of
all their conversations.

Prus was an easy man to talk to, he knew how to listen, and

she told him more about herself than she had said to anyone in years. He offered neither judgment nor advice. The distances between them narrowed imperceptibly until only the last, uncrossed boundary separated them, and she began to wonder, with regret, when that might be crossed. She had never had a reason to suppose that friendship could be possible between a man and a woman. The discovery, she admitted ruefully, had come a little late.

He told her about Lala Karolewska, and just enough about himself for both of them to know that they would not be lovers, and her sense of relief was so obvious that both of them laughed. Once more, it was clear, an accidental meeting had conformed to pattern, fitting everything that had gone before, and she was pleased to take the next logical step: to let him introduce her to the tense, disciplined world of an expatriate army, a society centered about an ideal that didn't have to be debated to death, where she felt, in characteristic English fashion, a wrench of envy and contempt. Prus and his kind appeared to inhabit landscapes of such uncomplicated harshness as to be monastic. She could see Ludo, or what she knew of Ludo, in every one of them. Their absolutes were simple, obvious, and unstated. No one among them intellectualized his role, or voiced complaint, or harangued the heavens to witness his distress, or showed concern about his own survival. (*We've the experience to suffer with discretion*, Prus had said in his amused, self-derisive manner, and she could believe it. *Point by point, century by century, and event by event, our history is a lesson in futility, you see.*) Such objectivity bordered upon smugness, she thought, and told him so.

—One says such things as if they didn't matter or one wouldn't be able to say them at all, he said.

—Please don't be introspective about things, she said. It's too painful to watch. And I don't really believe that you're as objective about it as you try to seem.

—Yes, you're quite right. I'm not at all objective about it. Caring about what happens to my country is the only thing left to me, and our friend Ludo is very much a part of that.

—In what respect? she asked.

—People can trust him and follow him without asking *why*. He looks beyond the obvious and he thinks about the things he sees. This hasn't made him popular in some quarters in the past.

—I don't see how it could, she observed. Particularly if he speaks up and says what he thinks.

—We've not done well in Europe since our independence in 1918, the general said. We've made serious errors. It's a complex question which needs some rethinking of who and what we are and what we ought to be. Ludo may suggest a new concept of Poland to the rest of us if he survives this war.

—But don't you need power, rank, that sort of thing, to become a leader of a nation? And doesn't that automatically change a man?

—It may not, he said. It depends on how little a man wants for himself. And on his sense of duty.

—And courage? she asked.

—Oh, of course, courage. That is often nothing more than fear misunderstood. I've done my best to teach Ludo the truth about courage, but he's the sort of student who outstrips his teachers. I've had to learn everything I know, you see. He knows as much by instinct. He is much more the man of the future than I ever was, which is why I want to spare him unnecessary disappointments.

—Can anyone do that for anybody else?

—One can try, he said. There are, of course, no guarantees of success. And the guiding hand has got to be a gentle one.

Then, smiling wryly, he nodded toward his pinned-up sleeve and amputated elbow.

—I think the gentle one is the one I lost.

Liking him, because he didn't make her feel like a citadel under siege, she said: I don't see you as quite the venerable father figure, Janusz. You don't extract a crippling price for the support you give.

—Yes, he said with a bitterness that astonished her. One does learn that much. But not, normally, before it's too late. Ludo could be the best kind of man if he makes the right choice at the proper time.

—And when would that be? she asked.

—Well, obviously, he said, smiling broadly. Before it's too late! (Then, seriously:) Before his sense of loss becomes the only thing that he is able to feel. Before he realizes that he might have made some bitter and diminishing choices in the name of his idea of duty, and that time is running out for him, and that he's going to spend some disappointing years staring into a shaving mirror in a lonely room. For some of us, that's almost an occupational disease.

Moved by his pained intensity, she murmured: You must have loved your Lala very much.

—I did. But not enough, I think.

—Was she at all like Ludo's sister?

—No. They were cousins, of course, but entirely different. Lala was quieter, gentler. Her capacity for life and living were . . . inspiring. Wlada was almost totally concerned with herself.

Knowing that she would hurt him, but needing to know the answer in order to complete her understanding of this man and, through him, of Ludo, she asked as gently as she could: How did Lala die?

—Stupidly. Horribly. Unnecessarily, he said. It wasn't at all inspiring.

—Perhaps there was nothing more that she could give you, she prompted.

—Perhaps not, he said. And perhaps she realized that I had nothing more to give to her. Still, that's not quite the point that I'm trying to make.

—The point you *have* made, my dear, is that, thanks to her, you've become a good man yourself, Ann said. And that you want someone, perhaps me, to do the same for Ludo. I don't think I can do that for anyone, but that's another story.

—Being a good man isn't enough, he said. No more than being a good woman is enough. Something more is needed. Love, gentleness, shared expectations . . . oh, just the ordinary human happiness, or what passes for it . . . that is, essentially, selfish. Good people are selfish, you know. They must be, to survive. But Ludo is capable of much more. He is capable of sacrifice for something greater than himself, and that's still the criterion for the best kind of man.

You wish him *that?* she asked. I thought you cared for him.

—More than I do for myself, that's certain, the general said. I want him to be useful to more than just his friends.

—And what does he want?

—It doesn't matter what he wants, the general said and shrugged, and she had another sort of vision of him and of Ludo and, perhaps, of herself as well. Such lives are too useful to be left to chance, he finished abruptly.

She found herself repelled by the charming yet austere faces that surrounded her in this transplanted Poland, which, she suspected, had been neither as ingenuous nor as stalwart before its displacement. Was there no end to these unmitigated gallants? she asked herself. Did they breed like mosquitoes in the bloodstained Polish soil? They seemed to live their lives as if only their last moments counted, and they insisted on that ecstatic immolation as their right, their part in the bloody pageant of their country's history. Turned from their courses, robbed of their vision of themselves as men who were free to choose their last moment, they'd have no more peace than unhallowed ghosts.

It was easier to find them fascinating than convincing, like a book written about something that didn't really touch the core of one's being, still easier to read their little labels and take them as reported in the popular press. They had brought a savage determination to the air war that still hung in the balance. Their pilots swung into battle with skill and enthusiasm that were beyond praise. Their contempt for death had made them the heroes of this British hour. Any thought beyond such skin-deep journalistic phrases might take her farther than she wished to go. Even so, she found their faiths infectious.

She wanted to ignore them, but there was no way to do that in England in those days. Of the three thousand and eighty RAF fighter pilots who were fighting to prove Britain's ability to resist the Germans, five hundred and thirty-seven were foreign volunteers. Of these, one hundred and forty-seven were Poles, one hundred and one were New Zealanders, ninety-four were Canadians, eighty-seven were Czechs, twenty-nine were Belgians, twenty-two came from South Africa, and another twenty-two from Australia, fourteen were Frenchmen, ten came from the Irish Republic, seven were citizens of the United States, two came from Rhodesia, and one each came from Jamaica and from Palestine. Of all

of them, the Poles were the most numerous, the most successful
in the air, and the most admired; one would have had to be blind
as well as deaf to pretend that they didn't exist. Thinking herself
at least half in love with one of them, and fond of another, Ann
found herself judging others according to their uncompromising
standards. These were too cruel even for her, she thought. When
she was not with Prus, she sat in the stuffy gloom of Derek's flat,
in what could have been any rich young bachelor's apartment, in
the smell of coal and dusty carpeting and polished brass and old
wood and leather and (in her own mocking terminology) surreptitious sin, and watched the sudden gleams and flashes in the
thick gray night and cursed her involvement. The thought of
spending all her nights alone—while the bright geometry of the
searchlight beams formed orderly cones in the London sky, and
the guns boomed and cracked, and the windows turned themselves into tuning forks—had become as distressing as the company of the displaced Poles.

August was half over before she faced the facts of her return to
London, not to some temporary and imaginary Warsaw, and she
realized that she had made no attempt to contact anyone she
knew, neither her family nor her former friends. She had never
had much retrospective mercy for herself, and now she recoiled
from an unreasonable hope that she was about to discover some
special meaning in her unplanned return. For her, this war was
awful, cruel, full of contradiction and futility; she would resurrect
none of her old illusions, nor did she want to construct new ones
for herself. For the Poles, the war was a Crusade, their reason for
being. The intensity of their commitment made her think of armored monks, and she needed neither a new faith, nor an Order,
nor a new Grand Master. They were a false start to her new life
in England.

Then came a night in which loneliness and surroundings which
were both foreign and familiar resurrected her most detested
memories—the Oxford years from which she had thought herself
reasonably safe. She listened to the thin distant wail of an air raid
siren out toward the East End and knew that others would follow
near, and very soon, and then she heard the tinny droning of an
engine in the clouds. (Ah, *he'd hardly have had time to reach
England, far less the London sky,* she thought.) And if there's

one thing I don't need at this of all times, she told her blurred
and darkening reflection in the rain-streaked window, it's another
single-minded hero. Not far from this flat was an old trysting
place, a cocktail lounge which she had been careful to avoid, and
she went there that night to exorcise her ghosts.

Outside, the air trembled to a distant air raid, the heaviest
since her return. It seemed unreal, something that couldn't touch
her or anyone she knew. She was aware, as most people seemed to
be aware, that this Battle of Britain, which had begun to capture
the imagination of the Western world as no stand had done since
the fall of the Spartans at Thermopylae, was a creation of Winston Churchill's brilliant rhetoric, yet the danger was a mortal
one nonetheless. No such thing had been planned by the Germans, who had simply wanted a campaign of attrition that might
destroy the Fighter Command of the Royal Air Force, give them
mastery of the air over the English Channel, perhaps provide an
opportunity for a cross-Channel invasion, and, above all, convince
the English politicians that Britain, with her armies wrecked in
France and her lifelines threatened, couldn't hope to win this war
now that she stood alone. One didn't have to know how to read
the headlines to see that Britain's fall appeared imminent. The
Germans were so sure of it that they demobilized some of their
reserves, and plans to move the Royal Family to Canada failed
only because King George VI refused to leave London.

In the debacle before Dunkirk, as Prus and his friends had
revealed, the Germans captured five hundred British tanks, twelve
hundred pieces of artillery, thirteen thousand motor vehicles, and
one hundred thousand rifles and machine guns. The RAF lost
nine hundred and fifty-nine machines in forty-two days of fighting
over northern France, Holland, Belgium, and the English Channel, among them five hundred and nine fighter planes needed for
the defense of the British Isles. Another sixty-six were destroyed
in Norway. Four hundred and thirty-five RAF pilots were either
killed or captured. British merchant shipping was going down at
such a desperate rate that all of it would be sunk by the spring of
1941 unless the neutral United States could be induced to replace
the ships, and to take up the burden of armament and supply.
In Churchill's view, it was essential to convince the American
Congress that Britain had not been defeated in the fall of France,

that this destruction of the Allies in the West was nothing more than an opening battle, and that the serious business of resisting Germans had scarcely begun. If the young fighter pilots of the RAF could stay alive long enough to force the Luftwaffe into a retreat, this would show the world that the needed massive American help in ships, money, new weapons, and foodstuffs—without which Britain wouldn't last a year—would not merely add to Hitler's stores of booty. The great air battles of September were yet to be fought, but people, if they talked about the war at all, no longer damned fighter pilots for their supposed invisibility at Dunkirk. They had already become the heroes of the hour which, in Churchill's phrase, would be Britain's finest.

Looking at a little gathering of pilots at the far end of the bar, she felt a wrench of memory, the fleeting touch of pity. How young they are, she thought, how . . . untried. The self-conscious boy who had moved to the seat beside hers had obviously made some sort of bet with his grinning friends. He wasn't much more than a uniformed child but to be with someone was not to be alone, and so she brought him back with her to the flat. In the flat, she stood before the windows, looking out, while he settled himself nervously in Derek's overstuffed armchair. Normally, Green Park wouldn't have been visible from these windows. There had been several small streets and mews between Park Lane and this part of Mayfair, but a Dornier filled with aerial mines had fallen there in July and now she had a view.

—I say, this is so terribly decent of you, the young pilot said, and she replied with an edge of bitterness in her voice: Decency has nothing to do with it, dear boy. Be a dependable child and bring the lady a whiskey and water.

—Where do you keep it? he asked with false bravado.

He had jumped to his feet and now peered about among Derek's trophies, bric-a-brac, Chinese cabinets, lacquered oriental boxes, Persian slippers, hookahs in which nothing more insidious than Player's Navy Cut tobacco had ever been smoked, stuffed hunting dogs, and wastebaskets fashioned from the feet of large thick-skinned animals. There was a film of dust over everything, and she didn't know his name, and she thought that it was proba-

bly best that way. There could be courage in anonymity, a form
of grace in submission to the inevitable disappointment, kindness
within oblivion.

—Damned if I know, she said harshly, destroying the moment.
This isn't my flat. But my brother is sure to have whiskey here for
his large naval friends. When he says, *Bottoms up,* he means it, if
you know what I mean.

The young man turned beet-red to the roots of his overlong
sandy hair, and blinked soft shocked eyes, and she said:

—You wouldn't be of the same persuasion, would you? Don't
worry, I'm not overly critical about that sort of thing. I've spent
years among people who think that a vegetarian is some sort of
pervert.

—No, of course I'm not! he said, then blurted on: Would I've
come with you if I were a homo?

—Why did you come?

—You asked me and I came, that's all.

—How very polite of you, Ann said and laughed and listened
to the sudden crash and clatter of the guns worked in the park
by the graceless young military women: the shopgirls and the
counter clerks and the milliners' assistants who had never made a
sound of their own before. In truth, she thought, nothing appeared to have changed for her, each of her moments was stale
with too much rehearsal, but everything was different for everyone else. She shuddered and the young man was immediately so-
licitous.

—Are you cold? Shall I look for a wrap?

—A goose just stepped over my grave, if you're familiar with
that country saying. I think I've just looked into a future in
which there'll be no place for me at all.

He had found the whiskey, filled a glass.

—This'll help, I think.

—It never has before, she reflected. I really can't see why it
should make such an enormous difference now.

He laughed uneasily, said: In the squadron, we drink to *the last
man to die.*

—How romantic of you. But I think that he must have done
that quite some time ago.

—I . . . beh-beh-beg your pardon?

—Forgive the lady's lack of appreciation for schoolboy heroics. Romantic gestures seem rather empty after a time, you see. One faces the facts of one's own life, after a certain age. One eschews illusions. Living among Frenchmen for ten years does knock one's nonpragmatic imperatives into a cocked hat, so to speak. Yet there remains a sort of aftertaste of hope, a will-o'-the-wisp that leads one into foolish, optimistic denials of one's own experience. It's all rather disheartening, if you know what I mean.

—I'm afraid I don't . . .

—Of course not. Why should you? The lady is talking to herself, I regret to say.

Quite as unhappy with herself as she was with the young man's accidental company, she darted from one set of accents to another, from the idiom and gesture of sculleries to the brittle brightness of Swiss schools, and the young pilot was suitably bewildered.

—I beh-beg your pardon?

—Nothing to do with you, dear boy. I was thinking of another pilot. He, at least, had the seasoning to rise to the demands of my more difficult moments. And like all men, he's never there when needed the most.

—I say now, give us a chance, what? the young man said and she laughed openly.

—Not today, my friend. One shouldn't expect a boy to do a man's job, particularly since most men seem to have forgotten what it is.

—Well, now, look here . . . , he said and she laughed and winked at him and patted his knee.

—No reason to be upset, dear boy. It's nothing personal. What I am saying is that sooner or later one stops living other people's dreams. One accepts the premise of inevitable disaster in all relationships. One knows, in the way that a priest knows his God, that the imponderable mystery behind every door is a solid brick wall. One does *not*, in any circumstances, attempt to turn back clocks.

—I fa-fa-fail to see . . . , the young man began and she nodded, said: One can believe that a Number Twenty-four bus will take one down Oxford Street to Tottenham Court Road, but one need *not* believe that it will be driven by the Easter Bunny. It's quite simple, really. It's astonishing how many otherwise intelligent people continue to delude themselves in the most absurd ways.

He had gotten to his feet and glanced at his wristwatch and cleared his throat and said, in the manner of a well-brought-up young man who understands nothing: Oh, quite. Of course. Well . . .

—Leaving so soon? she said. Well, the air raid does seem to be over.

—I hadn't meant . . . , he began, and she gestured toward the whiskey decanter and he refilled her glass.

—Not to worry, lad. I'm sure there's still someone at the Dorchester. It's not very late.

—It's just that I've to be back on station by tomorrow night, you see, the young man said. And . . . ah . . . one never knows when there'll be another spot of leave . . .

—And one does have to do one's bit for civilian morale, she said. Poke the old home fires, and all that. Yes. Well. I did have a similar idea earlier in the evening. But then something happened and the idea didn't seem quite proper.

—If I said something . . . , he said and reached for his cap and she said swiftly: No, no, you said nothing. You said nothing at all. Perhaps that's the trouble. Perhaps it's just that I've been stricken by conscience, suddenly.

—Ah, he said as though he had arrived once more in familiar country: So that's it? You have a husband serving in the Forces? Well, yes, I can see how that would make things uncomfortable for you.

—It's not that kind of conscience, she said. It's just that there are some things that not even a patriotic Englishwoman should do for her country, and that's bedding with a little boy who might very well be dead day after tomorrow. That's sort of like robbing the cradle and the grave in one ghastly gesture, don't you think?

Pale, wide-eyed, spilling whiskey on Derek's Persian carpet, the young man made a strangled sound, and then his face filled with blood.

—Wha-a-at?

—Sorry to hurt your feelings, and all that. But that's the truth of it.

He raged then, wounded and wanting to inflict a terrible injury in return.

—G-good Christ but you're a bitch!

—I've never denied it.

—Do you hate men, is that it? Are you some kind of pervert, like your stinking brother?

—Heaven preserve us from anything so gruesome, she said and walked to the windows and pushed aside the velvet portieres that concealed the night. Having loved an Italian, having lived among Greeks, Spaniards, fierce Basques, and venomous Moroccans, she fully expected the young pilot to throw her through the window. But he had broken down. He vomited into Derek's elephant's foot wastebasket and wept. She spent the rest of the night sitting on the floor before a pale coal fire while he slept with his head on her lap.

Why, in God's name, had she done it? What bloody-minded self-destructive impulse had driven her to this pathetic confrontation with herself?

I simply must stop thinking about the past, she told herself that night and on the several nights that followed, but the phantoms weren't to be dispersed without a special effort.

In the last week of August, as the Battle of Britain reached its critical stage, she departed London without leaving word for anyone and traveled to Scotland. She had no idea when she might be back.

CHAPTER XII

WHENEVER ANYONE asked Ann to describe her home, she said that it was an inhabitable space where she could be unnoticed, or at least ignored, and where she could hope to be more or less unaware of herself. Bellancourt was a large, square building with two uneven wings drafted as an afterthought, a lodge, a long, low garage in which the previous owners had kept sheep for some three hundred years, a perpetually drowned tennis court, and many climbing paths that led into the foothills of the Scottish

Highlands. It stood dead center in one thousand acres of gorse, sloped heather, long-needled pine, and mist. It possessed neither lawns, box hedges, mazes, formal gardens, rookeries, or roses, grace, beauty, or tranquility, nor anything else associated with the stately homes of England's noble rich. Since England lay several hundred miles to the south, this wasn't particularly surprising.

In the train, in the dispiriting night-long stench of cheap cigarettes and uniformed men and women, she thought that perhaps she ought to do something connected with the war. *Slacker* had become a term as abusive as *Conshie* had been in the First World War. But what to do and how to go about it? Driving an admiral's limousine seemed like a remarkably small sacrifice to preserve the British way of life. So did the shuffling of medical reports and inspecting bedpans. She couldn't imagine herself stamping around an antiaircraft gun in ammunition boots or polishing a searchlight, yet these were all minor acts of faith that called for compliance. In moments of real crisis, she knew by experience, one tends to cling to old clichés like an infant monkey to its mother's coat, yet the image of the time was a persuasive one: the armies of the Hun were poised to spring across the Channel on an unready Britain, and something simply had to be done about that.

In truth, the situation was nearing disaster. No one who lived in England at the end of August doubted that a great crisis was at hand. No matter how it was conceived, or when it began, the Battle of Britain had become a very real struggle for Britain's survival, bought with the lives of five hundred and twenty fighter pilots of many nationalities who died at the rate of about one hundred and seventy-five a month. It moved, almost by its own volition, from one of four distinct phases to another, so that the several separate but overlapping campaigns were thought of as one, and each of these was a step toward a final dramatic denouement.

Yet what could this be, other than defeat? Enslavement within those *new Dark Ages* that Winston Churchill had spoken of in June? The six-week German *Kanalkampf* against British coastal convoys in the English Channel had strained the RAF's Fighter Command to dangerous limits. One hundred of the RAF's ablest fighter pilots had been killed. The rest were exhausted. The brave young replacements fell out of the sky in dozens every day. Between July 1 and August 11, one hundred and twenty-four RAF machines were destroyed in the air and sixty-two in accidents on the ground. In the next twelve days, forty-four machines crashed when their worn-out pilots made mistakes on takeoff, and another hundred and thirty-five were shot down in combat. German bomber losses had been higher than those of British fighters from the start, but now the gap was beginning to close. Suddenly, the Luftwaffe's commanders saw a real chance to destroy the RAF's ability to resist, to gain control of the air above Britain's harbors, industrial centers, factories, and cities, and so to begin the process with which the waiting world had become so terribly familiar: the merciless and systematic German pounding of a helpless enemy into dust. They launched an all-out air offensive against radar stations, attempting to *blind* Britain. They attacked fighter airfields, giving the pilots and ground crews no rest. In the last six days of that disastrous month, all but a few RAF stations in England were attacked and many were wrecked. The radar chain that controlled British fighter tactics was pierced and disrupted at several points. Waves of German bombers droned in the English skies under the steel umbrella of massed Messerschmitts, and the fabric of defense began to crack. Yet no one, Ann least of all, would voice the thought that there might be wisdom in making peace with Hitler.

Indeed, she thought, strangely moved and determined that none of her pride would show, the best way to guarantee a British victory is to assume that Englishmen are willing to surrender. Scratch an Englishman (or woman, she supposed) and under the lacquer of bland self-concern and cultivated unimportance you'll find a raging patriot every time. She thought that the discomfort of the train jammed with men and women in khaki and two shades of blue, the stench of unwashed bodies, sweated wool, stale beer, and uneasy dreams, was small penance for years of national indifference. Her own sins of omission called for expiation; a weekend with her parents and their inevitable guests would go a longer way toward settling her accounts with the unforgiving island gods. No one who lacked a talent for self-entertainment ever came to Bellancourt more than twice, unless their incomes depended upon it.

What usually happened there was that everyone wandered alone in the round, sheep-infested hills, and then drank tea or malt whiskey at appropriate hours. The women sat in one of several drawing rooms and chatted about friends who hadn't come down for that particular weekend—a euphemism, since the distance involved in traveling from London required at least a fortnight for the visit. The men fired shotguns at small birds, played billiards, smoked cigars, and talked about the varieties of weather to be found elsewhere. On rare occasions, Ann would find an embittered ally wandering around the paneled stone galleries and hallways, but, most of the time, she could count on being quite alone. Her parents hadn't spoken to each other in Ann's memory, so that she could believe they might not even notice she was there.

Coming back to London might (or might not) have been a mistake. Involvement in the lives of others had always been a trap, the more dangerous if there were foreigners about. Coming back to Bellancourt was probably no different. Time will tell, she murmured to herself while renting a car that might take her the last twenty miles north of Aberdeen. And then she shrugged and assumed her most contemptuous expression because time, judged in her own experience, seldom told her anything except *I told you so*.

Ann arrived in time for dinner. The journey had been a dreadful twenty hours. The train had stopped twice in open fields while Midlands cities were bombed in the night, and then it was shunted into sidings while troop trains crawled past, and then there were the hours in Crewe while police and Home Guards came aboard to inspect ration books and identity cards in search of German spies. Some Norwegian sailors, a Czech pilot, and an Irish nun had had a particularly difficult time of it, she remembered.

She felt tired, clammy, gritty-eyed, and ravenously hungry and wanted nothing more than a hot bath, a little food, and a good night's sleep, but that was not the way that things were done at

Bellancourt. The food was Scottish and deplorable: broth in which mutton had been boiled, a few bony victims of that morning's shooting, then the mutton, carrots, and potatoes, then little cups of custard and blancmange. Her father and his friends sat at one end of the long refectory table, her mother and the women sat behind a barricade of candlesticks and artificial flowers at the other. Ann, a latecomer for whom no seating plans had been made, sat midway between the male and the female contingents, with Wally Hudson, her brother-in-law, at her left, and Mrs. Smallwood, her mother's transplanted Canadian crony, at her right. Derek, recently returned from Lisbon, sat across the table between Mr. and Mrs. Yellowstone, whom she particularly disliked. Originally Hungarian, they had made themselves more English than the King James Bible and seemed to live in permanent fear that someone might call their bluff.

Yet even Bellancourt could harbor a surprise, and she watched and listened to John Laidlaw at her father's end of the table with the confused feelings of one experiencing a familiar nightmare. In moments, the carefully stacked barricades of the years turned to rubble and she was—once again—at Oxford, a willing and fascinated victim of his manipulations, confiding in him as though he were a benevolent confessor (as well as her lover), while he arranged the destruction of one young idealist after another.

The Oxford images evoked by this ruthless politician, now surprisingly a Minister of the Crown, were those of noisy young men determined not to get killed in another war, and of some determinedly intelligent young women who trooped through John Laidlaw's rooms like the changing of the Palace Guard. They were too young and confused to know whether they were being loyal or disloyal, idealistic or subversive. Their communism was all the more fanatical because it was unschooled. Laidlaw, whom all of them had trusted as the only tutor who took his humanities to heart, had used her to expose the others, so that it had become important to her to remember them as noble and betrayed rather than as merely naïve. Now, listening to Laidlaw once again, watching the bland, self-assured face, she felt as though she were reliving a disaster.

—What is *he* doing here? she hissed, and Wally Hudson, who, along with Derek, worked for a committee chaired by Laidlaw at the Foreign Office, gave her an odd, hooded glance as he said:

—It's official business, I expect.

—Who's he going to drive to suicide here?

Cautiously, as if an attack upon his superior were a direct threat to himself, Hudson said: Aren't you being a little extreme?

—Yes, she snapped. There was a boy at college who found *him* extreme.

—Shepperton, he named the first of her lovers. Gerald Shepperton. I remember the case. Shocking thing, of course.

—Oh, quite, Ann said. Shocking. Terribly awkward for Mr. Laidlaw, as you can imagine. But how clever of poor Gerry Shepperton to have hanged himself on his own Paisley tie, don't you think? How do you suppose he ever thought of that?

—You shouldn't . . . ah . . . dwell on that sort of thing, Ann, Wally Hudson said. It was all so many years ago.

—And time cancels crime, does it? The years absolve us all? The trouble with idealism, cousin, is that some poor fool invariably believes the rhetoric. And then things get awkward for everyone. Everything works well enough if one remains a cynic.

—Oh, quite, of course, Hudson said uneasily.

—Yes. Quite. Well, there's not much to be done about it now, I expect. Spilled milk, and all that. I'm sure that Mr. Laidlaw didn't worry about it overlong.

—Perhaps one should be careful in picking one's ideals, Wally Hudson offered, and she could no longer conceal her contempt.

—Like one's love affairs?

—I really wouldn't know much about that, would I, Ann? he retreated.

Grinning as if her sanity depended upon it, Ann said: Well, I would. In detail. And that includes confusing physical attraction with those so-called spiritual values. One can delude oneself very nicely until people start hanging themselves on their Paisley neckties, just because they've been betrayed by their best friends and lovers. That's when things get awkward for everyone. Not much fun, you see, making love or college revolutions when things get that awkward.

—I'm sorry, Ann, Hudson muttered humbly.

—Why should you be? I never gave *you* a Paisley tie for Christmas.

It was no better at her father's end of the dinner table, where politics, finance, the economics of war, and the great air battles over southern England were being discussed. RAF Spitfires and Hurricanes had shot down thirty-five Messerschmitts earlier in the day, for a loss of thirty, and Mr. Yellowstone was moved to exclaim: Ours?

—No, Cousin Wally muttered. *Ours.*

Amused, John Laidlaw said: Really, Hudson! Are those the proper sentiments for a member of an inter-Allied liaison committee?

—One can work with the foreign beggars, Minister, Cousin Wally murmured. One doesn't have to like them.

—Quite right, said Ann's father. Exactly. Can't see what good they'll do us anyway. I mean, look at the damn Frogs. But we can't very well leave them to the Huns either, what? That's not the British way.

—Actually, some of them are quite useful at the moment, John Laidlaw said. The Prime Minister is delighted with them.

—Winston likes them? Ann's father said, astonished. Whyever would he do that? The man's English to the core, for all that damned American blood in his veins.

—Fighter Command has more than five hundred of them, including the colonials, and they're all good pilots.

—Foreigners? Colonials? Ann's father voiced the evident dismay of the Smallwoods and the Yellowstones. Whatever can Winston be thinking of?

—England's survival, I expect, said John Laidlaw. It *is* all rather touch and go at the moment, I'm afraid.

—Touch and balderdash! Ann's father exploded. Our chaps are beating the pants off the Hun and you know it, Laidlaw.

—Not quite, sir, I'm afraid, Laidlaw said. We keep this sort of news from the journalists, but I've toured fighter stations where terrified ground crews huddled in their shelters and forced the pilots to fuel and rearm their own machines during air attacks. The Hurricanes and Spitfires climb into battle among falling bombs and return to wreckage. It's all going to be a rather close-run thing.

—You really shouldn't be spreading despondency and gloom, John, Lord Bellancourt said. I mean, *that* isn't going to help much, is it? No, I should think that's the last thing we need.

—Sorry, sir, said the Minister. But it is rather a good idea to face unpleasant realities now and then, otherwise they might overwhelm us all. I remember my own feeling of dismay when I heard Air Vice Marshal Keith Park, who commands the fighter sector that's defending London, say the same thing to Churchill. I had gone with the Prime Minister to a briefing at Air Chief Marshal Sir Hugh Dowding's Fighter Command headquarters. The PM, who hates Dowding for refusing to waste all of his hoarded Hurricanes in the defense of France, attempted to humiliate him by speaking only to his subordinate, Park, and he was quite sarcastic when he asked when reserve squadrons might be sent up to stem the German onslaught. *We have none*, Park said simply and, for the first time since any of us have known him, Churchill was lost for words.

—Well, that's not our fault, Minister, said Mr. Yellowstone who, having been the treasurer of the Bellancourt interests, had now become a moving force in the Ministry of Aircraft Production. We're keeping up our end of it. The assembly lines are matching the attrition rate quite well.

—In aircraft, certainly, said John Laidlaw with an amused glance up and down the table. Unfortunately, we can't manufacture experienced fighter pilots in quite the same way. Our own chaps are deathly tired. Some of them have been flying six sorties a day since the first of July. Eighty of Dowding's best squadron and flight leaders are gone. His new men are going up against the Messerschmitts with twenty hours of Spitfires in their logbooks, and they're getting knocked down in their first fight. What's happened, you see, is that Goering's got our fighters into a meat-grinder battle that only he can win. According to Dowding's projections, his Fighter Command has only six weeks of life left at most.

—Damn the tricky Continental swine, Ann's father said, and Mr. Yellowstone coughed into his napkin.

—Trust the Hun not to play it fair, Cousin Wally murmured

in the sudden silence, and Ann looked at him with mild, apprecia-
tive surprise.

She wished that she could like him, as he probably deserved to
be liked, and she thought that she might have if he hadn't made
her feel hunted and pursued. He had grayed and narrowed since
she had seen him last. His mild eyes had darkened. The diffidence
of his earlier years had resolved itself into mere patience, and he
appeared to have become the sort of man for whom compromise
was a duty. She knew the kind well. Sooner or later, almost everyone she knew became resigned to smallness and defeat and to the
little daily treasons that sapped whatever youthful vision of themselves they ever might have had. His life, she thought, had become a day-by-day retreat. She thought him incapable of either
outrage or real devotion; he'd be committed to nothing more
than his own survival.

Time had passed, the dusk of evening had turned into night.
There was a smell of rooks and old chimneys in the high-ceilinged
room. Like Britain herself, she supposed, this cold room had the
unfinished elegance of a place where people lived slightly beyond
their means. The rich Turkish carpet showed unraveling threads;
a maid had missed a crumpled theater program under the
credenza; there were dark rectangles on the striped wallpaper
where portraits of Neville Chamberlain and some of her father's
other discredited political associates had been taken down. Some
small pieces were missing from the chandelier.

Fearing Laidlaw, or perhaps detesting her own contempt for
weakness, she could admit to fascination with his subtle exercise
of power, and she contrasted Hudson's troubled silences with the
peremptory self-confidence of the stronger man. Yet she didn't
want to judge her cousin harshly; she remembered his many attempts to render her a kindness.

—Sarcasm? she said softly. I wouldn't have expected it of you,
Wally. You've been changing on me, have you?

—In some things, I haven't, he muttered within his unsuccessful military moustache, and Ann, conscious of Mrs. Smallwood's
ears and Derek's fixed grin, said rapidly: Oh, for God's sake, hang
it up, will you? I'm not your damned retirement policy.

—I've never thought of you as that, Ann, Hudson said.

—Well, stop thinking whatever you have thought about me. It just won't happen, will you understand?

He ducked his head, blinked rapidly, and bowed over his food, and she thought with wry self-contempt that things hadn't changed since her Oxford days as much as she had hoped. She was still arrogant, still terribly injured. People were still getting hurt when she was around. She had loved neither Shepperton nor Laidlaw. She had barely begun to learn how to love herself.

—Ah, Hudson said then with that bitter and superior air that she loathed in all other Englishmen she knew. You've some other bloody little Continental on the string? As always?

—Dozens of them, of course, she snapped while Derek grinned derisively across the dinner table. As always. What did you expect?

In that odd, coincidental way that turns several private and seemingly unrelated conversations into one, Mr. Yellowstone cried out at that moment: But we've been knocking 'em down in dozens every day! How long can Goering keep up *his* fighter losses, then?

—Actually, our figures aren't quite as good as all that, John Laidlaw said. What's not generally known is that most RAF victories in the last six weeks have been against lone reconnaissance machines and unescorted bombers. Whenever we've come up against massed Messerschmitts, we've generally gotten the worse of it.

—That's damn disloyal, John! said Ann's father. I'm surprised at you. I'm sure that you're not speaking for Winston at this moment.

—Indeed I am, sir, the Minister said. Say what you like, our foreign volunteers are damn important to us now. For some of them, like the Poles, this is their third war against the Messerschmitts and they know their business.

—Poles? cried Ann's father. What the devil would Poles know about machinery? They still think that the fastest thing on earth is a horse! Isn't that so, Hudson? You know them, you've learned that dreadful language of theirs, which, I must say, is going a bit far. But am I right or not?

—Actually, they're doing quite well in the air, sir, Cousin

Wally said. They think themselves superior to machines, they're not awed by mechanical limitations, so they get more out of their equipment than anyone else.

And was it her imagination, then, that Laidlaw looked at her as he said, softly but with authority: They're something of a godsend to us at the moment.

—Only if you assume that God has a curiously perverted sense of humor, Mr. Yellowstone said unpleasantly, and Derek laughed and winked knowingly at Ann.

A godsend? That seemed a bit much, yet she *had* begun to think of Ludo as somehow providential. Why else should a man born in one part of the world, designed and raised to function in one specific set of cultural circumstances, meet a woman born in (and created for) a wholly different part, and why should they find themselves the complementary missing parts of each other's jigsaw puzzle, unless it were ordained? And shouldn't she at least trust God to know what He was doing? She had placed the various fragments of her life in much worse hands than that!

John Laidlaw, Gerald Shepperton, and at least a dozen other accidental lovers had offered an illusion of importance to a life in which paradox set the rules, and she was no longer willing to assume that any one person could direct her course. If they were such good guides, why were they always losing their own way? *You have something of a mind,* Laidlaw had said to her eighteen years ago, *and you can't expect it to remain content with the little that you seem to want to offer it.* Perhaps the time had come to try a different mental and emotional diet.

In the meantime, Derek was watching her, curiously amused, and, on an impulse, she stuck out her tongue at him. Damn him. Damn them all. And damn that odd, complex man she had found sprawled among the other flotsam on her private beach. Damn him more than all the others for bringing about a moment of impulse and renewed illusion. Oh, it was all such a bloody, *bloody* waste!

The thought that Laidlaw might be aware of her connection with Ludo was unbearable; it seemed to guarantee disaster. Yet if

Derek knew about it, and he did because she herself had mentioned it to him in Lisbon, then Laidlaw would know it too.

—I can't presume to speak for God, he was saying then. Keeping up with Winston Churchill's thinking is difficult enough. But I do know that German fighter skills are incomparably superior to those in most British squadrons, and that we've no other pilots as experienced as the Poles. They're much more highly trained than all but a few of our own prewar RAF professionals. And they hate the Germans.

—I still say it's dangerous to trust these foreign Johnnies with anything more complicated than a bayonet, Lord Bellancourt said. Clive armed his sepoys with spears in India, you know. A damn sensible thing.

—Nobody has to trust anyone very much, Laidlaw said. That's hardly the question. It's just a matter of using everybody where they're the most useful.

—Everyone in the know is quite aware that there's no such thing as a *Battle of Britain* anyway, Ann's father objected. It's just another of Winston's brilliant phrases, designed for the Americans. How did that go, by the way? *The Battle of France is over . . . a Battle of Britain is about to begin . . .* and then something about a *new Dark Ages* and *Britain's finest hour.* Winston always did make a bloody good speech.

—It may have been inspired rhetoric at the start, John Laidlaw said quietly. But there's a very real Battle of Britain now.

She heard them but she had ceased to listen. She thought it likely that everyone, including her parents, would forget within days that she had come home, and she looked forward to that hushed, gray quality of her interior air in which she could begin to come to terms with her unchanged world.

There was some thinking to be done here, that was clear. Bellancourt's one unfailing virtue had been solitude and time. She could walk the round hills and wait for the next inevitable accident to happen. Sooner of later, she knew, she'd have to seize control of her own life, however that might present itself to her.

And then . . . what? she asked herself in the cold gray after-dinner gloom, while the candles guttered and the fire burned down. One really couldn't be so professionally English as to say that life had to be lived because it was there. That wouldn't take into account her sense of uselessness, futility, and boredom. At least men invented wars to fight when they could think of nothing more intelligent to do. She had had no useful occupation since she had been her father's gun bearer in these hills at the age of twelve.

That night, there was a storm. Sometime toward midnight, all the electric lights went out in the house while white sheets of fire rippled across the sky, and when she rang the bell in her room nobody came. She went downstairs to the library, where (she thought) a fire might be glowing in the grate, but when she got there the stone hearth was cold. The storm raged on beyond the windows where, at one time, a cohort of imported gardeners had tried to impose a roseate English order on a Scottish moor, and she felt very much alone, huddled against the night and looking at cold ashes. And then she listened to the slow, precise fall of approaching footsteps on the granite flagstones behind her tall chair.

—If you're the family ghost, she said, go to hell.

—I used to go there quite often when I was a boy, John Laidlaw said quietly. But it's like taking your holidays in the Greek islands, do you know? It's quite middle-class if you visit more than once, and you certainly wouldn't want to talk about it to anyone you knew.

In the red glow of the thick votive candle he had set on the flagstones near his knees, his face was gaunt with shadow. He set about rekindling the fire.

—There, he said. It'll catch now. Whatever made your father buy this drafty old pile of stones?

—The need to be the baron that his title made him, I suppose, Ann said.

—Well, it's damned difficult to get a good night's sleep here.

—Oh? Ann said and listened to her own revealing bitterness. And here I thought it was your conscience that sent you snooping along the battlements at midnight.

—I'm not the Devil, he said. Neither am I God. I don't accept responsibility for other people's pain. I've no trouble with my conscience because everything I do serves a better cause.

—Gerry Shepperton would've been glad to hear that.

—He was told. He didn't care to listen. But I didn't come here to discuss undergraduates who thought that talking about a revolution was the same thing as making one. I came to ask you to do some work for me when you return to London.

—I wouldn't dream of it, she said.

—I think I might be able to persuade you once more. You'd really be doing the country quite a service.

—Sorry, Minister, Ann said. I lack my brother's capacity for malice or, for that matter, Wally Hudson's hopeless pursuit of a secure old age. You'll have to do without me in your Bellancourt collection.

—I think you'll find that you don't have any choice.

—Are you threatening me? Because if you've some sort of blackmail in mind, then you'd better know that old infidelities don't embarrass anymore. Not even in this dreadful household.

—Perish the thought, he said. I came to ask, not threaten. You've qualities that could be truly useful. In fact, I can't think of anyone I'd trust to do this job as well as you might do it. You always were an extraordinary woman, Ann, and now you've a chance to do something really important for us all. I wasn't joking at dinner when I said that this is going to be a difficult war to win.

—I can't quite see myself in a fighter plane, she said.

—What I've in mind may be a lot more useful than shooting down a few Huns.

—I don't drive cars all that well either, she said. I've wrecked three in five years and I've never been able to change a tire.

Patient, as he had always been with her, he went along with her necessary rejoinders.

—We draw our cars from the Ministry pool, he said. They come complete with girls called Daphne and Opal who drive them into lampposts. I've something else in mind for you.

—I will not polish searchlights, she said. I will not wear that awful battle dress. And I will not salute. I have no clerical qualifications whatsoever, Minister, as you should damn well know.

—Please don't call me Minister, he said. I've not become as pompous as all that.

—I feel a terrible need for formality, she said. It must be something in this awful air. Or perhaps it's a way to defend myself against men like you, who know more about me than I can think about with any degree of comfort. You do know that, John, don't you?

He shrugged, smiled, said: I've always known it, Ann.

—Ah, then you have thought about me now and then.

—You aren't an easy woman to forget about.

—Yes. Well. Oxford was a terribly long time ago, Minister, she said. Now, what do you think I'd be able to do?

—You've already started doing it. You know General Prus, don't you? You speak French and German?

She listed her accomplishments as if they were sins recited in confession.

—And some Italian, and a little Spanish, and a bit of good demotic Greek. And I've given up spying and reporting on my friends, Minister, if that's what you have in mind. One filthy little horror of that kind is enough with or without ivy-covered walls.

—Yes, that's quite out of fashion this year, he said seriously, and she could laugh again without affectation.

—Well, isn't that a comfort? But if I'm not to spy on anyone, drive your car, type your memoranda, or polish your desk, what would you want me for?

—I want you to be exactly what you've always been, John Laidlaw said.

—Bloody hell! said Ann.

—You're a cultivated, cosmopolitan Englishwoman who knows how to deal with Continental Europeans. By which I *don't* mean overtipping them. I need you to open doors for me, that's all.

—Back doors or front doors? Ann said. And what about the windows?

—Whatever has to be opened at a given time.

—Never again my bedroom door, Minister.

—That's taken for granted. You've the perfect background to create the sort of aristocratic social atmosphere in which all these professional democrats like Sikorski, Prus, de Gaulle, and Masaryk can feel at ease with me. You're the sort of Englishwoman they've admired for a thousand years without really knowing what it was they found admirable. I want them to think of me as Ann Bellancourt's friend, rather than as the Whitehall civil servant who controls their purse strings and may not, necessarily, have only their best interests in mind.

—And what will they think of you without Ann Bellancourt's aristocratic atmospheres? Ann asked, although she didn't really want to know.

—They view me, perhaps with some justification, as the sort of Englishman who has manipulated their histories for three hundred years. They call me *The Minister for Unpleasant Affairs*.

—Which is exactly what you are, Minister, isn't it? Ann said.

—We're English, Ann, John Laidlaw said and shrugged. We do have our duty.

—Over which the sun never sets, Ann said.

—Quite. And the moment that it does will be the end of Europe. Winston's *new Dark Age* has never been very far away, and it is only our English civilization that keeps it at bay.

—I don't know, Ann said. I'll have to think about it. *Minister for Unpleasant Affairs*, eh? That doesn't sound very encouraging.

—Political wit is seldom accurate, John Laidlaw said. In my department, I'm known as *Winston's other hatchet*. The reference is to Lady Churchill, I believe.

—What a horribly unfair thing to say about Clementine Churchill, Ann said. And what would I be called? Laidlaw's Circe?

—There's no reason for anyone to know that what you'd be doing is at all official. In fact, there's every reason for no one to know it. And it would be tremendously helpful in dealing with people like Sikorski, Prus, and some of their newer men that we don't know very much about.

—I do like Janusz Prus, she said. I quite like . . . the Poles.

—I know you do, he said and she waited for him to bring up Ludo's name but he went on: You'll like Masaryk, the Czech Foreign Minister in London. He's an excellent man. I think you'll like Sikorski. Winston might find him difficult to deal with, but he's the only real leader the Poles have at the moment. Your friend Prus is quite devoted to him, isn't he?

—Yes, Ann said. In quite the same way that the younger Poles seem to be devoted to Janusz.

—That's terribly interesting, Ann, John Laidlaw said. We weren't quite sure about that. You do see what a help you could be to us, don't you?

—I'm afraid I do, Ann said. No matter what you call it, John, I'm to be a spy for you again.

—Oh, that's quite the wrong way to look at it! John Laidlaw protested. I merely want you to be yourself, doing what you want . . . there's nothing *infra dig* about that, is there?

—I don't know, Ann said. I'll have to think about it.

Her tone of voice might have suggested doubt, but she knew that she had already made up her mind, and Laidlaw, unless she was quite wrong about his powers of perception, knew it too.

—John, she said in a firmer tone. Do you know what I've always thought about you?

—Yes. Most of the time.

—I don't believe I've ever hated anyone as much as I hated you after that mess at Oxford. Slit wrists, no less! Nobody needed to give *me* a necktie for Christmas! How's that for the imperturbable British upper crust? You were the first of my truly memorable disasters. But even then I thought you the best kind of imperial Englishman. You were fearless, ruthless, cynical, polished, and urbane . . . and no more to be trusted than I was myself. Yet there was always a cause under everything you did.

—Therein lies the explanation and the expiation, John Laidlaw said.

—Perhaps. I've rather given up on causes. Until quite recently, I thought that I had given up on people as well. But perhaps I haven't. I wouldn't want anything to happen to anyone I like.

—I don't see how that could happen, Ann, John Laidlaw said. We all want a decent Europe to live in after the war. We're all working toward the same ends. There's no way in which your new Polish friends could be disappointed in us or in you.

—I want your promise that I'll never have to betray anyone for whom I care deeply, Ann said. I simply wouldn't be able to bear the aftermath again.

—I can't imagine such a thing becoming necessary, John Laidlaw said. In fact, let me suggest in strictest confidence that the very best of your new friends can benefit quite considerably from what we've in mind.

—And who might that be?

They were silent then, for a time: strangers who shared a ghost. The pull of intimacy made them ill at ease. What better way to emphasize her suspicion of him than an object of common interest that neither would name? She told herself that he couldn't be aware of her affair with Ludo, yet she knew, even then, that she was lying to herself again. She was—she had to be—equally wrong about his continuing ability to harm her. Her fear of him had unhinged her objectivity, she was sure. Guilt made her censorious.

—If, she said, I did do what you want, not that I'm saying I will, I'd want two other guarantees. One is my own privacy. I wouldn't tolerate it if someone spied on me. My life must remain totally my own.

—I've never thought of it as anything else, he said.

—And finally, if I am to be your arranger of atmospheres or whatever you care to call it, I'd want to be sure that neither Wally Hudson nor my brother know anything about it. Like you, John, you see, I don't believe in giving anyone an unearned advantage.

—Of course, John Laidlaw said. I guarantee the confidentiality. So what's your answer, Ann?

She sighed and said in a voice that sounded tired and resigned, even to herself: Well, it *is* better than polishing brass mountings on a Bofors gun. I'll think about it, Minister.

—Thank you, Ann, he said. Give me a ring when you're back in town.

—I'll think about it, Minister, Ann said.

During the next few days, she wondered why she had allowed herself to enter Laidlaw's plans and thought of several explanations. Bellancourt and its cast had had its effect. It had been a painfully sharp reminder of how much she detested the insincerities, cruelties, and posturings to which she had been born. She felt far more at ease in a foreign air which didn't trouble her conscience, and the Minister offered an opportunity for service in that atmosphere. She needed to believe that Laidlaw's promises could be trusted despite past experience, that nothing she did for him would endanger anyone she cared for, or place her own self-respect in jeopardy, and that by being useful to her new friends (as well as to her country) she'd make amends for her Oxford past. She thought, although she wouldn't admit it to herself just yet, that in helping to bring together the Poles whom she continued to admire, with the sort of Englishmen whom she wanted to admire the most, she would be bridging whatever gaps existed between herself and Ludo.

In truth, and in the time's own air of recklessness and hazard, she didn't think that the alliance between the Poles and Britain could ever be threatened. Each side had begun to earn too much of the other's gratitude and affection. Laidlaw hadn't exaggerated the desperate nature of the battle at the end of August, nor who was proving the most useful in it. The Poles, and the First Canadian Squadron, went into action in that critical moment, and the battered British could finally draw a breath. Some hundred and forty Polish pilots had been flying with British squadrons from the start, but now they had their own independent squadrons, manned wholly by themselves, and, within days, their quality made itself felt. As the BBC and her father's *Times* and *Scotsman* reported, 303 Squadron (Polish) shot down fourteen Messerschmitts and crippled five others in its first day of combat, then six more fighters and ten bombers on the second day. Flying ten record sorties on the last day of August, Ludo's men destroyed eighteen German fighters. Nine bombers had been seen to smoke, but not to explode or plunge into the furrowed Kentish fields, so they were counted as "probables" rather than as confirmed victories, and the tide of the battle had begun to turn. Unlike the untried young RAF replacements, whose heroism could seldom tip the scales of victory against cold German skill, the Poles had brought into the battle the icy expertise of seasoned veterans. They had already shot down a hundred and thirty-eight German aircraft over Poland and forty-eight over France. They were remarkable marksmen whose first three squadrons took the top three places in the RAF spring gunnery exercises, and the British press exulted in their contempt for danger. Their practice was to close within one hundred feet of an enemy machine before opening fire, and they fought with no regard for their own lives or safety. Six of them died over London when, out of ammunition, they rammed German bombers.

Trying to understand their savage dedication, it was convenient for the journalists to say that they fought like madmen—madness being the only way to explain courage beyond ordinary under-standing—but their enthusiasm, spirit, and élan in battle infected everyone. They couldn't show themselves in an English pub without causing a storm of heartfelt and genuine applause. And Ann, of course, whenever she read or heard anything about them, saw each of them as Ludo.

With this in mind, and carried on the wave of general enthusi-asm, how could she doubt Laidlaw's purpose or question his mo-tives? Even her father, whose xenophobia had acquired the weight of a religion, began to make complimentary sounds about Polish fighter pilots.

She returned to London in the middle of September, a day to be known thereafter as *Bloody Sunday*. She telephoned Prus at the Rubens Hotel on Buckingham Palace Road, where the reorga-nized Polish Armed Forces in the United Kingdom had their gen-eral headquarters. He was delighted to hear from her again. He told her that Ludo had reached his squadron at about the time that she had gone to Scotland, but she had already read about him in her father's *Times*.

CHAPTER XIII

THAT DAY, which would be both the turning point of the battle and its most violent chapter, dawned in a cold mist over southern England. The clouds were variable at three thousand feet, there was a weak west wind that swirled among the buildings, and as the Hurricanes rose above the South Gate of Northolt Air Sta-tion, they were caught in the burbling downdraft. Their takeoff was toward the northwest, across trees and above the pretty, green, delineated suburb, and Ludo could bless the Rolls-Royce Merlin III engines, whose twelve liquid-cooled cylinders gave the humpbacked fighters one thousand and thirty horsepower to lift them steeply above danger. Even so, Wilchurzak was pulled down and crashed.

Gentleman Johnny Sommerset, the Canadian pilot and regular RAF officer who led them that morning, was talking with the ground controllers, who were reporting a mass enemy assembly over the French coast near Calais, and Ludo took a quick look around, then counted his men. Gerlach waggled his wings for him. Reszke nodded under his big bubble canopy and cocked his thumb upward in that half-mocking gesture they had all learned from the British pilots, and Frantisek, the Czech who pretended to a vast historic disaffection with the Poles but who had refused to fly with any other squadron, pushed open his canopy and lit a cigar.

—Two vector five, the controller's voice crackled in their earphones. Eagles One and Two, Maple Leaf One, you'll find forty bandits at eighteen thousand angels, fifty at twenty-six. Many more assembling. And for God's sake, Eagles, don't bugger the frequency for me, will you, please?

—Roger, Ops, Johnny Sommerset said, and then in French: Écoutez-vous, messieurs?

—Ask them if we're to expect anyone we know, Johnny, Reszke said.

Reinecke's orange-nosed Geschwader, known throughout the RAF as the Calais Gang, had been identified in the Calais region, and there were debts to pay.

—Just *Hell's grim tyrant*, I expect, the Canadian squadron leader said. But you can keep hoping.

—Now look here, Eagle One, do button it down! Why do you always have to talk so much? the controller said. Do keep the frequencies clear for instruction.

—The boys like to know who's coming out to play, Johnny Sommerset said. But we'll be good. Sorry to give you fits so early, Controller.

—Good hunting, then, and good luck, the controller said.

—And the best of British luck to you, old chap, Gerlach said in his terrible imitation of the English language, and all the others

laughed, and twenty squadrons of Hurricanes and Spitfires heard
the controller say: Aw . . . *bloody* hell!

They flew in silence then, and there was time to think. In the
nineteen days since the squadron had become fully operational,
his men had destroyed one hundred and twenty-six enemy aircraft
and fourteen "probables" and damaged nine others. Their score
for just the last four days was fifty to three. They had had their
first casualties on September 11 when three of them were killed
in a fight with an entire German Geschwader, of whom they shot
down seven. Gerlach was nicked in the foot in that scramble.
Straka, who had reached England only the week before, was
burned around the face when he collided with a Spitfire over
Tunbridge Wells. Reszke was shot down but landed safely by
parachute in a Kentish village. Since he was wearing only striped
pajamas at the time, he was unable to convince the Home
Guards that he was not a German and spent the night in a rural
jail until Johnny Sommerset could come for him next morning.
Now they were airborne again and flying against the greatest German armada assembled against London since the beginning of
the war.

The soft green countryside of England flowed smoothly under
them as they circled the gray smudge pot that was London, and
Ludo thought of the kindness and generosity he and his men had
found there, of the shy, friendly men who put the pints of beer
on the tables and then walked away, of the eager women, of the
quiet sympathy given to them by people who had no reason to expect anything but a disaster of their own. No one in Britain
doubted that this was the most terrible of their hours, yet they all
seemed to know that it was a wonderful one as well. The power
of the German Wehrmacht seemed almost mystical, yet their
stubbornness would save them. Just as the rout at Dunkirk had
been publicized as a heroic British feat, a miraculous rescue rather
than a staggering defeat, so this new felicitously named Battle of
Britain in which they were engaged would demonstrate Britain's
unbreakable resistance. The endless glory of the British people
must include the fact that they never doubted it.

Then they flew south over Kent and angled toward the Channel, climbing steadily to twenty thousand feet, where they cut to
cruising speed to save fuel. Their range was just over five hundred

miles. Their top speed was three hundred and twenty-eight miles an hour—the speed at which the Emils could cruise two thousand feet higher than the top altitude of the Hurricanes. Interception from below would be suicidal. Even so, the Hurricane was a wonderfully dangerous weapon after the P-7s and -11s that most of Ludo's pilots had flown in Poland.

—Guns, gentlemen, Johnny Sommerset said, and each of them fired a short burst from his eight Browning .303-caliber machine guns. The lights winked steadily on Ludo's panel and the stick shuddered lightly in his hand.

—I've a jam, Gerlach said.

—D'you want to go back?

—No. Perhaps they'll clear. Chief Auerbach would tear my head off if I went back for nothing.

—Keep your eyes peeled, gentlemen, Johnny Sommerset said. The Huns should be with us any minute now.

The ground controller called out urgently to the Canadians and the second Polish squadron and they veered sharply to the northeast, wagging their wings in farewell, and Ludo's twelve machines began to move into battle order. No orders were given; none were necessary. The flights formed, one behind the other, like steps rising into the sky behind the lead echelon. They'd have the sun in their eyes but there was nothing they could do about that. The Emils would hit them head on from above. Their one advantage was that the wood-and-fabric fuselage of the Hurricane was more resistant to cannon shells than the all-metal Emils. Half the time, the shells went right through without exploding and, after the first pass, they'd be above the Germans.

Someone (he thought it was Reszke) had begun to whistle. —*Wojenko, wojenko* . . . Little Lady War . . . And then (as suddenly) the whistling stopped.

—I . . . do believe we have company, Reszke said.

The Germans flew in tight order at eighteen thousand feet and about a mile to the north: forty Dornier Do 215 heavy bombers. Wing tip to wing tip, just like over Warsaw. . . . A small force of Bf 110 Zerstorers hung above them and about five hundred feet behind them. . . . The Emils would be on the roof, hidden in the pale sun at thirty thousand feet. It was ten-thirty in the morning and the mists had cleared.

Ludo peered upward, searching for the single-seaters, and then he looked down and saw small white creatures standing about in the peaceful fields, and thought they were sheep. Then he began to laugh and couldn't stop laughing because these were not sheep but men dressed in white and playing their game of cricket on a Sunday morning. He was moved by a wave of sudden affection for this strange, implacable, undemonstrative race which could ignore its own imminent destruction.

What the hell kind of a chance would mere bombers have against that kind of people? he thought, and then Ann's long, dark, well-bred face appeared on his mental screen, and he blinked away the image of the downturned mouth, and the black eyes that seemed like painful bruises pressed into her flesh, and focused on distance.

—Johnny? he said.

—I hear you, the Canadian drawled.

—Let's pass them, get the sun behind us, and shoot them in the back. I don't think they've seen us.

—I bow to your experience, Gentleman Johnny said.

—No, no, Eagle One! the controller shouted. Go straight in as vectored! I'll tell you when to cross sector lines!

—Bloody R/T's gone dead, Johnny Sommerset said. Did you hear something, Ludo?

—Nothing, Ludo said.

—Who do they think they are, bloody Nelsons? the controller raged but, in truth, it was impossible then to hear anything within the one vast sound of several distant battles drawing nearer. The airwaves were full of cries, exhortations, warnings and explosions, calls for help and blasphemous obscenities. The battle raged in a rough hexagon of sixty-by-eighty miles above East Kent, the Channel, and London's East End as more and more enemy formations went into the attack. The Germans came in waves of forty to one hundred bombers at various altitudes from eighteen to twenty-six thousand feet—two hundred and fifty heavy bombers with Stukas below them—and a great assembly of Messerschmitts flying over them.

Ludo's men sailed past the German armada like ships in review, then turned and attacked. They came down from the late-morning sun on the rear of the unsuspecting Germans, falling from twenty-four thousand feet in flights of three, one flight behind the other as if for target practice, and they were through the Zerstorers and among the bombers before one angry stream of tracers could rise up to meet them. They started shooting at a distance of two hundred feet and turned away only when the glass greenhouse-domes of the bomber crew compartments blocked their fields of vision, and shards of metal (flaps, ailerons, shot-away controls) rattled on their wings. They dived through the bombers then turned and attacked them from below while the German gunners were still peppering the Emils which had come down to help them. They shot down three Zerstorers and ten Dorniers on the first pass, three more on the second, and then the shattered enemy formation scattered and ran for home.

In his earphones, Ludo could hear an angry Viennese voice shouting: *Heiliges Sakrament!* By the smothered balls of the innocents, wait! There's only twelve of them!

And then the sky was clear and empty of Germans.

Throughout, as though it were unthinkable for him to do anything else, he had looked for Reinecke but the wily German had eluded him. Since that day when Reinecke's schoolboys had sent him down in flames over Warsaw, and then tried to kill him as he hung unconscious in the shrouds of his tattered parachute, he had fought them a half-dozen times, had shot down ten of them, had watched them kill five of his own men, but he had never come up against Reinecke himself. He looked for him in every dogfight with the orange-nosed Geschwader. The easy Viennese drawl was unmistakable in the ether. He knew by instinct that Reinecke looked for him with the same cold blend of curiosity and respect. But the fights were always too sudden, too swift, and neither of them could catch the other at a disadvantage.

The chase had taken them over the French coast, where they caught a formation of Heinkel He 111s gathering for another flight across the Channel. Without their screening fighters, the Heinkels had no hope of surviving a Hurricane attack. They scattered and fled. Then the Poles came under fire from German antiaircraft artillery which, in turn, scattered them, and they flew back to England in pairs or alone.

Alone, he hesitated only for a moment. Reinecke's forward field was temptingly near. He checked his fuel and armament, then climbed and flew northeast into France.

East of Calais, the ground mist and the morning fog and the sparse cloud cover thinned out even further, and he could look down at the peaceful French countryside, the warm brown fields and the straight, tree-lined highways that would always remind him of wrecked armies, defeat, and surrender, and he did his best to check his contempt as he flew above the sunbaked little towns in which life went on, untroubled, as if nothing had happened there only four months earlier.

Looking down, he saw a shadow skimming the poplars and hiding in the hedgerows and, at first, thought it to be his own. The dark, nimble cruciform hugged the land as he himself had once dodged among trees and haystacks to escape from the grinning Messerschmitts of Reinecke's first squadron, and then he knew that he had found a victim. It was a Fieseler Fi 156 Storch, an unarmed ground-liaison aircraft, and about as dangerous as a gnat. So slow that it could fly at thirty-five miles an hour without stalling, it could land in fifty feet without rounding out, and it could be shot down with an air rifle. Such kills were not counted in the RAF, although at least one foreign ace had made his reputation with seventeen of them.

He banked, cut his throttle, fell out of the cloud, and dropped toward the Storch as slowly as he could, watching the helpless German start his desperate dance of evasion among the trees and spires. Even so, he could be dead in moments, and both of them knew it. The press of all countries had turned fighter pilots into lone, knightly figures who fought chivalric duels in the sky, and that's the way they would ascend into romantic legend; the truth, as Ludo knew too well, was considerably different. Now and then, in the war's earlier days, there may have been moments of pity, of sympathy, of guilt, of rare human impulse, but these were long spent. Truth was, that the most successful of these quite unromantic heroes killed their enemies from ambush, diving at them steeply from the sun, and shooting them in the back. No fighter pilot ever questioned the fact that he would be a legitimate target while drifting, helplessly, in the shrouds of his parachute. German Red Cross float planes, Storches, and British Miles Master trainers and Lysanders were shot down (in passing, as it were) as a matter of course. If a pilot chose not to count such kills, that was his business; the killing, however, was sanctioned and expected.

Yet Ludo didn't kill the German in the dancing Storch. The spindly little airplane skipped out of his way, and he flew on, having neither time nor fuel to waste. As it was, and as the frenzied squawks in his earphones informed him, other and more dangerous enemies were running to their machines only ten miles away. It was his turn, then, to go to ground level and skim the hedges as he drew nearer to his goal. High overhead, rows of gray puffs blossomed out as AA-gunners opened up, less in the hope of hitting him than to show his path to the fighter pilots. The moments of his safety narrowed, and then they were gone.

He flew between trees, so close to the highway that the white summer dust boiled up behind him, and he could read the road signs and the advertisements for wines, hotels, historic landmarks, and the odd bathing beach. He had been there before; a wingless windmill on the left, and a rustic *auberge* on the right, signaled the new German hard-topped side road that wound toward the airfield, and he went up over the trees just high enough to clear them as he turned.

A quick check of his instruments then. The fuel-contents gauge had begun to blink, the oil-pressure wavered, and he switched on the electrically operated reflector sight and set all his guns to FIRE. The pines, beeches, oaks, and chestnuts were distinct, each branch and leaf sharply drawn as they bowed before his slipstream; and then they were gone, and he was in the open, and there were three orange-nosed Messerschmitts speeding toward him on the ground. He dipped his own scarlet spinner just enough to center his gunsights and pressed all his triggers. As the guns responded, and as the Hurricane bucked against the recoil, he pushed the throttle lever wide open and pulled back on the stick and burst into the sky through the oily black smoke of the Messerschmitt that blew up under him. Then he went straight up and over in the classic Immelmann turn, rolling out at the top of the loop so that he flew in the opposite direction. The two Messerschmitts whose flight leader he had killed had cleared the trees at the end of the runway and were climbing steeply right

into his gunsights. He tapped the throttle lever back and eased
the stick forward just enough to dip his guns toward them, and
steadied his machine with gentle pressure on the stick and opposite rudder. Each of his movements was consciously unhurried, as
if he had all the time in the world to set out his tools, and—
feeling neither anger nor pity nor elation—he shot them down
one after the other on that single pass from above and behind.
The second plane, hit from fifty feet right into the cockpit, had
been so close that Ludo saw the German pilot's mouth moving as
he cursed him.

They fell and burned among trees in great, greasy clouds of
black smoke edged with red-and-orange, and he wondered in an
offhand, disinterested fashion how old these two pilots might have
been. He doubted that their combined ages could have totaled
more than forty years. Fighter pilots on both sides were getting
younger every day (Urban, his own squadron's infant, had just
turned nineteen), and no experienced, battle-wary flier would
have climbed with such single-minded innocence toward certain
death as these two had done. Had one of them been Reinecke, or
his Austrian countryman "Joschko" Fozo, or Heinz Bär, or Max-
Helmuth Ostermann, or Wilhelm Balthasar, or Hans-Karl Mayer
(whom Ludo had shot down and killed only the week before),
his Immelmann would have been anticipated and the Messerschmitts would have been somewhere else.

These were dangerous skies. Climbing, he twisted, made unexpected irregular turns, listened to the angry German voices in his
earphones. Anywhere along the Channel coast, he could encounter men like Werner Mölders, Adolf Galland, Helmut Wick,
Herbert Ihlefeld, Joachim Müncheberg, Walter Oseau, or Hans-
Joachim Marseille—the "dog-collar soldiers" of the Luftwaffe
fighter arm who wore the Ritterkreuz at the neck and who had
shot down more than three hundred Hurricanes and Spitfires between them. Even in light of the odd Luftwaffe habit of multi-
plying air victories by three, these were not pilots to be taken ca-
sually, and all but three of them worked in the air zones assigned
to the Poles. Entering their air, one moved as cautiously as if
coming upon a wolf's lair in a forest; young pilots remembered
every childhood prayer at such times.

He gained height in tight, rapid turns among the bursting antiaircraft shells, and scanned the sky above him and behind him at each turn. The sun had climbed high enough to be dangerous but nothing came from it on this Sunday morning. Arriving alone, he had evaded detection until his meeting with the Storch, so that no sentry squadron had been sent to lay an ambush in the sun. He regarded the deadly little puffs of gray-and-black smoke around him with academic interest. At twenty thousand feet, a Hurricane offered a frustrating target; small, and moving swiftly, it was almost impossible to hit from the ground.

—Bark all you want, he said. The horse has been stolen.

Once more alone, a pale and dwindling speck concealed in the vastness of an empty sky, he set his course for home. He had killed three Germans. He had not been hit. It had been a rather ordinary Sunday morning.

Cold in his shirtsleeves, he switched on the electric heater, activated the air vents, and lit a cigar. Equally cold and gray and deadly and unfeeling, the Channel beckoned to him under wisps of cloud. The horizon tilted. He watched the forest of masts fixed in the Goodwin Sands, the rusting hulks of torpedoed ships in the Thames Estuary off Gravesend, the huge concrete gun forts on their spindly-legged towers, looking as though they had come, ready-made, out of the imagination of H. G. Wells, and beyond them the dark and smoky mass of London. He thought about Ann.

He wondered if he would run into her again. He supposed he might if she returned to England. London, particularly wartime London, was remarkably small for a metropolis of its size. There were only so many places where one could go without encountering England's terrible austerity, which had turned this glittering capital of an empire into a dull provincial town, and Ann was sure to know them.

He flew on, perfectly aware of everything around him, no matter where his thoughts carried him at any given moment. The deep, steady humming of the engine, the hiss of the slipstream through a loose rubber gasket in the canopy housing, and now, as he brushed against the edge of a cloud, the crystal droplets of rain on his windshield, were part of his most immediate world. He thought that if this were not to be his true and ultimate reality, he wouldn't want another.

Northeastern Sector Ground Control had spotted him then and queries crackled in his earphones, so he put out his cigar, clipped his helmet's chin piece and throat microphone in place, and identified himself.

The ground controller, an Irishman by his accent, welcomed him to England.

—And did ye have a nice little visit with the Calais Gang?

—I doubt they'd think so, Controller, Ludo said.

—Left them a bit perturbed, did ye now? Diminished, as it were? Well, the good Saints will forgive ye for working on a Sunday. There's nothing they like to hear more than the Devil gnashing his ugly, great teeth. You're clear at fifteen thousand all the way home, me bhoy.

—Thank you, Controller.

—And may the Saints keep you.

The lunar landscape of London's impoverished East End, where, on Winston Churchill's order, the Double-X manipulators who controlled all German spies in England had lured the Luftwaffe time and time again, so as to spare Whitehall and the homes and property of the rich, slid under his wing. Tenements that had become mass graves. Scorched ruins. A terrible triage had been practiced here on unsuspecting thousands so that something thought to be of greater value than they could escape destruction. He wondered what it would be like to live in a century and on a continent where ruins were always a consequence of antiquity rather than of premeditated murder. What would that sort of life offer as a challenge? What were its risks, and how would one prove one's dedications there? War was his home, he knew then, even if it had made him homeless.

Rounding the field to land, he identified himself as *Six, Eagle One*, his R/T designation as squadron commander, and gave the customary cryptic accounting of his morning's work.

—Roger, Six, Eagle One, the laconic towerman replied. Come in on five-six-oh and watch for the potholes. Ground wind tenner and gusting. Good show. Welcome home.

CHAPTER XIV

THE FEELING, after you've been shot at in the air and survived, after you've killed the man and destroyed the machine whose purpose was to kill you, is much like the euphoria that accompanies a bottle of aged vintage wine. Everything seems possible, nothing is quite believable, and nothing seems to matter. Yet this day was still too young to end without additional surprises, Ludo knew.

He made his wide, shallow turn, cut the throttle and heard the engine subside to a growling whisper, then looked out and down. The station had been attacked in his absence, the air was foul with ashes and dissipating smoke, and he could see fires burning all over the field. Auerbach's ground crews were beating out the embers with brooms and mattress covers. A crumpled Hurricane (Wilchurzak's) leaned against the wreckage of a NAAFI van that had invaded Northolt to dispense its battery-acid tea, pork pies, deadly sausages, and custard. Near the mess entrance, a large welcoming committee of ground crews, correspondents, and distinguished visitors in khaki had begun to gather. He looked among them for his own returned pilots, but there were still more of them in the air, coming in from the red-streaked mass of smoke above London, than on the ground.

Two of them angled sharply just in front of him—Zegar and Kawecki, to judge by their numbers—coming in on the last of their fuel over the tall trees at the edge of the field. Indeed, their engines stuttered and coughed as they thinned out the fuel mix at the top of their glide, and by the time they had hit the concrete, and then rolled and turned and braked before the hangars, their engines had died.

Both the machines were full of holes, their canopies shattered, the wings streaked with cordite above the gun ports, but both the pilots raised an arm in the two-fingered victory sign as the mechanics swarmed about their machines. Then, as the ground crews lifted them from their cockpits, something of the other picture of the battle presented itself. Another Hurricane appeared overhead, trailing smoke, and just before the machine became a ball of fire, a small black figure tumbled out of it. The flat white circular canopy snapped open above it and the man drifted out of sight.

Then the wheels of Ludo's own machine touched concrete, squealed, and rolled. Glass glinted in the hands of the cheering men who ran toward him with their congratulations.

They had all come out to watch for his return—Auerbach, Jacek Gemba, the injured Wilchurzak, the British station officers, the visitors, and the correspondents. He saw Loomis, who had appointed himself his chief chronicler, get out of a car. General Prus was stepping from another. Romuald Modelski had appeared near what looked like a reviewing stand and was glancing nervously at his watch. In the near distance, black smoke was boiling upward out of the fuel dump. It spread in the sky like spilled ink.

They had come out to meet him and now they ran toward him and each of them carried a bottle of champagne, because the news that had come down from London was simply astounding. What is it? he asked uncasily, his attention straying to the soiled sky. What *is* it? they cried. A dozen bottles of champagne were lifted toward him, and he took one, drank from it, and then pressed the icy glass against his forehead.

Up on the wing, and helping Ludo with his harness straps, Auerbach said: What is it, it's a victory. The biggest one yet. Maybe we won't be going home day after tomorrow, maybe it's too soon for that, but we will be going home someday, that's certain now.

—Oh?

A sudden weariness had fallen upon Ludo, the aftershock of combat. The concrete felt liquid and unreal under his boots, his hands closed and opened. A fist, cold as ice, had clenched in his stomach.

—Three dead men don't make any kind of victory, he heard himself saying, and then everyone was laughing and talking at the same time.

—*Three* dead men? Auerbach said, grinning. More like thirty, forty.

—No, more, much more! Urban babbled in his childish voice. We've finally beaten them. They're finished, Major, and not just for today.

Suddenly anxious, still searching the sky for Gerlach, Reszke, Straka, and the others, he told the young man not to be a fool. But then the story began to piece itself together. He began to listen. The words acquired coherence. He saw the images they created. No, not the hurtling aircraft, the flash of yellow fire and spirals of smoke, not the streaked sky, not even the cursing round mouth of the German pilot in his flaming cockpit, but as words printed upon a page. At noon, one hundred German bombers had finally broken through Dowding's line and appeared over London, and Fighter Command was claiming forty of them as destroyed. Ludo's men had caught another forty Dornier Do 215s just east of the city, shot down sixteen of them in less than one minute, and scattered the rest. Joseph Frantisek had shot down five Messerschmitts that morning. Reszke had destroyed three over the English Channel. Gerlach and Straka had accounted for five Heinkels between them. Ludo's own score for the day was six.

In the nineteen days beginning August 26, when the first two squadrons of the Polish wing had entered the battle, the Germans had lost four hundred and twenty-seven aircraft—more than a thousand of their finest aircrews and pilots—and that was more than even such a superb war machine as the Luftwaffe could bear. Frantisek had destroyed seventeen of them, more than any pilot in the RAF. Two of his fellow fliers in 303 Squadron were next on the roster of RAF high scorers with sixteen and fifteen victories each. Of the next ten top aces of Fighter Command, those who had destroyed between eleven and fourteen enemy aircraft, six were foreign volunteers and three of them were Poles. Of the thirty pilots, each of whom had shot down between five and ten enemy machines, eight were Poles flying with 303 and 302 squadrons. Each of the hundred and forty-seven Polish pilots who flew in the battle had destroyed at least two German aircraft in combat. Thirty of them were killed, seventy-eight were wounded, forty-two received high British decorations.

Later, as the excited babble of visitors and pilots suggested to Ludo, historians would mark this noon attack on London, on September 15, as the climax of the Luftwaffe's assault, the point at which the day's battle—and the greater battle of which it was a part—was finally won. Thereafter, the Germans would never come in strength against British fighters over British soil. They would attack English towns at night, and they would make deadly hit-and-run fighter-bomber raids across the English Channel, but they'd make no more mass daylight raids against a British target. It would be several days before Churchill said so, but everyone knew that Britain's most important crisis had been passed. In the next few months, the American Congress would approve the Lend-Lease Bill, and a great stream of arms, munitions, foodstuffs, raw materials, fuels, and medical supplies would begin to flow across the Atlantic. No one, no matter how young and optimistic, was able to say whether the war itself had been won in those ten hours on a Sunday afternoon and morning. Not even laughing Urban would go as far as that. But, if all he heard were true, Ludo knew that from that day on the war couldn't be lost.

The cheering young men who hoisted him to their shoulders and carried him toward the assembled visitors—the King and the Queen and General Sikorski, the ministers and the ambassadors who waved and cheered as wildly as schoolboys, the red-tabbed officers of the General Staff whose eyes were wet with tears—had every reason to congratulate themselves, Ludo knew, although their reasons and his own mightn't have been the same.

Their laughter was loud and nervous, traversing the scales. There was an element of astonishment in their huge satisfaction with themselves. Each of them had done better than he had expected; each was alive to laugh after the battle, and only Ludo seemed to know that a far greater and more decisive battle had to be fought inside each of them, and that he'd be fighting his own, unaided, to the death.

Auerbach looked steadily at Ludo and their glances locked. They knew each other too well for any dissembling; the bonds they shared had given them a closeness that other kinds of men could only imagine. Yet even those familiar gray eyes, crouched in their nests of wrinkles, couldn't grant Ludo the absolution he wanted.

Something had changed in the air in which he was moving. A

gulf, or perhaps a void, had appeared between him and his certainties. For the first time that he could recall, he was unable to take pleasure in his morning's work or pride in its result. Perhaps it was the persistent image of screaming young men lifted from shattered cockpits, of boys rather than machines who burned in the air, that intruded on any sense of satisfaction that he might have had. When a combat leader develops a conscience, he thought worriedly, it's time to look for a less demanding mistress than Little Lady War.

There was one fleeting moment when he wished that he could go back to that untrammeled innocence with which his young pilots went after their victories or, if not that far back, then at least to the simplicities of a patriot. But there had been too much death in his life for such black-and-white conclusions. The cold, unfeeling processes of war had become a river by that time, and he was far downstream, and there was no way to reverse his course. Despite the wild elation of the victory in which he had shared, he knew himself to have reached that point of physical and mental weariness in which conscience becomes the real enemy. As Auerbach murmured in his ear: What one wants and what's available just aren't the same thing.

Three Hurricanes landed then, one after another, and Ludo turned to watch them with a sense of gratitude, since they disrupted the trend of his thoughts. Each had been hit several times, and their gun ports were heavy with soot.

—That's Karcz, Kulesza, and Frantisek, Auerbach named the three sergeant-pilots. Lieutenant Matejczyk went to Tanglemere. Air-sea rescue pulled young Kozloski out of the water near Haesebruck. It looks like everybody's had a busy day.

—Lieutenant Reszke came down near Dover, Jacek Gemba said importantly, then flushed and explained. They telephoned to the mess about ten minutes ago, begging the major's pardon.

—Who was that who bailed out? Ludo asked. Did you see?

—Too high to spot his numbers, Auerbach said, and then the high-pitched whine of a fighter plane coming in too fast drew their attention upward.

—Coarse mixture, coarse mixture, the line chief muttered and began to curse, and everyone knew what was about to happen. Whether he was wounded or unconscious, or whether he had simply forgotten his landing procedures, the incoming pilot hadn't switched his fuel mix and, in another moment, he would be killed in flames.

Wilchurzak, who had sprained an ankle in his crash but was otherwise uninjured, began to hobble with desperate urgency toward the nearest parked machine, to find an R/T set and send out a warning. Then he stopped in midstep, stiff as a doll in white-faced resignation. It was, of course, too late for the pilot to do anything.

—Straka? someone murmured, and someone else said softly: Poor son-of-a-bitch.

It was just like tossing in a nightmare from which one can't awake, Ludo thought. You know that the moment is an unreal one, but the nightmare holds you a prisoner anyway. The Hurricane came on and then seemed to pause at the edge of the runway, suspended like a ballerina between *entrechats*, and then the wheels touched the ground and snapped off like sticks, the machine stood on its propeller and began to cartwheel, and struts and shorn wings and lengths of tubular frame and engine parts and fabric flew into the air. The fuel tank exploded and a monstrous fireball bounced across the runway, and then there was only a pool of greasy black smoke and red fire.

—There won't be enough left of him for a funeral, someone said. Damn. A hundred pounds of sand and two red bits of cloth in yet another coffin.

Loomis and Romuald Modelski had reached them together. The diplomat cried out: How could you let that happen? What will the British think? The King . . . the Queen . . .

—Who? Ludo said and, for a moment, he really didn't know what his brother-in-law was talking about.

—We didn't invite them here to witness a fiasco!

—We hadn't planned one for them, Ludo said.

Loomis tugged gently at Wilchurzak's sleeve.

—God, he said. I'm sorry. I know what you must feel. It's terrible to see someone you care for die like that.

—I hardly knew him, the young pilot said and shrugged the American's hand away.

As a frequent visitor to Ludo's squadron, Loomis knew that Straka and Wilchurzak had been inseparable, each fiercely protective of the other. But now, pale as he was, Wilchurzak had begun to hum a music hall ditty as he and Ludo and Loomis and Romuald Modelski, followed by Auerbach and Urban and the other pilots, and (at a respectful distance) by Jacek Gemba and several mechanics, began to walk toward the milling correspondents.

—You were like brothers, the American insisted. And aren't you engaged to Straka's sister? How can you be so cold and unfeeling about this? What sort of people are you, anyway?

—Take it easy, Loomis, Ludo said. You were in Warsaw. You know what we are.

—This is the worst possible impression to make on the British, Romuald Modelski said.

—They'll get over it.

Cold? Unfeeling? Indifferent to the death of friends? Nothing could be less true, Ludo knew. But who but one of their own kind could understand their notion of themselves as replaceable components of their country's history? Life itself had proved an enemy, meriting disdain. Rejecting their own injuries and the death of friends, they could always regard themselves as whole. Whether or not they failed in their tasks, their rejection of the *penalty* of failure would nullify every victory of their enemies.

The pilots walked in what seemed a comfortable silence, hands thrust deep into the pockets of their flying jackets, heads lowered against the sharp bite of an unseasonable wind that swirled among the hangars. Dark glasses concealed their tears, as they did Ludo's own. But, even so, he averted his head. The distinguished visitors had been ushered swiftly into the officers' mess. The flames behind them had been smothered with sand and an American bulldozer was pushing the debris and wreckage out of sight. The sky had clouded over; it would be raining soon.

Stung by their rejection of his sympathy, Loomis said: I wish someone would give me a simple explanation.

—If something has a simple explanation, Auerbach said quietly, it's not worth explaining.

Always afterward, when asked about that afternoon and evening that marked the high tide of the Poles among their Western Allies, Ludo would recall three conversations, one of them overheard. King George VI questioned him about RAF fighter tactics and listened attentively to his reasoned praise of the German *Schwarme* finger-four formations. He answered questions from the Air Minister, Sir Archibald Sinclair, about the merits of the Spitfire as opposed to the Messerschmitt Bf 109. The Spitfire, which was Churchill's favorite symbol for *Britain's finest hour*, was superior to all German fighters except at altitudes above twenty thousand feet, in which the Bf 109 excelled. Air Marshal Portal pointed out that Ludo's squadron flew early-model Hawker Hurricanes—the wooden, fabric-covered machines that made up eighty percent of Fighter Command in the battle—which made their success against the Messerschmitts all the more remarkable. Lord Beaverbrook, the Minister of Aircraft Production, assured him that the next available Spitfires would go to the Poles. John Laidlaw, a permanent undersecretary at the Foreign Office, invited him to lunch. But these were not the conversations that would stand out in his memory.

While waiting for General Sikorski to beckon him over, he had a drink with Prus, who remarked that Englishmen seemed to like him.

—Is that important, sir? Ludo asked.

—It could be very useful to us, the general said. We don't have as many friends among them as we should. Oh, it all looks very friendly on the surface, we're the very picture of Allied unity at war, but there's the future to think about, you know.

—A fighter pilot has to be very young to think about the future, Ludo smiled and said.

—All the more reason for you to stop rattling about in the sky. We've lots of friends today when we're needed, but we'll have fewer and fewer of them as the war goes on and we're needed less. That's a law of nature, I'm afraid.

—Then we'll just have to keep fighting all the harder, Ludo said.

The general laughed softly, said: Spoken like a soldier. But can we still afford to look at the world across the ears of a horse? Or, in your case, out of the cockpit of an airplane? No, my boy, there are other ways of doing your duty. You ought to consider spending more time on the ground.

—I'm a line officer, sir, Ludo said. I do what I know best. Politics is a mystery to me and I'd just as soon know nothing about it.

—Some of us think that you may have quite a talent for it, the general said.

—I don't write my own press releases, General, Ludo said and the older man laughed.

—Well, whoever does it must be doing a labor of love. Hardly a week seems to pass without there being something about you in London papers. Of course, I can't order you to march yourself into politics, but I know that General Sikorski would find good use for you. As a trusted aide to the general, who is chairman of the Allied Council, you'd have access to everyone who matters in this war.

Looking about the crowded room, hearing his laughing pilots, Ludo smiled and said: I think I already do.

—The view from the cockpit of a fighter plane is more limited than you think, the general said, and Ludo wished that this difficult conversation might end.

—I wouldn't even know how to begin to do anything else, sir, Ludo said.

—Practice takes care of that. Training, careful guidance. I watched you talking with Sinclair, Beaverbrook, and Portal. These are immensely powerful men and yet they listened to you with extreme attention. King George himself spent more time with you than even his extraordinary kindness required. You have a natural quality of leadership that such men identify immediately. God, man, do you think that men like Laidlaw would waste five seconds on an air force major unless they thought that he might be important to them in some way? They didn't become what they are by ignoring the obvious. General Sikorski has given us a leadership we can be proud to follow, but he has great difficulty in dealing with Churchill, who simply can't believe that a man of such rocklike integrity is entirely real. I speak for the general when I say that we must begin to develop a political leadership with which our allies may feel more at home.

—I've a responsibility to my pilots, sir.

—Is that more important than your responsibility to your country?

—Forgive me, sir, but to me they're one and the same.

—Yes, I suppose that's the secret, the general said softly. To love the people for whom you're responsible. I suppose that's why your men love you as much as they do and that's what all the others see.

—You are the one who taught me, General, that duty, service, and responsibility are indivisible, Ludo said. And that all of it is a matter of love.

—Yes, I suppose I did, the general said. We met in simpler times. Wars were uncomplicated then. The enemy was always in front and gallantry was just another way to test the value of one's own convictions. You could say then that love and life were interchangeable. If you loved something, you'd risk your life for it and military heroism made sense. Now, when bravery decides nothing at a conference table, when integrity has become incomprehensible and a politician is regarded more for his ambition than for his sense of duty, such simple notions have become absurd.

—Sir? Ludo asked, more troubled than ever before. How can you say this to me? How could I say that to my men? How can a soldier think that and still keep his sanity?

—No sane man can afford to think anything else in this century, the general said. You should have no illusions about the value of heroism. The dead are not ennobled by their sacrifice alone. They can be simply a waste.

Ludo watched and listened and wondered if the general knew that Lala too was dead. He thought that he did. The irony would be too cruel otherwise. Yet how could he continue to resist an idea that he himself had begun to believe?

As though the thought had crossed from his mind to the general's, Prus laid his artificial hand on Ludo's shoulder and touched his cheek with the back of his glove.

—I want to spare you the pain of finding that out for yourself when it's too late for you to do anything about it.

—It . . . may be already too late, sir, Ludo said.

Prus, always a complex man to be admired with caution, nodded and said nothing more.

The second conversation of the night that he remembered was one he overheard in the dense crowd of pilots, visitors, and correspondents gathered around the bar, where Jacek Gemba was pouring whiskeys, pink gins, and iced vodka. He heard his own name spoken first, and then Jacek's impassioned exclamation:

—I'd follow him to hell! There's never been a better officer in the service.

—With that kind of reputation, he ought to run for public office, Loomis said, and Derek Bellancourt smiled and said quietly: Oh? Do you really think so? And does he take his morning exercise by walking upon the waters?

—He likes to take walks, Jacek Gemba said.

—How introspective of him, Derek said and laughed. But it's all done on dry land, I expect.

—Why the hostility? Loomis asked. What's he done to you? It's pretty damn clear what he's doing for you, so why the bitchy cracks?

—Sheer envy, I suppose, Derek said and smiled disarmingly.

—Is there something official about your interest in him? I mean, you and your Minister don't usually go to visit your Continental dependents with bottles of French champagne. Nor does your Minister ask any old Allied major to break bread with him.

—My interest in him is purely personal, Derek said, laughing yet sounding as though laughter was a tactical exercise for him. I collect antiques. It's one of the interests I share with my sister. You might call it a family obsession. But I will say that some of his . . . ah . . . Continental doings have made him rather interesting. We're always looking for men among our allies who could be useful to us.

—I can't see how much more useful he could be.

—Oh, that, Derek said. Oh, of course. But one does have to keep the future in mind. One wonders, you see, how much of a political following he'd have if, let's say, something happened to General Sikorski. Would his people follow him into paths they might not entirely understand? There are so many questions.

—You haven't been reading my stories, Loomis said.

—Oh, I wouldn't miss one of them, Derek said. One wonders
though, reading them, why he needs an airplane to fly. And when
is he going to start raising the dead? It would solve so many of
our replacement problems.

The third conversation, one he'd never be able to forget entirely, was with Frantisek, the Czech hero of this British hour,
who seldom spoke to anyone at all. Of all the extraordinary young
men who flew with the Polish squadrons, Frantisek was probably
unique. The war that he was fighting didn't seem to have much
to do with the one in which the rest of Europe was engaged. He
had no respect for discipline, air tactics, formations, or orders
from the ground; he exasperated the commanders of all the British squadrons to which he was attached because he'd break away
and take off on his own at the first sight of Germans, whom he'd
attack and fight no matter what the odds, disdaining all help.
The Poles, whom he joined at his own request, allowed him to fly
with them as a *guest of the squadron* and to fight his private war
in any way that pleased him. The day's great victory had
confirmed him as the champion Emil-killer of the RAF and he
was celebrating it in his own fashion, playing solitaire at the card
table that had been set up for him permanently in the mess. The
game was a complicated one of his own invention. It took several
days to finish. He'd return to his card table after every mission.

A woman (wife? daughter? secretary-mistress?) of one of the
distinguished visitors, an exquisitely gowned and coiffured lady in
her middle years, had just ended congratulating him on his seventeen confirmed kills as Ludo came up to them, and the Czech's
mild gaze had thrown her into some confusion.

—But surely there must be some satisfaction in doing your job
so well? she insisted, and he said: I leave that sort of thing to my
Polish friends.

—But don't you have anything to avenge?

—Not since Munich, madam, the Czech said. You do remember Munich? That's when your Neville Chamberlain won
Peace in our time.

—Yes. Well, of course, said the lady. A terrible pity. So many of us were so sorry for the poor, brave Czechs.

—There were some people in Prague who were equally sorry, the Czech said. But one can't really share one's sorrow, can one. It doesn't travel well.

—Whatever could you mean by that? the lady said, grown haughty. What an extraordinary thing to say!

—It's quite an experience to fight in another country, wearing a foreign uniform, taking orders from people who don't understand anything about you and care even less. People who, by the way, may have had much to do with the fact that you don't have a country. You develop quite an extraordinary viewpoint.

—Well, said the lady. I must say, you're not very gracious. Or grateful. After all, Britain did take you in.

—Gratitude isn't in my contract, the Czech said. All I am paid for is killing Germans.

—Shocking! the lady said. How . . . utterly shocking.

She swept away, head held high, and Frantisek bent over his cards again.

—If you'd put the jack of hearts on the queen, you'd be able to pick up an entire row, Ludo said behind him.

—Oh, you know my game, do you? the Czech said.

—I've watched you play often enough. A bit hard on the lady, weren't you?

—She'll get over it. She'll just put it down to another primitive Slav, another bloody little Continental. Can't expect decent manners from any of them, you know.

—We've all learned the lessons of appeasement, Ludo said as evenly as he could. What is past is past and no apology can repair the damage, but there'll be no more Munichs.

—Well, we'll just have to wait and see, won't we, the Czech said with a smile in which pain seemed as evident as amusement. The British are the only people who have it in them to be truly generous to a defeated enemy, but they do tend to be rather careless with their friends.

Thoughtfully, Ludo looked up then and at a distance, standing beside Prus and General Sikorski, he saw Ann.

CHAPTER XV

THE RECEPTION, so ordinary if one was used to gatherings of this kind, had been going on for some time when she came into the room. She waited quietly in a corner while Romuald Modelski hurried off to bring her a glass of champagne, and she watched the animated little groups of uniformed men and handsomely gowned women and listened to the brittle scraps of their conversations.

No one, it seemed, was able to talk about anything other than the war, or people and events connected with the series of political and military disasters which had occurred in Africa and Europe. Loomis, perhaps pretending to be drunker than he was, was also the loudest in a group centered about Ludo. She watched her past-and-future lover's tall, straight back, noted the overlong hair that seemed to have grayed heavily at his temples, and didn't regret for a moment that she had arranged her own invitation. She knew that when she finally came face-to-face with Ludo, she wouldn't be able to abandon her own defensive brittleness for some time. He, she was sure, would continue to seek cover in taciturn evasion, as he was doing with Loomis. It was, she thought, in the normal order of relationships where two people, each confronting an unexpected hope, resist reality so as to avoid future disappointment and a new sense of loss.

In the meantime, she listened to his words and thought them soft and blurry, like lights in a fog.

—What are you after, anyway, Loomis? he asked.

And the American, struggling to hold in place the lines of self-indulgence that marred and masked his face, said: Would you believe . . . decency?

Prus took her by the arm then and led her to the small group gathered around General Sikorski, a group that included John Laidlaw, Brigadier Wadsworth-Jones, Sikorski's wife and daughter, the British ambassador to the Polish government-in-exile, Jan Masaryk (the Foreign Minister of the Czechoslovak government), and her own brother Derek. She had a moment to study them all on her way toward them, and she could see at once why Winston Churchill, whom she had known from her earliest days of childhood as her father's confidant and friend, would find the Polish leader impossible to deal with. Churchill's overwhelming desire to dominate resulted in a feeling of inferiority in regard to anyone in whom he could see no flaw, and when that took place there was no limit to his vindictiveness and wrath. He had always feared people to whom ambition was secondary to service. The Pole's probity and selfless dedication would be an affront to him.

Introduced, and exchanging the expected complimentary phrases, she was struck by the untroubled clarity of his gaze in which, by a paradox she thought typically Polish, innocence and arrogance negated each other. A handsome, well-fleshed man, and erect as all his military kind, he seemed both appealing and forbidding, and she slewed her eyes immediately toward Ludo and noted the same odd detachment.

And suddenly she wanted to shock and shake them all, to assert herself while there was still time. Laidlaw's bland, diplomatic smile sent lines from Blake running through her mind, lines about a smile of love and a smile of deceit, and *a smile of smiles in which two smiles meet*. A warning? A reminder of the past? All her distrust of Laidlaw returned in a rush, yet she had to admit to herself that his command of surreptitious power excited and attracted her enormously. If all her other men had proved to be, sooner or later, civilized artifacts of doubtful provenance, having been brought up to polite mediocrity, he (at the very least) was a genuine barbarian.

She was still her own woman; she hadn't yet become his arranger of aristocratic atmospheres (indeed, she wondered how anyone could arrange anything that might impress Sikorski), although this evening would be the start of it. She could still react with affection to people she liked. She wanted to warn Prus.

But at that moment, Ludo looked up, saw her, and she was immediately confused. One expects joy at such times. One assumes amazement. One doesn't expect resignation, as if something terribly important were being laid aside. Everyone was listening attentively to General Sikorski, who was outlining his vision of a postwar Europe—a powerful Central European Federation based on

the union of Poland and Czechoslovakia, under a joint Constitution that had just been agreed upon by Sikorski and the Czech
President Beneš—but all she could think of was: Why does he
look so stricken? Where's that bright flash of recognition, of anticipated pleasure, of *acceptance*? Thrown off stride, she listened
to the others.

—This may be the most important political idea in Europe
since Bismarck unified the German states, Jan Masaryk was saying. Russia, of course, will oppose it, which means that America's
leftists will attack it. But it may really put an end, once and forever, to German and Soviet expansionist ambitions.

—Didn't Marshal Pilsudski have the same idea? Laidlaw murmured then. As I recall, all of Poland's neighbors opposed it.

—And Britain opposed it more than anyone, Masaryk said.

—It seemed . . . premature, Laidlaw said.

—It was premature, said General Sikorski. The successor states,
as you call them, those that reappeared on the map after the dis-
integration of the Austrian, Prussian, and Russian empires, were
too intoxicated with their own new statehoods to accept submer-
gence in another, greater political entity. Pilsudski's federalist
dream seemed like a new imperialism. And the Old Man himself
didn't help matters very much in London and Paris.

—He was . . . unusual, to say the least, Laidlaw agreed.

—He was too impatient, General Sikorski said. He had little
sympathy for other people's feelings, and he wanted all his
dreams accepted without explanation. That sort of dictatorial
stance frightened all of us. All of us, you see—Poles, Czechs,
Hungarians, Roumanians, Bulgarians, Lithuanians, Letts, and Estonians—had only just struggled out of the grip of foreign empires. Poland itself had come together out of three oppressive foreign tyrannies. Consensus was impossible. Anything that seemed
a threat to independence was anathema. And yet, deep in our
hearts, we've always understood that we could have independence
only as part of a political union that was powerful enough to defend all and each of us.

—Once Germany is defeated and the Nazis are gone, Laidlaw
began with a reassuring gesture; and General Sikorski smiled at
Masaryk and said: Then there will be Russia.

—Czechoslovakia's natural ally, Laidlaw added quickly.

—Czechoslovakia's most unnatural ally, the Czech statesman said. There won't be any need for such alliances once Poland has a government we can respect and trust. As we trust and respect the government of General Sikorski.

—Oh, of course, of course, Laidlaw said at once.

—And once we're all part of a powerful federation, we won't need to depend on protection from outside, the Czech said, still smiling. Recent times have taught us that such protection is sometimes unreliable.

—His Majesty's government can only applaud such a possibility, Laidlaw murmured in a voice that Ann thought particularly hollow.

And then General Sikorski was asking Prus to bring Ludo to them, so that he might congratulate him in person and thank him for his work.

She studied Ludo then, as earlier she had studied General Sikorski, noting changes and wondering if they were for the better. It had been only eight weeks since they had seen each other, but she herself felt aged by months, if not years. Had he aged at all? The lines driven sharply past the corners of his mouth seemed deeper, darker; his cheekbones seemed sharper; there seemed to be a small tremor in the hand he raised in salute. But all that may have been the fault of insufficient light. War, which to her was a mindless, wasteful aberration that went against all logic and reason, was his element, she knew, and yet he too seemed to have been worn down to the core. What had made him and his kind such good copy for the journalists, she supposed, was their ability to fight a personal war while everyone else was simply caught up in, and struggling against, a great chaotic public donnybrook that didn't seem to mean more than the death of friends. They, the Poles, died too, of course. But, somehow, one didn't notice that so readily. She supposed that if someone mourned in a foreign language, and observed a ritual of grief rooted in the historical experience of another culture, it didn't seem quite real to anyone else. He would depend on affection to help him through his days but, as the war saw to it that there were always fewer persons for whom he could care, he would avoid and evade lasting emotional commitments.

It wasn't the most promising basis for that necessary mutual disarmament with which loving relationships begin or resume.

Still, she would try, she knew.

She was moved, pleased, and felt a touch of proprietary pride at the way in which powerful men deferred to her lover. General Sikorski's eyes and voice reflected such genuine warmth as to seem paternal. He, Masaryk, and the King had all decorated Ludo, and she wondered why Ludo seemed more embarrassed than honored by his new distinction. Prus, when she glanced at him, seemed equally embarrassed. Laidlaw's eyes seemed particularly watchful.

Alone sometime later, with the generals and ministers preparing to leave, and with the journalists and pilots looking as if they were going to make a night of it, she took Ludo by the arm and led him outside. Night had come. The Royal Couple and their entourage were long gone. The sky was red above London, where the day's fires were burning. He smiled at her and she thought: It'll be all right. His disappointing reaction to seeing her had been just a moment of uncertainty, shock, all perfectly human. Some disbelief, a touch of doubt, perhaps, and who could blame anyone for that in times such as these? Something was troubling him, perhaps a new choice that had nothing to do with his feelings for her. Perhaps he too had come to a moral and spiritual crossroad where he had to pause, look back over the distances he had crossed, and scan his horizons. In a time of violent and dramatic changes, what could be more natural?

Looking at her, he shook his head over and over, as if to clear it of persistent cobwebs, and rubbed his forehead with the gloved fingers of his injured hand.

—I don't understand this, he said finally.

—What's there to understand?

There is an awkwardness about renewed relationships, a wary ritual of maneuvering for position, of testing the air, of wondering if hopes may be justified or if barricades were necessary after all. She was appalled by her own stilted tone.

—You said you liked surprises now and then.

But he was listening only to himself.

—Do you believe in coincidences? Destiny? Things like that?

—Take my word for it, lover, Ann said. There's no such thing as a coincidence. God has it all well planned.

—Planned? But it's . . . illogical, he said.

—What does logic have to do with anything?

If she felt it necessary to shield her nervousness with harshness, his refuge seemed to lie in the destruction of the English language.

—But in France, it was all finished, no? And that was logical, yes? So why should I remember you? Why should I be reminded? But everywhere I go I am reminded of you, and I think about you. Ann, it is not a good way to be in a war.

She laughed then, honestly and with no artifice of any kind.

—Poor Ludo, she said. English is always your first victim when you lose control of the situation. But there's really nothing to be alarmed about. France was . . . France. We didn't have a proper fare-thee-well. The lady took flight, I'm afraid. So here we are again, given another chance to repeat our mistakes, and if that's not part of someone's grand design then I've misread all of my life's little lessons.

—It is still all too much for me to understand, Ludo said.

—Think less, she coined a parody. The gates of paradise are narrow.

Humorless, as he seemed to her at times, he couldn't follow her into imprecise images or ideas, so he asked, somewhat puzzled: What does thinking have to do with narrow gates?

—People with swollen heads get stuck in them, she said. Heaven is for the simpleminded. Well . . . let's see the new gongs. That's the RAF word for them, isn't it?

Ludo groped for and found the black oblong leather case in his tunic pockets, passed them to Ann, who opened them, took out the small enameled crosses, and cocked her head over them.

—That one I know, she said. It's the DSO, isn't it? Patrick has one. This other one . . . is there some significance to the fact that the ribbon is all black-and-blue?

But he had missed the point again, a simplicity and perhaps an innocence that she found endearing. Such light conversational touches as the English language could provide were, occasionally, beyond him.

—It's Polish, the Virtuti Militari, he said.

—Granted for military virtues, I expect. I see you're wearing another one of them. Have you been very virtuous to get them?

—Only in the military way, he said finally and began to grin in his turn.

—Thank God for that, Ann said.

Yes, she thought, it *will* be all right. It will be. Otherwise, everything *will* have been only a coincidence, and who'd need any more of those? London was glowing redly on the near horizon, sound rolled there like thunder, and the thin white beams of searchlights were sweeping the sky. There had to be a reason for something as unspeakable as that, it had to be a part of God's sensible plan; otherwise she'd be obliged to think that *everything* was merely a cruel accident. That (and here she took flight again from her own unreasonably reawakened hopes) would make life . . . unendurable.

Could he leave the base?

Yes, if he were back before dawn. Victory or not, the squadrons weren't on stand down, they'd fly in the morning. Indeed, even as they (Ann and Ludo) ran through the sudden rain toward the visitors' parking area behind the mess building, as the rest of the night began to acquire that aura of expectancy that quickens the blood, the party had begun to end. The correspondents and the ground-echelon officers would go on drinking, singing their schoolboy songs, playing their complicated games of soccer among piled-up furniture, walking on their hands. The pilots walked to quarters.

Then, as they squeezed themselves into the bucket seats of Derek's Morgan racer (with Ludo's long legs cruelly angled and wedged under his chin), she had a sudden sensation of déjà vu. She had been here before, had done this before in this very car, driving from a party to a borrowed flat with an accidental lover; driving through a sharp rain that angled right into the windshield, obscuring the dark road; watching the needle nudge the hundred mark as she bit her lips. Life expectancy could be mea-

sured in seconds at such times. Death . . . silence, peace, an end
to hopelessness and frenzy . . . would be instantaneous . . .

Ludo's sharp white profile looked like something chiseled out of
chalk. He seemed indifferent to his fate which, at that moment,
lay entirely in her hands, or (to conjure up the precise image, the
mot juste) under her foot on the accelerator. Would nothing
move him? Was he beyond the simplicities of fear? And of what
use would such a man be to her? The damned man was an affront
to everything that she had been taught to believe about herself
and yet she knew, even then, that he had come to his authority
through pain. The risks such men were taught to take were never
an investment.

The touch of his hand on her shoulder, a gentle pressure that
was both questioning and commanding, was (she thought) infinitely soothing. She took a deep breath, expelled it, watched the
speed-indicator needle drop.

—That, she said quietly, in control again. That is known as
doing the tonne. One hundred or better.

—Interesting, he said and she was free to laugh.

—Tell me about your trip through Spain, she said then. Was it
very difficult?

—Yes, he said. It was. How was yours?

—Nothing to press into a memory book. Oily food, horny
Spaniards, and lecherous Catalonian waiters. Madrid was a bore.
Full of sauntering Nazis and anxious Jews and greasy little men
talking about Spain's right to Gibraltar.

He paused then, choosing his words with care: My journey almost ended in Madrid. I saw a man there that I had met in a
hospital in Warsaw. He is the man who put me in that hospital.
A German. His name is Reinecke.

—You have a German friend? she asked. Now, isn't *that* unusual for a man in your line of work?

—He's not a friend, not exactly. In fact, he is my Enemy, the
one that I look for every day. As he looks for me. Both of us
know, I think, that nothing is going to happen to either of us
until we find each other in the air. I know this may be difficult to
understand, but that's what I think.

—I've had some such ideas myself, she said. Go on.

—In Madrid, we saw each other. He was in a café near the Prado, having coffee and cognac with some Spanish officers. I was outside, in the crowd, on my way from one railway station to another, and I caught his eye. He winked at me. He smiled. I don't know how he recognized me or knew who I was. The only time he had seen me, my face was wrapped in bandages. And I was, of course, trying to look like everybody else you might see on a Spanish street.

—More onions? she said.

—What? he said, distracted. What onions?

—Nothing, she said. Never mind. Go on.

—How could he have known who I was? He must have sensed what I felt. He must feel what I do. He must know what he and I are to each other in this war.

—Perhaps he saw your photograph somewhere, Ann said quietly, and waited, and then there was a silence.

—That's possible, of course, Ludo said at last. They keep intelligence files on some of us, just as we do on them. . . . But that wasn't the feeling I had at the time. I don't know if I'm making myself clear, but something very personal happened in that moment.

—Go on, she said.

—There was a shock, a moment of tension, Ludo said and shook his head and searched for better words. No. There was more than that. It was that ice-cold fraction of a second when a sort of miracle takes place in air combat. It's when you know that you are sitting dead center in somebody's gunsight, and that there's nothing you'll be able to think of fast enough to save yourself before you are hit, and that before you can begin to move you're going to be dead. Everything stands absolutely still. The air itself seems solid. There is no time to think. Indeed, there isn't any *time*. The mind tunes out and some entirely different force takes over, and suddenly you are saved. How? What happens? I don't know. But, I suppose, once you stop thinking you can move by instinct, and what you do by instinct must always be right.

—It seems to work that way sometimes, Ann murmured.

—Yes, well, Ludo said. That's what happened then. We saw

each other and each of us recognized that feeling. It was . . . (and here he hesitated as if embarrassed by the need for poetic imagery) as if we traded souls for a moment, if you can believe it.

Very softly, Ann said: I do recall one or two such moments.

But he was not listening to her then. Quite likely, he was hardly able to hear himself. He had stepped away from the conversation and was tap-tapping blindly down the dark path of his memory, moving reluctantly through the jumble of debris and deadfall that lay concealed behind his blue-green lenses. She couldn't follow him into all that wreckage, she knew, and find her way out again.

Then he was laughing nervously.

—An odd thing to have happened between enemies, don't you think?

—Perhaps not so odd, she prompted.

—No. Well. My journey should have ended there and then. But he obviously decided to save me for another time.

Impatient (she was easily bored by mystifications), Ann said: That makes you sound like something one keeps in a larder.

—That's it, exactly, Ludo said. Sooner or later, I will have to kill him and both of us know it.

—Now that *is* sick, Ann said and went on to lament only half in jest: Why do I attract twisted, honorable romantics? I had thought better of you.

—I know. I'm sorry. But that's what happened, you see.

—He's keeping you alive so that you can kill him, or he can kill you, in some sort of medieval battle in the skies? Pardon the confused metaphor, but there's a limit to what I'm willing to swallow in a bedtime story.

—We knew it in Warsaw, Ludo said.

—Nothing that happens there would surprise me, Ann said. But this is London. People don't think like that at this end of Europe.

—I heard him, Ludo said. He grinned from ear to ear and he said: *By the lost and found balls of Saint Anthony, how many lives have you got?* Then he distracted the others with a joke in Spanish and I could step back into the crowd.

—By the lost and . . . really, Ludo! Nobody talks like that.

—He does. And I knew exactly what he meant.

—Well . . . that's just sick, Ann said. I don't want to hear that kind of a story.

—I don't have any other kind, Ludo said.

Later, with the lovemaking over for the moment, the windows glowing red with the distant fires, and the beginning of a morning chill creasing about her back and shoulders, she said: Tell me about Portugal. Did you really steal a ship or a plane, or whatever it was?

—A plane in Lisbon. A ship in Casablanca. There's really not much more to say about that.

She laughed, not really amused: Are you being modest? Please don't become all English and modest. I told you what I think about that.

He shrugged, spread his hands, not at all displeased.

—I stole a whole squadron in Poland, he said.

—That's more like it. You're not a very principled sort of person, are you. That should stand you in good stead in London.

—Ann, he said and yawned. Couldn't we get some sleep?

She sat up among the tumbled pillows, said accusingly: Sometimes you sound more English than the Hudsons.

—I like your cousin, he said.

—You've met Wally Hudson? Yes, I suppose you would. He does have his moments, which is more than I can say for most of my abominable family.

—At least you have one, Ludo said.

—Is that important to you? she wanted to know. You seem to be a man who does well enough alone.

Once more evasive, he said: It isn't a state I'd have chosen.

—All right, then, she said. Keep your secrets. But there is one more story I'd like to know about. It's a murder story.

—Which kind of murder? he asked bitterly. The kind for which you go to hell, or the kind for which you get medals?

—I suppose it might qualify as a bit of both, Ann said carefully. It's someone you're supposed to have murdered in that hospital in Warsaw. To switch identities, or something.

—How . . . , he began and she, retreating from the numb fury in his face, said quickly, soothingly: It's a story Derek brought back from Lisbon. It's something the Germans have been floating, I believe.

—Oh, the swine, Ludo said.

He plucked the blue-green glasses off his nose with a swift, desperate gesture and she could see his eyes. The whites had yellowed, they were veined in red, and she thought (very frightened now) of old parchment maps, the kind one finds behind glass in museum cases. *Here be Dragons, here be Monsters, and here the Navigator has fallen off the edge of the world.* . . . She thought that she had never seen pain stamped so indelibly into flesh; it was as if a butcher's mallet had struck him between the eyes and shattered the twin prisms and disfigured him.

Alarmed, she said: It's just a German story. Why are you so upset? Nobody pays attention to any German stories.

—The swine are trying to pay me back for that funeral, Ludo was muttering then. Oh, the sons-of-bitches! No wonder Reinecke was amused.

—I don't know anything about funerals, Ann said. I only know the story's being mentioned here and there in some official places. . . . It's the sort of dirty little trick that Derek would pull, you see, and it's not something that anyone would do anything about . . . not normally, anyway.

—No, not normally.

—I'm sorry, she said then. I shouldn't have brought it up. Why are you so angry?

—Angry? he said and uttered a short, barking laugh. It's an entirely different kind of feeling.

—Because I do understand that sort of thing, she said.

—You're English, he said, cold as ice. Why should you have to understand anything?

And then she gave way to an anger of her own.

—Haven't you heard about slander? Defamation? she asked harshly and made a snorting sound of bitterness and contempt. There are whole peoples who make a wonderfully comfortable living for themselves out of lying about others! It's the only way that petty little men have of coping with someone bigger than themselves. If they did *not* tell their damned lies about you, if they couldn't gossip with their knowing smiles and make all their gleeful little comments about how undeserving you really are, if they couldn't reassure themselves about their own stature by pulling you down to their slimy little level, it would mean that you're just as dull and small and cowardly and unimportant as they are! I ought to know something about slander, damn it. And I do.

He said nothing and she went on in a softer tone, feeling unaccountably exhausted: Perhaps it helps them to master their own consciences. And if yours doesn't bother you . . .

He interrupted coldly. —Why should it? The matter is trivial.

—Then why are you so angry?

—A man who doesn't care about his own good name isn't going to be concerned about anyone else, he said.

She could laugh then, mocking gently.

—Believe me, lover. Slander is something you never learn to live with. Not entirely. But it does get easier year by year. And can it really make all that much of a difference in the end?

But she was quite sure then that he was unable to see her. He was staring through her and beyond her into some icy moment where she couldn't follow, and she thought once again of antique maps and legendary monsters and of a voyager lost at the far edge of his possibilities. Outside, a lost homeless dog had begun to howl, its voice mad with hunger, and the rain went on tapping and scratching at the windows like a wet gray beggar.

Later, he slept. She watched him as he turned and muttered in a nightmare and time seemed to be roaring in her ears. It's all right, she said to herself as much as to him. It's all right. When the main nightmare passes, the small ones will end.

PART FOUR

Foes and Lovers

Fanaticism consists in
redoubling your efforts
when you have forgotten your aim.

GEORGE SANTAYANA

CHAPTER XVI

THAT WINTER, as Ann would seek to understand it later, and then through the next year into the spring and summer of 1942, the war began to acquire a darker life and destiny of its own. It prospered with little seeming relevance to the fates of thousands killed in North Africa, in the skies above Britain and northwestern France, in the Atlantic and the Mediterranean and the North Sea and the Indian Ocean, and—soon enough—in the Far East and on the Russian landmass.

The war grew and spread; it maimed, murdered, and imprisoned tens of millions in occupied Europe, buried thousands in the rubble of their London homes. It slaughtered openly and it killed in secret. It plotted and manipulated and connived. Its face —so bright with a heroic purpose at the start—darkened with treachery, brutality, and greed.

Headlines . . . there was no comfort to be derived from bulletins or newsprint. The British and Italian armies swept back and forth across the sands of Libya. The French fleet was attacked without warning by its erstwhile allies and sunk at anchor at Dakar. In April 1941, the war consumed Yugoslavia and the Greeks. Thanks to Winston Churchill's fascination with *the soft underbelly of Europe*, twenty thousand Australians and New Zealanders were sent to destruction in Greece and in Crete just at the point when they were about to annihilate Italy's North African empire. On June 22, the war engulfed Hitler's eastern partner —the Russian Colossus—with results that would doom Ludo and his kind.

In December 1941, when the Japanese attack on Pearl Harbor redefined the war and gave it a new American identity, the threat to Poland's future could be seen quite clearly by those among the Poles whose business it was to know about such things. They were aware of American ignorance about them; they were soon to become very much aware of the hysterical adulation by which a highly vocal leftist minority in the United States—a powerfully entrenched and influential population of misguided libertarians who still addressed their prayers to Lenin and Trotsky—transformed the murderous Joseph Stalin into a benign *Uncle Joe*, and all witnesses against him into *fascists*.

Yet if one were to believe the headlines of the times, then all of the Allies, not merely the Poles, seemed to be heading for catastrophe in that season of disasters. The British Empire fell apart in Asia. Hong Kong was lost. India was in turmoil. Malaya and Singapore, along with a British-Indian army of eighty thousand men, fell to a small corps of twenty thousand Japanese. The Royal Navy's *Prince of Wales* and *Repulse* were sunk by Japanese bombers, and the heavy cruisers *Cornwall* and *Dorsetshire* followed soon after in the Bay of Bengal. Thirty-six thousand American and Filipino troops marched into Japanese captivity with the surrender of Bataan on April 9, 1942. Corregidor fell on May 6. In North Africa, the fortress of Tobruk surrendered to the Germans on June 21, along with nine generals, forty thousand seasoned British and Australian soldiers, and mountains of munitions, and General Erwin Rommel (soon to be Field Marshal and darling of the German Army) prepared to invade Egypt. On the same day, which marked the first anniversary of their invasion of the Soviet Union, General von Manstein's soldiers broke through the defenses of Sevastopol, drove the Russians out of the Crimea, and began their advance to the Caucasus and the lower Volga.

As Ludo said bitterly to Ann, it was a fine year for wooden and enameled crosses. It wasn't a good year for a warm and loving relationship to flower and grow.

In her bed, in her bath, on Derek's Persian carpets, jammed against the refrigerator in her kitchen, in theater cloakrooms, in the backseats of taxis and across the hood of her borrowed sportscar, in country lanes and hedgerows, once in a train compartment, they fell on each other with the desperate savagery of a bayonet charge across open ground, as if to assert, once and for all, their simple human triumph over a sinister and disembodied war that continued to defeat them. As the war's mechanical convulsions spread across the globe, and as less attention was paid to the bright clear-cut purpose of the war's beginning, and more to its darkening and demeaning nature, so their assault on each other's bodies acquired an opposite, fundamental intensity, as if to reaffirm an earlier stage in human evolution.

But if their nights were right, they knew that their days were terribly wrong, and there seemed to be nothing that they could do about it.

He told her the story of a 1919 cavalry charge in the Ukraine, a hopelessly romantic gesture in the face of barbed wire and machine guns, where, in the midst of unbelievable carnage, the stallions of the officers began to mount the mares of the privates in some sort of primordial spasm of affirmation of life over death. (*It knocked the charge into a cocked hat, of course, but Holy Mother of God, what better time to preserve the species? The poor damned brutes died grinning from ear to ear.*) She didn't laugh. Indeed, to her own astonishment, she burst into uncontrollable tears.

—It's only a story, Ann, he tried to console her.

—I hate that kind of story. It's ugly, cruel, and degrading. It reduces everything to animal functions. And it's not even true!

—It happened, Ann. I was there. Prus was also there. Ask *him*, if you can't believe *me*.

—I don't care whether it happened or not! Just because it happened wouldn't make it true! Oh, don't pretend that you don't know what I'm talking about. It's all so . . . diminishing. Things are confused enough between us without that sort of thing.

—I'm not confused about us, he said. I know exactly what I feel.

—Oh, yes, she said bitterly. Whenever you can afford to think about something other than the war!

—It isn't something one can forget these days, is it? he did his best to soothe her. But I think about you as often as I can.

—Then why can't I feel any commitment from you? Bed is all very well, but . . . dear God . . . even *that's* beginning to feel like a historical transaction. I've been trying to understand this distance between us ever since we met. My own commitments depend on it, you see. If you and I could achieve that necessary closeness . . . if you could meet me at least halfway . . . if I thought I could depend on you and not be left stranded in an emotional vacuum from which there's no way out . . . I'd be glad to clean house of all my encumbrances, let go of the past, and live for the future.

Touched by a sudden jealousy, he asked at once: You have another man?

—No, not a man. Of course not a man! But there are other things in which I'm involved. Call it my war work, if you like. Entanglements of that kind. They too are . . . diminishing. If I could feel that sense of safety and support that comes from a true commitment, I'd get rid of all that dreadful nonsense. And then there'd be nothing to stand in the way of a decent, normal, loving, ordinary life.

He sighed, averted his face, said with that bitterness that appeared more and more frequently in his voice: It's too soon to talk about life. The war . . .

—Oh, damn the war! she cried. Too soon to be human? Too soon to stop living other people's lies? Someday I'll have to tell you my story about Laidlaw.

—A confession, Ann? I'm not very good at hearing confessions.

—I really have a need to make that confession. But don't worry. I can't do it until I'm sure of you. No, my dear, it seems closer to being too *late* for a human impulse rather than too *soon*. But, dammit, Ludo, couldn't we at least give it a try?

—Is that still possible?

—Well, by God, she said and noted her own uncertainty. If it isn't, if the possibility of it is out of the question, then why are we still bothering to keep ourselves alive?

—Instinct? he asked in reply. Hope? I don't know. I thought you might tell me.

For quite some time, ever since she had begun to do her work for Laidlaw, she had been collecting Ministry of Information propaganda posters that dealt with eavesdropping and spies. On the framed poster above their heads, the one that overlooked her bed and warned against loose talk (and suggested the danger of shared confidences and threatened retribution for a moment of incautious closeness), an open mouth was spewing swastikaed torpedoes at a sinking ship. They both looked at it and grinned helplessly at each other.

She sighed, pressed her lips together, fell back on her pillows. After a moment, her hand moved to his chest and began to trace the scars and ridges there. In all that time, he had been careful not to move at all.

—I do so want to try, Ann resumed. And you do too, I know. The sad truth, lover, is that neither of us can think of the other in purely romantic, sentimental terms. We can't be merely silly with each other; there's too much at stake. Each of us is a desperate romantic in his or her way, but this romanticism embraces far larger ideas than a relationship between a woman and a man.

—I do love you, Ann, he said (*confessed*, she thought, would be the better word in that penitential moment), but I find it difficult to feel anything.

—Well, now, she said. That's not entirely true. You do feel a deep sense of responsibility toward your young men.

—*Mea culpa.*

—Responsibility *is* a sort of love.

—That isn't something I ever think about, he lied and cursed his necessary caution.

—I hate the image of star-crossed lovers, Ann said then. It's a cheap, melodramatic way out for Victorian lady novelists who suffer from a failure of the imagination.

—Is that what we are?

—I'd rather think not. Our bedtimes have been far too imaginative for Victorian lady novelists.

—Won't that do, for now?

—I suppose it has to. Ah, if that's all there was to this loving business, there wouldn't be anything to be concerned about. Otherwise . . . well . . . don't *you* think there should be something more?

—I don't know, he said.

—Because, she said. If that's all there was to it, everything would be too easy to be worth the trouble.

Cautiously, yet driven to make at least that much of a commitment, he offered what had begun to be his personal slogan: It'll happen if it's supposed to happen.

—I hate fatalists too, she said.

—Few of us can control our fates entirely, he observed. And never in a war.

—You could, Ann said. If you wanted to.

Stubborn and resentful under pressure, he had become impatient. —Who've you been talking to? That idiot Loomis?

—No, not that idiot Loomis who, by the way, isn't as much of an idiot as you think. But to Prus and Laidlaw and your own General Sikorski. They all say the same thing, that you've always been able to make your own way, no matter what the circumstances. That you're an unbelievably strong and stubborn man, and that you live by a code that's entirely your own, but you don't understand the difference between compromise and defeat. I mean, that's almost the basis of your legend.

—People, he muttered, are not legends.

—I agree. So could we try to live like ordinary people? Could we start to have something important to say to each other? I mean, the war doesn't have anything to do with you and me as people. It exists outside us. It lives its own life. It can control our lives only if we let it.

—But the war *is* our life, he argued. There isn't any other kind of life for anyone at this moment.

—It's a fraud, she said. It's a lie. It's a nightmare. It's a mad dream that's poisoning everything around us. It doesn't have anything *real* to do with either one of us.

—It's real enough to me, Ludo said.

For many men, she knew, especially in wartime, their accidental women were as replaceable as used socks, and all too many women employed their lovers as though they were bits of costume jewelry of no particular value: this one to go with this dress and occasion, this one with another. It was the safest way to love when nothing was certain; it guaranteed that the lines of retreat were always open and protected. But it wasn't the simplest way to live.

Month by month in that revelatory year, as absolutes and verities crumbled and as innocence receded, she became increasingly aware of a need for simplicity and order, and for that oddly poignant sense of belonging in the spaces she happened to occupy. She had begun to crave peace, a life of no surprises and no further changes, perhaps even a life of mild, complacent middle-class

conformity whose preoccupations were as undestructive as they
might be mindless. She could detect a note of desperation in that
unexpected longing for everything that, before the war, had filled
her with impatience and contempt. Said in its simplest terms, she
had begun to think herself unable to live without Ludo once the
war was over, as—in what must have been his own earlier, innocent existence—he had been quite unable to consider living without a sense of destiny, duty, honor, and pride.

He, in turn—she thought—needed her because her English life
promised him more than his own; it would seem easier, less of an
unmanageable burden, more convincing, and not without its own
wry shibboleth or two. In his own culture, which was so utterly
demanding in its bloody rituals, and in its endless call for human
sacrifice in the name of history, all the commandments were as
rigid and imperishable as if hammered into granite tablets. *Thou
shalt* and *Thou shalt not* governed every possible human aspira-
tion without regard for human frailty and need. There was never
a provision for forgiveness, nor was anyone allowed to forget who
and what he was, where he had come from, and which debts he
owed. In her life, she thought, he'd find room for welcome argument.

If he hadn't given her life as much thought as Ann, perhaps,
demanded, it was because he had resisted the need to question his
own, she was sure. But once he had begun such questioning, it
must extend to her. She thought that he'd be more forgiving
about her transgressions than about his own; in that thought lay
the promise of the trust she wanted. For this reason, more than
by any design of Laidlaw, she pressed him to declare himself as
hers rather than his own.

—Show me who you really are and what you can become. I
want to know whom I'm willing to trust. You come into my life
like some improbable hound of heaven, you change everything
that I've believed about myself, you make me feel and think
about things I'd never been able to imagine, and then you talk to
me about horses in the Ukraine! I mean, God, lover, by this time,
shouldn't there be more?
—What more must you have?

—Honesty, to begin with. I want to be totally open with you about everything, but how can I when I've almost no idea what you are? Yes, I know, I know. . . . You've lost your family, your friends have been killed, the future of your country is more uncertain every day. . . . I'm not sure I'd ever be able to understand entirely what that means, but it must be a terrible sort of burden. Even so, are you beyond commitment to anything but war?

—I'll do what I can, Ann, Ludo said.

—When? Ann asked. When will you begin?

—When the war is over.

There was a rustling and a creaking and a click of lighters, and Ann's throaty chuckle merely underlined the desperate quality of her voice, shocking in her own ears.

—Well, she said doubtfully. I suppose that is *some* sort of a beginning. I suppose that a declaration of *future* commitment from a man like you is almost as good as a solemn treaty. But I've a sudden premonition of disaster.

Troubled, but struggling not to show it, Ludo asked mildly: What disaster, Ann? Is there something you're not telling me about?

—Oh, my dear, she said and laughed bitterly. Isn't there just? But you're right, of course. It *is* just the war. It's nothing to do with us.

She could feel a peculiar sense of freedom then, as if all the lessons of her life had been finally confirmed, and her illusions could be laid to rest along with all of her admonitory ghosts. But this mild euphoria was a deceptive one because the war—*the damned war*, as she always put it—intruded in a new, mysterious way that had begun to threaten everything he valued.

In London, disquietening reports had begun to reach the government of General Sikorski; a quarter of a million Poles, released by the new Polish-Soviet treaty of alliance from Russian labor camps and prisons, streamed to the assembly points of a new Polish army in the Soviet Union, but there were almost no officers among them, and all inquiries as to the fate of some fifteen thousand of them (captured by the Russians in Poland in 1939) brought evasive answers. All trace of them appeared to have vanished, and those Poles who were reaching the new army on the middle Volga brought tales of massacre. Almost immediately thereafter, almost as if ordered, a strange elusive whispering campaign began to defame the Poles.

Ironically, as Ann was well aware, their standing in Britain had never been higher. The spring and summer of 1942 had been halcyon months for Ludo and his pilots. By midyear, they had chalked up their five hundredth victory above the English Channel, and Loomis, the sight of whose byline Ludo had begun to dread, had made the most of it. His story about Ludo's return from the Dieppe beaches with twenty yards of hardened copper wire wrapped around the tail assembly of his Hurricane (he had, apparently, dived under high-tension wires to massacre a German reinforcement column) was read into the record of the House of Commons. Gerlach, who was shot down by Focke-Wulfs while escorting a mixed British, Polish, and Canadian bomber strike on Bremen, escaped from a German prisoner-of-war camp, sailed a skiff across the Baltic to Malmö in Sweden, and made his way back to Britain by the summer's end. Reszke, whose combat record rivaled that of Ludo, was promoted on his thirtieth birthday and given a new Spitfire squadron of his own. Wilchurzak, who to no one's great surprise married Straka's sister, the orphaned Marylka, flew as Ludo's wingman until he was killed in a fight with Reinecke's Calais Gang shortly after Christmas.

They were still liked in London, admired and praised; there were still medals for them at Buckingham Palace, pictures in the *Post* and the *Illustrated London News*. The Battle of Britain still burned brightly in too many memories for slander, hostility, and suspicion to take root; but something had shifted in the air around them, a dark rearrangement of forces began to take place; something malignant, not yet identified but growing, began to seep across the Atlantic from America and to spread in England.

—*What is it, and who's doing it, and why?* she had asked, and Ludo was immediately evasive. He didn't know. He couldn't identify the source and origin of endemic hatred because bigotry had never been a part of his own commitments. He couldn't understand what had begun to happen, nor how he and his kind could defend themselves.

—How does one fight air? he murmured in reply. I can follow tracers to the gun that fired them, see where they're coming from, and destroy the gunner. But words? Whispers? Lies? How does one fight them?

Reminding him of what she had once told him about slander hadn't made either of them feel better.

Jan Masaryk, whose father had helped to bring about an independent Czechoslovak state after the First World War, explained it best to her by saying that politics began where heroism stopped. At which point, he said, unable to do anything heroic, a man would sometimes rise to greatness by compliance with the verdict of history rather than by defiance, stubbornness, and insistence on honorable resolutions.

It was a warm evening, the last in that disastrous June that marked the high point of German success in North Africa and Russia, and they were standing by the open window of her expensively redecorated flat, watching the women of the antiaircraft batteries planting petunias around their revetments. The quiet flow of relaxed political chatter filled the rooms behind them, and he had just voiced some of his own fears about his country's future.

Then suddenly Masaryk asked: Who do you think is the most heroic statesman of our time?

—Well, she said and looked around the room, pleased that the conversation was taking a less gloomy turn. There's usually one or two to be found right here. Haakon of Norway? Spaak? Yourself? Peter of Yugoslavia?

—I didn't say *the most tragic.* I said *the most heroic,* Masaryk said quietly.

—General Sikorski?

—A knightly man, the Czech said thoughtfully. Austere in all his dedications, honorable, and selfless. But can he make decisions that might deny his own humanity? Everyone is first a victim of his own culture, you see, and then of his history, and only then of his enemies. It takes an extraordinary man to wrench himself and his country out of this cultural and historical context into a contradictory course.

—Winston Churchill, then? Ann asked and smiled and nodded toward Prus, who had begun to walk across the room toward them, and then she felt a touch of pity for him. Like his leader—indeed, like Ludo and the rest of them—Prus wouldn't know how to compromise if his life depended upon it, she thought.

—Certainly, Masaryk said. A romantic giant. But the man I've in mind is Charles de Gaulle.

—Oh, come now, she said, laughing. *Le Grand Charles?* No one can take his posturings seriously. He thinks he *is* France.

—That's why everyone must take him seriously. He sees centuries where the rest of us see people. When Winston Churchill decided to sink the French fleet at Dakar, and kill two thousand Frenchmen without warning, just in case the Germans found a way to gain control of those battleships, de Gaulle never flinched. He gave his consent to this brutal, cynical, and unprovoked massacre of his countrymen because he could look beyond the tragedy, and judge the alternatives, and because he was willing to accept the terrible moral burden of this sacrifice. It takes more than just an ordinary man to think in such terms.

—But that is terrifying! Ann said.

—That, he said softly, is greatness. That's why Churchill admires de Gaulle and will fight to the death for him, no matter how much the Americans despise him, and why he'll always distrust and resent General Sikorski, who is too pure a hero to make such decisions.

—Heavens, she said and gave that necessary artificial laugh she found so demeaning. What a dreadful reason to admire a man. But what does that have to do with your uneasiness about your country's future?

—The Poles may soon be facing a crisis of that kind. We may not be able to stand beside them if they insist on taking an unbending view. I admire General Sikorski. Indeed, any talk about a Central European Federation would be impossible without him. But, for the first time since I met either of these men, I wish that de Gaulle was Polish.

She laughed, a brittle sound, uncertain and spiraling. She heard other laughter, sharp as broken glass, that came from the group around Ludo. Watching him, as she had watched him through the recent months, and trying to remember when she had last seen an untroubled smile on his harrowed face, she was struck by conviction that no matter what she did, the war would defeat her.

Laidlaw's eyes brushed against her gaze with gentle irony, moved on. She thought Ludo looked ill, and fear—quick, irrational, persuasive—made her cold as ice. He had changed and, she knew, that change would continue; the silences between them would become longer and more frequent. In that one harsh, bitter year in which, by yet another irony of history, the Russians had become the Poles' accidental allies—the year in which the nature of the war around them underwent its changes—Ludo seemed to have stepped beyond graveness where she couldn't follow. She too had changed, of course. But her progress seemed to have taken her on an opposite course to Ludo's; abreast at the moment, soon they'd pass each other and move out of sight.

Masaryk had turned to talk to someone else, and she began to listen to other conversations. She moved toward Prus and, unaccountably, she was alive with hope. She had always wanted everything to happen at the precise moment when she needed it, and —if it didn't happen just like that—she'd assume that it couldn't happen. But if you really wanted something, if . . . in Masaryk's phrase . . . you were willing to accept a heavy moral burden, and take the necessary risks and judge the alternatives correctly, then you could make it happen by sheer will.

Even now, even in this puzzling time when the war acquired its dangerous new personality, the Poles were not wholly without hope, she thought. Could she do any less? When a weapon was knocked out of their hands, they looked for other weapons. One of the weapons with which they pressed their claims among the new American arbiters of their fate was the great moral authority of General Sikorski with four million Polish-American voters; it was a weapon with which even Roosevelt was obliged to reckon.

Another was their projected union with the respected Czechs. Their final weapon, the one on which they had always been able to rely, was the continuing exemplary service of Polish airmen, soldiers, and sailors who fought beside the British on every front in Africa and Europe, and who, in this beginning of their fortune's crisis, fought harder than ever to prove themselves and their country worthy of remembrance. If, in the end, these weapons should prove unavailing, at least they'd know that they didn't have to blame themselves. She could do no less. The lesson which they taught was suddenly very clear.

She wanted to tell Prus then (at once! immediately! while the illusion of hope still made a terrible sort of sense!) how afraid she had become for Ludo, whose legend seemed to have acquired the weight of a cross. But Prus seemed burdened with an uncharacteristic fear of his own. He was to leave for Moscow the next day to search for the missing fifteen thousand Polish officers, and for a million and a half other Polish soldiers and civilians who had vanished in the cold white spaces of the Soviet Union, and he was ill at ease about what he might find.

—Lots of bears and such, I expect, she said and listened to her own uneasy, insincere laughter.

—I hope that's all I find. The rumors we've been hearing here are . . . disturbing.

—Oh, well, she said and made a brief, dismissive gesture. You know what rumors are worth. I'm sure you'll find everyone is all right. What could have happened to all those people, after all? I mean, if they were prisoners of war?

—In Russia, anything can happen, he said gloomily. When you are dealing with the Russians, you must always be prepared for the worst. It's . . . not just a different civilization, you see. It's a different world. Our way of thinking is quite incomprehensible to them. And theirs, thank God, is unimaginable here.

—Oh, come now, she said. Can it really be as bad as all that? There's not *that* much difference between people.

—We've known them for a long, long time, he said. We've been at one kind of war or another with them for five hundred years. It's not as if we'd just read about them in a book.

—Why do the Russians hate the Poles so much, then? she asked and he seemed puzzled for a moment.

—I don't think they hate us. In fact, I think there's a sort of grudging admiration in their feelings for us. We're always in their way, you see. We're always causing turmoil in their empires. They have nightmares about our influence among their own people. All Western notions come to them through Poland, including the one about man's right to determine his own fate, and any of the Eastern European peoples they control—like the Lithuanians, the Ruthenians, the Byelorussians, and the Ukrainians—look to us for that Western air they must breathe to survive as nations. They've tried to swallow us for five hundred years and we've always stuck sideways in their throats. And, as Stalin said last August to General Sikorski, when we went to Moscow to sign our treaty of alliance, *The Russians have ruled in Warsaw only once; the Poles have been three times in the Kremlin.* It's not the kind of thing that means much in Washington and London, but it's something that no Russian would ever forget.

—You've friends as well as enemies in Washington and London, she said to encourage him, but he would be neither encouraged nor comforted.

—We're treading a very dangerous line, he said. Our proposed union with the Czechs is the beginning of a wall that would keep the Russians permanently out of Central Europe, and they can see that as clearly as if it were written in the sky in letters of fire. I think Stalin would do anything to destroy General Sikorski, wreck us in Washington and London, and continue his policy of dividing all of us against each other. But if there's one lesson that you British teach in your own brave genius for survival, it's that survival, pursued steadfastly to the end, must lead at least to a *kind* of victory by the denial of the fruits of victory to the enemy. That way, at least, not all the lives are thrown away for nothing. We've been taught for a thousand years that our lives are nothing, that they're worth only what they're spent for. I wish it were possible for us to learn something else.

She seized her opportunity then, because it would most likely be her last.

—I must ask you to do something for me. I've never asked you for anything before. But we are friends, and friends should always stand by each other and help each other, shouldn't they?

—That's what one would like to believe, he agreed.

—It's about Ludo, of course, she said. He has to stop flying. If he keeps flying, he'll destroy himself.

—Has it occurred to you that this might be what he wants?

—You told me once that it didn't matter what he wanted. That he must be useful to more than just his friends. You know how useful he could be to you in this difficult political climate.

—Yes, I know. But he is yet to realize it for himself.

—Then give him time to do that! Have him taken out of the air where, day by day, he loses more of himself. Each time one of his pilots dies, a part of him dies as well! How much longer do you think he can go on doing that?

—Perhaps he's stronger than you think, Prus said.

—And perhaps he isn't! Perhaps he's just as vulnerable as anyone else! His concern for his pilots has become obsessive. He actually feels that he owes them their lives.

—I know the feeling, Prus said.

—Then you should know exactly what I mean!

—I also know what it means for him to fly, Prus said and made a weary gesture, and she could see how old he had become. A fighter pilot is the only kind of man for whom any kind of personal victory is still possible. And as long as Ludo believes that wars are won in combat, there is nothing that I can do for him.

—Look, she said, pleaded. If you can't have him grounded for his sake, or even for your own, do it for me. I need him. I never thought I'd hear myself say this to anyone, least of all myself, but I do. I know that it's an absurd discovery to make in the middle of a war, but I want to open myself to life without fear of loss. For better or worse, I've picked on Ludo as my vehicle to that end, but I can't even reach him! He mustn't, he absolutely mustn't fly.

—I'll see what I can do, Prus said.

—Thank you. Thank God and thank you. You're a dear man, Janusz, do you know?

—Dear? he said with an ironic bitterness she hadn't expected. *Costly* is, perhaps, the better word. As in the price a woman pays for her commitment to a single-minded man who is first a soldier, then a patriot, and only then a human being who might be responsive to her needs. Almost any other kind of man must represent a better life to a woman, I should think.

—That might depend on the woman, she observed.

—Yet I know that *any* woman deserves more than that.

—Women are people. People make their choices. And not even the American Constitution guarantees more than the mere pursuit of happiness.

—No doubt.

—Yet Lala loved you. I am sure she must have, Ann felt compelled to say.

Prus had begun to hum the song about Lady War that she had heard so often among the Polish pilots, a song to which they had given an ironic meaning, and she pressed on, anxious to secure her advantage.

—You know that General Sikorski can use some help in Whitehall. You know how Winston Churchill feels about the general, and you probably know why. I can't think of a man among you who'd be less likely to irritate him than Ludo. He fascinates Churchill. Laidlaw is cultivating him. For some people, he is everything they think of when they remember the Battle of Britain. And that's the sort of imagery that Churchill understands very well.

—Don't ever let Ludo know that we've had this conversation, Prus warned. He'd never forgive you.

—It's worth the risk, she said.

—Are you sure, Ann? Are you really sure? Because when you begin to manipulate another person's life, especially a life like Ludo's, the penalty of failure can be an extreme one.

—I think that he's my last chance to be the kind of woman I was meant to be. Or ever wanted to be. Nothing else seems worth the effort it takes.

He nodded, kissed her hand, departed. Then there were only the last of her guests to speed on their way.

She felt quite spent and very frightened then. She stood by her window, looking out into the darkening day. The treetops in the park fell away like gapped teeth, and she heard again the wail of a siren. A lone German bomber was droning overhead and the guns in the park began to buck and bellow, and shrapnel rattled on the rooftops and among the leaves.

If only it were possible to live in gentler times, she thought. If this depleting war didn't intrude into every nook and cranny of her life, threatening every hope . . . If that old, abandoned sense of untroubled English permanence could be resurrected so that plans, hopes, and expectations could be trusted, then she'd be able to continue trusting in God's will. But, it seemed to her then, life could no longer extend believable promises. The night was thundering redly in the east. Hatred drew nearer, measured by the minute. Above, torn clouds caught fire and a comet fell, trailing flames.

CHAPTER XVII

IN JULY 1943, leaves became available again. The weather, always unpredictable in England, had turned to ground fog and rain and low cloud, and whole days passed without a Messerschmitt or Focke-Wulf sighted on patrol. Ludo's pilots became irritable because they were bored. They had time to think and sometimes a passion of homesickness got into them and they mourned lost friends.

Their Hurricanes were taken away from them and sent to training squadrons, and they waited impatiently for the Spitfire Mark IIBs with which they were to be re-equipped. Finally, Johnny Sommerset (who had become group captain and station commander for the six fighter squadrons of the two Polish wings) sent them all off to London for a weekend's recuperative wildness and distraction. Ludo had taken the early morning train with Gerlach and Reszke, pleased to be getting away from flying for a while, yet ill at ease because he wouldn't be returning to the squadron. He had orders to report for reassignment to the headquarters of General Sikorski. On the following Monday, he was to go on reassignment leave (fourteen days in which to find a Lon-

don billet and move his belongings). Gerlach was promoted to replace him as the squadron leader.

—Any idea of what you might be doing from now on, sir?
Reszke asked, and he shrugged silently, and Gerlach said swiftly:
We'll always have a machine for you, you can be sure of that. I'm
having the reserve bird painted with your numbers. And your red
spinner, of course. It's yours anytime you get tired of flying a
desk.

—I'm tired of it already and I don't even know where it is,
Ludo said.

—Well, you know where to find us, Gerlach said. At least,
most of the time. We're going to miss you, Major.

—I'll miss you, he said automatically and, suddenly, he was
quite sure that without him to look after them their parting
would be permanent.

The flat green English suburbs rolled past the windows of their
third-class carriage, but he thought of another countryside, made
greener by its loss, and a soft curse hissed out before he could
stop it. *You owe it to us, Ludo,* Wlada had said to him in a forest
clearing and he had felt, again, the quick hot lick of irritation because he prided himself on owing nothing to anyone, the dead or
the living, memory least of all. When you owe nothing, you are
independent; you are free to make all your own coldly calculated
decisions about everything; you're never obliged to render an accounting. If ever a manual had been written for the maintenance
and operation of a life such as his, that would have been in it, he
supposed.

What do I owe and how do I pay it? Ludo thought and listened for an answer among the grim and unsmiling young pilots
who would never need to ask themselves that kind of question.
Owe? Pay? And of all the possible times, why now? Having found
something with Ann for which he thought he might want to live,
he could no longer feel contempt for death, yet the war demanded continuing disdain.

In November 1942, the war's deadly tide began to turn. A great
American army stormed ashore in French North Africa, under an
unknown general named Dwight Eisenhower. The Afrika Korps
of Field Marshal Erwin Rommel had run into forty acres of artillery, planted wheel to wheel near El Alamein on the Egyptian

border, and the Germans' African adventure was over. In Russia (the Russians had now become the heroes of the hour), a huge trap was sprung upon the Germans in a place called Stalingrad, and three hundred thousand German captives vanished in the tundra at just about the time the Polish army of General Anders, an army of starved scarecrows and ragged human wreckage released from Russian prisons, began to make its way to the Middle East. They came without their officers. In April 1943, the Germans announced a grim discovery in Russia: twenty mass graves, hidden under the pine and spruce of the Katyn Forest, containing the bound and gagged bodies of the murdered Poles and the doom of Ludo and his kind was sealed.

At once, almost as if on cue, a violent anti-Polish campaign broke out all over Britain. Slogans equating Poles with Nazis appeared on the walls, right under whitewashed demands for an invasion of the Continent to relieve the pressure on the Soviet Union. Mobs invaded Polish military hospitals in Scotland and threw wounded soldiers and airmen into the streets. Poles were caricatured in the public prints as dupes of German propaganda. They were insulted and assaulted in the pubs, where there were no more cheers or free drinks. English and Scottish girls who married them, or who went out with them, were pelted with garbage. Special teams of British and American information officers began to tour public meetings, schools, union halls, and military bases to explain why the Poles didn't really have a right to that half of their country which the Russians had seized in 1939. The Russians announced themselves outraged by the request of General Sikorski for the International Red Cross to investigate the Katyn massacre, and broke diplomatic relations with his government. A Polish Committee of National Liberation (the nomenclature was still innocent and unrevealing in those days) appeared in Moscow as the provisional government of a future Poland, and it was only a matter of time before Washington and Whitehall would recognize that collection of expatriate Communists, most of whom had left Poland long before the war, as Poland's legitimate government. The Czechs, reacting to pressure from President Roosevelt (who, in turn, was acting on behalf of Stalin, on the advice of Communist sympathizers in the State Department), took fright and canceled their proposed union with the Poles. Isolated among their allies, who began to treat them as if they had been enemies from the start, a quarter of a million Polish airmen, soldiers, and sailors in the West were about to become an army in exile, fighting for a homeland to which they'd be unable to return.

Ann said, as even the most sympathetic of the Poles' critics in England and America had begun to say: But why did you make such a fuss about that Katyn business? Granted, the Russians probably did it. Why not wait until after the war to ask questions about it?

—Because the murders were discovered now, Ludo said. Not after the war. Because General Sikorski is not de Gaulle, who can ignore a massacre of his countrymen. Because the Russians would have found any pretext to destroy Sikorski. Because we're human and we don't look at dead men as numbers in a ledger. Because we thought that we could rely on your sense of morality and justice, if not your gratitude.

—Well, of course you can! she said. We're not as venal and corrupt as all that.

Struggling to contain his bitterness and anger, he explained as patiently as he could that the enmity and brutality of Russians was nothing new in his countrymen's experience, that for the Poles there were two sets of enemies in this war—as, indeed, there had been through their history—and that while he and his kind would do their duty to their Western Allies, always and in all circumstances, they should not be asked to do the impossible.

—We can accept adversity with contempt, he said. But you shouldn't ask us to endorse our own humiliation.

What he didn't tell her, what he could neither forget nor ignore nor dismiss from his consciousness in any other way, was that the name of his brother Janek had been listed among the victims of the Katyn massacre. His body had been exhumed by the Germans with nearly seven thousand uniformed corpses found in the first two of the Katyn graves.

—Still, Ann said. It all seems rather ill-considered, politically naïve, to say the least. If, as you say, the Russians were just waiting for a pretext to set up their own Polish puppet show, why give them the chance?

—They'd do it sooner or later anyway, he said. Now, at least, we're still necessary to you. And we're armed.

—Would you turn against us, then?

—Don't be ridiculous, he said angrily. We're not all suicidal. And *we* do not betray our allies in the middle of a war! No. No. There's still some hope that things won't end too badly. We still hold some cards, as long as there is fighting to be done. And we still have General Sikorski.

—Can one man do so much for you? she asked wonderingly.

—He unites us, he said. He has great influence in the United States, you know. As long as we have him, President Roosevelt must be careful with us.

—You could replace Sikorski in your generation, she said suddenly, and he began to laugh.

—Why should I?

—You *could*, you know, she insisted.

—Ann, he said through bitter laughter, are you being wifely? Are you ambitious for me?

—What's wrong with ambition? she asked. The higher you rise, the more you can do for your people. Even Janusz Prus thought that the time had come for a new leader among you, one with whom our own politicians might feel more at home. And Janusz is totally devoted to General Sikorski.

—They're two of a kind, Ludo said.

—And you're a third, she said.

—There's a saying among us that no man's youth dies until he murders it. You're old and useless only when you've betrayed your own youthful vision of yourself. Ah (and here he laughed in a way that made her heart constrict), if it weren't for our devotion to our own ideas of what we and our country ought to be, we'd have been wiped off the maps a thousand years ago.

—But does anyone else know who and what you are? Ann asked. And if you can't tell them in some way that makes sense to them, why should they care, Ludo?

Thinking about Wlada, Norwid, Janek, Straka, and Wilchurzak, and about the many other pilots who had died, he said: I thought we *had* told them.

—Not in a way that anyone but you could understand, she said.

In the train, going up to London, her words turned and twisted in his memory like Hurricanes in a dogfight, so that they seemed to hang before his eyes everywhere he looked. The days when smiling English travelers would offer their seats to Polish fighter pilots were long gone. The windows in the corridor where he stood, jammed between drunken black American truck drivers and gloomy British soldiers, were dark and smeared with fog. Rain splashed against them and ran like muddy tears.

Wlada, Norwid, Janek . . . the ghostly roll call rattled in his head. Straka and Wilchurzak . . . Karcz (burning over Calais), Kulesza (drowned in the North Sea), Zegar (whose time had run out only the day before) . . . Frantisek, not yet dead but dying in a London hospital . . .

Reszke, he noted, was looking at him with concern.

Wlada, he knew, was dead, starved to death in Russia, but he didn't even know where, in that vast Soviet graveyard of Polish hopes, her body was buried. Piotr was alive, in Egypt with the Anders army, preparing to join the recent invasion of Italy, but everyone else he had loved had been taken from him.

He wondered, looking from one of the grim young pilots to another, which of them would be the very last to die, and knew that without them, and without all the others, there'd be no home to which he'd ever be able to return. Twice now, when he was very tired, he caught himself addressing Reszke as *Norwid*, and Gerlach as *Piotr*, and it was only a matter of time before the youngest of them, Urban, became his replacement for the murdered Janek. He knew that by the laws of nature he should have gone first. As the oldest brother, he had been sworn to protect the younger, whose claims to life were newer, therefore better, than his own. But he had failed to save any of them, time and time again, and this failure brushed against his conscience no matter how impervious to any other feeling he might have become. Brave, unquestioning, obedient—yet (he thought) trapped in their destiny like sparrows among the ruins—Reszke and Gerlach had become the sole remaining reason for his own survival.

Then the softly rolling English landscapes fell away and the train wound through a bleak industrial wasteland that was a perfect setting for images of disaster.

There was a moment in the last week before he went on leave that was degrading and (in the end) revealing. Never before had he lost control of himself to such an extent. He had come back from a sweep in the Pas de Calais, where his squadron had run into an ambush. Sixty-six Focke-Wulfs, the sum of Reinecke's orange-nosed Geschwader, had fallen on them out of the sun as they went to ground level to strafe canvas dummies parked as decoys on an airfield, and Ludo lost five men. It was their first defeat since they had come to England. Coming as it did on top of all their other humiliations, it drove the pilots half mad with frustration. Ludo blamed himself, his preoccupation with matters that had nothing to do with the job at hand, the distraction of his fatal fascination with Ann, and his own growing bitterness.

—You're making me kill my own youth! he had raged at Ann.

—What the bloody hell are you raving about? she raged in return. Am I to blame because you've lost your grip? You're forty years old in a game that calls for the stamina and reflexes of a twenty-year-old boy. You've said that yourself. You've no business rolling about the sky in an airplane. If you can't keep your mind on your job, then start flying a desk! I can arrange that for you with no trouble at all!

—Oh, yes, he said bitterly. You British are damn good at arranging things. But that's one arrangement you're not going to make.

—Don't you dare to speak to me like that, you bloody little Pole! she screamed at him and was immediately aware that she had gone too far, but her pride wouldn't allow her to step back. What makes you think you can blame anybody else for your own damn failures?

—Ah, so it's come to that, has it? he shouted. You're joining the chorus?

—I don't join anything! she cried. Neither am I a stiff-necked throwback to the nineteenth century who misreads his own nostalgia as political reality! Get off your national cross, will you? If you lack the will to take charge of events, you've no right to complain because life mistreats you. And if you've no stomach for life as it is, rather than as you dream it should be, then have the courage and simple decency to blow out your brains and be done with it! Has no one ever told you that pathos is boring?

Stunned by the onslaught, Ludo felt relief.

—What brought that on? he said.

—You did. I did. The damned war. I don't know, she said truthfully. If there's one thing that drives me berserk, it's people who enjoy their own suffering. There's just so much of it that nobody asks for.

—Events, he said. Yes. Well. I've been thinking about that. But how can I turn myself into a politician?

—There's not much to it, she said, relieved in her turn. Believe me, I know. All you need is ruthlessness and cunning and contempt for everybody but yourself. People will assume that you're fit to lead them if you look as if you might know where you're going.

—There's a saying among us that a Pole may not know exactly where he's heading, but he always knows where he is coming from. We wear our country's history like an overcoat.

—Is there really such a saying? she asked and put her arms around him.

—No, he said and sighed. I just made it up.

—I thought so. You see? You'd make an excellent politician. It's a lot better than looking tragic and hitting out at people who care for you the most. All it takes is courage and decisiveness and you've never lacked that.

—Lately, he said, I've wondered.

—Then don't, she said. Act. Seize an opportunity. Otherwise, you'll only have yourself to blame for all the tragedies you want to prevent.

Wondering, he asked: How do you know so much about things like that?

And she, immediately on her guard, said: Practice. Intuition. Call it what you will.

In the train, remembering, he thought that Ann must have touched the lives of many men in just such a way. They had met neither too soon for him to recognize his opportunity, nor too late. Age had not yet extinguished all their optimism. Yet if their nights were right, the days were terribly wrong and both of them knew it. War—his damned trade, as she called it—had become that exalting and depleting mistress that sent his adrenaline flowing with a rush.

—No mere woman can compete with that, she said to him on one of those rare days of closeness when everyone speaks the truth.

—If that's your rival, it's your only one, he said.

—For the time. For the moment. And it's quite enough. I don't compete, as I've told you once before. It's all or nothing for me, lover. I am not a hobby. I'm willing to take you on as a full-time job, but I've got to get back at least as much as I give. Otherwise, my own reserves will be exhausted in short order, and then what'll happen?

No longer willing to defend himself (he had been badly shaken by his defeat in Reinecke's ambush), Ludo would offer no excuses for himself.

—I can't give you what I haven't got.

—Oh, you've got it all right, lover. You've got it. I know it when I see it. But you're obviously not a man for more than one commitment at a time.

—And what about you?

She chose to mock herself.

—I'm a woman. Women don't waste much time in burying their dead. One does have to go on with the business of living, don't you know.

The day, the first day of his leave and the last as a squadron commander, had scarcely begun. Its outlines were unpromising

and shrouded in the rain and fog, and he tried (in vain) to anticipate its course.

The headlines, over which the early morning passengers were
nodding in a second-class compartment, were thick with Italy's invasion and the savagery of German resistance in the mountains of
the peninsula. There had been an American landing in the
Solomon Islands, a thousand-bomber raid on Essen, Hamburg,
and Cologne. In Moscow, the Russians had fired a hundred salvos
with two hundred guns (or perhaps it was one hundred guns and
two hundred salvos) to celebrate yet another massive victory on
their way to the west. Each day, victory by victory, the Russian
armies rolled closer to Poland. Soon (it wouldn't even take a
year!) the Red tide would engulf his country once again, bringing
with it a Communist puppet government, the Red Militia, the
midnight knock, doors kicked in at four o'clock in the morning,
prisons and the firing squads in cellars, endless deportation trains.
Once more, as so often in his country's history, private destinies
would be one with a public fate, and there'd be no Poland to
which an exiled army might return.

He closed his eyes against the grim and deadening landscapes
of industrial London and against the walls with their insulting
slogans: SECOND FRONT NOW! HELP RUSSIA! HANG THE POLES! How
to remain proud in humiliation, he wondered. Perhaps the young
men knew. He didn't. His throat constricted and his eyesight
blurred.

—Is anything the matter? Reszke said.

—No. Nothing at all, he lied.

—It's really going to be strange to fly without you, Major,
Gerlach said. Of course, I'm glad to get the squadron. Glad and
proud. But it just isn't going to be the same thing. We're going
to miss that scarlet spinner of yours in the lead echelon.

—I'll will it to you, if you like, Ludo said.

—I'd rather you had kept it. I wish we could've stuck together.
I didn't mind when Reszke started playing squadron leader on his
own, that just made us a better squadron, right? But I've a feeling
things won't turn out too well with all of us scattered.

—You'll manage, Ludo said.

—What worries me, though, Reszke said. Is what we're doing
really going to count? I don't mind any of it if it'll mean some-

thing in the end. But the English don't even know who we are.
How are they going to remember us when the shooting's over?

—Fondly, I hope, Gerlach said. I do my best in spite of the sulfur they put in the tea.

—We'll think of something to remind them, Ludo said.

—But what will they *think*?

—They don't think, Gerlach said. There are only six opinions
in the English language. Ask them about the Germans and they'll
say: *Best infantry in the world.* The French? *A nation of actors,
the worst of whom are on the stage.* The Italians? *Half of them
have operatic voices and the other half sings.* Paris is *that place
where it always rains on Bastille Day.* The American Revolution? *The best thing that ever happened to the British Empire.* I never worry about what they think.

—You might have to worry about it when the war is over,
Reszke said.

—I doubt it. I doubt it very much, Gerlach said. I'm not as
good a pilot as all that.

—Well, Reszke said. I worry about it. No matter how carefully
it's explained to them that Poland wasn't a Dostoevski novel full
of debauched nobles and their suffering serfs, that no one there
lived in a mud hut on a diet of vodka and potatoes, and that
there's no reason why I should be struck speechless at the sight of
a double-decker bus, they just won't believe it! They smile and
nod their heads and keep on asking if there was a cinema in Warsaw. If we shoot wolves in the streets in winter and if I've ever
eaten marmalade before. They take pride in explaining that in
England newspapers are published every day and that milk comes
in bottles. Who, in God's name, do they think we are?

—They think what their politicians tell them, Gerlach said.
What they read in the *Times* and in the *Daily Worker*. And
now, of course, they think what the Americans make them think.
This is a country where a man once said, *England expects every
man to do his duty*, but all they're saying these days is *Got any
gum, chum?*

—Be serious, Reszke said. This isn't anything to make jokes
about.

—So who's making jokes? People will think of you what they
want to think. What's convenient for them. What makes them

feel better about themselves. There's nothing you can do about that.

—But we've got to get them to see us as we are! Reszke said. Otherwise, why should they give us a thought when the damned war is over?

—There's no reason for them to do anything of the kind. As far as they're concerned, God is an Englishman. They're made in His image. Everyone else is some kind of animal that walks on its hind legs. Just learn to wag your tail, and you'll be all right.

—Goddammit, Gerlach, Reszke cried. I'm trying to say something I think is important!

—And you think I'm not? Listen, I tried to explain Poland to some kindly maiden ladies who invited me to tea in a parsonage. It was just after we landed in England, so it was a real act of charity on their part. I said that life in Poland was a tragedy for those who could feel and a comedy for those who could think, and that it was the only country where, if a boy told his parents he planned to be a poet, they were pleased to hear it. I said that we were taught to interweave a personal destiny with a public fate and that we tried to live in the center of our best and bravest selves. I thought that covered it all quite well. Well, you never saw such embarrassed people. You'd think I had pissed in their silver ornamental teapot! I mean . . . they were hurt! Here they were, you see, doing their Christian duty on behalf of a picturesque denizen of the fucking steppes, and he's telling them about a land of poets? He's making statements that sound as if they might have come out of a book? So I stuck a stick of celery in my ear and drank my tea through a cube of sugar clenched in my teeth and everybody loved me. I still get postcards from that vicar's wife.

—What's the point of the celery? Reszke said.

—Well, what the hell else was I going to stick in my ear? They didn't have carrots, Gerlach said.

—You're a fool, Gerlach, d'you know that? Reszke said, but he was smiling and the tension had begun to ebb.

—Of course I am, Gerlach said. If people laugh at you, they're not obliged to feel afraid of you. If they're not afraid of you, they leave you alone. I keep my serious moments for the Focke-Wulfs. None of us have to explain anything to the Calais Gang.

—And isn't that the damnedest part of it? Reszke said and

laughed bitterly. The only people who still seem to remember who and what we are, and what we can do, are the bloody Germans.

—Well, that's the other side of the medal, Gerlach said and laughed. If people *don't* laugh at you, you'd better be damn sure you can hit them where they hurt the most.

Then they were silent and, perhaps, embarrassed, and Ludo was quite sure that he would never see any of them again. He wanted to reach out and touch them, as he had reached out to his brothers on the morning that the war began, as if this fleeting human contact could ensure their continuity and safety, but this time he held himself in check. Reszke had flown with him for more than twelve years, Gerlach for seven, Auerbach had been a dependable constant in his life since Ludo was sixteen. Grounded, moved by orders he hadn't solicited, he was stepping out of their lives. This, too, was a sort of dying, he supposed.

He knew that he should be feeling some special sort of grief; sorrow is a very human attribute, after all, and all partings bring pain. But, he thought, there was a limit to the amount of moral agony that a man could be expected to inflict on himself while on leave; he made sure that none of his thoughts and feelings would show to the others.

For a time, for a long moment that none of them wanted interrupted, they stood on the sidewalk outside the railroad station and talked about things that didn't matter to them. A man called Arthur Koestler had written a new book titled *Arrival and Departure* and this had a certain symbolic meaning for them. Reszke, a theatergoer, couldn't make up his mind whether to see *The Patriots* or *Tomorrow the World*; he thought that Noel Coward's *This Happy Breed* might be the best choice. The rain kept falling. The wind whipped up the short utility skirts of the scurrying English girls and they looked at their legs.

Nothing, Ludo thought, not even the weather, had changed since he had last come up to London, and he couldn't remember the names of all the dead pilots whose funerals he had attended there.

Walking away from the station in the day's soft rain, Ludo knew that thereafter his own life would be different. A chapter had closed, a clearly defined purpose had vanished, an identity on which he had relied had come to an end. Whatever happened to him from this moment on would *have* to be different; life itself might be new.

A taxi wasn't to be found. The rain had dwindled to a wet drizzle, the kind that Ann described as *Scotch mist,* and he walked all the way from Victoria to Mayfair, listening to the sharp clicks of his leather heels echoing from banks and government buildings. He passed the soiled monuments of statesmen and military heroes: marble and limestone and cement and ornamental railings, and names that no one bothered to remember. Pigeons, he thought wryly, are the final beneficiaries of great deeds.

Then he was climbing the two familiar flights of carpeted stairs, and then he stood in a paneled hall under a groined and coffered ceiling where the lackluster shades of another century hung between the arches, and then he was rattling the polished brass lion head beside the discreet nameplate, and then the door opened.

CHAPTER XVIII

SHE HAD CROPPED her black hair very short, in keeping with the austerity of the times in which there were no shampoos or lotions, and soap was rationed, and hot water was measured by the inch in bathtubs. With her tanned, olive coloring, the strength and length of her face, and her luminous black eyes in which, with just a touch of imagination, he could see the Spanish sailor whom a passionate Irishwoman had pulled from the wreck of an Armada galleon, she looked like a young man: Mediterranean, ready to guide you among Moorish treasures, sell you a fake antique and offer you his sister, pick your pocket, and send you out in a cousin's taxi (with a leaky radiator) to look at pyramids in the desert. All other women he had known, he knew, would be merely insipid in comparison, and, of course, all similarities to young men ended at her neck.

Time had given weight and substance to her body. She was (he thought) one of those rare women who, exciting and appealing in their youth, become beautiful only in maturity, and what had once been a gamine impertinence of breast and hip and thigh, and glint of eyes and dark sheen of hair, acquires the satisfying reassurance of kept promises. One needs to be only marginally romantic to know that such women, rightly limited in number, provide a man's full ration of human possibilities. Met too soon in frenetic youth, they are easily lost; met too late, they'd underline the awful emptiness of age. For years after their passing, often for the remainder of a life-span, a man will be wholly inaccessible to any other women, who will appall him with their insufficiency. He will remember life lived at optimum intensity, at its highest speed, and neither loss of innocence nor the end of opportunity will have much to do with the regret and wonder that combine to form his final gratitude. Crudely, wryly, as in his memory of war, he will say to himself: *I have seen the elephant; I know that it exists,* and time and again, in the most unlikely of middle-aged moments, he will feel the lined and brittle skin around his mouth crack into a smile.

Ann brought him a drink. She sat down beside him on the disordered ottoman where they had made love. Once more, the sirens had begun to wail their warning of intrusion in the clouds and, after a moment, he could identify the pulsing drone of the lone Dornier Do 17Z: the two weak, underpowered Bramo 323s were unmistakable, fading in and out. Willy Messerschmitt had cornered the best engines for his Emils, and the poor old Dorniers had to do with whatever was left.

Listening, looking toward the ceiling, Ann said: They don't come much in daylight anymore.

—It's not a raid, he said. It's a reconnaissance machine. They've found a way to take photographs through clouds.

Naked, she said: How very vulgar of them. But not through roofs and ceilings, I hope?

—Wouldn't you like to be Hermann Goering's pinup?

—And be drooled over by a fat Hun? What a revolting thought.

—You don't mind, though, if I do some drooling?

—For some strange reason I don't quite understand, you seem to have earned the right. I wish, though, that we had our own flat to do our drooling in. This one is Derek's, you know. I'm never quite at ease with the thought of Derek's malevolent little presence near me. Or any other of the malevolent presences that occupy so much of my life these days. What would you say if I got a flat for us somewhere else?

—A home, Ann? I wouldn't know what to do with it.

—Yes, I know you've lost one. And I am opposed in principle to being a replacement. But I've my own qualities to offer, as you do, which makes the whole thing original rather than a replacement. It's the difference between using someone for a moment's pleasure, for distraction, for an interruption in a dull, despairing sort of hanging-on at the far edge of reality, and whatever possibilities can exist between two people. Believe me, darling, it's all as much of a surprise to me as it seems to you.

The guns in the park began to fire then, and the windows rattled, and the glasses chimed on the cocktail table, and Ludo said: I think that reality has just spoken to us.

Ann said, at once: That sort of reality has nothing to say to women. How long was it until you knew exactly what you wanted?

—You mean, in life?

—Yes. In life. If *life* has anything to do with the way we're living.

—I don't know that I ever did, Ludo said.

She laughed quickly, averted her face, said in a particularly bitter voice: Well, you're only forty. You've time to decide what you want to be when you grow up.

—Whatever it is, he said, it looks as if it'll be happening on the ground. I'm no longer flying. This is my reassignment leave. I'm to report tomorrow to General Sikorski.

—Thank God for that, she said and added quickly: You've done enough, you know. It's time you let some of those young men of yours get some of the glory.

—That's the last thing any of them want.

The afternoon had moved toward its end and the day had darkened. High over the clouded heart of England, a machine turned into a ball of fire and began to fall, and he rose on one elbow to watch it through the window.

—Did I ever tell you my favorite fantasy? he asked.

—Mmm . . . no, I don't believe you did. We've acted out a number of them, here and there, but you've never stated your order of preference.

—It's to do with flying, he said. You fly and you meet everything you've ever hated and feared and despised. Imagine a plane carrying Hitler, Stalin, all your own corrupt politicians . . . and, along with them, everything about yourself that you find difficult to live with . . .

—All in one neat little package, she said. How convenient.

—Yes. You meet it, and you dive on it, and you press a little red button, and you change the history of the world.

—And your own, of course?

—For whatever that's worth.

—It's a nice little fantasy, she said. But it *is* only a kind of wishful thinking, isn't it? I mean, nothing that you can do in the air can really make that much difference, can it? And life, whatever that might be, *is* lived on the ground.

—I can't imagine what that kind of life could be.

—Try it, you might like it, she said brutally and he began to laugh.

—Are you playing prophet, or is there something you know that you haven't told me? Because there's no reason for my being grounded, as far as I can see.

—Someone must have thought that you'd be more useful in another job, Ann said and rose on her pillows to reach for a cigarette.

—I'd hate to think that I'm as much a victim of forces beyond my control as everyone else I know.

Suddenly angry, or (he thought) afraid of something he didn't understand, she said sharply: What makes you think that someone is manipulating you? Or, if they are, that it isn't for the best? And didn't you once say that things happen if they're supposed to happen? Sometimes it's better not to question *everything*. And, anyway (and here her voice softened and she laughed a little), since when have *you* started to question your fate?

—Since it ceased to coincide with my vision of myself, I suppose, he said.

—Really, she said and laughed, although this laughter had no humor in it: Isn't that asking for too much? I mean, do you know *anyone* who gets to be and do only what they want? Dreams are all very well, my dear, but sometimes reality must be faced before it overwhelms us all. And, sometimes, it's necessary to give your dreams a bit of a helping hand.

Not yet suspicious, but wondering, he said: Do you know something about all this, Ann? Did Prus say anything the last time you saw him? There wasn't any warning about my reassignment, you see. No one said anything. There wasn't even a suggestion of anything in the wind.

—Why should I know something? she asked evenly. It seems that I can't even order and organize my own life very well.

They were using the same words to speak of different things; language had become suddenly less a means of communication than a vehicle for misunderstanding. The guns barked and bellowed in the park.

She said: I really should've known better than to fall in love. It leaves a person so utterly defenseless. Loss, the kind that you can't live with, becomes so very easy then. Wouldn't you think that at my age, and with my experience, I'd know better?

—What does that have to do with what I am saying?

And then both of them were staring at each other, struggling to be understood over the maddened roaring of the guns, and quite unable to hear one word that was said.

—*I said*, she said, and *All that I meant was*, Ludo had begun and saw that she was no longer listening to anything. She had begun to stare past his shoulder; her long, uncompromising mouth twisted into an ugly wound, and then she scrambled for a sheet with which to cover herself and shouted (*screamed* was the better word, perhaps, because of the pain that he saw reflected in her eyes): *What are you doing here?*

He slid away from her, turned, and looked toward the door that they had been too preoccupied to secure, and saw the short, balding, narrow-shouldered man who was regarding them with slack-jawed idiocy. He noted (and recognized, of course) the thin, schoolmasterish, disappointed mouth, the unsuccessful military moustache, and the petulant gestures with which the shocked intruder had begun to stab the air. Hudson's features seemed to have been designed for someone larger than himself.

Two hectic spots of color appeared on his white well-bred face, and he seemed to be groping for invisible weapons.

Unaccountably, Ann began to laugh. Her laughter, muffled under bedclothes, bordered on hysteria.

—Oh, God, she mumbled through her sheet. Well. Now you've another enemy who'll join plots against you. Is there no end to these damned accidental appointments with disaster?

The shocked and painfully embarrassed British officer had begun to retreat.

—I beh-beh-beg your pardon, he was muttering stiffly. I . . . had no idea.

—I just bet you didn't, Ann said, sighed, and sat up, clutching the soiled, damp sheet to her breasts and neck. Is this another of John Laidlaw's brilliant, unnerving little moves?

—I . . . I . . . I . . . , Hudson stammered, and Ludo felt both embarrassment and pity. It was as if both of the men had come, suddenly, face-to-face with the worst kind of treason: the betrayal of their best hopes and favorite illusions, and something of each man's vision of himself as well. Reaching for his borrowed robe, Ludo was conscious of the other's murderous hatred, injured vanity, and violated pride.

—I'm . . . terribly sorry. I was just . . . passing by.

The Englishman wouldn't look at Ludo.

His vague gestures in the direction of the tumbled ottoman were meant to hide both his embarrassment and his shock, but Ludo looked beyond them to the bitter envy of the disappointed lover, to years of longing and waiting for the rewards of love given and of resentment for love denied, and to the deep, corroding anger at the illusive quality of affection. Ludo's own palms were moist and hot, and he knew that the fleeting touch of compassion that brushed against his conscience had less to do with this angry visitor than with himself.

—I just bet you were only passing by, Ann said. What's John Laidlaw up to, then? More filthy little blackmail? Well, you just run home to your master and tell him it won't work!

—I'm sure the Minister has . . . ah . . . better things to do than to . . . ah . . . concern himself with this . . . ah . . . sort of thing. What would give you an idea he'd even know about it?

—Bitter experience with your rotten master, Ann said. I don't believe a word you've said so far, you snooping errand boy. John Laidlaw had better have a damn good explanation for me. My life was to be private!

In full retreat, Hudson said: I don't know what you're talking about, Ann.

—I just bet you don't, Ann said and gave a brief, ugly laugh. I just bet. Well, come in, come in, if you're coming in. Close that drafty door.

To make peace and to quieten his own uneasy conscience, Ludo said: Perhaps you'd better tell me what this is all about.

But Ann was listening only to herself.

—I told him I wouldn't stand for this! He gave me his word! Why can't you dirty little snoopers *ever* be trusted to do anything you say? You can tell your master I'm done with his filthy puppeteering!

Hudson, who was making a desperate stand of his own on whatever dignity he could salvage, said in his high, quavering voice: I don't even know where he is.

—I know where he is, Ann shouted. And if I know, why don't you? You're his poodle, aren't you? His fetch-and-carry dog? Ring him up in bloody Gibraltar if you have to, but I want him to know right now that I'm finished with him! Let him find himself another arranger of civilized atmospheres!

—Please, Ann, Hudson began to say, then stopped. The twin red circles on his long white face gave him the look of a tragic clown; his prim little mouth had twisted. The sad eyes had watered. It was clear he would no longer try to defend himself, and Ludo looked to his own defenses. It *was* too late to be human, trusting and believing . . . to stop living other people's lies.

Ann left the room then, wrapped in her hasty sheet, and he and Hudson regarded each other with mutual dislike.

—I'm sorry, Ludo said.

—For what? Hudson asked. For having witnessed my humiliation? Yes, I should think you would be sorry, being what you are.

—If I could think of something that might make you feel better about all this, I'd say it, Ludo said. But there really isn't anything to say.

—Shut up, you bloody little Continental, Hudson said. I don't want to hear anything *you* might say.

—Look, Ludo said, as reasonably as he could, there's no point in making matters worse. If you can't be civilized about this, why don't you get out?

—I told you to shut up, Hudson said. Who the devil d'you think you are, to talk to me like that?

—I'll stand at attention if you like, Colonel, Ludo said. If that would help matters.

—Shut up, you swine. Just shut your damned superior Continental mouth. Anything you might say to me had better be done before witnesses from now on.

He had recovered his British cloak of superiority before a lesser mortal, and Ludo shrugged, reached for his clothes, and began to dress.

—I'm sorry, he said. Perhaps if this hadn't happened, we could've been friends.

—Friends? With you?

—In another time, Ludo said. Under other circumstances.

—In England, Hudson said, we choose our friends with a lot more care than that.

—I know it's been a shock, so I'll say it again: I'm sorry. Ann and I love each other. When people love each other, this is what they do.

—Shut up, you silly little puppet, Hudson said.

—Now, that's one thing I've never been, Ludo said and felt anger rising.

—That's all you've ever been, you silly little man, Hudson said. Tell me one thing, though. Did you get Ann to pull the strings to get yourself transferred out of combat? Or did she do that on her own? Not that we care about it all that much, but we did wonder how you managed it.

—What are you talking about? Ludo asked.

—Well, they do say that the victim is always the last to discover that he's been played for a fool, Hudson said.

—Get out, Ludo said.

But Hudson wasn't done.

—It seems that you're even more of a puppet than we thought.

I never did understand how the Minister could take you seriously. I thought you were just something useful to keep Ann from kicking over the traces . . . something to be kept in storage, as it were, in case we needed to replace a more important puppet. But you're a lot *less* than that, aren't you? No, not a top-drawer puppet at all. Nothing that important.

—Get out, Ludo said.

—In due time, said Hudson. Tell me, what does it feel like to know you're not a man at all? That you've been artificially constructed out of string and newsprint? How did you ever manage to keep a straight face at Buckingham Palace? It must have taken either unbelievable vanity, or an innocence that borders on idiocy, and I don't believe that even a Pole could pretend to be so naïve.

—That's enough, Ludo said.

He had become progressively chilled and the insufficient electric heater in the fireplace had nothing to do with that. Clues that he had ignored reappeared to mock him; questions suggested answers he didn't want to hear. But once set in motion, the process of disillusionment can't be reversed or stopped.

—Oh, it's not at all enough, Hudson said. It's hardly a start. If there's anyone here who should be sorry for anyone else, it ought to be me. But then a man who'd have his lady friend pull strings to help him dodge his duty is hardly worth a moment of compassion. What happened, Major? Did you lose your nerve? Or did you finally realize what a fool you've been? But no, I don't suppose it could've been that. Not even a Pole would have the nerve to hope for something better than the run you've had.

—No one pulled any strings for me, Ludo said.

—How would a puppet know?

In another moment, Ann would return and it would all be over. He didn't know what he might say to her. Had she said something about puppeteering? Things that she could arrange? Every word that had ever passed between them acquired a new meaning, and he felt a sick, mad rush of blood to his head. He wondered what had happened to his instincts, which had never failed him before.

He didn't blame Hudson, whom he thought to be just another

middle-aged man confronting the end of his most treasured illusions. He was aware, grimly and with self-contempt, of what must be the ultimate vanity: to accuse another of naïveté because he lived a life composed of different choices from one's own. He had assumed that just because his commitments had been absolute, and that his own loyalties had been beyond betrayal, so were those of everybody else. . . . Obviously, his education had lacked a whole world of cynical experience.

He hated to ask, but he had to know: What does Ann do for your Minister?

—I leave you to make your own discoveries, Hudson said in a voice in which contempt was struggling with pity. But I'll tell you this much: Ann's loyalty will be always to herself.

Then he nodded bitterly at the poster of the sinking ship and the swastikaed torpedoes. —Quite a good message to keep in mind these days, don't you think?

—Oh, for God's sake, get out, Ludo said.

Ann did return then with a bottle, glasses, and a small lacquered tin of American gingerbread (courtesy of Loomis), but Hudson was already halfway down the stairs. In the minutes that they had faced each other, each man had learned that he had been betrayed and also that he had betrayed himself.

Then the rain ended. The catastrophic day had passed into evening; it could not be rescued or recalled. A bar of electric fire was glowing in the grate among the dead ashes, and the wind was moaning quietly in the chimney like a sleeping old dog.

There was probably a simple explanation for everything, Ludo thought. There usually was. One merely had to look into it, exercise charity and reason, and suppress one's pride. But he was quite unable to think of any explanation with which he might live.

Looking into his face with no expression, Ann said in a harsh, uninflected monotone: It's not what you think. And you shouldn't bother about what *he* thinks. It doesn't matter what anybody thinks.

Her sheet had fallen and she made no attempt to retrieve it, but, for all that he cared, she might have been a statue made of copper or bronze. He could see each of the small harsh lines at the side of her mouth, the deep shadows under her suddenly aged eyes, the beaded line of sweat on her upper lip. A small vein in her temple had begun to pulse, and the rigidity of her back and shoulders proclaimed the end of all her expectations.

—Time for another English lesson, he said. The word is not *think*. The word is *believe*. If I'd been able to think, I'd be unable to believe what I'm thinking now.

Beginning to assemble her defenses, she said: I thought that soldiers weren't paid to think.

He shrugged contemptuously and said: That's a civilian notion. It comforts them, I think.

And she said: And you feel that I've betrayed you in some way, is that it?

—It doesn't matter what I think, he said. Does it? Did it ever? Once faith has cracked, it can't be plastered over. Deceit lives a long time after the event. And understanding doesn't bring forgiveness.

—Damn you for an archaic son-of-a-bitch, she said. Who the hell are you to judge anyone?

—I don't judge, he said. I'm not paid to judge anyone.

—No, you're not, she said. You're paid to kill people. And some of them you murder, free of charge. Well, I'm not one of your willing victims.

—I didn't kill Kaminski, if that's what you're talking about, he said. I don't know who did. It was either Auerbach or Bettner. I accept the responsibility, but I didn't kill him.

—That's what all the heroes say when they've been caught with their decorations down, she said.

—Haven't you got that turned around a bit? he said quietly. Who is the cheat and liar and manipulator here?

—It isn't what you *think* or *believe* or whatever the word, she said desperately. It was all supposed to be a lot more innocent than it turned out to be—because I didn't mean to do you any harm.

Speaking, each faced an opposite wall. As chance would have it, his was the wall with the confiding mouth and the sinking ship. They wouldn't look at each other, in just the way that Hudson had avoided looking at Ludo, as if neither of them could trust his or her own ability to command belief.

—I'm not a priest, he said indifferently. I'm not paid to give absolution.

—How about compassion? Understanding? Something human that a woman might be able to use in a difficult moment? There are no service regulations for an ordinary, decent, unheroic life in which people live and love and make mistakes and hope for the best and struggle from one awful disappointment to another. Even you must believe in someone, don't you think?

—I don't need anyone, he said.

—Now you're lying, she said. I know that's a lie. Why do you have to be so utterly unbending? It isn't easy for me to talk to you like this. I've just as much pride as you have, perhaps even more. But you just won't make anything easy for anyone, will you. Not even for yourself!

—That is the least of my concerns, since you've been taking care of all such matters for me.

—I can explain all that, she said. It was a mistake but an honest one.

—And I'm not paid to hear confessions, Ludo said. ·

—Well, you'll hear this one, Ann said and walked toward the ottoman and sat down on it with her long, dark, naked back to him, and he was moved by such a powerful longing and affection that it took all his will to hold him where he was.

—I'd like to think that whatever you do about all this, Ann said, you'll do it with some understanding of what really happened. I could, perhaps, live with your hatred but not with your contempt.

Unemotionally, as though it didn't matter to her whether or not he believed anything she said, she told him her entire story.

Night had come by then. The sky was clouded over and there was no moon. Their only light was the insufficient red glow from the fireplace, where the electric heater rattled and creaked. His skin was dry, cold, and unresponsive to the touch; hers would be no different, he supposed.

The shadows mocked him with his own illusions. There seemed to be only derision to rely on as a shield. Again, the scornful line was echoing in his head: To have had such hopes, such illogical expectations . . . Faith, obviously, was for fools and trust was for children.

—I really had something quite different in mind, she said in conclusion. I wanted you to see that there was more than just one way for you to do your duty, and Laidlaw had nothing to do with that. I believed that I was helping you to get what you deserve and, at the same time, bringing you down from your damn clouds to where I could finally mean everything to you. I couldn't touch you up there, don't you see? If I was using you for anyone's private purpose, it would've been my own. . . . And couldn't you, at least, *listen* to what I have to say?

He heard her, but he wasn't listening. In his mind, he had already stepped away from her. There, in that cold, private space where he had been able, now and then, to live only for himself, something extraordinary began to happen. He was sixteen and running away to war. His father was muttering advice designed for another century. His mother had hung a holy medal around his neck and made sure that he had extra socks packed in his knapsack. Zosia waited by an apple tree to say her good-byes. Wlada began to cry. His brothers stared at him with awe and with envy. Dedication to unprofitable ideas had not yet become a source of malice and amusement, and people who continued to govern their lives with ideas that were beyond immediate calculation were not yet scorned as impractical romantics.

Had all of that been real? Had it really happened the way that he remembered it? Or was that just part of a one-thousand-year-long nightmare in which infrequent light ebbed only so that another long night could begin? And, if that were so, who but a madman or a mystic would insist on his right to such dreams? And if it weren't so, then why were these dreams invisible to everybody else?

She waited for him to say something, but she must have known that almost everything they had said to each other was discredited, and that no further word would ever be trusted. Once a single brick has crumbled in the complex structure of faith and affection, then the whole edifice is as good as ruined.

She asked, in a voice grown difficult with violated dignity and pride: Will you, at least, stay the rest of the night? Tomorrow you can go wherever you like. But . . . much as it irritates the lady . . . much as she despises herself to have to admit it . . . she doesn't want to be left alone just now.

—Why not? he said coldly. It's too late to look for a bed anywhere else.

Their night went on, hour after hour, and neither of them could elude consciousness. Names, places, faces passed endlessly before his mind, and vanished. The light in the windows was blue-gray, edged with scarlet, before Ann's bitter silence turned into an uneasy, muttering sleep. He studied her then as though she were an object of great value that was taken from him and he didn't know whom to blame for the loss.

But what if war was his true home? he thought. And could a homeless man expect any other? Triage, by which a battlefield surgeon decided life and death by choosing those among the wounded who seemed more likely to survive the knife, and leaving others to die unattended, was an established practice of civilized warfare and, he supposed, of life itself as well.

But it was not so simple when the life abandoned was one's own.

CHAPTER XIX

HE DRESSED QUIETLY, taking care not to wake her, and made his way toward the Rubens Hotel, where he was to report to General Sikorski later in the day.

Outside, a thick yellow fog had stained the warm, damp air. The royal standard hung limp above Buckingham Palace and a policeman stationed near the main gates gave him a measured, calculating look. Ominous shapes rushed toward him through the fog and swerved aside at the last possible moment to avoid collision, and he went on beside the long gray palace wall, muttering alternating apologies and curses.

Because he didn't know anyone else in this part of London, and because he couldn't find a restaurant that would be open so early in the morning to serve him a breakfast, and because his brother-in-law lived in nearby Chelsea, he made his way there, wondering—as he did whenever he thought of Romuald Modelski —what Wlada could have seen in him.

At fifty, Romuald was something of a family joke: a cuckold who had condoned his wife's careless infidelities because some of them helped to advance his career. People thought him shallow, bigoted, treacherous, and a bit of a fool, but his talent for political survival was beyond reproach. In the twenty-one years of Poland's independence, he had worn the colors of every major political party, being in turn a member of the Peasant Party, of the National-Democrats who displaced the Peasants, of the Socialists who supported the Pilsudski coup, and of the nonparty Camp of National Unity created by the heirs of Pilsudski. Now he was a Christian-Democrat dedicated to the federalist ideas of General Sikorski whose protocol secretary he had become that year. To think that he might have to spend months, perhaps even years, in such company, made Ludo's stomach lurch.

The door to Romuald's flat was opened by a butler—he would, of course, have a butler—a gray-faced little man with pale, thin hair and anxious eyes, who ushered Ludo into a beautifully appointed morning room and asked him to wait. Count Romuald was dressing. While waiting, Ludo read his *Times*.

The headlines were full of names and places that he didn't know. New Guinea and Rabaul. Salamaua in peril. Landings on Rendova. In the United States, where aircraft production had reached an astounding eighty thousand machines, laundry workers had been declared essential to civilian morale and were to be exempted from military service. In the Manhattan Center, three thousand persons had heard Earl Browder, general secretary of the Communist Party of the United States, call for the destruction of *the dark and sinister forces* that were accusing Russians of imaginary crimes and undermining the antifascist alliance. In the Ukraine, the Red Army took ten towns and seventy-two villages in one week and rolled one hundred and fifty miles closer to the Polish border.

Then Romuald was standing in the open doors, posed against the sun in exquisitely cut black cloth, silvery pinstripe, and dazzling Oxford linen. The gold pince-nez, which he affected for its air of *dernier siècle* distinction, dangled from the lapel of his coat like a decoration.

—Ludo, he said in a voice that contained no pleasure whatsoever. How delightful to see you. To what do I owe this unexpected visit?

His eyes were small, black, full of cunning and malice, and Ludo thought: What have they ever seen? Have they ever watched the survivors of a combat mission drifting in?

Ruthless, conscienceless, and adaptable to the end, Romuald would survive until Judgment Day, along with the cockroach and the shark, Ludo thought, and the *rightness* of this survival didn't astonish him at all. To think that such men would live through the war, to emerge into power, to poison the public air once again, and to influence the image of the nation, was almost more than he could stand that morning. But he knew that such men as Romuald won whatever game they played because they always found scapegoats on which to blame their disasters.

—I came because I had nowhere else to go, Ludo said.

—How very flattering, said Romuald Modelski. But if you've come here to shave and bathe, to make yourself presentable for your appointment with the general, I hope you've brought your own shilling for the gas.

—I'll give you thirty, if that's your standard fee.

—One will do, Romuald said. And I expect that you'd like some breakfast?

—If it doesn't cost me too much, Ludo said.

Anger, that touch of savage hatred that he felt whenever he thought of Romuald with Wlada, had ebbed and only a muddy residue of self-disgust remained. Who was he to despise anyone this morning? Contempt, he thought, can be just as demeaning for the man who feels it as for the man at whom it is directed.

He followed Romuald into a sunny dining room, where the sad-eyed butler served a sumptuous breakfast.

There was Canadian bacon, fresh Australian butter, eggs from the country, grapefruit from California, and pumpernickel toast. Whatever horrors of war might trouble the diplomatic corps in London, starvation obviously wasn't one of them.

—Rationing, Romuald said as he ate, is the best thing that ever happened to the ordinary Englishman. Do you know that seventy percent of the working class never tasted butter before the war? Or bacon? Now that it's rationed, they've got to eat it along with everybody else.

—Why not? Ludo said. Since they're getting killed along with everybody else.

—So Noel Coward tells us, Romuald said. So *Mrs. Miniver* informs us. Actually, the British have lost more people in traffic accidents than in battle. They've had 387,996 men killed, wounded, or taken prisoner, since the war began, including the hundred thousand that the Japanese captured in Burma and Malaya, the sixty thousand that Rommel captured in North Africa, and the thirty thousand who surrendered with the French. They've had 588,742 knocked down by taxis in the blackout. We lost more than that in the first ten days of the war.

—Which *you* spent eating brioche in Paris, Ludo said.

—And a good thing too, said Romuald. At least some of them weren't eaten by the Germans.

—I wonder what Wlada had to eat in Russia before she starved to death, Ludo said.

—I wonder, Romuald said. More cream in your coffee?

—Damn you, brother-in-law, Ludo said. Why do you always make it so easy to dislike you?

—Because you've always made it so easy for me not to care, brother-in-law, said Romuald Modelski.

—It's . . . *obscene* is the word, I think . . . to watch you here in this expensive flat paid for by British money, wearing your Savile Row suit, eating food that most Englishmen haven't seen in three and a half years, and listening to your sarcasms.

—Your Anglophilia has been noted, Romuald said. Two lumps or three?

—What?

—Sugar in your coffee?

Nothing, Ludo thought, nothing that anyone could do—in war, revolution, genocide, pestilence, or earthquake—would shake the equanimity of this professional survivor, because he simply had no eyes for anyone but himself. Victims were merely digits with an appropriate number of zeros behind them. He had a vision, then, of the world destroyed: mountains of wreckage, no life in the ruins, and the last representative of the race appearing in the smoke: Romuald, a slice of buttered pumpernickel in his hand, complaining about the dust on his patent leather shoes.

One fights a war for causes, and the cause must be always undefiled and above suspicion, otherwise the necessary sacrifices are a foolish joke. One has to live with a sense of rightness at all times. But Romuald presented the other side of the heroic medal; the thought that anyone might have died to preserve him was unbearable.

Romuald went on talking as he ate and Ludo felt the start of a sick, pounding headache. His stomach, always the seat of fear, tightened in a knot. So there are still such people among us, he thought, those gentlemen of impeccable manner and disastrous notions who had sat down to war as though it were a bridge game, and who, having forgotten that the laws of antichance guarantee disaster, could take such awful chances with the nation's life. Somehow, the image of Sikorski had led him to believe that the bad days were gone.

—Seriously, Ludo, Romuald was saying. With your . . . ah . . . *connections*, you could write your own ticket, as the English say. Transfer into the RAF and you'll be a group captain tomorrow. Which, by the way, might be in the wind, in any event.

—My connections, as you put it, have been disconnected, Ludo said.

—How very stupid of you.

—For once, we agree.

—I happen to know that there is quite considerable interest in you in certain quarters of Whitehall. I've done my best to encourage it, of course. We are related, after all, and one must look ahead.

—I'm sure you'll manage that, Ludo said.

—Politically speaking, our situation has become quite serious. Our . . . shall I call them *ill-advised?* . . . inquiries about the Katyn massacre were just the pretext Stalin needed to wreck us with Washington and Whitehall. Suddenly, we're terribly short of friends. Now that it's too late to do anything about it, Sikorski wants to take our case directly to the American people, and

Roosevelt is furious. And as they say in Whitehall nowadays, *When Roosevelt is furious, Winston Churchill growls.*

—Politically speaking, Ludo said, I don't give a damn.

—Of course, Romuald said. How could I've forgotten? The pure hero is above such things as politics. How very pleasant it must be to look down at everything from thirty thousand feet. Not wise, perhaps, not even very helpful where you could really matter, but pleasant. I envy you the luxury of your conscience.

—Thank you, Ludo said.

—Of course, some of us can't afford a conscience. Some of us must make practical decisions. When a cause seems lost, one must find another. One listens very carefully to any idea that might offer something both practical and useful. Do you have any idea of what I'm talking about?

—Laidlaw, Ludo said.

—Laidlaw speaks for Churchill. Churchill won't even speak to our General Sikorski. There are quite a few people in our government who think it's time we gave Churchill a man who won't make him feel like a devil dipped in Holy Water. I think it's a situation where your cooperation would be useful. Your one-word answers don't help.

—Sorry, Ludo said.

—You still believe in miracles, is that it? Let me tell you something, brother-in-law. This is a world where principles always give way before expediency, where the lives of friends are a matter for negotiations, and where gratitude lasts only as long as there's a need. You can still risk your life for something in which you believe, but only a fool expects sacrifice to bring any reward.

—I'll keep that in mind, Ludo said.

—Do so. And if it doesn't strain it too much, give some thought to where and how we'll be living after we've lost this war. The time to ask such questions is before you're desperate for an answer. The time to make yourself useful to influential friends is before you need them.

—I'm sure there's nothing I can tell you about that, Ludo said, but Romuald seemed to have forgotten him for a moment.

—We won't be going back to Poland, that's getting to be more certain every day, he reflected. Our British friends are considering a twenty-year pact of friendship with Stalin, and his price is

Poland. In America, we have mortal enemies who'd be glad to
bury us no matter what we did. Our real enemies don't shoot,
Ludo. They write in newspapers. They advise their President.
They dangle votes before their politicians and, in the meantime,
they work for a revolution that no longer exists! Any future *they*
decide for us is bound to be a nightmare.

—Have you no faith in General Sikorski?

—I have faith in nothing that I can't control, Romuald
Modelski said.

—There's something the general said I've never forgotten,
Ludo said. *If we're to be the kind of people who have a right to
expect understanding from others, then we have to start our own
renewal with ourselves.*

—Yes, Sikorski does make everything sound simple, Romuald
said with scorn. The last man I've heard of who tried to love His
enemies found Himself hanging on a cross. Perhaps the next time
you're up there in the sky, you might ask Him if it was worth His
trouble.

—Ask Him yourself, Ludo said.

—I would, but He's had nothing to say to me for years. And,
anyway, looking at His career, I wouldn't take His advice about
mine.

Outside, the fog had lifted. A pale sun appeared. The damp,
drying air smelled of coal smoke and tasted of sulfur, but Ludo
took in deep, chaotic breaths as though it were the sweetest air
he had ever breathed. The night had set him up for the ambush
of the day and he had to get away from it.

Prus would have been the man to see at that moment. But
Prus too had fallen victim to the Katyn massacre, and had no
more power to influence events. The revelations of the Soviet
crime had infuriated Churchill, since they had angered Roosevelt,
and something had had to be done to assuage this rage. And since
Prus had been head of that Polish Military Mission in the Soviet
Union which had searched for the missing officers until they were
discovered in the Katyn graves, his head seemed like the one most
suitable for rolling. In the bitter uproar of denunciation in the
British press, which heaped scorn upon the victims rather than

the murderers, even General Sikorski had been unable to save his old friend. The frightened politicians of Sikorski's Cabinet demanded Prus's resignation from the Army. With his dismissal, and after breakfasting with Romuald Modelski, Ludo knew that he was finally alone.

It was too early for him to report at the Rubens Hotel, but he went there anyway, as though some kind of reassurance might be found among the stern, familiar military faces, where honor, duty, and a sense of service were non-negotiable. More than ever, he believed that General Sikorski would find the right way, reverse the catastrophic course that the war had taken, and lead them all to that independent Poland where a new kind of nation would rise from the ashes. The alternatives were unthinkable.

But as he walked into the marble lobby, where a large American flag had been hung that morning to commemorate an ally's Independence Day, he saw and heard only evidence of fear, anger, and despair. He saw a gray-haired colonel weeping into his clenched fists, and a gnarled, beribboned sergeant-major sitting as though transfixed, and he watched armed and shouting officers milling on the stairs.

—What's going on here? he asked a wide-eyed orderly at the reception desk, but the young man seemed unable to speak. What's happened?

Speaking through tears, the duty officer told him that General Sikorski had been killed.

—What? Where? How?

But the distraught staff officer could tell him nothing more. All he knew then, all that anyone seemed to know, was that the converted Liberator bomber in which General Sikorski had been flying from the Middle East had crashed near Gibraltar and that the general and his staff were dead.

—*Finis Polonia*, said a weeping major, and another officer told him to act like a man if he were unable to act like a soldier.

Africa . . . Gibraltar . . . plane crash . . . sabotage . . . accident . . . assassination . . . tragedy. The words bumped into each other like empty freight cars coupling and uncoupling in a shunting yard. He thought of long trains whose journeys were over, breaking up. Neither he nor anyone else he saw seemed to have any further purpose or direction.

—Well, that's the end, said a youthful colonel. There is no more hope. From now on, we're in the hands of the Old Guard again.

—Be quiet, said an older colonel. I order you to control yourself and set an example.

—Ah, by all means, said the younger colonel. We must set examples. I'm sure everyone will be impressed. But will they be impressed enough in Washington and Whitehall? That's what I want to know.

—Will you please control yourself? cried the older colonel. Will you remember who you are? Think of your dignity as an officer!

—Oh, dignity, by all means, of course, said the younger colonel. That's going to take care of everything.

In the glass of the large framed portrait of General Sikorski that hung behind their heads, Ludo caught sight of his own distorted features. The skin under his eyes was empurpled as though he had been branded with hot irons, his cheeks were papery and gray, and an unhealthy splash of livid color was spread across his forehead like a stain.

—Does anyone know what actually happened?

—Oh, it's you, said the older colonel, whom Ludo recognized as an old acquaintance. All that we know is that the general is dead. His plane crashed on takeoff in Gibraltar.

—A clear case of murder, said the younger colonel.

—Don't pay any attention to him, said the older colonel. He's become unnerved. We don't know how the general was killed. We only got the news a half hour ago. They're still diving for his body and his briefcase. There were some terribly important papers in that briefcase.

—But, don't you see? They had to have him killed! said the younger colonel. It stands to reason they'd do that.

—Oh, do keep quiet, the older colonel said.

They were absurd and they were pitiable, and the fact that a man was dead (that, in fact, all of their hopes for their country's future had suffered a crippling blow) didn't make them any less ridiculous.

—Our Eastern Allies murder half of our officer corps, said the younger colonel. Our Western Allies murder our commander-in-chief. We really have some extraordinary allies in this war, don't you think? I wonder what we've done to deserve such allies.

—These things are not related! cried the older colonel, whom Ludo knew to have been a hopeless but persistent admirer of Wlada. Toporski, tell him that these things can't be related! One thing is a coldly planned, premeditated murder and the other is a tragic accident! We must have *that* much faith!

—Which is the murder and which the accident? said the younger colonel. And what's the difference, in any event? There's a point beyond which coincidence fools no one.

—One must have faith in something, said the older colonel, and the younger one said: *Balls*.

Ludo freed himself from the clutching fingers of the older colonel, went upstairs to the *adjutantura* where, he expected, he would receive his orders. He didn't really care what they were. The simple military motions he was making wouldn't erase the tragedy, he knew, but they might save his mind. When he got to the office of the adjutant-general, he found it shuttered and locked. In the outer office, a beautifully uniformed young woman looked at him dry-eyed, and he searched his memory for her name.

She helped him with a smile that he found more chilling than anything he had seen downstairs.

—Marylka, she said. Jan Straka's sister. Jozef Wilchurzak's widow.

—Of course, he said. Forgive me. The last time we saw each other was . . .

—At my husband's funeral, she finished the sentence.

—Yes.

—And at my brother's before that.

—You . . . look well.

—Yes, I know, she said.

She had changed. She had become prettier, he supposed, but the feeling of which he was most aware was a sick sense of horror. Her pale hair had been cut as short as a flapper's; she had filled out and coarsened. A long tongue kept darting between painted lips and small teeth smudged with lipstick.

She nodded toward the inner door as she said: If you're looking for *him*, Major, he's in the hospital.

—Don't tell me there's been another accident?

—Perhaps, she said evenly, then shrugged prettily. Perhaps not. He went out through the window. It couldn't have happened more than half an hour ago.

—What the hell is this, Ludo said. Ancient Rome? Are we all supposed to fall on our swords, or something? Has everyone gone mad?

—Grief is hard to take if you're not used to it, the young woman said. At least, I suppose so. And when you think that there's still something you can lose . . . well . . . you do things like that, don't you think?

—I *am* going mad, Ludo murmured quietly.

The long pink tongue had snaked out again in the corner of her mouth and the dry eyes acquired a quality as bright as glass.

—It was . . . exciting, she said. It made me feel . . . strange.

—Was he killed? Ludo asked.

—Oh, no, she said. It's only four stories to the pavement and one has to fall from much higher than that to be killed, doesn't one?

—I don't believe any of this, Ludo said.

—I don't see why not, she said and smiled and showed her sharp white teeth, and once again the long pink tongue came out to touch the corner of her mouth. You've seen it all before, haven't you? How many times have you seen it, Major? Fifty? A hundred? More? You and I ought to understand each other very well.

Then she said softly: Why don't you take me to lunch and we'll talk about it? Suddenly, I feel terribly hungry. I haven't . . . eaten anything since last night.

—Some other time, he mumbled, stepping back.

—What's the matter, Major? Do I remind you too much of my brother? Or my dead husband? Or of the dozens of other young people you've seen killed? Don't you think I'm owed something for *my* suffering? Believe me, the dead make poor company at night.

—Find someone your own age, he said brutally and couldn't face her terrible, twisted smile.

—They don't last long enough these days, she said and he backed out into the corridor.

There, as he hurried toward the stairs, Loomis caught him by the sleeve.

—Wait, the American said. I've got a message for you. Will you wait and listen, for a change?

He looked at the well-fed, well-meaning American face, smelled the alcoholic breath, and his stomach heaved. What had Lala seen in this long-distance expert on European disasters? She had been tragic by choice, and her death had been a fitting one for the accidental sort of life she had been permitted, and it seemed unforgivable that she should be mourned by no one better than that.

—The AFLACC people want to talk to you at the Foreign Office.

—What AFLACC people? he asked bitterly. Are they like the Stalag people or the Oflag people? And since when have you become a British errand boy?

—Aw, come on, Ludo, will you? You know who I mean. Laidlaw and that bunch. I've just come from Whitehall. They're having some sort of a flap there, and everybody was arguing about you.

—I've nothing to say to any of them or to you.

—Hey, wait a minute, Loomis said. I'm only trying to do you a service.

—Do us all a service, Ludo said. Make friends with the Germans. Then perhaps we might be able to win this damn war.

Loomis stepped back with a placating gesture and smiled uncertainly and said: Hey, hold on there, pal! I'm not your enemy. In fact, I'm probably a better friend than you realize. Look, this is an awful thing that's happened, I know that, but it's also a hell of an opportunity for you . . .

And Ludo thought, enraged: Why did nothing tragic and irrevocable ever happen to these arrogant, complacent American meddlers? Why were they immune to disaster? They came to war as though it were a football match on a Saturday afternoon and they didn't even know the rules of the game. If it was true that their sick, deluded President was about to hand half of Europe to Stalin and the Russians, then he wanted to see them convulsed in a national agony of their own before he was dead.

—Hey, take it easy, Loomis said. I know you've had a shock, but, Jesus Christ, getting mad at me won't bring your general back to life. And it wasn't me that killed him, anyway.

—Excuse me, Ludo muttered and pushed past the American correspondent, who followed him, asking with concern: Hey, Ludo, wait a minute. Are you sick? What's the matter, Ludo?

The question trailed behind him in the stricken air as he stumbled down the stairs into the crowded lobby.

Behind him, Loomis cried out: Will you please listen while there's still time to do something about all this? You have to make the best of it, don't you see? You've no other choice under the circumstances.

Under the circumstances, Ludo thought, and at this of all times, Sikorski's death had become too much of a coincidence. Yet murder? *Murder?* That remained inconceivable.

In the tiled white cubicle of the downstairs toilet, he fell against the wall. Everything seemed to let go at once; he could not stop trembling. Romuald's cynical face seemed to hang before him everywhere he looked. Marylka offered her own nightmare smile, and his heart felt as though it were about to explode in his chest. He neither could nor would think about Ann.

What was he to do? What was anyone to do? Outside, old colonels were bickering about dignity and faith, understanding little. Upstairs, a corrupted child had turned her back on life because death was so much more believable. His own eyes were invisible behind their dark lenses, so that he couldn't see how near he had come to collapse of his own. He held his maimed hand cocked high across his upper chest as though expecting an attack.

Words had wearied him. Thoughts refused to form. No ideas presented themselves to suggest a trustworthy direction. He longed for that near-mystical and inexplicable moment that occurs in combat when the mind ceases to function and the body receives its orders from an unknown source, and the best possible course of action is taken without plan. One either lives through such a moment to emerge, safe and sound, on the other side of doubt and delusion, or one fails to live and, either way, there are no more questions that need to be answered.

When he came out again, everything had changed. Discipline had reasserted itself rapidly. The desperation had given way to a softly murmured embitterment and anger, and as he watched the senior officers of the General Staff moving among the others, as he listened to their competent professional voices and watched their calming gestures, his own thoughts steadied and his purpose hardened.

He got his orders then. Colonel Bydlinski, whom he remembered from Wlada's gatherings in Warsaw, and who had been Sikorski's chief of personnel, brought him the mimeographed sheets, with a smile designed to mask all feeling.

—It's all quite useless now, of course, the colonel said. We'll have to think of something else for you to do. But I thought you'd like to see what the general had in mind for you.

The orders were for Ludo to accompany General Sikorski to the United States, where they were to begin a two-month-long speaking tour at the gathering of the Polish-American societies in Chicago, to mobilize American opinion in the Polish cause, and to bring the pressure of four million Polish-American voters to bear on the White House.

—He could have done it, I think, Colonel Bydlinski said. He was good at that. It might have worked, don't you think? Of course, now we'll never know.

—Could someone else go in his place? Ludo asked.

—I'm afraid not. Roosevelt couldn't refuse to admit General Sikorski to the United States. That might have cost him the upcoming election. But the Americans have already told us that they can't guarantee the safety of anyone else.

The afternoon went on, became evening, and turned into night. The crowds grew in the lobby as the news spread among the billets in Kensington and Pimlico and Wimbledon and Chelsea, and in the service clubs in Queen's Gate and Trafalgar Square, and in the dance halls and in the theater lobbies, and soon several thousand soldiers stood in silent ranks outside the hotel and waited for orders.

He thought then that if someone were to tell them that General Sikorski's death was not an accident, that it would free the leaders of America and Britain to act as ruthlessly with Poland and the Poles as their political needs might require, and that Stalin could now undoubtedly have his way, they would storm the palace across the road in an act of vengeance that would ignore any consequences. It was, of course, inconceivable that this would take place.

Retreating from the crowd, wanting solitude in which he might come to terms with his own sense of shock, he found himself in an angle made by the hall reception desk and a small jungle of tall potted plants, but, even there, he wasn't left alone. Officers made their way to him to ask his opinion and advice, and to listen with profound attention to anything he said. Suddenly, he noticed Loomis at his side again. He tried to ignore him.

—Hudson was right, Loomis murmured. You do have the magic.

—What magic is that?

—People want to follow you, Loomis said.

—And where do you suppose I might lead them? Ludo asked wearily.

—I don't know, Loomis said. I've never been a leader. Whenever anybody wants me to take them anywhere, I call for a taxi. At least that way, I don't wind up as everybody's sacrificial lamb.

—Better that than a Judas goat, Ludo said.

—Are you talking about anyone I know?

—I don't know who you know, Ludo said. And I don't really want to talk to you at all. I've become very tired of the English language.

—That's too bad, Loomis said. Since that's the language in which all your important decisions are being made. It wouldn't do you any harm to talk to the AFLACC people.

—Not in English, Ludo said. I'm not listening anymore to anything said to me in English.

—Then you and your friends had better start practicing your Russian, Loomis said.

—We don't surrender as easily as all that.

—I know it, Loomis said sadly. Don't you think I know it?

—I don't know what you know, Ludo said.

—Lala died in my arms, did you know that? Loomis asked and made a vague, apologetic gesture and went on: Well, that's not quite true. She died in Prus's arms. I sat in the rubble and I made a speech. I don't know what I said and, anyway, nobody understood me since I spoke in English, but the gist of it was that I had had enough of useless sacrifice and all that damned, stupid, and unnecessary dying. I wanted to know if Prus was finally satisfied, if his Polish passion play had had its appropriate sacrificial victim, and if we could now call a halt to all that honorable killing and go home. He didn't listen. I know he didn't listen. Why is it impossible for you people to listen to reason? When will you learn that you can't live any longer in a world that doesn't exist?

—It exists as long as we do, Ludo said.

—So, for the sake of pride, you're going to pull it down on top of your heads? This is a world of reason, Ludo. Nobody wants to understand the way you people live and nobody can. It's too difficult for us. But you just won't make anything easy for anybody, will you!

Brutally, Ludo asked: Didn't Lala teach you anything?

—Only about myself, Loomis said. And who wants to be taught that at my age? But maybe that's why I'm trying to be your friend.

—You want to save us so that Lala's death can have some sort of meaning, is that it? And so that you can live with your own image of yourself?

—What are you saying? Loomis cried. I can't even save myself!

—Then leave us to work out our own salvation, Ludo said.

Then the night gave way before a blue-gray morning, and the electric lights went out one by one. Years, rather than hours, seemed to have passed between that dawn and the preceding noon, and the silent ranks of waiting officers, and the massed soldiers, sailors, and airmen outside looked shabby and worn.

Upstairs, in what had been the private offices of General Sikorski, the first of several conferences had come to an end, and the new commander of the Polish Armed Forces in the West, General Sosnkowski (who, even at that moment, was being described in print in the United States as a Nazi agent) came down the stairs with the new civilian Prime Minister, Stanislaw Mikolajczyk, and the grim-faced members of Sikorski's staff.

They left for an immediate conference with Churchill at 10 Downing Street, but he, pleading an attack of indigestion, refused to see them. In the meantime, the story of General Sikorski's tragic accident began to appear in the early editions of the London papers.

Among the dead were the general's daughter, Zofia Lesniowska, who had accompanied her father to the Middle East; General Klimecki, the Army's chief of staff; Sikorski's operations chief, Colonel Jarecki; a courier from the underground Home Army in Poland named Jan Gralewski; Navy Lieutenant Ponikiewski, the general's adjutant; Adam Kulakowski, who was the personal political adviser to Sikorski in his role as Prime Minister of Poland; Lieutenant Colonel Victor Cazalet, M.P., a member of the British House of Commons and critic of Churchill, who was the British liaison officer to General Sikorski; Brigadier J. P. Whitely, M.P., military adviser to the British viceroy of India and friend of Sikorski; and nine aircrew. The captain of the Liberator bomber, Czech Flight Lieutenant Edward Prhal, survived.

What was never reported, and what three hundred thousand angry and embittered Poles in Britain and the Middle East were ordered never to discuss, not even among themselves, were some odd coincidences, and strange events that made the nature of their leader's death open to question. General Sikorski had gone to the Middle East to inspect the Second Polish Corps—the army of one hundred and eighty thousand men and women rescued from the Russians—and to confer with its commander, Władysław Anders, who had spent eighteen months as a tortured prisoner in the Lubyanka prison, and who was quite prepared to lead his army back to Poland, arms in hand, past whatever enemy might stand in its way.

A lean, leathery, taciturn man, he was known to be the key to Sikorski's plans, which the commander-in-chief had discussed with no one, and no one would ever know what these two men talked about during Sikorski's visit. In his private papers, published after the war, General Anders would make only a passing reference to that six-hour meeting. Leaving the meeting, General Sikorski turned and said to Anders, within hearing of several Polish and British officers: *You are my man, then?* And Anders assured him that he would do his duty.

In the Polish Air Transport Command aircraft that carried him westward, General Sikorski transcribed the notes of this meeting in his own hand, placed the notes and their draft in his briefcase, and chained it to his wrist. The aircraft landed to refuel at Gibraltar. Almost at once, it was declared defective and unsafe, although its Polish aircrew didn't think there was anything wrong with it. A new machine was to be provided in the morning.

Met at the airfield with full British military honors (a Royal Marine honor guard, a brass band in shining regimentals, the staffs of the three services lined up for inspection), General Sikorski accepted the governor-general's hospitality. He and his party dined in the governor's private quarters, where they were joined by an emissary from the British Foreign Office in London, who had arrived in Gibraltar the day before to intercept Sikorski. During the dinner, the general received a top-secret cryptogram from England, asked for immediate transportation to the British Isles, and he and his party took off in a converted Liberator bomber staffed by a British aircrew whose first pilot was a Czech officer of the RAF. The general's own Polish aircrew, headed by the veteran Colonel Izycki, swore that they never left their quarters that night, but the British explanation was that the Czech pilot and his British airmen were the only crew they could assemble at short notice. The Czech flight commander was the only person who survived the flight. He reported that the controls failed shortly after takeoff. The Liberator crashed into the sea, within sight of Gibraltar, and the general and his party drowned in fifty feet of water. Colonel Izycki's men were sent to England the next day in their own machine which, apparently, had not been defective after all.

No one would ever be able to determine the cause of the crash, nor the nature of the urgent message that prompted General Sikorski to make that wholly unexpected journey. The British signal logs for that night were destroyed in an accidental fire that broke out in the Naval Communications Center the next day. No message, however, had been sent from any Polish government or military sources. No explanation was given as to how the injured Czech pilot of the Liberator, whose converted cockpit could be entered only through the passenger compartment, had escaped from the aircraft while everyone else drowned. Royal Navy divers found the plane intact, its doors and portholes locked, and its fuselage substantially undamaged, but most of the bodies were not recovered for several days. The body of the general's daughter was never recovered; it had, apparently, floated out of its locked, temporary grave. The general's own body lay for several days in a warehouse, in the furnace heat of a Mediterranean summer, before a Royal Army Medical Corps surgeon could examine it, and only then was it boxed for delivery to its countrymen. It was carried to Britain aboard the Polish destroyer *O. R. P. Orkan* and arrived in Plymouth on July 7, 1943. By that time, the body had decomposed so rapidly that it had burst through its wooden coffin and had to be sealed in lead. The lead coffin was never reopened in England. This was to avoid any suggestion of suspicion. Prime Minister Mikolajczyk felt that he and his vilified government couldn't risk yet another breach with their Western Allies.

General Sikorski was buried, after ceremonial services in Westminster Cathedral, in the Polish airmen's cemetery in Norfolk. Ludo was captain of the honor guard.

CHAPTER XX

THE DAY OF THE FUNERAL had dawned as a brilliant one. It was one of those miraculous days of an English summer which confirm the notion of England's immortality. The sun gilded the simple white crosses. The breeze was frivolous among the flowers and dead leaves. The kings and queens and presidents and prime ministers, and the ambassadors and generals and diplomats and soldiers, stood bathed in light under a sky of such translucent blue that it denied the possibility of anyone's dying. Rain clouds were moving slowly inland from the sea, and an electrical storm flashed behind them like a warning beacon, but Ludo knew that there couldn't be any rain that day.

It took several hours for everyone to disperse afterward. He and Prus and Reszke and Johnny Sommerset, and Brigadier Sir Hugh Wadsworth-Jones and Derek Bellancourt of the AFLACC office, and (at a slight distance) Loomis and Romuald Modelski, stood talking quietly on the sidewalk outside the cemetery gates as if unwilling to be left alone. The curious English passersby, moved by that instinct for the proper thing that had allowed them to civilize an Empire, stepped up to one or another of the Poles to tell them how terribly sorry they all were.

They spoke in tones designed to honor the dead even as they dismissed all the dead from memory, in voices that bore just the amount of gloom required at a funeral, and Ludo stared longingly at the sky as if the sight of it would armor him against them. The feathery white contrails unfolding in the blue, marking the trails of invisible machines in crystallizing vapor, swept on, silent as death itself, and he wondered what there was left for him to do.

Sikorski was dead, one among millions whose names rang like a dirge, and perhaps what Winston Churchill said about him earlier in the morning in a message to the Polish people and, in particular, to the Polish Armed Forces in the West, was all that had to be remembered. *Sikorski is dead,* Churchill said in a voice so deep, so shamed and stricken that it had struck a chill. *His efforts and your sacrifices shall not be in vain.*

Prepare yourselves to die for Poland, the measured phrases rolled. *For many of you to whom I speak must die, as many of us must die, and as he died, for his country and the common cause. In the farewell to your dear leader, let us mingle renewed loyalties.*

We shall not forget him, Churchill said. *I shall not forget you. My thoughts will be with you always.*

Yet none of them could doubt any longer—neither the nervously polite Englishmen nor the dispersing Poles—that this dirge would be forgotten in no time at all. How else could the world survive, unless it could murder its own memory and conscience? The sun would rise and set, Ludo knew, and the world would continue to spin on its axis; a greenness had already begun to return to the land. The rusted wreckage of Hurricanes and Spitfires

would sink in the soil, and grass and vine and sapling would rise
to deny that anything of note had happened in that oddly skewed
moment of time, and all the witnesses to that moment who had
died for something, but whose deaths will have accomplished
nothing, would be mute, so that no one would learn the lessons
they taught.

If anyone had asked Ludo then who or what had been buried
in that sealed lead coffin, he'd have said: Truth, faith, honor,
Poland, a man's ability to believe in such things as Righteousness
and Justice, and every other illusion for which men had died. The
war would run on, he knew, for months—perhaps even years—
but it would be nothing more than ordinary killing from that moment on, a matter of habit for which there was no cure. Its purpose was dead for him. In that grave lay more than just one
man's decomposing body. As in the gloomy desolation of the
Katyn Forest, so here, in the midst of England's celebrated centuries of civilization, hope had died.

As though the thought had traveled from his mind to that of
Prus, the general looked up at the sky and said: There are worse
things that can happen to a man than getting killed in war.

—Such as what?

—Such as living in a manner that negates everything that
means anything to him.

—You sound as if you envy General Sikorski, said Romuald
Modelski.

—I think I'm happy for him, Prus said. At least no one will
turn his life into a lie.

—Perhaps the less said about that, the better, said the brigadier. One doesn't want to feed the rumormongers.

—Neither can anyone afford an inflexible position, Romuald
Modelski said. We are no longer living in the nineteenth century.

—Some things can't be compromised, no matter what the century, Prus said. You learn about that sort of thing when you've
been a soldier.

—You learn about the other if you've your future in mind,
Romuald Modelski said.

—And if there is no future? Ludo asked.

—Oh, there's always a future. Unless you decide that you don't want one. Then, I suppose, you put a bullet in your head. I suppose General Prus will tell us that that's also something you learn about when you've been a soldier. Personally, I never thought it worth considering.

—Not many people do, Prus said.

—Not many people choose to die, Ludo said. A great many of them do it, nonetheless.

—Quite, said the brigadier. It's just as the Prime Minister said this morning in his valedictory for General Sikorski. *Soldiers must die,* he said. What is it that they're supposed to die for, though? I can never remember.

—*To nourish the country which gave them birth,* Brigadier, Derek Bellancourt finished the quotation.

—Yes, well. That's what it's all about, then, said the brigadier. To nourish the country.

—With all the nourishment this one's been getting in the last few years, it ought to be rather overweight, Loomis murmured, and the brigadier said: What?

—Loomis believes in the adage of *Albion Perfide,* I'm afraid, Sir Hugh, said Romuald Modelski.

—Oh, he does, does he? said the brigadier. A damned odd thing for an American to do.

—Well, sir, Derek said with a sideways glance at Loomis. He's rather an odd sort of damned American.

—Quite. Scribblin' fella, said the brigadier. I expect that's what makes the difference. Be a good chap, Derek, and get my car, will you? The Town Hall ought to be a good place to meet, I expect. You'd never get the Bentley through this mob.

Derek smiled, saluted, turned about, and vanished in the crowd that flowed through the cemetery gates, and Ludo thought of Ann, whom the younger man resembled. The war seemed very far away then, yet near, as the moments of his private history were always close to hand, and he wondered if it were not too late to look for new beginnings. He knew himself to be in great danger of becoming the sort of dry, cold, solitary man who had attended too many funerals which, along with his years, would chip away his ability to care for anyone convincingly enough even to fool himself. War, which cannot brutalize a really decent man, may, nevertheless, destroy a mind or numb it to every gentle instinct, he knew. But, he wondered then, is that kind of injury always irreversible?

He yawned.

All through the funeral he had been unable to stop himself from yawning. The drums, the lowered regimental standards, the massed trumpeters playing the "Last Post" and the traditional, interrupted call of the "Trumpeter of Krakow," the crash of final musketry . . . all this had threatened to bow him to the ground.

Yawning, he was reminded of a man he had known, an officer who had been cashiered out of his regiment for cheating at cards. Ludo had sat with him through the long night before his ceremonial degradation while the man packed and talked and yawned, and didn't try to explain himself or justify his actions, and Ludo hadn't been able to understand why this disgraced man should act in such a normal, unaffected manner, how he could seem so detached and bored and indifferent to the dissolution of his life. Then the man had excused himself politely for a moment and gone to the bathroom and shot himself through the head. No longer able to count on a past that he cared to live with, he had averted an unacceptable future. The prayers, eulogies, muffled drums, and valedictory volleys fired over Sikorski's grave pointed to an unavoidable future of his own, but Ludo had no idea what his immediate days would bring. Without love, mercy, honor, trust, and faith, there would be little left of his former vision of himself in any event, and he wondered if he'd still be able to intervene in the destiny of others. In that past which was no longer quite believable, his advice, orders, or example had turned some lives into other courses and, occasionally, deferred some young man's doom. But as the war had aged, as its idealism had dimmed and given way to ordinary waste, so his own influence on events had narrowed until only selfish choices were left to him now.

Was it too late to turn it all around? And, in that reversal, to move toward a wholly new destiny, perhaps even a life in which affection might take root? As the last echoes of the funeral volleys drifted from his mind, he struggled to finally face the reality of his wars, his life, and to cut the skeins of memory and tradition that held him to his past. But he knew that in any new assessment of himself he'd find himself desolate.

The brigadier offered Ludo and Romuald Modelski a lift back to London. There was a need for them to have a talk, he said.

—Thought we'd have lunch and then drive on up. Derek's scrounged some enormous steaks from the Americans for us, and we thought we'd have them done up at the Fox and Bucket.

—I've not much of an appetite just now, Brigadier, Ludo said.

—Wonderful steaks, though. Never saw so much meat in one piece since the war began. Didn't quite know what to do with 'em at first. Eat 'em? Frame 'em? Put 'em in a glass case at the War Museum? Say what you like about our Yank allies, but they do run to nice meat now and then.

—It's nice to be app-preciated, Brigadier, Loomis hiccoughed and said.

—Perhaps the general could use a lift to London, Ludo said and turned to where Prus had been standing, but he had stepped into the blue-and-khaki crowd that flowed between the sidewalks toward the center of the town.

—There's no use looking for your mentor, brother-in-law, Romuald Modelski hissed in Ludo's ear. You're quite alone now to make your decisions.

Indeed, Ludo thought that he had never felt more alone than now. A major segment of his journey had come to an end; what lay ahead could only be surmised.

Once more, he looked for refuge in the sky. A flight of rooks rose from the trees on the other side of the cemetery and wheeled in formation. A flight of Spitfires flashed silver-and-white at fifteen thousand feet. All he needed was a perfectly ordinary miracle to take him across the reefs and shoals on which his thoughts had beached themselves and splintered. Was God in his lighthouse? He believed in God as he believed in the movement of the planets; he didn't need functional analyses to know that the moon controlled the tides and that God intervened in human affairs. But no help came from the sky that morning.

—A damn sad thing about Prus, said the brigadier. Brilliant soldier, a wonderfully decent chap. Too bad he got himself mixed up with the wrong people, eh? Could've made a brilliant career for himself if he'd listened to the right sort of people.

—That's always the trouble with his kind of people, said Romuald Modelski. Men of such narrow loyalties as his are the last thing that's needed nowadays, wouldn't you agree?

—Eh? Oh, quite. Quite, said the brigadier. One must take the broad view of things, as it were. Still, it *is* a shame.

It was all said for his benefit, Ludo knew, and he wondered what would be asked of him, what he would be offered, and what he'd do about it. In the mood of the moment, he neither knew nor cared. The sky, when he glanced up at it again, was empty; the Spitfires were gone. The rooks settled, cawing, in the trees.

In the meantime, they had begun to talk about the Middle East, which had become a dumping ground for British civil servants and military officers who had failed their masters but who were too well known, or too well connected, to be forced into a straightforward resignation.

—Worst monkey house in the Empire, said the brigadier. Can't trust the Copts, can't talk to the Gyppos, and can't stand the damn Jews. Just about the only civilized company between the Nile and the Euphrates is the crocodile.

—Were you ever stationed there, Sir Hugh? Romuald asked, and the brigadier recoiled: Good God, no. The Mid is where the War House sends all the misfit odds and sods they'd rather not have cluttering up the landscape anywhere else. Worst set of stations in the Empire. Just about the only things you don't boil there before use are gin and your socks. Only chaps that go there are the wayward Johnnies who don't know how to do the right thing. Fate worse than death, I'd say.

Then they too became part of the great gathering of soldiers, airmen, and sailors who had come, with or without orders, to pay their last respects to General Sikorski. The crowd swept them down the dusty street into the town, each man the equal of another in shared grief and gloom, paying no heed to rank or its privileges. Their group split up. Romuald clung to the elbow of the brigadier. Reszke walked with Johnny Sommerset. Ludo found himself shoulder-to-shoulder with Loomis.

—I never thought I'd feel sorry for Prus, Loomis said to him. I just didn't think he was human enough to feel anything, so why waste sympathy on him? But the way they served him up in Whitehall . . .

—This has all happened to him before, Ludo said. He was a national hero when he opposed Pilsudski in 1926. Both he and Sikorski could've split the country, started a civil war, and they could've won it. But both of them preferred to accept forced retirement and obscurity rather than ruin what was left of unity in Poland.

—And now they've both been put out of the way again, Loomis said. Don't you find it kind of a coincidence that both Prus and Sikorski would be gone within a week of each other? And that the people who benefit the most by that coincidence are anxious to talk to you? Doesn't that give you any ideas at all?

—What I think, and what I'm willing to talk to you about, are two different things, Ludo said.

—Just as long as you're aware of what's in the wind, Loomis said and shrugged.

Impatient, Ludo glanced sideways at the American then, and suppressed a biting reply. He saw the dry graying cheeks, the lines of disappointment etched as if in acid around the corners of the mouth, the glow of fanaticism in the wet eyes of the alcoholic. How in God's name could *he* set himself up as anybody's conscience? Loomis's shabby trenchcoat, a symbol of his own romantic vision of himself, was slung over his shoulders and the empty sleeves hung like broken wings.

—What *are* you after, Loomis?

—I told you before. Decency. Something clean to take out of this filthy business. A conclusion one can live with. I wouldn't think I'd have to explain that to you.

But Ludo no longer cared to hear anything that anyone said to him or about him. He was no longer an airman among his own kind, no longer a man whose life contained the love of a woman; he had no worthwhile expectations of any kind.

It was then one of those coincidental moments that can be understood only in afterthought when there is both the time and the solitude to isolate and examine the overheard phrase and to give it both the relevance and the significance it deserved. The crowd had begun to pass under the arched vault of historic gates which caught and magnified voices and sent them booming back, and Ludo heard the icy cynicism in Romuald's voice as he said invisibly: . . . *and if he declines, you can send him off to the Western Desert. Events have gone far beyond anyone's private sense of right or wrong.*

—The Minister can be very persuasive, said the brigadier.

—And if he fails again?

—Then someone else will pay the price of his convictions.

And then the crowd's own booming passage through the arch shattered all their voices, and then they were in the town's main thoroughfare, and both Romuald and the brigadier were inaudible again.

Ludo knew both his challenge and his danger then, and looked about, withholding all judgment, but the war-weary, disillusioned faces in the crowd communicated nothing he wanted to see. A part of his mind urged discipline and caution, the virtues which his father had attempted to instill in him. His father, whom he had never remembered as vividly as now, had known that his sons would always veto caution in favor of ferocity, and that Ludo, the most gifted of them all, could be as savage and implacable as a ferret. A rage, as of barbaric ancestors, lived deep in his system, and now he felt its familiar stirrings. The concrete under his thin-soled dress shoes seemed as brittle as glass.

One era had come to an end, he knew. Another hadn't yet begun. In the gray haunted no-man's-land between a past that couldn't be recalled and a future in which he wouldn't be able to live, only the dead seemed to be able to speak to him with authority.

PART FIVE

So Shall It Be at the End

And Samson said to the lad who guided
his steps: Suffer me to touch the pillars
which support the whole house, and
let me lean upon them and rest a little.

JUDGES 16:26

CHAPTER XXI

THAT AUTUMN, and then into the spring and summer of 1944, Ann's life acquired a desperate and dispiriting monotony that seemed to derive less from her chosen circumstances than from the runaway encroachments of the war. Ludo was gone, shunted out of sight into the Egyptian backwaters of the conflict, and, by all accounts that reached her now and then, was drinking himself into oblivion in a rented house in Gezira on the Nile. Janusz Prus spent his days in the isolation of a rented room near Turnham Green. She made no attempt to contact either of them. She lived from one distasteful dawn to another, feeling as though an arctic night had slid across her wasted days, and she took care not to think about what must follow.

The war, as portrayed in BBC bulletins and headlines, was still a crusade. In reality, it had become something altogether different. Because she was who she was and did what she did, she heard and knew much more than the manipulated public, and sometimes felt herself living beyond her times, looking backward, aware of the duplicities, the betrayals, and the uselessness of every honest effort. In November 1943, at the Teheran Conference, Churchill had finally buried his vision of a reconstructed, manageable Europe and agreed that the Continent was to be invaded in France, not through Italy and the open coasts of the Mediterranean, thus making sure that the Western Allies would be unable to reach Central Europe before the Russians got there.

As John Laidlaw told Ann during a brief resumption of their old affair (she had been close to a nervous breakdown in July and August and reached out for his unsentimental strength), Stalin had been infuriated by the Anglo-American invasion of the Italian mainland and threatened to make a separate peace with Hitler unless a wholly new invasion was mounted in France. He had sent Vyacheslav Molotov, his best hatchet man, to open peace negotiations in Kaganrog behind the German lines, and he saw to it that Roosevelt heard the appropriate rumors.

—You should have been there, Ann, John Laidlaw related. It

was a masterful performance. Without the need to say a single word, that damned old cunning murderer raised the specter of a hundred and forty German divisions freed for service in the west and, at the same time, he made it clear that with Russia out of the war, and perhaps even going back to being Hitler's silent ally, Roosevelt could forget about winning his fourth term. You can imagine what all those shrill American leftists would make of a war without Russia in it. Roosevelt's political power base would be totally disrupted. You can be sure that he got the message.

—I don't think I want to hear any more of this, Ann said.

—Oh, but the best is yet to come! The joke, you see, the cunning peasant joke, lay in the fact that the Kaganrog negotiations didn't have a chance! The Russians won't settle for less than half of Poland, and the Germans, whom God in His wisdom must have deprived of the last of their wits, went on demanding the Ukraine! It was all a wonderful little play-within-a-play, enacted in the wings, so to speak, to distract the actors of the main drama staged in Teheran. And Stalin did it all with one cold glint in his fearsome eyes, one angry pout under his walrus moustache, and a brace of faithful servants in the American State Department who made sure that Roosevelt heard what Stalin wanted him to hear.

—I *don't* want to hear any more of this, Ann said.

Laidlaw, however, was now speaking only to himself. She envied him his freedom from conscience, his Victorian certainties, and his ability to live in the world as it was and not as romantic fatalists might want it. Walking up and down the room in which she still saw Ludo everywhere she looked, she had found him her best distraction from an image of herself that she couldn't bear.

—One has a tendency to laugh at the Russians, he said admiringly. One makes little jokes about their atrocious suits and their appalling manners. One thinks of them as somewhat childlike in their primitive brutality. There's this extraordinary compulsion to pat them on their pointed skulls and say: Now, look here, Ivan, that's not the way things are done in civilized societies; you really ought to let your betters manage the world as they've always done; why don't you just pop back into your picturesque little village and bugger a goat? And then suddenly you realize that you've been the poor old goat all along. Still, to give the murder-

ous old devil his due, Stalin had the measure of his man at
Teheran, which is more than can be said for Roosevelt.

—Couldn't you have warned him? Ann asked.

—Winston tried. Roosevelt wouldn't listen. With the Ameri-
can presidential elections less than a year away, he had something
more important on his mind than the fate of seven European na-
tions. And, since in Winston's mind Roosevelt has become the
Empire's only hope, we didn't argue as much as we might have.
Stalin got his way. The Western Allies would quietly undermine
their own successful Italian campaign and invade northern
France. Russia would be free to *liberate* the Baltic republics,
Poland, Czechoslovakia, and the Balkan countries. The Red
Army would have the honor of taking Prague, Vienna, and
Berlin. A government friendly to the Soviet Union would be in-
stalled in Warsaw. In exchange, our great and glorious Soviet ally
would stay in the war and President Roosevelt might count on
four more years in the White House.

—And what about all the people who have trusted us and
who've depended on us?

Impatient with what he must consider a sad but unavoidable
sacrifice, the Minister made a dismissive gesture.

—Straws in the wind, I'm afraid, he said. Not really good for
anything except to show which way our winds are blowing. A
pity, of course.

—Yes, she said. A pity.

—You're concerned with your . . . ah . . . Polish friends? he
asked in a gentler voice, one that acknowledged the existence of a
human element in the processes of history.

—Shouldn't I be? she said bitterly.

—If you must, he said. There's not a great deal that we can do
for them. Roosevelt actually said to Stalin that Russia could do
anything she liked with Poland and the Poles, provided that she
didn't start doing it until after the American elections.

—A pity the Poles had been led to believe something different
all these years, don't you think?

—They had their duty, he said. We have ours. Winston's responsibility is to the future of the Empire, and he'll do battle
with Stalin and Roosevelt for no other cause. And if that means

that he must swallow his pride in the process, and hold some damned American politician's coat while that historical illiterate consents to the enslavement of a hundred million people, Winston will do it.

—*We shall not forget him*, Ann drawled out the deep, rolling phrases of Churchill's funeral promise to Sikorski. *I shall not forget you. My thoughts will be with you always.*

—You didn't make any promises to anyone, he consoled her. You just behaved as though we meant to keep them, which, at the time, we did. It's . . . disappointing for your former friends, I'm sure. But then they're used to being disappointed. Their sense of doom puts meaning in their lives, something that most civilized people have learned to live without.

—I've yet to learn it, then, she said.

Receptions, lunches, formal dinners, stand-up cocktail parties, theater parties, gatherings of temporary friends, ambassadors, prime-ministers-in-exile, youthful American major-generals: the war went on. Poised, interested, perfectly groomed, aloof, and challenging, she gathered spite-filled, condemnatory glances from short-skirted women who were obliged to paint orange imitation stockings on their legs. The black market nylons she wore sold at ten pounds a pair.

What could she think of this war, knowing what she did? How could she feel anything but contempt for herself and hatred for her kind? Brave young men and women went on dying in Europe for whatever ideals were most precious to them while three old men (one a cynical patrician, one a vicious killer, and one a fading nineteenth-century romantic) whose one shared quality was a ruthless dedication to power at all costs, were carving up the European continent to suit themselves. Flat on the ottoman in Derek's apartment, from which every trace of Ludo's presence had been carefully removed, she made her mind as empty as the nights allowed but, even so, sleep seldom came before dawn.

There were no dreams, no nightmares. Her sleep rivaled the depth of death but lacked its permanence. She would awake morning after morning, recoil at the possibility of breakfast, and carry her teacup to the window while the BBC announced the day's distant, antiseptic victories. A hundred thousand Germans killed after their surrender at Sevastopol. Two hundred thousand Crimean Tartars whisked into the Siberian tundra because they had welcomed Germans as their liberators. Ten thousand tanks grinding back and forth across the plains of Kursk. A thousand British bombers obliterating Hamburg. . . . Two thousand, three hundred tons of bombs were dropped on Berlin.

In the gray wintery park, two weeks before Christmas, the bulky army women had decorated their revetments with holly and ivy. *We are but warriors for the working day*, she quoted as she watched their domestic bustle around their instruments of war, but her own war, lacking all aim and purpose, had become a matter of boredom and indifference.

The war went on, with or without her aristocratic atmospheres. London had filled with raucous pink Americans, Lucky Strikes, Camels, Wrigley's Spearmint, Hershey bars, the jitterbug at the Hammersmith Palais de Dansc, fleets of sinking condoms in the Serpentine, and (soon enough) brown babies. Exquisitely balanced between love and hatred, the New World had come to the rescue of the Old.

(Popular wisdom, *vox populi Deique*: What's wrong with the Yanks? They're overpaid, overfed, oversexed, and over here. . . . But thank you, Lord of Hosts, for the Blue Bonnet Margarine, Spam, Canadian bacon, and B-17 "Flying Fortress" bomber.)

The war went on. The patched, overmended, shabby wartime clothing began to match the gray texture of undernourished faces in which the lines of unsupportable worry were etched deep as scars. Irritability and a curiously inverted, self-deriding anguish had replaced whatever human sympathy and warmth had existed in another time. The city's upward grin was somewhat marred by the black gaps of ruin.

If anyone were to tell the desperately injured people of her city that the war might go on one minute longer than it had to, for whatever reason, or that peace had to mean more than just the mere ending of hostilities, or that British fair play and national honor demanded additional privations for the sake of solemn

promises and treaties, they'd tear him limb from limb with their
bare hands, she was sure.

And the war went on.

In January, an Anglo-American corps landed at Anzio on the
Italian coast, twenty-five miles south of undefended Rome, with
only two platoons of German communications troops and one bicycle company of Italian Black Shirts between them and a bloodless occupation of the Eternal City. They waited on their beaches
while the Germans brought Panzer Grenadiers from Russia, para-
troopers from Westphalia, Alpine sharpshooters from the Tyrol,
and Tiger tanks from Paris; waited, at first incredulous then
resigned, while the batteries of deadly Eighty-eights were dug into
the Alban Hills that overlooked their beaches; waited until the
combined chiefs of staff in Washington and Whitehall decided
that they had waited long enough. Rome fell five months and
twenty thousand lives later. It was time enough for the Russians
to break into Poland.

Names, places, numbers. Geography and arithmetic paved the
way for history. In February, Soviet armies crossed the prewar
Polish-Soviet border, and there began mass roundups of the resistance forces, shootings, deportations. Censorship guaranteed discretion but, even so, she knew how to read the absent truth in
the headlines.

On May 12, with the road to Rome open once again, and the
great German bastion of the Gothic Line outflanked eighty miles
to the south, the Second Polish Corps of General Anders was
thrown against the fortress of Monte Cassino, the fortified Bene-
dictine monastery, and its surrounding mountains. In the six days
of savage fighting against the First German Parachute Division,
and SS Hitler Youth, and punitive battalions who neither expected to be spared nor tried to surrender, two thousand Polish
soldiers were killed and three thousand wounded on the precipi-
tous slopes which two Allied armies had failed to take in three
months. When the smoke finally lifted to reveal the Polish flag
flying above the ruins, and this unnecessary battlefield was returned to stillness, this Polish corps, which had marched to Italy
out of Russian prisons, had virtually ceased to exist.

Joyful Rome was freed on June 4. Two days later, the greatest air-and-sea invasion force in history debouched upon the beaches of Normandy, a thousand hostile miles between them and Berlin. Two army corps, withdrawn from Italy for the *Champagne Campaign* landed on the French Riviera. In Normandy and Brittany, British, American, Canadian, and Polish divisions began their long and painful journey to the Rhine.

Names, places. Arnhem . . . the great airborne fiasco . . . the Polish Parachute Brigade of General Sosabowski slaughtered when dropped on a Panzer corps. One hundred thousand Germans, bottled up in the closing of the Falaise Gap, surrender to the First (Polish) Armored Division of General Maczek. In a town named Lublin, in the former eastern provinces of Poland, the Russians install their committee of Communist expatriates as the provisional government of the country.

And the war went on.

Names, places, dates. Numbers of dead and missing that were as meaningless in the ecstatic headlines as the distances astronomers estimate between galaxies and planets. Her skies were black, without stars. She had declared a vast, inner armistice. Indifferent to her destination, unable to help herself into fresh perceptions of a life that had become a matter of regretful habit, she withdrew her forces from the war.

In September, V-2 bombs began to fall on England.

But there were other dates, other places which didn't quite get their proper mention in the headlines. On July 20, the German generals attempted to kill Hitler, failed, and died on meathooks. On August 1, the irresistible Red Army reached the Vistula at Warsaw and Radio Moscow called on the Polish Home Army in the city to rise against the Germans. The Poles rose, as much in expectation of early assistance from the halted armies of Marshal Rokossovsky (a Sovietized Pole) as in the hope of liberating their nation's capital, and installing their legitimate government before the Russians could bring in their puppets. For two months, the city fought and burned while the Russians waited. They helped by dropping bags of flour and ammunition (without parachutes) from ten thousand feet. They refused permission for British and American transport aircraft to supply the city in their zone of war. Polish bomber crews, flying a one-way suicidal mission from Italian airfields, brought the only help and died in the process. When all resistance had been crushed by Germans and Ukrainian SS volunteers, when Warsaw had become a ruin and one hundred thousand Poles had died or were driven to captivity, and when the Home Army had ceased to exist in Warsaw, the Red Army entered a city in which nothing moved.

Paris, in which not a single ruin marred the neoclassical façades, was liberated on August 25. Athens was freed on October 14. In November, Roosevelt was re-elected.

And the war went on.

—It's interesting to watch someone impose his will on others, John Laidlaw said to Ann. One can't help wondering what course events might have taken if Winston's vision of a postwar Europe had been understood by anyone but Stalin, if the Mediterranean campaign had been properly supported, and if there hadn't been a Normandy invasion. But power is an art form which follows its own rules. Authority has a remorseless, self-serving logic of its own.

—I don't want to hear this, Ann said.

—You find speculation tiresome?

—As tiresome as you. As tiresome as my own image of myself.

—Forty-six is far too young to begin to die, Laidlaw said. But then you always *were* given to unreasonable emotional commitments. Distance, my dear, is the key to longevity. Distance, and the realization that every noble gesture has been made, that there is nothing new to be discovered, and that no reverence needs to be reserved for the unknown.

—I don't want you to come here again, Ann said.

—Another *adieu*? Pity. I thought that, eventually, we might be able to establish a useful, civilized *modus vivendi*, complete with book and candle, in which neither of us would have to be entirely alone.

—I wouldn't marry you if you were the last man in Europe,
Ann said.

—It's just possible that I am, he said thoughtfully. Pity about
the other. I suppose that it *is* the memory of the other?

—There is no other. There'll never be another.

—Pity. You offer quite a lot. I too have much to offer. After
the war, there will be nothing left, you see. Not undergraduate
romanticism, not even German fascism to be incensed about, not
even an Empire. There will be only the Americans. It's likely to
be a terribly dull sort of life.

—Oh, she said furiously. I'm sure you'll find some little country
to manipulate and betray.

—I'm afraid that the only little country that I might know well
enough to manipulate is going to be our own. And that will have
been betrayed quite adequately enough.

In December, she accepted her first dinner date with Loomis.
For no reason that she'd ever want to explain to herself, she asked
him to take her to the Polish Hearth.

—The atmosphere isn't very happy there these days, he offered
doubtfully.

—Indulge me, she ordered.

—You're the doctor. I suppose that if one falls off a horse the
thing to do is to get right back on another one. But it all seems
like masochism to me.

—That's a rotten analogy, she said.

—I'm a rotten person. Luckily, this is a rotten world, so I've a
good chance to make it to a comfortable old age.

—Have you no illusions?

—This year? Nary a one.

—But there were other years, she observed.

—Eons of years and acres of illusions, Loomis said.

—Name your most recent one.

—The possibility of love.

—Yes, that's a good one, she said. That's quite a remarkable illusion. It's an expensive one, though, don't you think?

—Well, it's the best there is. If you want quality, you've got to pay for it. There are all sorts of secondhand illusions you can get at half price, but who'd want one of those?

—God, but you're a fool, she said and was finally able to smile at him. Is that how you've survived your acres of illusions?

—Oh, I had nothing to do with that, he said. I can't take the credit.

—Some of them died in Warsaw, I understand, she prompted.

—Oh, things die there all the time, he said. That's the place for it. You could say that Warsaw is the cemetery of European illusions.

—You make it sound like an elephants' graveyard.

—That's just what it is! Hopes go there to get buried. The damned thing about it is that they're never entirely laid to rest there. They keep popping up.

—Don't talk about politics, she said.

—Hmm. You've had enough of that?

—More than I can bear.

—Poor Ann. You really have had a time of it, haven't you, he said. Ah . . . are you expecting someone to join us?

—No. Why would you say that?

—You keep looking around.

She looked for Ludo everywhere: in a swirl of clouds, the fold of a curtain, the slant of rain along the vacancy of windows, in the fall of gray December light. Someone had said to her in the long-ago days when she was still able to wear her disguises with conviction, that the death of self-love was death to the imagination, but, obviously, he hadn't known what he was talking about.

At night, she sat on the ottoman hour after hour, shoulders as sharp as the forward edge of a folded wing, staring into the imitation warmth in the marbled hearth. The Minister (she wouldn't honor their failed intimacy by thinking of him by his Christian name) was right to this extent: she didn't need to reserve any reverence for whatever was still to happen to her, but the tears seeped between her lashes anyway.

Because she thought of Ludo first and foremost as a man in love with his (and his country's) past, indifferent to the future, she saw him in her mind's embittered eye as a quiet pacer of foggy battlements in Egypt, a watcher of night fires around desert camps, a reader of premonitory skies. Wakening into the cold, unpromising English dawn, she imagined his restlessness in a hot, jasmine-scented night under palms or, as seemed more likely, hunched over some terrible, sugary Palestinian wine at five pounds a bottle while a dispirited, tawny, naked girl writhed in a belly dance. The more uncomplimentary the images, the better, she supposed; yet, even so, the nights were unendurable without him.

Damn him, damn them all. The Poles had had their fair chance. A choice had been offered. Half a home was better than none, as the Minister had said, and if he (they) refused to compromise their vision of themselves, if they insisted that all the promises be kept and that their entire country be returned to them, they had no one to blame for their betrayal but themselves.

She knew, because the Minister had told her, that Winston Churchill had tried, until the very last, to give them some vestigial remnant of a home to which they might return. The idea that he might be the gravedigger of the Empire, as Roosevelt was of Europe, was quite maddening to him, yet his love of the heroic could not accept the image of stark betrayal. In begging the London Poles to agree to the dismembering of their country as Stalin had insisted, and to cooperation with the Soviet puppets, he risked more than they were able to imagine; Roosevelt, who had become so accustomed to imperial powers that life without them would have been unendurable to him, was barely able to conceal his American distaste for the Empire of Britain. But they (Ludo) wouldn't (couldn't, she supposed) hear anything but the pulse of their remorseless history. It was to be everything that their own battle flags commanded them to live by, honor and fatherland intact, or nothing. . . . And so it would be nothing.

She had been present, hidden behind the lacquered oriental screen in the bay window of the Minister's office, when the offers and requests were made to Ludo. It was the price she had demanded for the aristocratic atmospheres she had provided. She had sat in the dusty, speckled air, breathing the scent of some unknown, red-bloomed plant which twitched whenever a fly landed on its leaves, while the Minister and Derek conferred with her lover. He sat (she watched him through a crack in the screen that decapitated a fire-breathing dragon) as still as though he had become part of the carved, antique mahogany which the Minister affected, frozen in time like the poised riders in the hunting prints, while the soft voice of the tempter droned on. Split in her loyalties, pinioned (as he would be, she was sure) between reason and emotion, she couldn't believe in the measured unraveling of the solipsist arguments. Loving him, despite her own savage disappointment in him, she wished him the best and the worst simultaneously, knowing that any choice would be fatal to him. She thought, in idiot flight from truth or absolutes into that safe dimension where the spirit shelters from the temporal world, of Christ on the mountain, of proffered crowns and kingdoms, of the rough, winding track that leads to destiny. Blasphemy didn't help. His face wasn't Christlike, in any event. The Minister performed with expert correctness and facility; he (Ludo) seemed to have turned himself into stone.

They talked (the Minister and Derek) and she knew that whatever they had wanted to accomplish had been doomed to failure from the start because they didn't understand his terrible simplicity. He (Ludo) could do what they wanted only if he believed that what they proposed would give his country a measure of freedom, a modicum of dignity, a possibility of hope. His own pride would mean nothing to him with such stakes on the table, she knew; why else would he have come there in the first place? But they dealt with him as they would have done with one of their own kind. They tried to bribe him with honors and distinctions, and then to hint at blackmail. Oblique remarks were made about a burned man who had been murdered in a Warsaw hospital, courts of inquiry, the possibility of disgrace. Glittering rewards were displayed. The Polish government would have to be reorganized to face facts, rather than to continue living in self-deluding fictions, and to accept a Poland which (as the Minister delicately put it) would be *shifted considerably to the west*. An important politician had been found who was willing to cooperate with the Lublin Communist Committee and pressure was now being put on the London Poles to make him their Premier. If he could have a popular military hero as his Vice-Premier, much of the Polish problem could be solved. The trouble was,

the Minister confided, that the Polish armies in the west refused
to follow this man of singular vision, so that his lone compliance
would merely mock and irritate the Russians.

Whom would the Poles follow? Never a man who, in their esti-
mation, would crack their unity in the face of treason, never a
turncoat civilian politician whom they couldn't trust. Sikorski's
death had deprived them of their leader but, contrary to every expectation, had not shattered their determination. Their ranks and
minds were closed to pressure as to arguments of reason. They
were quite willing to condemn themselves to exile in order to
haunt whatever conscience could be found for haunting in the
west. . . .

Because he said nothing, because his darkened face displayed
no emotion, they must have assumed that they had found a sympathetic listener, she supposed, and found herself believing that
he would consent to lead the recusant Poles. They would trust
only a bona fide military hero, as the Minister suggested: a man
who demanded nothing for himself, who had lived as they had
done in an atmosphere of hazard and value, and who was, perhaps, unaware that he had done anything remarkable. . . . *In
short, a hero*, the Minister had said and inquired politely: *I mean,
isn't that the Polish way? Or have we misunderstood your
Telemachan sense of military fidelity? And, if so, is there a reason
why we should concern ourselves with you any further?*

Listening, she watched and knew the full extent of the cynical
manipulations in which she had played a part. Ludo could have
no further doubt about it. Nothing about him suggested the fury
that he must have felt; only his face appeared to have grown thinner, more cruel and cold. She knew that in some way she had to
make amends so that, if nothing else, he'd hate her less.

Toward the end, Derek was sent from the room. The pretext
was sherry, or perhaps it was tea. Outraged, and barely able to
suppress her furious exclamation, she heard the Minister describe
the advantages of marriage to herself, a world of wealth, unassailable position, and (if that's what one wanted after the exer-
tions of a war) unlimited leisure. Like his indomitable master, the
Minister was ready to sacrifice anyone for his cause. Ludo rose, saluted, bowed politely, and left.

—What did they offer him, anyway? Loomis asked.

—Nothing he could value.

—But what?

—I forget the details. Instant promotion, high rank, in any event. The Polish government would be forced to endorse whatever they promised. He was to be a Vice-Premier, or something. There was to be a very handsome pension if, in the end, he decided to settle in the United Kingdom.

—And all he had to do was induce the Poles to follow him back to Poland when the war was over?

—In substance, yes.

—Not bad for a major who's been frozen in grade for eleven years. But, of course, he refused.

—Of course, she said and felt her heart miss a beat.

—The poor, damn, bloody fool, Loomis said.

—Yes, she said quietly and fixed her eyes on her plate. He does make a clear conscience rather difficult.

What she heard then, astonished, was a half-strangled sob. Indifferent to vanity, and curious about all the varieties of grief, she put on her glasses and looked at Loomis with greater attention. He wore a neat, dark three-piece suit in conservative striping; his face had been equally diplomatic and elusive, a mask worn as a disguise. In the harsh, unforgiving light of the dining room it was now rubbery with barely hidden pain; an inner wound had opened. His eyes were as pale as candles guttering on a grave.

The Thames fog, thick as curdled milk, seeped into the room through cracks around the windows, and with it came the graveyard stench of coal smoke, rotted vegetation, and damp night. Somewhere in the United States, she knew, he had a rich wife who owned a newspaper, lovers, stocks and bonds, a mansion and horses, a bought-and-paid-for husband whose career always hung in question. His competence in doubt, his image of himself reduced, he clung to a single palatable memory: Lala had loved him. He had no reason to expect another affirmation of his manhood.

—Why are you so concerned about the Poles? she asked.

—Why are you? he muttered.

—I'm not, she said and felt the hot, sharp intake of her breath; never before had the truth been so physically painful to her and, for some reason she didn't understand, nothing but the truth would do at that moment.

—I'd have thought, he began, but she cut into his argument: Loving one of them is difficult enough, she said brutally. Caring for all of them would be madness.

Working his way upward out of gloom, past the debris of his own crushed hopes and toppled illusions, he said finally: It's quite the opposite for me. I'm driven to do something for all of them, though God knows it's pretty damn near impossible to pay my kind of debt.

—You see love as a debt? she asked.

—That's what it is, he said. Nobody has the right to love anyone unless he's strong enough to protect them.

—There's not enough strength in the whole world for that! she said. Are you trying to become a martyr?

—I'm not a Catholic, he said. I think martyrdom is merely suicidal. But I'm Irish enough to know that you pay your debts in one way or another.

—Well, I'm Anglo-Irish enough to know that there's no satisfaction to be found in other people's causes. Good God in heaven! It's hard enough to find any in your own!

—What about seeing to it that a truth is told?

—Good God, she said. Next you'll be talking about faith, charity, and hope!

—Isn't that what we're talking about? Loomis said. Faith in our own ability to do something about a terrible injustice? Charity toward our own failings? Hope for our own future?

—In *this* world? she asked then. What in hell's bloody name do you expect a mere individual to do?

—In hell's bloody name, he has to do something.

—These are just *words*, Loomis! she cried out. Quite properly devalued! No sensible human being hears them any longer with anything but amusement.

—Somebody trusted *you*, he said. Whether you like it or not, you've got to do something about it.

—I don't have to do anything about anything! she cried.

—Yes, you do, he said. And you know it. If you want to think of yourself as a decent person, despite everything you know about yourself, you've got to give it a try. Otherwise, you might as well cut your throat and be done with it.

—Oh, leave me alone, she said.

She felt cold tears running down her cheeks and moved to conceal them. Not all her words were worthless; some had acquired a very costly meaning, despite devaluation. Churchill, as everyone who knew him would attest, wept when confronting *greatness, nobility,* and *honor. Trust* and *faith* (with their attendant *faithfulness*) continued to disarm her, yet she knew that any tears shed in their behalf would have to fall in mourning. In the cynical lexicon of the times, which, warped by pragmatists and sentimentalists alike, derided all but the most material concepts, such terms had become a cocktail party joke. *Heroism* was an idea aged in wood. *Courage,* if talked about at all, had to be preceded by adjectives like *blind, lunatic,* or *mindless,* implying an affinity for destruction. Humanity and sensitivity were the provinces of the noncourageous. Sensible people, the sort of whom everyone was supposed to approve, took no risks.

She watched the winter day dissolve, the December light fading into snow, the clean white coverlet melting into cindery slush the moment it was laid. Her own future seemed as unappetizing as the gravy congealing on trimmed bones on the dinner plate before her. Ludo's faith had been genuine, antique, coming toward him as a gnarled survivor might struggle up, step by stubborn step, out of the imprisonment of history. While hers was . . . what? An occasional mask to be worn in a confessional?

—Damn them, Loomis muttered finally. I wish they'd get just one thing into their proud, unrealistic heads.

—And what might that be? she asked, regretting the evening.

—That there're no second chances in the evolutionary process. The only rule is: Adapt or die. But they insist on being what they've always been.

—I think there's something quite splendid in that, she said.

—Oh, certainly. Splendid. Spectacular. Inspiring. No wonder Roosevelt called Poland *the inspiration of the nations.* But that didn't stop him from accommodating Stalin, did it? No, it didn't. Because there are other ways of looking at it all. What can you think about a people who see their country's salvation only in resurrection that follows crucifixion? Isn't there something a bit monstrous in that? They take pride in thinking of themselves as *the Christ of the nations*. But what about everyone who has to die to fulfill that terrible destiny? I don't think that's particularly splendid.

—So what else would you have them do?

—That's just the point, he said. That's the terrible part of it. There's nothing else they can do, being what they are. Trying to love them, or to care about them, is like contracting an incurable disease.

After their dinner, they walked across the park toward the West End, then along Piccadilly to the Haymarket and down the long sweep of marble steps and pavements to Whitehall. The city, lightless and silenced for the night, gleamed silvery in the sudden moonlight.

She took his arm because he needed reassurance among these past centuries which she took for granted; her path was clearly marked among the pillars, pediments, soaring spires, and equestrian metal. He was another accidental foreigner to be guided there, while she never felt more certain of herself than when conducting strangers into her own past.

At the Cenotaph, he paid his passing tribute to the unidentified bones buried there after the First World War.

—Sleep well, my friend, he murmured and she glanced sharply at his ravaged face and saw there, in the trick of gaunt light, something of what he might have been when young and proud and thin-lipped and possibly as predatory as Ludo himself.

—He's not asleep, she said. He's dead.

—Poets hold otherwise.

—I don't hold with poets. If people would stop thinking of death as something noble, they might begin to understand the disgrace of war.

—Why should they bother to do that? If there's one thing I've learned about wars, it's that they aren't real at all. They're all a madman's dream and we're just something that populates a nightmare.

—What do you think you are, then? she asked. Some kind of sick figment of God's imagination?

—Say rather the Devil's, Loomis said and laughed. When nothing else makes sense, then a sense of humor makes a fair substitute.

—It's a little early for me to think like that, she said.

At the Embankment, they leaned over the ballustrades to stare at the black sluggish river thick with debris and mist, and she saw it as it had been in the week of her return from Bellancourt to London, a lagoon of fire, the docks melting into the crimson water, the sky rent in a continuous explosion.

—Were you here during the Battle of Britain? she asked, then went on with a wry, apologetic grimace: But of course you were. I remember all those stories you wrote about Ludo.

—*Mea culpa,* he said and tapped his chest with a mocking finger. I've done my share to glorify the unspeakable.

—There, she said and pointed downriver as a tourist guide might do. Beyond Tower Bridge. The Pool of London was full of burning barges. Lambeth and Vauxhall were two huge fireballs. Woolwich and Lime House were flowing with hot lava. The clouds were red because of all the cinders.

—Yes, he said, remembering in his turn. You could read a newspaper at midnight right here where we're standing.

—What did the Germans call that awful week?

—*Adlerangriff,* he said. The Eagle attack. It all seemed rather touch and go then, didn't it?

—Not to us, it didn't. No one doubted that we would win, you see. We all believed Winston. Say what you like about him . . . or us, I suppose . . . we really were quite splendid. If that was *not* our finest hour, it'll do until the next time the Spanish Armada sails into the Channel.

—*We shall defend our island, whatever the cost may be,* he quoted the grand Churchillian phrases. *We shall fight on the beaches, we shall fight on the landing grounds, we shall fight in the fields and in the streets, we shall fight in the hills; we shall never surrender.*

—Somebody had to bend American public opinion, she said. Otherwise, how would we have got all those *Bundles for Britain?*

—And the ships, he said. And twenty thousand tanks. And the Eighth Air Force. And a million and a half men to win your damned war. I know, I know, it isn't going to be really won. Not by you. Not by us. The Russians will win it. We'll be the conquerors, but Russia will be the only victor. Britain is going to be the surviving hero. And the losers are going to be the Poles.

—Damn you, she said. Why do you always see the dark side of everything?

—Because it's the truth.

—Truth? How would you know what's true? Every man and woman has been looking for truth since the world began, and you think you've found it? Didn't you just say that there were other ways of looking at things?

—Yes, if you want to soothe a troubled conscience. You can always say that if someone got killed in a plane crash it's his fault for not taking a train.

—Oh, get off it, Loomis! Either shut up or talk about something else.

—Of course. Why not? Why not the real subject you want to talk about? Why not about Ludo? You helped to sell him down the river. Would you like to do something to get him back?

The pose, if not the substance of contempt, had always been her most accessible refuge and her surest weapon, and so she raised her head and stared down her long, straight aristocratic nose at this persistent, not-so-grand Inquisitor.

—And how, pray tell, do I do that? she asked.

—Humble yourself, milady, he mocked her. Go on your knees to Whitehall. It's your cousin and your little brother and your friend Laidlaw who decided that a desire for honesty was dangerous and had to be hidden in the desert. Once they were sure that Ludo would always be a political liability in England, and useless to their plans, they sent him to chase sand flies in the Delta. Christ, Ann, isn't that obvious? Would *you* want him around if you were in their place?

—Because he wouldn't do what they wanted from him, it doesn't mean he'd raise a riot against them, she argued.

—But how would they know that? The only motives they'd ever understand are their own. They've never trusted a friend in their entire lives, so why should they suddenly begin to trust a declared enemy? Believe me, they got rid of him all right, and they can get him back here just as easily. All it would take would be a *pretty-please* from Lady Ann. So what about it, lady?

—I . . . can't do that, she said.

—So much for love among the upper classes, he said and began to laugh. How could I've forgotten? Pride. The stiff upper lip. The things that aren't done. One doesn't *ask* for anything, since privilege is a God-given right. You'll have a bad time of it, my dear, when this quaint little island becomes a debtors' prison after we've won your war.

—That's despicable, she said.

—Tell me about it, madam, he said, his wet eyes gleaming. Words are cheap. I should know. I make my living with them.

—Leave me alone, she said wearily.

But her own conscience wouldn't give her peace. No medieval hell could burn with hotter fires. Her life had been constructed around savage pride, a ruthless and uncompromising image of herself which had allowed the most extraordinary excesses in the name of independence. Her first responsibility had been to herself and she had gloried in it. She was her own favorite penitent and confessor; never before had she failed to give absolution to herself.

Now, God in heaven, this capability was gone. In loving Ludo, she found herself obliged to love the ideas which he represented and to defend them as fiercely as he did himself. All of her own carefully raised defenses had crumbled at that instant; naked in her own eyes, she couldn't shield herself against her own future.

Loomis talked on and she began to listen, heard words and weighed them, saw a possibility of making amends.

—To bring Ludo back, she said. To restore his command. To expose that whole filthy Laidlaw business and all the dirty doings that are a part of it, that might make you and me sleep a little better. But what will it do for him and the rest of them? They've been wiped off the board months ago; nothing can change what's going to happen to them.

—Not necessarily, Loomis said. What's being done to them works only because the few decent people who still have a conscience in the USA and England don't know anything about it. That can change overnight if the Poles do something that nobody can conceal, dismiss as insignificant, or ignore. Three hundred thousand armed and angry men carry a lot of weight, you know. They can still shake the tree if they all get behind a leader they can trust.

—They'll never mutiny, she said. If that's what you're saying. When loyalties conflict, that's when their professional honor takes over. They simply act like soldiers then.

—Soldiers are simply armed people, he insisted. When people get angry enough, they make themselves heard.

—Nobody is heard unless there are people who're willing to listen, she said bitterly. And there's not a soul anywhere who'd pay attention to them if it means that the war will last one day longer.

—Then at least let these poor betrayed bastards register a protest! Loomis cried. Don't let them just vanish in the goddamn pit without a sound! They came into the war because they thought that their destruction would be remembered later, that the sound of their fall would be so great that their loving allies would be unable to forget it and so restore their country. Can't they at least go out of the war the way they came in? I mean, Christ, can't they get *something* out of this damned slaughter?

—What's left for them to get?

—An image! he cried. A way to be remembered! Some single great gesture that no one would be able to forget! Something to say that they were here all these years!

—A gesture? she murmured.

—Something to shake the bastards who betrayed them, he said. An act of sacrifice and courage, perhaps. I don't know. But I can't think of anyone but Ludo who'd be able to come up with something of that kind.

—That's utterly insane, she said. He's done quite enough.

—Let him decide that, Loomis said. Let him complete his destiny in his own way. Sure as hell, he's not doing it getting drunk in Egypt!

—Sweet God, she murmured. Do you know what you're asking me to do?

—Save him, perhaps, Loomis said. Or let him save something that's even more important to him. Dammit, Ann, don't you know anything about these poor wretches? That's what their lives are for. . . . They don't know how to live unless they've something they can die for.

—But that is mad! Inhuman! she protested furiously. Nobody can think like that.

—You should've been in Warsaw the day Lala died, Loomis said.

His voice now stuttering with emotion, he pressed her to the limits of endurance and then, she knew, beyond her ability to think. Reason stood for nothing in the face of what he had to say; logic acquired meanings beyond her comprehension. In her mind's eye, she could see dim roads that spanned vast distances toward a fixed, dark goal, a man advancing toward his destiny, and suddenly she didn't want to have anything to do with it.

—I think we owe it to him, don't you? Loomis said.

—Owe? Owe? How dare you say that to me? she cried and thought of Ludo muttering in a nightmare. *I owe nothing!* she said, quoting him precisely, and knew that this was just as untrue for her as it was for him.

Cursing herself for a romantic fool, and for a believer in a wrathful God and a medieval Devil, she knew that she would bring about Ludo's return to England, if not to herself. If that were to be her assigned role in the drama of his destiny, she'd play it and be damned. It involved nothing more than arrangements made through friends, lovers, acquaintances, and family connections; it was as simple and as natural for her as taking a deep breath. Thereafter . . . a word that need not have anything to do with the hereafter . . . she'd have no further role to play.

As a Catholic, she could understand a life that had evolved toward a single purpose. The death on Golgotha made more than just simple legendary sense; it dealt with quite immediate human needs that transcended symbols. Step by step, a long and difficult road had narrowed into a single moment in which the sum total of a man's years could shine forever through the murk of history. The involuntary, Christlike image that she had scorned while listening to Ludo's hour of temptation no longer seemed as blasphemous as it had; indeed, she could accept it as part of his truth.

And the war, which would go on regardless of anyone's choices, might possibly be made to have a kind of sense.

CHAPTER XXII

SNOW AND ICE swept Europe all of the next week. In the east, ten Russian armies, thirteen thousand tanks, twenty thousand pieces of artillery, and two million men burrowed into the frozen banks of the Vistula and peered westward through the fog that had settled over the Continent. In the Ardennes, in the still forests through which the Germans had burst in 1940 to overwhelm France, and in the widely scattered stone villages and farmsteads and small provincial towns with names like St. Vith and Malmédy and Bastogne that no one had ever heard of, cold and bearded American infantrymen warmed themselves at their own peat fires and complained about yet another Christmas away from their homes.

Nothing moved in the deep white forests. No bird could live in the frozen air. The track of the fox and the spoor of the wolf were the sole occasional reminders that life, in all its deadly urgency, went on despite an icy armistice. Behind the resting, sleeping, bored American soldiers in the icy outposts, men who looked much like themselves but who were something altogether different, were mining bridges, altering road signs, and preparing ambushes. In front of them, invisible in the fog, two Panzer armies spared from the quiet Russian front, ten armored and seventeen motorized divisions, two thousand tanks, and a quarter of a million men were creeping toward them. The war would go on.

In London, queues formed at cinemas to watch Laurence Olivier in a British propaganda version of *Henry V*, Clark Gable and Walter Pidgeon in *Thirty Seconds Over Tokyo*, Ray Milland in *Ministry of Fear*, George Cukor's *Winged Victory* (featuring Jeanne Crain), Alfred Hitchcock's *Lifeboat* with Tallulah Bankhead, Barbara Stanwyck in *Double Indemnity*, Humphrey Bogart and Lauren Bacall in a propaganda version of Hemingway's *To Have and Have Not*, and Clarence Brown's *National Velvet*, starring a captivating twelve-year-old Elizabeth Taylor.

In the patient queues outside tobacconists' stores, fishmongers, and bakeries, in the music halls and service canteens and pubs, trains, fogged parks, and darkened streets, people sang "I'll Walk Alone," "Count Your Blessings," "I'm Making Believe," "Don't Fence Me In," "I've Got a Lovely Bunch of Coconuts," "Rum and Coca-Cola," "Sentimental Journey," and "It Could Happen to You."

"Have Yourself a Merry Little Christmas," people sang and said: "Spring Will Be a Little Late This Year."

John Laidlaw was in Washington, preparing for the next conference of the three war leaders which was to be held in February in a Crimean holiday resort named Yalta; Wally Hudson, whom she thought her best bet for asking a humiliating favor, was in Italy, still serving as liaison officer with Anders's army; her brother Derek, whom she feared and detested even more than Laidlaw, would have to act as her private deus ex machina, she supposed. But she had one more man to see before making her difficult pilgrimage to Whitehall, and on the afternoon of December 16 she went to Turnham Green, where, in a small gray house, indistinguishable from a row of other small gray houses, General Janusz Prus had begun his enforced retirement.

The day, as she would recall it later, seemed full of warnings, admonitions, prophecies.

She paid them no attention as she walked through the wilted front yard to his door, thinking only that there was no other man whose advice she could trust because he was the only man she knew who had nothing to gain from advising others.

She rang the bell, heard its strident clanging in the depths of the house, then listened to slow footsteps approaching the door.

He would have changed, of course, in the two years since she had
seen him last. My God, she thought, had it been two years? The
war had gone on, altering everything, yet if one looked around, if
one could weigh events and judge the quality of one's inner air,
then it might seem that nothing at all had changed. She waited,
ignoring premonitions, while he came to the door; here was a
man who had gone beyond tragedy time and time again and had
emerged undamaged on the other side. She could think of no one
else as a possible exemplar. She could confirm her every decision
in his quiet assessments.

Then he was standing in the open doorway, grinning down at
her, and she, in turn, was grinning up at him, and it was as if no
time at all had passed since they had last gone together to see a
play. It had been a tasteless American propaganda farce, called
Jacobovsky and the Colonel, in which the Poles were pictured as
archaic buffoons, possibly gallant in an antediluvian sense but absurd in the twentieth century, while the sweet, unassuming, gentle, and mistreated Polish Jew wandered about the stage like an
unheard voice of reason in a world of cruelty and folly. They
had felt then as though they had witnessed an obscenity, and she
recalled vividly the pain in his eyes. It was only then that she had
begun to understand what the campaign against the Poles had
been all about.

But, obviously, time had passed. He had grayed and his body
had bowed at the shoulders. The eyes were the same thoughtful,
patient blue, but the face around them had worn and whitened
until it seemed that the skull under it would emerge. He wore a
khaki cardigan, the missing arm pinned under his elbow, and the
wool had begun to unravel around the buttonholes. His long
polished riding boots were gone, replaced by carpet slippers, but
his tie was neatly knotted, his shirt thickly starched, and his
flannel trousers were pressed to a knife-edge. Only the large white
hand he had raised in greeting seemed to belong to another man;
she couldn't fail to notice its uncharacteristic tremor.

—Ann, he said with the quiet formality of a man who is never
undermined by the unexpected. Come in, my dear, come in. How
very nice to see you.

Suddenly nervous and sure that he could have nothing more to say to her because he was no longer a part of the war, she said: You sound as if you had expected me.

—In a way, he said softly. In a way. Friends do come to see me now and then. We sit about, planning new careers as tobacconists and waiters. And you . . . well, I knew that sooner or later we'd see each other again.

—I really don't know why I'm so nervous, she said.

—Well, he said and stepped aside so that she might enter the dank little hallway, and climb the dark, steep stairs. This isn't quite the sort of place you're used to, I expect.

—Can *you* get used to it? she asked, touched by shame and pity.

Surprisingly, he laughed.

—I am a soldier, he said and waved his arm around the drab walls of the little room where she stood, appalled by the sagging wickerwork and an iron bedstead and flowered chintz and the pink fly-blown shade on the single light bulb. I've spent at least a third of my life in ditches. I can think of at least a hundred times when this place would have seemed palatial.

—You really don't belong in this century, do you, she observed, and he began to clean off the rickety card table on which awls, hammers, oiled twine, brass tacks, and brads had been positioned with military precision into orderly stacks and piles.

—My new trade, he said. At least it sustains a temporary illusion. Will you take some tea?

—Please, she murmured, taking care not to look at him.

He took a metal teapot off the single ring and went to get water and she looked about the drab room and felt tears starting. So that's how it was going to be for all of them, she thought. The thin gray light seeped through a dusty window, a twisted tree displayed skeletal branches. *Go thee now, faithful servant, to thy earned rewards.* Snow had begun to fall again outside.

Waiting for his return, she took a short unguided tour among his mementos, picking up maps and putting them down again, touching stacks of papers. If it were true that a man's character might be read by the environments he creates for himself and by the trivia he retains through the years, then this confusion of the past and present might have spoken volumes. Maps, papers, folders, worn books, polished riding boots, the tangible spoils of a life at war; at first chaotic, they began to show a private sense of inevitability and order. The tools of a new trade, as what? Furniture repair? Shoemaking? Surely a far cry from anything he had imagined for himself. A curved Circassian dagger was hanging on one wall, a framed print of a darkly sorrowing Madonna on another. She examined a yellowing, affectionately signed framed photograph of a moustached man, another of Sikorski, another of an intense young man in Alpine gear, another of a young woman with braided blond hair who stood waist-deep in a field of wheat. She noted a framed display of medals under glass . . . a group of self-conscious young men in old-fashioned, high-collared uniforms, leaning on large curved sabers and striking a pose . . . Ludo's boyish face was unmistakable among them.

Prus had come in so softly that she hadn't heard him; his voice made her jump.

—Bric-a-brac, he said. How the French language dignifies the trivial!

—If all this were trivial, you wouldn't have it here, she observed.

—Hmm? Well, perhaps not, he said. The milk has turned, I'm afraid. Will you have lemon in your tea?

—Thank you, she said. Who are all those people? I recognize General Sikorski, of course. And Ludo. When was that picture taken? How old was he then?

—Nineteen, I think, he said. A perfect age for heroic poses. Life is endless then and the future smiles from ear to ear. He and this other fellow here, chap by the name of Bettner, are the only ones in that photograph who are still alive.

—And this, she said and pointed to the young woman in the wheat field, is Lala?

—That was Lala. The boy with the alpenstock and ropes is my son Adam. The man with the moustache is the old marshal, Pilsudski.

—The one that you rebelled against in 1926?

—I loved him, he said simply, then went on in a voice tired with too much repetition: I didn't rebel against him. I opposed something he set out to do. I think he always understood that, at least I hope he did.

—He doesn't look particularly lovable, she said.

—He died in 1935, a cantankerous and disillusioned old man who had the only political plan that might have saved Europe from this war. Like Sikorski, he wanted to unify all the nations between Germany and Russia into one defensible political entity, but your Lloyd George feared a strengthening of France's natural allies and destroyed the plan in the League of Nations.

—He signed his photograph: *To my dearest and most loyal friend,* she said. And yet you opposed him?

—Friendship is one thing, Prus said. Duty is another. One can love a man and treasure his vision and still say no when this man allows his personal ambition to threaten the country. Pilsudski staged a coup against the legitimate government. It was a weak, corrupt, and inefficient group of squabbling politicians, but it *was* the government. A soldier is not a politician. He doesn't have the luxury of going against his oath. But that's an old story, often told. You didn't come here to hear about my disappointments and mistakes.

—I don't really know why I came, she said.

—You've never lied to me before.

—No, she said. I . . . came to talk to you about Ludo. He . . . should be brought back to England, don't you think?

—To do what? Prus asked.

—Can't you be a little less abrupt about all this? she pleaded. This is so difficult for me to say. A friend, someone who knows him, suggested that I owe it to him. So that (she went on desperately in the face of his judgmental silence) he doesn't die *a cantankerous and disillusioned old man!*

—There is some other way of dying you have in mind for him? he inquired politely, and she cried out, shocked by his careless tone: No, of course not! Oh, I don't know what I have in mind! But someone should do something, don't you think?

The small wartime one-band radio set banged and clattered with the artificial Latin rhythms of Edmundo Ross, and he turned it down, and then began to pat his pockets in search of his cigarette case. A search for his lighter gained him some more time. A feeling that she should leave at once, mixed with a sudden vision of what would happen if she did not leave, seemed to paralyze her. She looked about with a mild sort of desperation and fixed her eyes on the photograph of the youthful, cheerful, and believing Ludo, seeing him with a sharpness that had been quite impossible when they saw each other every day.

In the meantime, Prus had found his cigarette case and lighter, offered her one of five hoarded Passing Clouds, and lighted one for himself.

—In the Napoleonic wars, we were led by Prince Józef Poniatowski, he said quietly. When the French lost the battle of Leipzig and both our cause and Napoleon's was as good as finished, the Prince jumped into the Elster River, horse and all, and drowned. The horse also drowned. He, that is to say Prince Józef, not the horse, is said to have done so, crying out: *God has entrusted me with the honor of the Poles, I shall render it only unto God.* I don't know if God heard him, or what He thought of that remarkable gesture, which seems to have been excessive even for those days. But no one else appears to have been listening. Thereafter, Poland vanished from the maps of Europe for a hundred years.

—What does this have to do with bringing Ludo back to England? she asked.

—Not much, I expect. It's just another piece of useless historical baggage that most of us seem to carry in our heads. This friend of yours, who is so interested in arranging a suitable destiny for Ludo, he said, glancing up. He wouldn't be an American, by any chance?

—Yes, she said and sighed and, despite herself, glanced at Lala's photograph. He . . . is terribly concerned. He feels he has a debt to pay.

—And, like all other sentimentalists, he'd like someone else to pay it for him, Prus said. Well, why not? It's a very economical way to buy a clear conscience.

—Neither Loomis nor I want Ludo to die, she said gently. I just don't want him to end up like this.

His eyes, in which mild irony and pity seemed to be blended in equal proportions, followed the sweep of her hand along the drab walls as though he'd never before noticed the framed memorials to his own vanished life, and she knew that what he was seeing was lost fame, authority, power, and the love of a woman who had left him before she was killed. She was sure then that he himself was going to die; no matter how lightly he treated the historical gestures of his kind, he wouldn't live a moment longer than he had to. Suddenly faint and short of breath, she leaned against the bookcase and put her hand on a sharp, jagged piece of shrapnel wrapped in tissue paper. Whom had that killed and why, that he should carry it about with him? And who would do that, other than a man who needed to celebrate death rather than life? It was as if she had brushed against death herself and she recoiled with a sharp, bitter cry.

—I'm sorry, Prus said with his quiet smile. Did you cut yourself?

—No, she said. It's I who should be sorry. I . . . shouldn't have wasted so much of your time.

—What else am I to do with it? he asked. I've far more than one man's ration, when he's unemployed. Ah, the water's boiled. Now we can have our tea.

Then, later, with the too-strong tea drunk out of two chipped coronation cups, and with the day darkening, he told her about himself and why he was there, but she knew that from Laidlaw anyway.

She wanted to leave then. The small, damp room with its scattered mementos, its framed photographs of the dead and soon-to-be-dead, and above all, the dull remote droning of his lifeless voice created an image that, she knew, would haunt her for years. He would not help her to justify her decision about Ludo, but he was showing her what to do nonetheless. As Loomis had so accurately described his disappearing kind: with nothing left to die for, they'd be quite unable to find a reason for living.

Six paces this way, then right-about-face and six paces in the opposite direction, he walked up and down the imprisoning room. His head was bowed. His arm was tucked behind him. His fingers had clenched. She heard, making every effort not to listen, as he explained the end of his career, which, as she knew very well, must have been the practical equivalent of life.

—I had hoped that we'd have no more need for our historic gestures. But, obviously, that's a better way to be remembered than the epitaphs written for us in New York.

—It's so unfair, she murmured and knew her words to be inadequate, and yet she didn't want to encourage his awful speculation.

—As long as there's still some service that a man might render, he said and passed his fingers gently along the edge of a frame, the one that preserved under glass the image of Lala, there is a reason for a man's existence, don't you see? But when all possibility of usefulness has ended, so has the need to live.

—Can't the man live for his friends? she asked, thinking less of Prus than of herself and Ludo. For people who love him?

—That's not enough, Prus said. The cause must always be greater than the man.

Abruptly, he changed the subject, asked: Did you ever wonder why we resisted the Germans in September 1939?

—For the same reason that everyone else resists an invasion, I suppose, she said. To defend your country.

—No, he said sharply. We had no hope of winning. Our leaders knew that our allies wouldn't lift a finger while we turned our country into a heap of rubble. Two days before the war, I saw a French directive that forbade any penetration of the German border deeper than three miles. Our Secret Service stole that order from German staff files. The Germans knew that they had nothing to fear from our allies when they turned their entire might against us. We had a choice of surrendering, as the Czechs had done, or of a war that would destroy our country. We chose national destruction. We did so in the hope that our resistance would be so spectacular, and the sound of our fall would be so unforgettable, that it would register on our allies' conscience, so that, when they had finally defeated the Germans, they would remember our terrible sacrifice and put our country back into the map of Europe.

Then he said: The Austrians welcomed a new, pragmatic world with brass bands and flowers. The Czechs swallowed their pride and let the Germans swallow them with a tragic smile. Our allies weep for the Czechs as a fallen bastion of democracy, and all the damage done to Prague was one broken window. We buried Warsaw in rubble and corpses, and all that anyone will remember of it after they've won the war is that, somehow and for no reason that anyone can see, all those years of misery began with us. They aren't likely to forgive us. Someone should remind them how this war began and then how it ended.

—What was it all about? he asked, addressing the silent photographs on his walls. Why did we do it? Five million of our people are dead, a million and a half were left behind in Russia, but no one sees it necessary to give them a thought. They're only Poles, you see. They're not part of someone's necessary legend. To say anything about them, other than to libel them and question their worth, wouldn't serve the needs of Soviet propaganda. It wouldn't serve the purposes of a private hatred.

—Please, she said. Please. I don't want to hear any more of this.

—Of course not, he said. But there are people being born in Poland today who'll never know what it's like to live in freedom among their own kind. What can we do today to remind them, twenty years from now, of who and what they are? It's necessary, you see, for us to do something at least once in every other generation to remind ourselves that we're Poles, no matter who rules us. One hopes that there is something in the blood . . . something that transfers the ideal from one generation to another, but since when have hopes been enough? What kind of an example can we leave them? What can we do to make ourselves remembered?

—I don't know, she said.

—Did you know, he asked quietly then, that my brother Michal committed suicide in 1939?

—No, she said, no longer caring to conceal her tears or to divert him from his course. I'm sorry.

—No need to be. Romantics make their own best natural victims. They live in a world in which it's still possible to die for an idea. He was a man for whom such words as *honor* and *motherland* were a matter of perpetual inner argument. He used them as a yardstick to measure every thought. When the Russians stabbed us in the back and no one in the West protested, he did what his conception of honor demanded and he blew out his brains. I've . . . never been able to decide whether his death was the highest act of courage, representing the most supreme conception of duty, or just the simple egotistic impulse of a deranged mind.

—I suppose it's what he thought that counted, she whispered.

He walked to his photographs, peered at them as if each carried a private message.

—There he is, he said and pointed to a small face among the other youthful faces which stared intently at the camera. Next to Bettner. That's Abramowski beside him; he died at Katyn. Abramowski's son Abel was killed at Monte Cassino. Ludo's brother Piotr was also killed there, by the way. Michal's son Pawel was murdered in Poland by the Ukrainians. My own son . . . was caught in Austria by the outbreak of the war. He was a mountain climber, you see. He loved to climb mountains. He was a championship skier, too. Anything to do with height, I suppose.

—Please don't say any more, Janusz, she begged, but he didn't hear her.

—Ludo taught him to fly gliders. He would have flown with Ludo, I am sure, if he hadn't been caught in Austria by the war. The Germans tried to use him as a means of forcing me to cooperate with them. They couldn't get anyone to form a collaborationist government in Poland, you see, and they thought that I, with my particular history, might be inclined to work for them if they held Adam hostage. It's quite amazing how many people make that kind of a mistake about us. I suppose that's because they're unable to understand us; they can attribute only their own motives to us. They've never had to learn the lessons of our history.

—Why should they? she murmured through her anticipatory grief, averting her head to conceal her tears. They're your lessons. It's your history. We've all evolved in a different way.

—Adam killed himself, the general went on. He jumped off a mountain. The Germans said that he died in a climbing accident, but I know that he committed suicide rather than force me to choose between my duty to my country and to him. It seems there are examples everywhere one looks.

Then he sat in silent contemplation of his dead. The small damp room—like his life—she knew, had become a cell whose door would open with no more pressure than was needed to pull the trigger of his service pistol. All that one needed was will, a certain sort of judgment, and a steady hand . . . and then all turmoil would cease. All that one needed to avoid the future was the

strength to reject it. As far as he was concerned, she knew, he had
already joined the people on his walls.

Quietly, unnoticed, she left him, went outside.

There, in the darkening street, snow fell and turned to sleet.
The ice underfoot had begun to melt into wet, gritty patches, and
her wartime utility boots were soaked through in moments. She
tripped on an icy curb, felt her ankle turn, hobbled on. Somewhere in the thick yellow fog, great armies had begun to move, as
the streamers on the news vendors' kiosks informed her. The war
would go on, as blind and directionless as she. Her face was wet
with tears that froze, hot as fire, in the icy wind.

. . . NAZIS BREAK OUT IN ARDENNES, GREAT BATTLES RAGE IN
BULGE. . . . MONTY'S OFFENSIVE HALTED AS AMERICANS REEL. . . .
RED ARMY RACES WEST. . . .

She felt as though a handful of hot coals had been flung at her
eyes with the speed of bullets. She had left Prus behind, locked
within a silence of a depth that she wouldn't have been able to
imagine.

Blinded, she slipped, tripped again, staggered, fell. The pain in
her hip was sudden and sharp. The bruise, she thought, would be
black and ugly. It was quite fortunate, in a way, that no one
would see it.

—Oh, dammit all to hell! she wailed in sudden rage, grief, and
hopelessness, and watched a worried policeman hurrying toward
her.

—Easy does it, missus. 'Urt yerself? No? Upsa-daisy, then. Let's
get yer 'ome to a nice cuppa and a cozy fire. 'Ave ter be careful in
weather like this. You'll be hallright, then?

—Certainly, she said.

. . . Certainly. Why not? Nothing in her life appeared to have
been more certain than her need to put an end to it. There was a
stale smell to it, as though it were an unventilated room in which
frightened people had sheltered too long. Prus, with his talk of
historical examples, appeared to point to the only logical solution,
but then logic hadn't had much to do with anything for years.

Ludo was gone; their lives couldn't intersect again. He was as
good as dead, nailed to a cross of his own conception of who and

what he was. Only fools, fanatics, and people for whom it was important to masquerade as martyrs wouldn't let their dead alone. Only the hopeless attempted to join them.

—This is some kind of an obsession, she murmured then as her vision cleared.

—Hmm, the policeman said. Maybe we'd better 'ave a doctor take a look at yer, missus . . .

—No, she said. Thank you. I'm perfectly all right.

—Well, he said doubtfully.

—No. Really. As you said, Constable, a nice cup of tea by the fire and my feet up and all that. Right as rain in no time at all.

—Well, if yer think so, missus . . .

—Certainly, she said. Why not?

Certainly. It was so wonderful to be certain about something.

CHAPTER XXIII

LUDO RETURNED to England in the last week of April aboard the *General Black*, a U.S. Army troop ship which a whole generation of young Poles would remember as the one that ferried them to life in a new country, to an aptly named status as persons who had been displaced in geography and time. But in this time, on this clear and sunny April morning with the war entering its final convulsions, the gray transport carried one thousand Polish soldiers who had spent five years in German prison camps, and three thousand Italian prisoners of war who had volunteered for farm labor in Britain. Both the Poles, for whom the humiliation of captivity had ended only so that a far more profound distress could begin, and the Italians, whose liberation from fascism was assured by their captivity, were escorted by a company of Royal Marines. Neither group had seen the gray-green shores of England before.

He (Ludo), for whom an entirely different period of confused detachment had come to an end, for whom an exile in the seamy fleshpots of Cairo and the hovels of Jerusalem had ended with a telegram that ordered him to London, stood in the port wing of the flying bridge beside the Marine major and the Bersaglieri colonel commanding the Italians, and watched the vast gray harbor, so triumphantly different from his first cold and foggy glimpse of it in the summer of 1940. He had come full circle once again, but his history was unlikely to repeat itself. In a week or two, the war would be over.

—So this is England, said the Bersaglieri colonel. Mussolini promised us that we'd see it someday. Of course, he also promised us an African Empire and the Mediterranean for a private lake. Still, one kept promise out of three isn't to be despised.

He was a tall, craggy, theatrically handsome man, with the face of a dissolute Pope; his long mobile hands made swift, emphatic gestures.

—*Giovinezza, giovinezza,* he hummed in derision, and the joyful, youthful, optimistic notes of the Young Fascists' song drifted like smoke in the crystal air. Thanks to God and His Mother, the lunatics are back in the asylum, and no longer running a mad world.

—I expect you've had quite enough of that, sir, said the Marine major.

—Indeed I have, said the Bersaglieri colonel. And so has the world.

—Pity it didn't have enough of it five years ago, said the Marine major. An awful lot of good chaps have gone up the spout. But then, I suppose, it's been worth it, what? No more Hitler and all that and . . . ah . . . Mussolini. A stiff price, but worth a victory, eh? Of course, it must seem rather odd to you, Colonel.

—Oh, quite odd, said the Bersaglieri colonel.

—I mean, you did start out on the other side, didn't you? said the Marine major.

—Yes, said the Bersaglieri colonel, and Ludo heard the amused contempt with which a civilized man would view the caperings of madmen. The point is to finish on the winning side in time for the Victory Parade. War is short and life is long, if you'll pardon a parody, and everyone is too embarrassed to think about it a moment longer than he must. Are you . . . ah . . . a professional military man?

—I don't quite know what I am, said the Marine major. I was in school before the war. A place called Bryanston in Dorset, not too far from here. . . . We used to ride our bikes along the downs a few miles to the east on Sunday afternoons. . . . It does all seem like a century ago, doesn't it?

—And you, Magiore?

—I did not bicycle here on Sunday afternoons, Ludo said.

—Ah, a professional, said the Bersaglieri colonel. So am I. I lost two regiments in Africa, one after another. Of course, they weren't Bersaglieri.

—Of course not, said the Marine major, who must have been all of twenty-four years old. Everyone knows about the Bersaglieri.

—We wear the plumes of eagles in our hats, said the Bersaglieri colonel. We are trained to move everywhere at a run. It's very useful training for an army which is always outgunned, out-maneuvered, and outnumbered. We may not always win our wars, but we've never lost one. It's quite the opposite of your experience, I expect, Magiore.

—You might say that, Colonel, Ludo said.

—I've always sympathized with *La Polonia*, said the Bersaglieri colonel. So brave, so devoted, so tragic. So dedicated to its idea of freedom. In Italy, we say that freedom is not in our blood because freedom *is* our blood. Which is why it's too precious to spill in a war.

—I envy you your civilization, Ludo said. I also envy you your geographical location.

—Yes, said the Bersaglieri colonel. God knew what He was doing when He placed us all where He did. Imagine what might have happened if He had put the English Channel around Poland. Or if He had given Warsaw to the Italians and Rome to the British. Imagine the kind of world we would be living in if the Acropolis stood in Moscow.

—Oh, I expect we'd have sorted ourselves out somehow, said the Marine major.

Not much had changed in the twenty-one months that he had been away, and yet everything was different.

He watched the young, strong, unconcerned American sailors busy with ropes and hawsers as the anchors dropped, watched the

Poles and Italians forming on the decks with their British escorts, and he was conscious of all the ironies of the moment.

Always afterward, he supposed, no matter where or when or in what manner that *afterward* might manifest itself, he would remember that moment of return to England by its smell of smoke drifting in the dusty sunshine, the soft April wind that blew the desultory rubbish about the piers, the bleak formations of former enemies who had never had a reason to war on each other among desert dunes. In moments, his twenty-one months among sand flies, flying ticks, and unspeakable diseases were gone as if they had never existed. Gone like a stone into water and dead before drowning. The wind was not the desert *khamsin* that drove people mad. The air, for all its industrial foulness, was bracing and crisp. He took deep breaths. He had not expected to be here again. Whatever power had interceded for him was worth at least a dozen candles in a church.

—Well, said the Bersaglieri colonel. I don't suppose we shall see each other again, Magiore.

—I suppose not, Ludo said.

—It's been a pleasant voyage.

The Royal Marine major had stepped away to supervise the deployment of his company on the forward deck (there was some confusion about which of the foreign formations should have Sten guns pointed at it and which might resent it) and the colonel's dark, knowing eyes glittered with amusement.

—And, like all interludes, it ends with no one quite remembering what it was all about. No more brave music. The parade is over. The comedy is finished and all the kings and princes and clowns and gentlemen-at-arms are taking off their makeup in the dressing room. And then, in a day or two, they will begin rehearsing their new play. Do you know Italy, Magiore?

—No, Ludo said. Not even from the air.

—A beautiful country. Poor, of course. All beautiful countries are poor. A rich country is always ugly, don't you think? It has to make itself ugly to become rich, which is why Italy is magnificent. Poland, I imagine, must be much like that?

—Poland, Ludo said, is a ruin.

—But magnificent, eh? Something to make your blood run quicker and to swell your heart? Believe me, I am a Roman, I know about ruins. They can be the most beautiful things on earth. Painters flock to paint them, tourists gape in wonder, and you can lace your boot on a stone on which Caesar rested in the Forum. Of course, you have to win your wars in order to enjoy your ruins. They are quite painful from the perspective of an exile. Are you planning to become an exile, Magiore?

—I hadn't planned it, no, Ludo said.

—But you will not be returning to Poland now that the Communists are moving into it? They are a people without a sense of humor about history. I am, of course, a Communist myself. All Italians are Communists because all Italians are artists and art demands the rejection of personal property. But as an Italian Communist, for whom history is an art rather than a science, I wouldn't advise living among people who are deadly serious about anybody's history. Such seriousness invariably proves deadly to everybody else. Come to Italy instead, Magiore. Italians have a natural appreciation of the heroic. We have, you see, a wonderful sense of humor.

—My brother is buried at Monte Cassino, Ludo said.

—All the more reason for you to settle there, said the Bersaglieri colonel. You can be as tragic as you like among us and no one will think any the worse of you.

—Is that the only choice left? To be tragic?

—That is the same as being dull, said the Bersaglieri colonel. Dull and boring. One must pay homage to the comic element in tragedy. Italians appreciate the heroic because we're always conscious of its irony. *Viva la comedia!* Our ruins show us every day that the final purpose of all great civilizations is to become a tourist attraction. Come to Italy, Magiore, and see what happens to the greatest tragedies of history, and then perhaps you won't feel so badly about your own.

On the foredeck, surrounded by their escorts, the two columns had begun to move toward the gangplanks leading to the pier. The three thousand Italians went first: small, olive-skinned men, each shouldering a small bundle of possessions, each anxious to look as unmilitary as he could because their war was over. They had been made to fight in a war which had meant nothing to them, and they had seen their German allies become fierce enemies, and they knew better than to attach themselves to symbols of allegiance.

The Poles . . . ah, that was another story. Some had been in German prisoner-of-war camps since 1939. Others, caught on the Polish borders in 1940 and 1941 as they attempted to make their way to the Western armies, had come from places such as Mauthausen, Gross Rosen, and Auschwitz, where a hundred and fifty thousand of their kind had died. Yet others, coming from the ruins of Warsaw after the uprising, had been liberated from prison camps in southern Germany and Austria. Why couldn't they accept the thought that their war was over? What made them as they were? Why did they insist on marching in step among the indifferent gawkers on the quayside? They wore bedraggled bits and pieces of every kind of Allied uniform and headgear—Scots bonnets and Canadian forage caps seemed to be the favorites—but each had managed to fashion some kind of red-and-white cockade, or an eagle cap badge cut from the lid of a fruit salad tin, or the anchor emblem of the underground Home Army molded from prison bread. Their boots, felt slippers, cracked shoes, sandals, and rope-soled convict footwear slapped the gray concrete of the pier, suggesting a parade of ghosts risen from their graves. Their gray faces were split by ghastly smiles and . . . God help us all, Ludo thought . . . they had begun to sing.

> Don't bring us by a miracle to our fathers' land!
> Neither by English grace nor angelic power.
> Let us win Her ourselves, so that She will be ours:
> Our fathers' land, bought with our blood and bones
> So that our children's children may have homes
> Where they will know what it is like to be
> A Pole among his own, free among the free.

—Italy, said the Bersaglieri colonel. Remember, Magiore. It is a country where one may contemplate the past without allowing it to undermine the future.

—I'll remember, Colonel.

In the train that carried him from Southampton to London, a rattling string of dilapidated third-class carriages which, judging by the slogans scrawled along their sides, had only recently been used as a troop train, he watched softly rolling green-and-brown hills, woodland, sheep and cows, thatched villages, and white-washed walls hidden among the hedgerows. He counted telephone poles so as not to think. He watched elderly station porters planting flowers along the platforms of country whistle stops. He read the slogans painted on the carriages as they reflected in dusty station windows: BERLIN OR BUST! NEXT STOP BROOKLYN! and (the most telling of the lot) DON'T CHEER, GIRLS, WE'RE BRITISH.

Because his khaki cotton desert uniform was too thin for an English April day, he had borrowed the sky-blue topcoat of the Canadian wing commander who ran the RAF personnel movement office in Southampton, and his fellow passengers treated him accordingly. A pink-cheeked schoolboy offered him a seat. An elderly matron in tweeds and walking shoes proffered a copy of the latest American novel, *Forever Amber*. An Anglican minister tried to engage him in discussing sheep farming in Australia (one colonial being interchangeable with another) and a moustached, red-faced businessman offered him newspapers.

They were all kind, considerate, thoughtful of his imagined needs, and interested in hearing what he thought of England, its weather, and its cooking, and whether it was true that Canadians felt closer to Americans than they did to their British past. No, he said (trying to remember what Johnny Sommerset had said about such things), Canada would never turn her back on England because the idea of an imperial past gave a young country a historic link with the Magna Carta, the Mother of Parliaments, Hadrian's Wall, Piccadilly Circus, and the Victoria and Albert Museum.

The schoolboy, scarlet with embarrassment and shyness, wanted to know if Ludo had killed a tremendous lot of Germans, and the red-faced businessman admonished him at once: Our chaps don't kill people. It's the Huns who do that. The Huns and the foreigners and all those Continentals. Country's crawling with them nowadays. Our chaps only inflict casualties on the enemy.

—Then, please, sir, said the scarlet schoolboy, how many Germans did you . . . ah . . . inflict?

—Forty, Ludo said.

The boy blinked. The businessman swallowed and quickly

looked away. The elderly matron in tweeds smiled in embarrassment. The Anglican minister plucked at his collar with a long
white finger. The lurid word seemed to hang among them long
after its moment and each of them felt stained and soiled by it.

—That is . . . ah, ahem . . . most commendable, said the cler-
gyman and licked his dry lips. Forty. Ah. Yes.

—Damn rotten Huns, muttered the businessman. Deserve all
they get. Bombed Coventry, didn't they? And that place in
Holland?

—Rotterdam, murmured the minister, shaking his head sadly.

—Rotterdamn, that's it, said the businessman. Damn rotters,
all of them. Oh, the poor damn Dutch.

—And Lidice, said the elderly matron in tweeds. Didn't they
bomb that or burn it to the ground or some frightful thing like
that?

—That's right, said the businessman. That's just what they did.
Poor old Czechs. Bloody Huns. No need to feel sorry for that lot.
Forty, eh? Well, I'd say that was . . . a damn fine show.

Had he spoken in terms of millions, or hundreds of thousands,
had he talked about the extermination of Polish Jewry, or the
murder of two million other Polish citizens in the one hundred
and twenty concentration camps that the Germans had set up in
Poland, or of the three hundred and fifty thousand Polish children taken from their parents to be brought up as Germans, or of
the three hundred thousand prisoners of war and deportees
worked to death at farm labor in German factories and on German farms, or of the two million lost in the Siberian wastes of
the Soviet Union, or even of the three-quarters of a million Polish
soldiers dead on battlefields scattered through Africa and Europe,
they would have clucked sadly and shaken their heads and gone
on to talk about more immediate matters. Vast numbers are incomprehensible to the uninvolved. But he had mentioned a figure
easy to understand. Forty. A man had killed forty other men. Almost anyone can imagine forty corpses. It is quite possible to
come to terms with that.

—Frightful, frightful, the minister said. Thank the good Lord
that it's all coming to an end.

Ludo closed his eyes. He could pretend to sleep then because he knew that no one would say anything to him for the rest of the way.

London, a city he had locked from his mind, had changed most of all. There was a weariness in its cool spring air; people moved and spoke painfully and slowly, as if both thought and gesture had finally become too difficult. There were more ruins now than during the Blitz; the flying bombs couldn't be decoyed to fall among the hovels of the poor, they left their black spoor everywhere. It was a reminder for anyone who might be able to forget that Germans could come up with terrible surprises until their final moment.

Hitler, as the newspaper headlines announced, was dead in his chancellery. Roosevelt had died two weeks earlier, complaining of a headache. America had a new President, of whom no one expected a great deal. In Italy, the German armed forces had laid down their weapons and, in Germany, the Americans had crossed the Elbe and halted fifty miles from Berlin so that the Russians, who were a hundred and fifty miles away at the Oder crossings, could be the first to enter Hitler's ruined capital. The Third U.S. Army was brought to a halt nineteen miles from the Czechoslovak border so that Prague too could fall to the Russians. The supreme commander of the Allied forces in the West, General Dwight Eisenhower, was scrupulous in carrying out the terms of the Teheran agreement.

In February, in an old Tsarist pleasure palace on the Black Sea, there had been yet another meeting of the three war leaders and the fate of the Poles, the Czechs and the Slovaks, the Letts, the Lithuanians and Estonians, and all the peoples of the Balkan countries had been finally decided. In exchange for a promise to declare war on the Japanese, Stalin acquired a greater European empire than all the armies of all the Tsars in history had been able to conquer in five hundred years.

To make one sound, to speak one word in protest, to acknowledge the facts of treason and betrayal by denouncing them, would be to break the dam that held his rage in check. And what would happen then? Would he attack bystanders with his bare hands?

The schemers and connivers and manipulators kept themselves safely outside the killing grounds, one didn't encounter them above the English Channel. What was there left for anyone except some singular act of premeditated violence which would say, clearly and beyond dismissal, that defeat was unacceptable in victory? That millions had died in the name of an ideal that had to be respected?

Prus, whom he had loved and whose example he had followed since he had been no older than his brother Janek, had shot himself through the head with his service pistol in a dingy room, Ludo knew, and—with that shot—he had saved himself from obscurity. Simple despair in the face of exile wouldn't have been enough to cause him to do it, nor had he ever thought personal tragedy profound enough to unhinge the mind. That shot was not meant to be heard around the world, Ludo knew. Only one man—himself—had been supposed to hear it and he tried to understand the message it contained.

Someday, he thought in the silence of his rage, someone would understand it and explain it to a world which, for its own unrelated reasons, might have matured beyond amusement or indifference. Someone, perhaps yet unborn, who would be looking backward from the future in order to understand the complexities of his time, might unstitch the fabric of historical lies and weave all the tangled skeins together into a new whole. The truth had to be more than the annotated pseudo-accuracy of historians. Perhaps Prus's message had been one of hope rather than despair. Perhaps that violent act that sent a bullet crashing through his head was meant to say that no life was worth as much as the idea for which it could be spent, and that defeat was always a matter of consent. Men, Prus had been saying, were quite properly perishable, but their ideas were not.

London, the great gray city where flowers grew in the occasional ruins, had begun to gleam and glitter in the pale April sun. White cirrus in the west suggested rain by nightfall.

He thought of broiling days, freezing nights: the months in the Western Desert, the abrupt blackness of an African nightfall, the truth in poetic imagery whereby a dawn did, indeed, rise like a clap of thunder, and the vast antihuman emptiness of uninhabitable landscapes where the mere idea of life seemed inconceivable.

Ah, there were just too damn many ghosts, he thought; there was no room for them all in either memory or conscience.

Entering the cold, dank lobby of the Rubens Hotel, he shivered suddenly in his desert clothing. The weather, the treacherous temperatures of an English April, had nothing to do with the sudden ice that seemed to have invaded his veins. In the pale sunlight that slanted through the windows, everyone he saw seemed to have become a ghost, a transparent shadow reflected in the mirror of another time.

—To hell with it all, he muttered, and the elderly colonel, who had been one of Wlada's unsuccessful suitors, cried out immediately: Ludo! I thought you were dead. What grave did you spring from?

—I don't know, Ludo said.

—Come in, my boy, come in. Sit down.

Colonel Bydlinski led him to an office where, from behind a barricade of files and sagging towers of paper, he could regard Ludo sadly with red-rimmed rheumy eyes. He had been a lecturer in moral philosophy at the General Staff College in Warsaw, and a permanent yellow tear hung at the inner edge of his monocle.

—Such times, he said. Such times. Well. What can I do for you?

Ludo handed over his orders and the colonel tossed them into a wire basket.

—That's all as good as over now. We're being reorganized into something called the Polish Resettlement and Rehabilitation Corps. We're all going to be taught how to be tailors and shoemakers and furniture repairers. Of course, there's tremendous pressure on everyone to go back to Poland, since there'll be a million demobilized Englishmen looking for jobs in another month. Our allies still haven't learned that the more pressure you put on a Pole, the harder he'll push back. Have you thought of something you might want to do?

—What *is* there to do?

—Not much, to tell the truth, said Colonel Bydlinski. The chief of staff and I are looking into a tobacconist's shop in Chiswick. Our demob pay will just about cover the down payment.

Quite a few of our officers are going to be working in the Cadbury warehouse. And it seems there's a need for porters on the London Underground. It's either that or going back to Poland.

—Have you considered that?

—Good God, haven't we all? No matter who rules it, it's still our country, isn't it? I've spent forty years in service to my country. I don't suppose they need lecturers in moral philosophy over there just now, but I could've made myself useful in some other way. So I got ready to go home and that, believe me, didn't make me popular in London. Your brother-in-law called me a traitor. Anyone who made his peace with that Communist gang in Warsaw, like Premier Mikolajczyk has thanks to British urging, undermined our protest and gave a semblance of legality to Stalin's puppet show, according to Romuald. We were to live abroad forever as a living symbol of international injustice. Romuald said that he'd rather shoot himself than become a traitor. Then something funny happened, call it a stroke of irony. Romuald was offered a post as Vice-Minister for Foreign Affairs by the Communists in Warsaw. I was informed that I had been sentenced to death in absentia for *antidemocratic activities*. So now Romuald is going back to Poland and I am going to be selling cigarettes in Chiswick.

—Prus found a different answer, I am told, Ludo said.

—Not everyone is suited for heroic gestures, said the elderly colonel. Besides, there's been enough killing, don't you think?

—Perhaps not, Ludo said.

—I don't blame Janusz Prus for what he did. He had a certain vision of himself, and he did what that vision commanded. I don't know, and I don't want to know, what your vision will order you to do. I only know that my destiny has led me to Chiswick.

—Each to his own, I suppose, Ludo said.

—Quite, said Colonel Bydlinski. Quite. Oh, absolutely. No one can do more than his sense of responsibility permits. We all define our duty according to whatever's still possible for us. But I don't have to say that kind of thing to you.

—No, you don't, Ludo said.

—Yes. Well. As you said: *Each to his own*, no matter how little that might be. There's nothing left to do, in the military

sense. It's just a matter of days before Germany surrenders. Today's what . . . May first? In two days, we're all to do something
to mark the anniversary of our Constitution, but no one quite
knows what we ought to do. Air activity in Europe is to end four
days later. So you have six days to do what you want with your
life. After that, the choices will narrow.

—There are no reassignment orders for me, then?

—No one is being assigned anywhere. There are no more orders. Why don't you go back to Northolt to wait for demobilization? It might make things a little easier for you to finish the war
among your old friends.

—The squadrons are still there, then?

—Oh, yes. Reszke has the wing now. He's a lieutenant-colonel.
But I don't suppose that'll embarrass you? No, of course it
wouldn't. I'd go to Northolt if I were you, Ludo. At least you
won't have to wait for the end alone.

Outside, he lighted a cigarette, and coughed, and his vision
blurred. He couldn't stop trembling. The hot desert sun and the
diet of drugs that had kept typhus at bay had thinned out his
blood, and the mild English spring day chilled him to the bone.
Where to go? What to do? How to mark his presence?

Around the corner, across the street from Victoria Station, a
Belgian whore informed him of a variety of delights available for
five pounds, and a policeman frowned at him, and the marquee
of the Odeon announced the latest American war epic: *They
Were Expendable*, starring Robert Montgomery as the commander of a PT squadron. The boom and roar of traffic threatened to unbalance him. The evening had come. And suddenly he
couldn't remember his name, or where he was going, or what he
was supposed to do; his identity had vanished, along with his
sense of direction. London itself appeared to have vanished.
There had been so many foreign cities since he had left Warsaw,
that all of them seemed to have become one, and all the names
and faces that crowded in his memory—Piotr, Norwid, Janek,
Wlada, and Lala and Prus . . . Zosia . . . Straka and Wilchurzak
—had become one accusing face.

—Is everything all right, sir? the policeman asked, and Ludo struggled to get himself under control again.

—Yes. A touch of the fever, I expect. Be fine in a moment.

—Where are you going, sir?

—Northolt Air Station, he remembered.

—That'll be on the Central Line. Take any Circle train to Notting Hill Gate and change for a West Ruislip train on the Central Line. There's a stop at Northolt. Then you can catch a bus to take you the rest of the way.

—I know, Ludo said. I remember.

—Ah, you've been there before, sir? I expect you have. Lots of Canadian chaps there, these days. Are you sure you're all right, sir? You look a bit pale, if I may say so, sir.

—Fine, Constable. Thank you.

—Because if there's anything I can do . . . my duty, you know, sir.

—Well, we all know what that is, don't we, Ludo said and did his best to smile.

—Indeed we do, sir, the policeman said. Well, here's your train, sir. Good-bye and good luck.

He saluted, a not-unkindly middle-aged man with a chestful of good ribbons from another war, and Ludo remembered just in time to change his Polish two-finger salute to the broad Canadian one that matched his borrowed coat. A not-unkindly man but a suspicious one, as all policemen were supposed to be, he'd lose all his kindness if he was confused.

Then there was only the quick rhythmic rattle of the rails, the whine of electric motors, intermittent flashes of darkness and light. He had never taken the Underground to or from Northolt before, feeling as he did about enclosed spaces, and now the whole weight of the city seemed to settle on him. Soon after the change at Notting Hill Gate, the train emerged into the gray night and ran on the surface, but his short trip through the catacombs had left him bathed in sweat.

Now hot flashes blinded him. He couldn't stop trembling. The sweat that glued his capband to his forehead became a stream. Yes, he was ill: there wasn't a doubt about that, and the disease was an incurable one; Napoleon Bonaparte's Polish Legionnaires, dying of yellow fever and loneliness and disappointment in Santo Domingo, had known all about it.

A woman's voice, blending concern with fear, said crystally: Is he ill? Is something going to happen? Shouldn't we do something?

He took off the Canadian wing commander's coat. Under his own stained and crumpled colors, he could breathe easier in the fetid air.

—It's a Pole, said the man who sat with the woman, then went on with embittered harshness: He's probably drunk. Drunk in the middle of the day. Shocking. Dirty little Pole.

—Northolt! The station is Northolt! 'Urry along now, please. . . . Mind the doors!

As always when it rained, there wasn't a taxi to be found. He walked, carrying his soft American Val-Pac bag and, eventually, he came to the line of chestnuts, oaks, and beeches that marked the edge of the heath where, beyond the gorse and bracken in the near distance, he could see the South Gate where Wilchurzak's Hurricane had crashed on Bloody Sunday, the bays and revetments, and the parked machines. Vast, gray, striped in browns-and-greens, the air station rolled away from him in the moonlight, its far edge disappearing into open country. The roundels and the checkerboards hung limp in the rain from their silver flagpoles.

He felt as suddenly impoverished as if his most precious memories were being taken from him, and bitterness followed him into the officers' mess where he managed to obtain a plateful of American cranberries, powdered scrambled eggs, fried Spam, and a slice of gray bread. "Taps" wouldn't be sounded for another hour, but because this was Sunday there were no pilots on the base.

He sat alone in the empty dining room, hunched over his unappetizing meal. It was a homecoming nonetheless, he thought.

Jacek Gemba appeared behind his chair, a pot of fresh-brewed coffee in his hand, and they exchanged greetings for some moments, asked about each other's health, but Jacek's normally frank and open gaze kept drifting from his own.

—They say that we won't be going home when this war is over, Jacek Gemba offered finally as he poured the coffee.

—Who, Ludo snapped, tells you things like that?

Startled, the boy stammered: Why . . . ah . . . everybody says it, beh-begging the major's pardon. Chief Auerbach says . . . I mean, what with the Russians moving in again and all . . . Well, sir, how *are* we going to get home?

—We'll go home, Ludo said automatically. Don't worry about it.

—Because . . . you know, you remember, sir . . . it's like we said that day when we was in that graveyard, before we got across the river and all . . . if we don't get to go home, then what's all this been for?

Too tired and distracted to stop himself in time, Ludo said: What can I tell you, lad? I don't know myself.

Jacek Gemba, who had never been a waiter at the Europejski but only said he was, as if to dream of something could transform an unpalatable reality and make him what he wished to be, stared at Ludo with enormous eyes.

—You don't know sir? But if you don't, who does? It's got to have been for something, sir. Otherwise, how come we got into it all in the first place? That's just plain stupid, sir! Even I know that.

—Perhaps to dream of something is as good as having it, Ludo said. Don't you think?

—Ah, Jacek Gemba said. That must be another of them *metafory* that you was talking to me about the day before the war started, sir. Is that what it is?

—It probably is, Ludo said.

—Still, Jacek Gemba said stubbornly. I want to go home.

The long room, dark so late at night, was full of memories and mementos, and each of these spoke of a purpose that no one had needed to question or discuss before. A shattered airscrew hung above the artificial marble mantelpiece. Its spinner was orange. The red-and-white checkerboard of the Polish Air Force insignia hung on one side of it, the red-white-and-blue RAF roundel on the other. Frantisek's card table, complete with his last unfinished game of solitaire, waited in the corner. Prewar Polish travel posters hung along one of the two long walls. A small forest of

black-and-white Iron Crosses, each with a date scratched into the
enamel, grew in neat graveyard rows along the length of another
wall. Thirty-two of them, edged in brilliant orange, were for the
Calais Gang, and Ludo wondered whether Reinecke's young men
sat down to their breakfasts of powdered eggs, gray bread, and er-
satz coffee among their own collection of checkerboards and roundels.

—We *will* go home, he said and fixed his eyes on the clean
white space reserved for Reinecke among the Iron Crosses, quite
sure that the Viennese had just such a space reserved on a wall
for him. It's been earned for us by all those who won't be going
home, do you see? In one way or another, we'll make them
remembered.

—So Chief Auerbach says, sir, the young man said softly. But
what're we going to do about all them Russians? Nobody's going
to help us against *them*.

—We'll do what we've always done, Ludo said shortly.

—Hmm. Yes, sir. And what might that be? Fighting and
killing and (here he nodded his close-cropped head toward the
Iron Crosses) dying, and like that? It's all part of them *metafory*,
I expect, but it seems to me we ought to be doing a lot more
than that.

—What's all this talk about metaphors? Ludo said.

—You know, sir. It's like what you said, sir. Like when you've
got to do things you don't want to do, and love things that you
hate, or you go mad?

—Did I really say things like that to you? Ludo asked and felt
nausea rising.

—Yes, sir, Jacek said, grinned, and poured more coffee. So what
I was thinking, sir, why don't we stop fighting them Germans and
start on the Russians? The Germans are as good as done for, everybody says. But nobody's even started thinking about them
fucking Russians. So why don't we just get on with it, beat them,
and go home? It's taken me a long time to figure out about them
metafory, but I see it all now.

—If only it were all that easy, Ludo said and began to laugh.
God, if only that was all there's to it.

—I don't see what's all that hard about it, sir, Jacek Gemba
said. I mean, didn't we beat the sons-of-bitches in all them other

wars? Chief Auerbach's been telling me about how he and you and poor old Chief Wyga and old Lieutenant Bettner chased the sons-of-bitches all over the Ukraine. So . . . what's to stop us from doing that again? More coffee, sir?

—No, Ludo said, no longer laughing. That's enough.

The food had become tasteless. He pushed his plate away, rose, and went outside. Rain still fell; the ground mist had thickened. Small acrid clouds of exhaust hung above the fueling and arming bays where engines were roaring.

Then he was listening to a marching song and, for a moment lifted from its context, he thought himself once more a sixteen-year-old boy who had believed in glory.

The late-shift ground crews were marching back to barracks. Their hobnailed boots beat out a long-remembered rhythm on the concrete runway, and he thought that he must have heard this harsh affirmation of their lives for at least half of his own. They came out of the rain, out of the night, in long ranks of tight military fours that seemed to stretch back to his own earliest moments. There seemed to be neither a beginning nor an end to their patient column. The duty sergeant gave them an *Eyes right* as they came abreast his improvised reviewing stand on the steps of the mess, and the wet white faces snapped toward him, the eyes and teeth glinting, and he stood at the salute long after the last file had vanished in the darkness around the main gate.

What could he say to them, Ludo thought, if there'd ever be an opportunity to say anything? That their years of service, their work and devotion, had all been for nothing? That the dangers of their various journeys would make interesting reading in somebody's memoirs? That dedication is its own reward and that true glory lies less in the success than in the attempt? They'd be embarrassed for him; they'd think he had gone mad.

The mist had swallowed the dark ranks, but he could still hear the echoes of their song, the immemorial rhythm of the hobnailed boots. A dead white moon hung over the city, where the barrage balloons swung like prehistoric mammals in a silver haze. His ears were full of softly muffled drums and ceremonial volleys, and then he heard a key trumpet scatter its cheerful notes in the deepened darkness. It was the call to quarters, lights out. The trumpeter played "Taps."

CHAPTER XXIV

THE NEXT NIGHT, which was the eve of their Constitution Day and also the night before the Polish squadrons were to stand down for good, dinner in the mess was particularly quiet.

What was there to say? Within a week, they knew, they'd be on their way to demobilization centers where they'd be given a month's pay, a mass-produced civilian utility suit, a cheap felt hat, and a railway travel warrant to a British town or village of their choice. Thereafter, they'd be on their own.

Ludo knew hardly anyone at the long U-shaped table, and looked from one of the sixty young, untried, troubled faces to another, and felt the slow, thick swell of pity, memory, grief, and disappointment. Of the squadron which rose to fight the Germans over Warsaw on the first day of war, only he and Reszke were still alive.

Gerlach, he had been told, was dead, killed in a brawl outside the Allied officers' canteen in Trafalgar Square after he and Urban—gloomy and on edge after a bitter political argument with some Americans and Frenchmen—had thrown a beer bottle at the portrait of Stalin that hung, along with that of Churchill, Roosevelt (draped in black), and Chiang Kai-shek, at the back of the bar. They had been beaten with chairs and bottles, and kicked with paratrooper boots, and Gerlach died on the sidewalk of internal injuries, and Urban lay in the hospital with a broken back.

Reszke, whom he had always considered a boy, looked middle-aged. His hair had turned gray. Ludo's own face, glimpsed in the windowpanes among the travel posters, seemed like the face of a man pulled out of a wreck. As a guest of the mess, he sat on Reszke's right, his back to the trophy wall. The forest of Iron

Crosses had grown in his absence. The centered spot reserved for
Reinecke seemed like a reminder of unfinished business.

—Whatever happened to him? he asked.

—Who? Reinecke? He's gone up in the world. Made brigadier
after the last Luftwaffe shakeup. A hundred and seventy victories
to his credit. But they moved him and his orange noses to the
Russian front after their generals' coup against Hitler. For all I
know, he's somewhere in Siberia, looking at white bears.

—How long has it been since we first saw those damn orange
noses?

—Five years, eight months, and a day, Reszke said.

—Seems like a pity not to finish the job.

—A lot seems like a pity, Reszke said. Every night after dinner,
I sit here alone and I look around, and I see all the people that
we started out with, but none of them have faces. I can't
remember what any of them looked like. I hear Gerlach talking
about his celery and carrots. I see Papa Bettner. I have arguments
with Wardzinski and Borowicz about things like courage. I listen
to Straka and Wilchurzak bickering about which part of the
country is more patriotic than another. None of it ever leads to
anything, but it does pass the time.

—You've changed, Ludo said.

—Of course I've changed. I'm five years, eight months, and two
days older than I was when we flew to Warsaw to pick up the
reserve pilots and the new machines. I've killed three dozen men
since then. I've attended eighty-seven funerals. I haven't had anyone to laugh at since Gerlach was killed. I imagine that I look,
feel, and sound just like you did at your sister's party. The last
few years have been . . . *an educational experience,* as Papa
Bettner used to say. I can't imagine what it was like to be a
young lieutenant who was sure that he had nothing more to
learn. But I'll tell you one thing. If I had a chance to do it all
over, even if I knew how it was going to end, I'd do it again.

—Of course you would, Ludo said.

—The war itself . . . well, I don't know. That doesn't mean
much to me anymore. I don't even want to think about it. But
those few weeks in 1940, that Battle of Britain, that's worth
remembering, don't you think?

—It *has* to be remembered, Ludo said.

—We were worth something then.

—We still are.

—To whom? Not to Poland. There isn't any Poland. To our allies, then? We're just part of a nightmare they want to forget as fast as they can. To ourselves? We've lost more people in this war than all our Western Allies between them, and what's it been for?

—Sooner or later, someone will remember.

—I don't expect to be around to see it.

—Oh, I don't know, Ludo said. You might be. But what I think matters is that we should leave Poland something to remember. There'll be whole generations born and brought up to think that we did nothing here. Stalin has robbed us of our country; his puppets will see to it that everyone else in Poland is robbed of his pride. We ought to give our future generations something to remind them of who and what they are.

—Fine words, Reszke said and shrugged. But what do they mean? People who lose a war don't get to tell their story.

—Yet perhaps something can be done, Ludo said. Perhaps we can do something to remind everyone of those days when, as you say, we were worth something to them.

—What would you suggest? Reszke asked bitterly.

—I don't know. But I'm not ready to accept defeat, any more than Prus was ready to do it. Perhaps we could all go up again tomorrow, don't you think?

—What for? A valedictory visit to our days of glory? They are long gone, and so's whatever glory there was. We'll go up if you like, but I don't see that it's going to do anyone much good.

—Maybe it'll remind us of what we had set out to do, Ludo said. These young men of yours weren't with us in the Battle of Britain. What have they got to remember? Why don't you leave them something other than a feeling of futility? Surely, you and I owe them that much.

—Owe? Reszke said derisively. That's the last thing I ever expected you to say.

—There *is* a debt to be paid, Ludo said.

But Reszke wasn't listening. He had got up and, caught up in the stream of his own memories, began to pace up and down the room.

—A valedictory flight? he said. Well, why not? Perhaps it'll be something that'll say we were here. That we've nothing of which to be ashamed, that we didn't fail anyone, least of all ourselves. If nothing else, it'll be a good way for all of us to say good-bye to each other. Is that what you had in mind?

—Something like that, Ludo said.

—All right, then, we'll do it, Reszke said. We'll fly a last patrol in our old Battle of Britain sector. There's only the two of us in this room who ever went to visit Reinecke and the Calais Gang after Sunday breakfast. We'll buzz his field again. We'll go to Abbeville and Ostend. Maybe as far as Dieppe?

—And Major Toporski can lead us again, a young pilot said.

—When did he ever lead you? Reszke snapped. You were still carrying schoolbooks when we fought the battle.

—Begging the colonel's pardon, the young pilot said. But he's always led us.

Reszke fixed his cold gray gaze on one young face after another, noted the tension and expectancy, then his eyes met Ludo's. He smiled.

—Yes, I suppose he has, he said. I agree. Major Toporski can lead us all again.

They cheered then. It was, Ludo thought, as if their wasteful war had ended in a victory after all, and he wondered what kind of innocent, boyish memories they could be carrying out of it. His own had become something with which he didn't want to live.

After dinner, he drank pink gins with Johnny Sommerset in the British mess, where, one after another, the British and Canadian pilots stepped up, saluted him, and asked for the privilege of buying him a drink. They knew his legend just as well as the Polish pilots, and they were anxious to show their affection and respect.

He smiled and nodded and nodded and smiled, moving from one group of polite and friendly Englishmen to another, and he watched their painfully restrained embarrassment and listened to their shy good wishes. He knew that he was making them uncomfortable, that they were ashamed of their politicians, so he went outside.

Dawn would come soon: his last as a pilot, he supposed. The

sun, as yet invisible from the ground, flashed from the underside of a silvery bomber passing high overhead, and he read it as a sort of signal to settle all of his accounts with the past.

It was then about four o'clock. His stainless-steel American PX watch, a replacement for the jeweled musical timepiece he had lost when Reinecke's humorous sharks had caught him over Warsaw, had stopped before midnight, but a blue-gray edge began to define the tree crowns at the east end of the field. The chimneys and the rooftops of the sleeping town also acquired definition, and the air was fresh, and his head was marvelously clear.

For years, there had been no time to feel, little time to think of more than the needs of the moment. Men and their ideas seemed to live only in that fragment of time that framed action, and when those swift seconds vanished, there was no way to say that they had ever existed at all.

He was alone, responsible only for himself; this day was his own to do with as he wished. And yet the air he breathed seemed filled with a myriad of particles of light as if a whole constellation had fallen around him, and each of these bright fragments was one of millions of nameless young men who flew with songs and laughter, full of loyalty and devotion to their various countries, not anxious to die but unafraid to do so, their lives having the value of history's legal tender. They filled the sky with an antique sense of valor as simple as legends.

The sky, which he regarded as both his home and his destiny, was spectral like the oceans of the *Flying Dutchman*, and the air was bright and hard as crystal in his lungs once more and, for an extravagant moment, he was aware of a remote possibility of redemption for himself and his kind.

Sooner or later, someone would recall what had happened here. Someone would tell their story. And if they could only find a way to leave the war in the same way that they entered it, with the same spirit of dignity and courage, then the years of war wouldn't be a waste.

Someone called out to him then, and he turned and watched as Jacek Gemba trotted out of shadows, a thermos flask of coffee in one hand, a mess tin in the other.

—Hot coffee, sir, he said. And it's real, too! Mister Sommerset sent it over from the jam-eaters' mess.

—Why are you always pouring coffee into me? Ludo asked with mock severity. Doesn't it ever occur to you that I might want tea? And don't you have anything better to do than to gallop about the field in the middle of the night?

—It's not my business to figure out things like that, sir, Jacek Gemba said. I'm an orderly. An orderly makes coffee. I figure if you want a change, you'll give me an order. But I always brought you coffee before you went up, so I wasn't going to miss doing it this time.

—I think when God made you He discontinued the production model, Ludo said. Thank you. That's fine coffee.

Heels clicked. Teeth flashed in pleasure. The regulation phrase didn't seem as foolish as it might have sounded at another time:

—*Ku chwale ojczyzny.* By your order, sir.

—And that's what everything's been for, hasn't it, Ludo said.

—What has, sir?

—*Ku chwale ojczyzny. So that our country may be honored and praised.*

—That's what it seems to have been for, sir, but it's not for me to figure things like that. It's like Chief Auerbach used to say, sir. You keep your mouth shut and your asshole tight and you do your duty, begging the major's pardon. And when it's done it's done, and that's all there's to it.

—What are you going to do when the war is over? Ludo asked.

—I'm going home, sir. There's a lot of work to be done there. There's all that rubble to pick up, and land to be cleared, and there's all the houses to put up again. And, who knows, sir, maybe I'll get to be a waiter at the Europejski.

—I'll miss you, Jacek.

—And I'll miss the major. Jesus, I will, begging the major's pardon! But that's the way things are. Some of us can go home and others can't. Nobody'll put *me* up against a wall over there. Nobody'll send me to look at white bears. And . . . to tell you the whole truth of it, sir . . . I can't live on them *metafory*, if you know what I mean. I mean, I've got to live where I belong.

Ludo nodded, averted his face, sniffed the air, and said:

—Looks like a fine day coming.

—Yes, sir. A fine day for the celebration, Jacek Gemba said.

And then, because Ludo looked momentarily confused—

because in their language the words for *celebration, sacrifice, ritual,* and *observance* were often the same—Jacek Gemba went on, grinning from ear to ear:

—*Jutrzenka,* the third of May, sir. *The Dawn of the People.* When everything in the country is made new and everybody knows that better days are coming. Of course it's never good for long, is it, sir. I mean the fucking Russians come in and turn everything upside down for us. But it's all bright and new for a little while and that's what counts, doesn't it?

—I think so, Ludo said.

And then, because small groups of pilots appeared at the edge of the field and began to walk, in the blue light, toward the dark machines parked in their revetments, Jacek Gemba said:

—Looks like it's time to go, sir. Shall I get your flying jacket and the boots?

—Please. Thank you, Ludo said.

And then he was alone again and walking toward the high, questing nose of a Spitfire with a scarlet spinner angled against the reddening light above its revetment. Gerlach had kept his promise, he noted in passing: his machine was waiting. He stepped into the mounting stirrup in the fuselage and swung into the cockpit. The automatic self-starter whined and fired at once, and he watched the needles come alive in the altimeter, airspeed indicator, artificial horizon and vertical speed gauge, compass, fuel and oil-pressure indicators, oil-temperature and fuel-contents gauges, the supercharge pressure gauge, and the revolutions counter. He grasped the stick with its molded grip and trigger buttons, and hefted the helmet with its heavy earphones, oxygen mask, and throat microphone. Near his left hand was the chunky throttle lever and, on the other side, the red emergency-release knob that unlocked the canopy in flight. He smelled the engine's hot breath and the fresh paint and the new soft leather. The little red-and-white Polish checkerboard was painted just aft of the wings, next to the RAF roundel, and another decorated the softly rounded tail, and his own family coat of arms (a red lion rampant, with castles and crescents) overlooked the forty Iron Crosses in eight neat rows of five that marked his witnessed victories, and he felt himself neither a stranger nor a foreigner there.

Running up the RPMs, he went automatically through his preflight instrument check like an honest workman testing the sharpness of his tools. His fuel calculations included the day's wind, drift, and ground-speed estimates, which Auerbach (also an honest workman who took pride in his trade) had already crayoned on his cockpit slate. The engine's roar was as steady as a healthy heart, an untroubled mind, and he throttled down and leaned back in the narrow box seat, and closed his eyes where tears had started.

A dream bird, he thought, remembering quite another time, a morning much like this one, in a forest where he had waited for the war to start. He thought again, and for the last time, of the young men who had waited with him. He had thought himself beyond the reach of feeling but, obviously, it wasn't so; he wept as freely as a child in the smell of hot metal and the gently shuddering machinery. All his ghosts were finally laid to rest. Then he watched Reszke's pilots manning their machines.

They would take off, he knew, the way they had trained themselves to do: raising their landing gear while still on the ground, tucking their wheels under their bellies the moment that the tails of their machines rose above the runway. That was their signature, the panache of the Polish squadrons, a way to say: We are born to danger and so, look, see how we despise the possibility of our own destruction. Then: straight up at full throttle and only then, angled at forty-five degrees at two thousand feet, would they begin to bank and turn toward altitude.

He watched them as they swung themselves into their cockpits, the red new sun flashing from their goggles, and he remembered —indeed, how could he do anything but remember!—that this was their day. May 3, a day of hope meant to be the beginning of a whole new era, lived in the consciousness of all his countrymen as the dawn of new dedication and commitment. It was a day on which a Constitution had been voted, and freedoms were conferred, and universal brotherhood had been declared among all Poles of all kinds and classes, and it was also a day when traitors in the pay of a Russian Empress had called in Russian armies. The day which dawned on May 3, 1791, ended in a night that lasted a century and a half. Then as now, hope and doom had played in ironic counterpoint. Which of our days (he thought) could be more Polish? Which said more about us? Which, recalled through dark centuries as if it had dawned only yesterday, made all our generations into one? The young pilots, now settled in their cockpits and looking toward him, didn't need to be reminded about that.

Now, buckled into the familiar box seat, the airscrew hurling shards of light into the scarlet morning, and the rich, hot stench of lubricants and oil corrupting his air, he raised his arm above his open canopy in a sweeping motion and heard the loud, exultant roar of motors as the throttles opened, and watched, for a detached fragment of a moment, as the lean, dark, dangerous machines edged out of their revetments. Could there be ever again a day as laden with purpose as this one? In moments, he too was out from among the sandbags and bumping along the Tarmac, and sensing the sixty streamlined masses of armament and metal that formed a wide, back-swept V around him. Then he was running at full throttle toward the South Gate.

At once a part of his machine, he was free of doubts, questions, human motives, follies. His hands moved without orders from his brain. Ground-speed and RPM gauges reported his mechanical attitude and he snatched up his wheels just as soon as his tail wheel was clear of the ground.

Birds, caught in the massive slipstream of the rising squadrons, whirled down and away. Clouds were pierced and entered. The earth—silent, dwindling, spinning around the needle of his compass—relaxed the clutch of gravity and, finally, released him. Then he was free again in his own element, among his own kind.

They flew due east, straight toward London with its prismatic gleams and glitters and green splash of parks and black-and-white corridors of asphalt and gray Portland stone, into a rising sun which, looking lacquered as if wet from the sea, turned the barrage balloons into inkblots. The morning images were immediately clear.

England in late spring. Pale sunlight glimpsed through intermittent clouds on the green-brown quilt. Cricketers on the town common and sheep on the heath. Children who interrupted their berry-picking in the hedgerows to wave at the Spitfires. It wouldn't be a bad country to live in if one could do it with a clear conscience and of one's own will. Far to the east, in the outermost corner of the sky, he saw a vast, glittering armada of silvery bombers assembling above the thatched pastorals of Norfolk. It was midmorning and the Americans were going to work.

Except for the Americans, it was all as he had seen it in that remote August and September of 1940 which, as everyone had supposed then, would never be forgotten. The fleets of heavy bombers had been German then. The landings had been weary and the takeoffs urgent. The runways had been pitted and the fancifully camouflaged concrete buildings were scorched, as likely as not. Other than that, nothing seemed to have changed. Cows grazed, children waved, the land looked drowsy in a mildly irritated way, as though it had been awakened accidentally from an inoffensive dream. But this serenity, he knew, was a deceptive one. The English might be upset to hear it, he supposed, but they were among the most impassioned people on God's earth, and capable of the most extraordinary sacrifices for the sake of their own continuity.

Time seemed to reverse itself then and the years flew backward as London slid majestically under them, and he saw the smoke and the fire again, and heard the cough of cannons and the stuttering machine guns. It was October 1940, the time of the Blitz, and eighteen thousand tons of high explosives had been dropped on London. Stepney and Shoreditch, the heart of the cockney East End, were piles of burning rubble and more than thirteen thousand Englishmen and women lay dead in the ruins. More than eighteen thousand lay in the hospitals and twenty-five thousand more were homeless, living in schools and churches. The propaganda of the day said, *London can take it*, and, surprisingly, it did. Sleepless, drained of emotional energy, listening for the first threatening howl of the sirens, the ill-fed, badly clothed, often terrified but never hopeless people went about their work, survived, accepted devastation as part of their lives, remained unpanicked and so, eventually, unconquered. How could one hate them? How could one do anything but admire them? For all their carelessness about the fate of others, in all their vast failures, they had accomplished more than anyone else had done in the war's most widely publicized successes.

He could regret none of his past commitment to them. Indeed, in that commitment lay whatever success of his own he might have been able to carry from the war. He'd have been proud, he thought, to have been born among them so that he might feel and think and continue to live as they did and would. But he had been born elsewhere, his sources lay in other ruins—where the rules for living were considerably different—and his path had been marked out for him before he was born.

Then London was gone; huge, timeless . . . a moment in history, an indelible memory fashioned out of stone. The Thames had left its banks behind and had become a sea. He ordered a change of course. The squadrons turned as one.

He watched them then as if they were pieces on a chessboard or, as seemed the more appropriate image, playing cards spread out for an unfinished game of solitaire: five squadrons in fifteen flights of four, each flight shaped like an inverted L and gleaming with refracted light—red, blue, gold, and purple—with the pair of machines represented by the short leg of the L flying in front and just below the long one . . . sixty Spitfire Mark IXs in alternating layers of four, eight, thirty-six, then eight, and then his final foursome . . . moving, with what must have seemed to the watchers below as majestic indifference, in softly humming air. His was the high flight, the Man on the Roof, and he, as the moving pinnacle, was the controlling mind.

It was quiet at thirty thousand feet, silent above earth's echoes. In such a silence you can hear your thoughts. On just such a morning five years, eight months, and three days before, he had led his squadron of ten PZL-24s into Prussian air. There had been just as little reason for optimism then as there could be now, although those reasons hadn't been the same. The war—that cruel, enigmatic mistress—had held out a promise. *Be faithful*, she had said, *and all will be well.* . . .

Then they flew south along the French coast, the sun in midsky on their left.

CHAPTER XXV

IT WAS, PERHAPS, ten o'clock in the morning when he heard the
Germans. He heard them long before he saw them so that this,
too, had the quality of a revisited experience. They were somewhere between the squadrons he was leading and the Dover
coast, west of the sun, and still invisible. Incredulous, he peered
into the still-empty sky, sure that he'd see specters, skeletal machines, dead men at the controls of ghost ships, as he listened to
the soft, drawling coffee-cream voice ordering stragglers into close
formation.

—By the smothered balls of the innocents, Reinecke said
clearly. Will you please close up? I know that you're the last of a
bad lot, the scrapings of the barrel, but, by the horned balls of
Saint Hubert, will you at least *try* to look like the Luftwaffe? It's
the last impressions that count!

And a small, incredibly young voice said tremulously: *Jawohl,
Herr General. Zum befehl* . . .

He thought then: No, this couldn't be happening. Not even in
something so full of coincidences and the unexpected as an air
war. Surely, this was a trick of the imagination. His heart had
merely missed a beat . . . there had been a momentary blackout;
perhaps the oxygen pump had failed for a moment. . . . But the
skin had begun to prickle on the back of his neck in that exact
spot where, as tradition held it, the gunsights of the enemy would
center as he dived out of the ambush of the sun.

He ran through the R/T frequencies, searching for a dispassionate controller who might tell him what radar had reported,
but the Germans had obviously come under the radar screen. His
earphones communicated only distant cracklings until he crossed
the Luftwaffe operational band again. There, a voice of almost
feminine sweetness was singing: *I once had a friend. But a bullet
flew toward him through the air. I once had a friend, now he's
gone.* And then, suddenly, all the Germans had begun to sing.

Angered, as if on Reinecke's behalf, he began to curse them.

Didn't they know they were giving themselves away? That, even if no electronic devices had caught them as they skimmed the waves, they'd be damned well caught and pinpointed by their voices. And why in hell didn't Reinecke, a man of such immense command experience, tell them to shut up? Ah, but (he thought then gravely) they knew what they were doing. Call Death by name and she'll come. Anytime. Especially in the air.

Reszke, leading the low squadron four thousand feet below him, was waggling his wings with a sort of frenzy and, one by one all along the line and layer by layer, the Spitfires began to bob and rock from side to side, silently acknowledging the alert.

He twisted around and looked toward the sun, but there was nothing in the danger zone. Now was the moment for Reszke to resume command; he was, after all, the wing commander here and, Ludo admitted wryly to himself, every decibel the lieutenant-colonel. But the low squadron remained where it was and, looking down and around, Ludo saw white faces turned upward toward him.

Very well. So be it, now as in the beginning. He'd lead for the last time, the way it should be done to leave that necessary right impression. As Reinecke was sure to agree, when there is nothing more that can be done in war, when it is lost and only the bequest of a gesture remains to be made, then one *is* concerned about the way one leaves the stage. But, for some moments, he was unable to think.

On the horizon was a glistening haze. He was aware of an intense, disarming lassitude. There was a sort of deathly stillness in the air. The squadron . . . *his* squadron . . . didn't any more exist. They were a tradition of ghosts. The voices of the Germans were stronger and clearer, their song had become an ironic hymn to wasted valor and discredited purpose, and then at last he saw them: twenty-seven black and gun-metal-gray cruciform shapes sliding against the watery blue-gray background of the Channel . . . a picture page torn from a history book. They had begun to climb gently toward an altitude where the last margin of their safety would be taken from them, where Spitfires could strike them from above and then turn below them. Normally, he thought, a group commander would be shot for a trick like that.

The high, metallic voices went on singing, revealing their position and their purpose. Since radio silence was unnecessary, he switched the R/T set to SEND, said in a voice that, despite all control, trembled in the ether: Battle order. The squadrons will attack from the right. By flights, squadron front. Colonel Reszke will begin on order . . .

—Heads up now, children, Reinecke said softly. We're one minute away from the English coast. You are about to see the famous white cliffs of Dover which, I assure you, are a sight you'll want to tell your grandchildren about. So heads up. Look like something that used to give the English nightmares. By the incinerated balls of Adolf Hitler, let's give them something to remember.

At thirty thousand feet, the Spitfire bucked and trembled as if impatient in the thinner air and Ludo wanted to protract the moment as long as he could. He could sense the subtle change in the pitch of motors, the deepening growl as the long, questing noses of the Spitfires lifted above the Germans; it was as if the machines themselves had scented their prey and had begun to purr their satisfaction in advance. The armored windshield shimmered slightly in front of his eyes, and the controls trembled just a little under his resting hand.

—Easy . . . easy now, he murmured as the squadrons rose around him, closing up. Wait for the word.

He too, he knew, was waiting. But for what?

Far below and nearing, a thin white edge appeared on a darker landmass, a chalk mark drawn between the blue-gray water and the brown-green island: Dover and its cliffs . . . a landmark sought so often at the limits of fuel and endurance.

—Attack, attack, attack, Ludo said.

In moments, in what were surely fragments of a second, the air was full of hurtling aircraft, white streaks of vaporizing coolant, the stuttering roar of cannons and machine guns, red fireballs and the brilliant streak of tracers, and the thick oily coils of black smoke.

—*Trup! Trup!* cried the Polish pilots, anticipating the effect of cannons.

—Lead them, lead them! Reinecke commanded. *Ach,* by the sainted balls . . .

In moments, Ludo was left alone with the high squadron, high in the cold, thin air above the churned cirrus and the soiled blue. Below lay chaos, fire, shredded metal, black-and-red explosions, machinery that twisted, turned, swooped, rose, and fell. A greenish Heinkel was disintegrating with a sort of stately, theatrical indifference. He watched as large pieces peeled and flew off the fuselage and cockpit covering, as streams of smoke boiled out of the engines, and as a great sheet of flame rose from the bomb compartment. Slowly, carefully, as if savoring the moment, the Heinkel dived and fell, lost its shape in fire, hit the sea with a burst of white foam, disappeared. A Dornier rose on one wing and seemed to hang suspended for a moment on a string of tracers, then fell heavily to the left, spun, and dived. A Spitfire had begun to twist at the end of a coil of smoke . . .

—High squadron, Ludo said. Attack!

At once, his wingmen rolled, dived, and vanished, and he was alone.

High above the pull of the earth's disappointments, lifted above malice, bitterness, and betrayals, he eased the stick back and cut his RPMs and held his Spitfire at the edge of a stall. The oil-pressure indicator waved slightly, then settled. A large white bird, perhaps an albatross (ah, but what would an albatross be doing in these latitudes?) followed his course a few thousand feet below, then veered away and left him undisturbed. He was alone, the sky was his to do with as he wished, the weight and pressures of the earth had crumbled in thin air; he knew that he would never have to kill anyone again.

He could play, then, and did. First, a shallow turn in which he opened the throttle and watched his speed increase. The motor gave a deep warning growl and the machine bucked as if to register annoyance, but he said, *Steady, steady,* and then dropped the scarlet nose still further. The airspeed indicator needle swept around and around the face of its clock. The fuel gauge blinked its scarlet eye at him. He pushed the throttle lever wide open and pulled the stick back and soared into a loop. Then up and over, and up and over again . . .

England and its horizons vanished. There was nothing left but the dazzling and untroubled sky in which there was no anger, no malfeasance, but only a cold disinterested intelligence which might approve of his little show. Still as the air trapped in a magic moment, he hung suspended in his straps at the top of the loop, savoring both the lack of motion and the sudden silence, and then the earth was rushing up to meet him in the howl of the wind and the roar of the engine. A red jagged thought presented itself for his consideration: Why not just keep going? Straight down into the inhospitable soil where so many of his friends had found their involuntary homes, where all their various journeys had come to an end among funeral volleys and the music of valedictory trumpets. . . . But his hands and feet were obeying other, older orders then, and he throttled back, pulled out, kicked his way out of a sudden yaw, and opened the throttle to come around again.

A stall turn, then, using the momentum of the loop. As the red nose went up, he throttled back and held the Spitfire dead still in the air for a fraction of a moment that, in his own stilled mind, stretched into time beyond infinity. There were no boundaries before him then. No one's horizons set a limit on his possibilities. The sky was a blue-white cloudless pool into which he could plunge and be eternally refreshed, where there were never any shadows to threaten and confuse.

Then the machine had fallen on its back.

Down and down, while the airspeed indicator needle threatened to wind off its pivot screw, back toward the earth and all its grim realities, back to his duty and responsibility and to the sense of unavoidable doom, he fell at breakneck speed. His entire body seemed to have become filled with the whistling sound of the slipstream, and an icy wind hissed against his face. He was aware of cold sweat under his flying helmet, the stench of oil, and the fluttering admonitions of his indicator needles.

Down and down, while the earth moved swiftly to meet him in midair . . . ah, but (he thought, and felt an icy grin congealing on his lips) that was too cheap a way to fulfill a destiny. He pulled out, opened his throttle, and went into a slow victory roll, coldly amused at the thought that this was probably the hardest of his victories, the one that he had won over himself. The scarlet spinner, with its pale aureole of light that splintered off the airscrew, looked as if it were permanently fixed to the revolving, hard-edged, black-and-white horizon, and he kept it there with gentle stick pressure until the world was lying on its back. . . . Then the roll was completed and he flew straight and level again, with the sky above him, knowing that there was no more earth under him, nor ever would be, and that he'd never need to come down from the sky.

Below, the battle had taken itself off toward the French coast, and the choppy waters of the Channel had closed over the wreckage. The light seemed very bright, defining the moment, and he watched the shadow of his own machine flitting quickly and silently across the iridescent top of cumulus lit by the sun behind him. He watched the solitary Junkers moving toward England.

Reinecke . . . of course it would be Reinecke, to judge by the broad yellow stripe of a general's personal machine painted on the tail . . . was as alone as he. What could he be thinking? Death had eluded him again. Something far worse awaited the Viennese: defeat, the end of everything that had meaning for him, no matter how illusory those meanings might have been. What sort of home awaited *his* return? The Junkers droned on toward England, its crew compartment shattered and pilot exposed, its ventral gondola and gunner shot away, its engines bleeding glycol and white smoke.

Slowly, he dropped toward the German.

A time check, then, as regulations demanded. It was ten-oh-six in the morning; the fight had taken almost seven minutes. The date was May 3, 1945, a Thursday. It was exactly five years, eight months and four days since he and Reinecke had met. That day had been a Friday, he remembered.

Both of them, he supposed, had come to the end of their possibilities. The war was over for each of them separately and for both of them together. But even then, he thought, there was something more. There would be always something more; duty never ended. It made no difference whether this was duty to one's country, to one's conception of manhood and its obligations, to a former enemy or friend, or—in its final meaning—to oneself; there was always something.

A quick check of his instruments then. The instruments were

steady. He throttled back to increase the rate of his descent and to prolong the intervening time. Falling toward the German, he began to count.

On one, he thumbed the safety catches off his triggers. On two, he switched on the reflector sight. On three, he released the canopy catch and pushed the bulbous dome behind him on the count of four. On five, with the cold air whistling past his face and the altimeter reporting eleven thousand feet of altitude, he took off his goggles and unclipped his helmet and detached the microphone and dropped them into the whistling air. On six, he leveled out two hundred feet behind and, perhaps, ten feet above the tail of the Junkers, and saw the small, black-helmeted, goggled head of the pilot turn to watch him coming, and then a black-gloved hand rose above the shattered Plexiglas dome. On seven, with the distance narrowed to one hundred feet, he brushed his fingers gently across his firing button but didn't press the triggers. On eight, he drew abreast of the vast black-edged hole where the Junkers' crew compartment had been, and where one helmeted man sat alone while another slumped back dead in his chair. The German pilot's face was turned toward him and his lips were moving. On ten, he made an aileron turn to ram.

. . . Somewhere below him, or perhaps within him, a city was burning. A city or a village. A red mouth opened in a brilliant smile and he heard the pounding of a giant pulse. He was sixteen and running off to war while cavalry trumpets played, and a voice was calling *Loo-do, Loo-do,* and dwindling in the distance. The past advanced toward him, saying: *Welcome home.* He fell toward its fires.

EPILOGUE

Victory Parade

GERMANY SURRENDERED on May 7. May 8 was proclaimed Victory Day in Europe after five years, eight months, and eight days of the war. The Japanese laid down their arms on August 10. History's greatest war (in the sense that it was the bloodiest and the most destructive, and covered a greater part of the globe's land-and-ocean surface than any other war) had come to an end. The Victory Parade was scheduled for September.

I had come from the hospital where Ludo was dying to the hospital where Ann was beginning to recover, and I thought of the report I would be making to the Minister that evening, and of the great march-past of the victorious nations which I would watch with Loomis from my office window. There were to be a hundred thousand troops, and five thousand aircraft were to fly overhead, and a million persons were expected to line the route of march. There would be no Poles in the parade, of course. With their Army, Navy, and Air Force disbanded, their government dismantled, and no one left either to lead them, unite them, inspire them, or simply tell their story, the Polish chapter was considered closed.

Ann looked quite well although pale and drawn, and her large black eyes looked all the greater and deeper for the shadowed pools in which they lay. I hadn't wanted to talk to her about Ludo, at least not just yet, but the subject came up on its own.

I had brought flowers and the latest novels: George Orwell's *Animal Farm*, a fanciful little political allegory in which some animals were said to be more equal than others, and *Brideshead Revisited* which, in its doomed mannered lives and sense of a world well lost, seemed to reflect many people's feelings at that time. We didn't know it then, of course, but a whole era had ended for us; a way of life that had served us well for centuries was one of the victims of the war. Not even Churchill could have been sure that day that his blind faith in the Americans, to whom he had surrendered control of the war in Europe, would cost Britain that Empire (and that Europe) for which he had been willing to sacrifice whole peoples and nations, so that our final victory would be assessed by history as yet another celebration of a concealed defeat. But, as I now recall that bright, cool yet sunny day in London, and the strange silence in which vast crowds watched the preparations for the triumphant march, I was aware of an overpowering feeling of regret. Something of great value had passed beyond recall, and we were all impoverished in our celebration.

Ann took the books and flowers, glanced at them, said that she was grateful, and asked me not to come to visit her again. The war, she said, had created too many distractions. She didn't want her life disrupted by anyone or by anything again.

I asked what she would do once she was well again, and she said that she didn't know. The house above the beach near St. Jean-de-Luz was still there. Derek had gone to look at it and found it untouched. She might go there, she said. Or she might go elsewhere. It really didn't seem to matter to her very much. The only thing of which she was sure was that she didn't want to live in England anymore. So . . . perhaps Cyprus, once again?

—Although who can tell if we can still live like that? she said. There doesn't seem to be much of a percentage in being British anywhere, these days. Everyone is so anxious to get rid of us. About the only people who still bow and scrape are the bloody Germans. And if I wanted to live among ruins I'd move to the East End.

I tried for the last and final time, and said that I could help to make her inner loneliness unnecessary; life could be much less dreadful if you had company in it. And she said, unsmiling and indifferent: And who would help you?

Then she said: No. That sort of thing is over for good. I am quite done with that. It's just too foolish to expect that whatever bright, brief interludes in futility one stumbles upon now and then can have much effect on the way things have always been. One might as well stand in the path of the Flying Scotsman and order it to stop.

Then we heard music, a song played on the loudspeakers in the public wards: "Till the End of Time."

Her face became quite contorted then. She said, with no inflection in her harsh, concealing voice: He hated that. Chopin. He couldn't stand Chopin. He said that Chopin would always remind him of defeat. He said that this was all they played in that hospital in Warsaw before the city fell. He said that they always play Chopin in Warsaw when there is nothing else left for them to do. What happened in that hospital, anyway? Did he kill that man? He said he didn't, but it's hardly the sort of thing anyone would admit.

—I don't know, I said. Auerbach and Bettner both swear that he didn't, but they're both rather unreliable where he is concerned. Nobody really does know, I suppose, and perhaps that's just as well. I certainly don't know as much about him as I should.

—What will you report to the Minister about him, then? Ann asked.

—What he wants to hear, I expect. It probably all happened pretty much like that anyway. After all, nobody needed to ram that German bomber, the thing was all shot to pieces, anyway, and it would have fallen by itself in another minute. It must have been some kind of a derangement.

—But if the Poles are no longer much of a problem to anyone, if the emergency is over, why bother to make any report at all? Can't it all just be dropped and forgotten, along with the Poles themselves?

—It's . . . . a matter of principle, I suppose, I said.

—Principle? You? Laidlaw? Derek? Or even me, in my small contributory way? Isn't that rather stretching things a bit?

—Well, if not exactly *principle*, then policy and practice, I said. An inquiry had been set in motion. It can't be closed without a report by the assigned investigating officer. If the inquiry remains open, so does the case. And we're all anxious to forget about it as quickly as we can.

—Well, I can't speak for England, she said. That seems to be more of a lost cause every moment. But there'll always be a Whitehall. The sun just wouldn't dare to set over that. And then, of course, there is your own future to consider.

I agreed that this was, indeed, one of the considerations and why this report had to reflect the desired truth.

—In this case, I think it safe to assume some sort of a temporary lapse of . . . oh, how shall I put it . . . the rational faculties? A failure in the processes of logic? A sudden coming together of all his . . . ah . . . frustrations? A sense of futility that he, as such a very positive man of action, wouldn't be able to tolerate in himself? In any case, it's all just for the record, for the files. Nobody'll ever need to see the report. The matter is so unlikely to come up again, you see.

—Yes, it is unlikely, she said in a voice so lifeless that I could hardly bear it, and then she went on: What you're not asking, what you've never bothered to ask anyone, I expect, is why people try to kill themselves at all. They do it from a sense of failure. No, not their own failure because they may not have failed in what they had set out to prove to themselves. They may have achieved everything they hoped for. They may have reached a final definition of their worth, their personal assessment of their own value, their *price*, if you like. But life may have failed *them*, don't you see? It may have proved itself unworthy of *their* efforts, and so a fitting gesture must be made.

I said as gently as I could that I had never understood the suicidal impulse. I was a man of basic needs, simple motives, understandable conventions; the need to assert myself in some sort of dramatic act of frightfulness had never been a part of my makeup. I had little sense of what the French call *the histrionic view of history*, or history as a theater whose third act is always in revision, and, until I was able to speak from experience, I'd have to go along with the established view.

She gave a barely perceptible nod, a dismissive gesture that contorted her long, colorless lips in a sudden spasm, and I left soon after. The audience—painful and unsatisfactory for both of us—was over. Leaving her to her haunted speculations, I thanked God for my own untroubled, undemanding English simplicity, the instinctive knowledge of what was right or wrong, practical or foolish, disposable or useful. It was only when I had reached the street that I realized that at no time during that awful, impersonal visit to the woman I'd love until I was dead, had we referred to Ludo by his name. It was as if he no longer needed one, as if he had acquired a quality that transcended the need for personalization, that he had become something greater than any individual could be, something . . . lasting.

I had no negative feelings about Ludo at that moment. I thought that he might have been right when he had said to me, on that disastrous day when I had blundered into Ann's flat, that, under other circumstances, we could have been friends. Perhaps we could have. Perhaps the distances of culture might have shrunk with time; perhaps we might have traded tolerance, exchanged understanding, shared the lessons of our civilizations. I doubted that he and I would ever have had a great deal to say to each other without restraint and caution; our frames of reference, background, upbringing, and tradition were too far apart for that. Each of us was turned toward a different sun, springing from different soil. But I could admire his dedication to his country and his sense of responsibility to the men he led, and to those simple-seeming but infinitely complex loyalties that marked the good soldier. He was, I thought (in Loomis's favorite phrase) a good man; good in the sense that, even in his errors, he took a stand against whatever seemed evil and corrupt. He wanted his own kind, whom he loved, to be better than they were. In a time of madness and unreason, he had been a silent witness for a simpler truth. His passing too was a matter of regret.

I thought then of Frantisek's phrase which I had overheard during that reception in Northolt on Bloody Sunday, in the midst of the carnage and glory that had been the Battle of Britain, in which the Czech had categorized Englishmen as being both nobly generous and forgetful. Were we like that? History seemed to suggest that we were; there had been many Munichs. But couldn't history's verdicts ever be reversed? Surely a people who could create an Empire such as ours, who could civilize four continents and half of another, and whose native sense of decency and justice had been the fulcrum upon which Europe had kept its precarious balance for more than a century, could write their own verdicts.

Ludo would hardly last the year. It was a miracle that he had survived his injuries as long as he had, although the superb care given to him by RAF surgeons had more to do with that than all the masses offered on his behalf. Not all of my Minister's persuasion could stop Winston Churchill from going to see him. The King himself expressed hopes for his recovery. The thought that I would be writing his epitaph tonight, and my reasons for writing it the way it had to be written, seemed to go against everything I'd ever held dear. Death—whether his or mine or that of an era

—would no more solve that problem for me than it would for Ann.

In my office, I put the kettle on the ring to boil for tea, and went through the papers on my desk that had been marked for urgent attention.

The matter which (according to the Minister's angry scrawl on the cover page) seemed most immediate, was a combination petition and threat, signed by the finest and best-known of Britain's air aces, demanding that the Poles who had flown beside them in the Battle of Britain be allowed to take part in the fly-past over the Victory Parade. It brought to mind another pilots' revolt on behalf of the Poles in the months immediately following the battle, when Censorship refused to pass the Air Ministry statement that 303 Squadron (Polish) had shot down more German aircraft in just nineteen days of fighting than any other squadron in Fighter Command throughout the three-month Luftwaffe assault. All squadron leaders tend to be jealous of their units' records (their own fitness reports depend on high combat statistics), but everyone in the RAF wanted the Poles to have the credit they had earned. There was a lot of petty, bureaucratic wrangling, I remembered, and finally Censorship agreed to a watered-down acknowledgment which said it was the Polish High Command that claimed the top scores. But that didn't matter. The RAF pilots knew perfectly well who had done what, and now, apparently, they remembered long after everyone else had found it convenient to forget.

What had struck me the most forcibly about Ludo's pilots in those days was that they seemed more like a family than a group of strangers who had been brought together, far from their own homes, for the awful purpose of fighting another country's war. Like any family, they were more dependent on each other than they realized. Ludo cared for them as if each were a younger brother entrusted to his keeping; they, in turn, would have followed him anywhere he led. Later, when it became so necessary to discredit them and to discount their merit, I heard them talked about as ruthless mercenaries, no better than the enemies they killed and no more worthy of compassion than the Nazis.

But in those telling days when, in Churchill's own words, the fate of civilization rode on the wings of men such as they, no one could doubt their devotion to the common cause, nor their affection for the British people for whom they risked their lives.

I seemed to see them then, and to hear them too. The strange, mournful songs they sang at every opportunity, their dreadfully mangled version of "It's a Long Way to Tipperary" and "Knees Up, Mother Brown," the roar of their machines. In this odd, perverted war which everyone except America and Russia appeared to have lost, they had destroyed one thousand four hundred and sixteen enemy machines. Three hundred and forty-three of them had died. They had shot down one hundred and ninety flying rocket bombs. The list of names in my hands was a long one, more than three hundred RAF fighter pilots had signed the petition, and many of their names would ring forever like victory bells in Britain: Kent, Johnson, Akroyd, Bader, Townsend, Sommerset . . . each had fought and destroyed the equivalent of several German squadrons . . . each had a lasting claim on Britain's gratitude. And what of the Poles? Looking out of my office window, I wondered if they were standing in the crowd, in their cheap, ill-fitting demobilization suits, waiting again to hear the roar of aerial motors. . . .

At once, time seemed to telescope for me. I stood by my window, the petition in my hands, looking out at the final preparations around the Cenotaph . . . the Horse Guards in their scarlet cloaks, the wreaths and flags and flowers. I listened to the distant booming of massed drums and the roar of motors. From the rich, deep colors of this glorious day rose the memory of another.

June 18, 1940. The French had fallen. The world had held its breath. Winston Churchill spoke.

I heard him still, the passage of five years notwithstanding; that deep, drawling voice, its measured phrases resonant with confidence and power, as he addressed the British people—and the American Congress—from the underground command center of his war. I heard him, and my heart beat up, and the breath caught in my throat as it did then, and my eyes filled with hot and angry tears.

The Battle of France is over. I expect that the Battle of Britain is about to begin. . . . If we fail, then the whole world, including the United States, including all that we have known and cared for, will sink into the abyss of a new Dark Age . . .

And then, with what I knew to be a savage joy of battle in his indomitable heart: *Let us therefore brace ourselves to our duties, and so bear ourselves that if the British Empire and its Commonwealth last a thousand years, men will still say: This was their finest hour.*

And then, three months later, as proud of the RAF and of all the peoples of the British Isles, and as humble in his gratitude as I had ever heard him: *Never . . . in the history of human conflict, had so much been owed by so many to so few.*

In the scale of the vast slaughters that had made this war the most terrible in history, the Battle of Britain had been a little fight, yet I knew that to me it would always be the pivotal point in the history of our times. Without it, what would those times have been? Having moved near the seats of power, and made to contemplate not merely the legends but also the bewildering maze of past circumstances and future consequences, I felt as though I had lived through those days in a brightly illuminated hall of mirrors out of which I was looking upon a sable jungle and raw night.

There had been so much courage and devotion, I thought as I waited for the Victory Parade to begin. We had been shown so much selflessness and love within the everpresent context of hatred, fear, duplicity, and death, that this final ceremonial irony was difficult to bear.

In just a few more hours, the street below my window would fill with battalions, battle flags, regimental banners, brass bands, martial music, hobnailed boots by the thousands striking sparks off the pavement; the air above would darken with machines. I would be looking down upon wildly cheering crowds. I would see the victors: British men and women, Americans and Russians, the French, the Chinese, turbaned Sikhs, Goums in striped cloaks, Norwegians, Czechs, Yugoslavs, Abyssinians, men of all colors from every corner of the Commonwealth and Empire, the gallant

Canadians, Danes, and kilted Greeks. I would see Italians who had been enemies for part of the war, Turks who declared war three days before Germany's surrender, Portuguese, and Brazilians. I would see the Arab Legion's Camel Corps and Cypriot muleteers. I would see no Poles.

Ludo would soon be dead and forgotten as quickly as it could be arranged; the Minister was quite determined that this should be so. His men, those who had survived, wouldn't fly over the Victory Parade no matter how many petitions were signed on their behalf, for in the final balancing of the ledgers, made many years and miles away from the time and place in which they had fought, their great and simple acts of sacrifice were blotted out.

Yet I knew that I could never make my peace with such a conclusion. This was a story that had to be told. Without it, where would justice be? And if we were, as history and its ghosts were suggesting once again, forgetful of our friends, how could we expect the world to remember the debts owed to us?

Everyone has his moment, I knew, the time for a gesture which might be meaningless for anybody else but which, in the context of one lifetime, illuminates all his years. Ludo had had such a moment. What was mine? For I too was a man, a soldier of a kind, an Englishman conscious of my duty to those civilizing British influences that had given meaning to so many European decades.

I knew then that I would tell this story. The Minister would be sadly disappointed in the report I'd make. There would be time to spare in that cheap boardinghouse in Camberwell Road on half-pay retirement, in that small room perched on top of a musty staircase where no one would ever want to visit; there would be years to fill. The kettle whistled then, and I turned from the window and went to make my tea. Behind me, in the distant swell of cheers, I heard the start of the Victory Parade.